SOLDIER A: SAS

BEHIND IRAQI LINES

PRELUDE

Just after two in the morning the Kuwaiti Customs and Immigration officials playing cards at a table in the concrete administration office of the Al-Abdaly checkpoint were distracted by a rumbling sound approaching from the border of Iraq. Lowering their cards and removing their cigarettes from their lips, they glanced quizzically at one another as other officials, who had been dozing at their desks, were awakened by the increasing noise.

The floor began shaking beneath the men's feet. At first bewildered, then slowly realizing that the unthinkable might be happening, the senior official, an overfed, jowly man in a dusty, tattered uniform, dropped his cards onto the table, stood up and walked to the door. By the time he opened it, the whole building was shaking and the distant rumbling was rapidly drawing nearer.

The Customs official looked out of the doorway as the first of a convoy of 350 Iraqi tanks smashed through the wooden barriers of the checkpoint. Shocked almost witless, he dropped his cigarette and stared in disbelief as one tank after another rumbled past, noisily smashing the rest of the barrier and sending pieces of wood flying everywhere.

Fear welled up in the official when he saw shadowy figures in the billowing clouds of dust created by the tanks. Realizing that they were armed troops advancing between the tanks, he slammed the door shut, bawled a warning to his colleagues, then raced back to his desk to make a hurried telephone call to Kuwait City, informing his superiors of what was happening.

He was still talking when the rapid fire of a Kalashnikov AK47 assault rifle blew the lock off the door, allowing it to be violently kicked open. Iraqi troops rushed in to rake the room with their weapons, massacring all those inside and – more important from their point of view – blowing the telephones to pieces.

As the spearhead of Saddam Hussein's military machine rumbled along the 50-mile, six-lane highway leading to Kuwait City, troops were dropped off at every intersection to capture Kuwaitis entering or leaving. Other troops disengaged from the main convoy to drag stunned Kuwaiti truck drivers from their vehicles and either shoot them on the spot or, if they were lucky, keep them prisoner at gunpoint.

Simultaneously, Iraqi special forces, airlifted in by helicopter gunships, were parachuting from the early-morning sky to secure road junctions, government buildings, military establishments and other key positions in the sleeping capital.

Moving in on the city, still out of earshot of most of those sleeping, were a million Iraqi troops, equipped with hundreds of artillery pieces, multiple-rocket launchers, and a wide variety of small arms. Stretched out along a 200-mile front, obscured by clouds of dust created by Saddam Hussein's five and a half thousand battle tanks, they endured because they were motivated by months of starvation and their growing envy of Kuwaiti wealth.

In air-conditioned hotels, marble-walled boudoirs and lushly carpeted official residences, the citizens of Kuwait were awakened by the sound of aircraft and gunfire from the outskirts of the city. Wondering what was happening, they tuned in to Kuwait Radio and heard emergency broadcasts

3

from the Ministry of Defence, imploring the Iraqi aggressors to cease their irresponsible attack or face the consequences. Those who heard the broadcasts, Kuwaitis and foreigners alike, went to their windows and looked out in disbelief as parachutists glided down against a backdrop of distant, silvery explosions and beautiful webbed lines of crimson tracers. It all seemed like a dream.

Thirty minutes later, as the early dawn broke with the light of a blood-red sun, the grounds of the Dasman Palace were being pounded by the rocket fire of the Iraqis' Russian-built MiG fighters. Even as the Emir of Kuwait was being lifted off by a helicopter bound for Saudia Arabia, his Royal Guard, pitifully outnumbered, were being cut down by Iraqi tanks and stormtroopers. In addition, the Emir's half-brother, Sheikh Fahd, who had nobly refused to leave, had been fatally wounded on the steps of the palace.

While Hussein's tanks surrounded the British and American embassies, his jets were rocket-bombing the city's airport, illuminating the starlit sky with jagged flashes of silver fire, which soon turned into billowing black smoke. Two guards died as Iraqi troops burst into Kuwait's Central

Bank to begin what would become an orgy of looting.

By dawn the Iraqis were in control of key military installations and government buildings in the capital, Kuwait's pocket army was fighting a losing battle to protect the invaluable Rumaila oilfields and thousands of wealthy Kuwaitis and expatriate Britons, Americans, Europeans and Russians, trying to flee to Saudi Arabia, were being turned back by the Iraqi tanks and troops encircling the city.

Having returned to their homes, the expatriates heard their embassies advise them on the radio to stock up with food and stay indoors. Those brave enough to venture out to replenish their food stocks saw Iraqi generals riding around in confiscated Mercedes while their troops, long envious of Kuwaiti prosperity, machine-gunned the windows of the stores in Fahd Salem Street, joining the growing numbers of looters. Soon reports of rape were spreading throughout the city.

Before sunset, the invaders had dissolved Kuwait's National Assembly, shut ports and airports, imposed an indefinite curfew and denounced the absent Emir and his followers as traitorous agents of the Jews and unspecified foreign powers.

No mention was made of the Iraqi tanks burning in the grounds of the fiercely defended Dasman Palace, the sporadic gunfire still heard throughout the city as loyal Kuwaitis sniped at the invaders or the many dead littering the streets.

Even as the sun was sinking, torture chambers were being set up all over the city and summary executions, by shotgun or hanging, were becoming commonplace.

By midnight, Kuwait as the world knew it had ceased to exist; the armoured brigades of the Middle East's most feared tyrant stood at the doors of Saudi Arabia; and thousands of foreigners, including Britons, were locked in hotels or in their homes, cowering under relentless shellfire or hiding in basements, attics, cupboards and water tanks as Iraqi troops, deliberately deprived of too much for too long, embarked on an orgy of looting, torture, rape, murder and mindless destruction.

1

On 1 January 1991, almost four months to the day after Saddam Hussein's bloody take-over of Kuwait City, an RAF C-130 Hercules transport plane secretly took off from RAF Brize Norton, Oxfordshire. It was transporting members of the SAS (Special Air Service) and the SBS (Special Boat Squadron) to a holding area in Riyadh – the joint capital, with Jeddah, of Saudi Arabia – located in the middle of the country and surrounded by desert.

Though the SAS men were pleased to be back in business, the fact that they had been called back to their Hereford base on Boxing Day, when most of them were at home celebrating with family or friends, had caused some of them to voice a few complaints. Now, as they sat in cramped conditions, packed in like sardines with their weapons, bergens, or backpacks, and other equipment in the gloomy, noisy hold of the Hercules, some of them were passing the time by airing the same gripes.

'My missus was fucking mad,' Corporal Roy 'Geordie' Butler told his friends, in a manner that implied he agreed with her. 'No question about it. Her whole family was there, all wearing their best clothes, and she was just putting the roast in the oven when the telephone rang. When I told her I'd been called back to Hereford and had to leave right away, she came out with a mouthful of abuse that made her family turn white. They're all Christian, her side.'

'Don't sound so hard done by, Geordie,' said Corporal 'Taff' Burgess. 'We can do without that bullshit. We all know your heart was broken a few years back when your missus, after leaving you for a month, returned home to make your life misery. You were having a great time without her in the pubs in Newcastle.'

That got a laugh from the others. 'Hear, hear!' added Jock McGregor. 'Geordie probably *arranged* the phone calls to get away from his missus and her family. Come on, Geordie, admit it.'

'Go screw yourself, Sarge'. She's not bad, my missus. Just because she made a mistake in the past, doesn't mean she's no good. Forgive and forget, I say. I just think they could have picked another day. Boxing Day, for Christ's sake!'

But in truth, he'd been relieved. Geordie was a tough nut and he couldn't stand being at home. He didn't mind his wife – who had, after all, only left him for a month to go and moan about him to her mother in Gateshead – but he couldn't stand domesticity, the daily routine in Newcastle – doing the garden, pottering about the house, watching telly, walking the dog, slipping out for the odd pint – it was so bloody boring. No, he needed to be with the Regiment, even if it meant being stuck in Hereford, doing nothing but endless retraining and field exercises. And now, with some real work to do, he felt a lot happier.

'What about you, Danny?' Geordie asked Corporal 'Baby Face' Porter. 'What about your missus? How did she take it?'

'Oh, all right,' Danny answered. He was a man of few words. 'She understood, I suppose.'

'I'll *bet* she did,' Corporal Paddy Clarke said.

Sergeant-Major Phil Ricketts smiled, but kept his mouth shut. He knew Danny's wife, Darlene, and didn't think much of her. Danny had married her eight years earlier, just after the Falklands war. Having once spent a weekend leave with Danny and his parents in the Midlands, a few weeks before Danny proposed to his Darlene, Ricketts felt that he knew where Danny was coming from. Always intrigued by the contradiction between Danny's professional killer's instincts and his naïvety about personal matters, he had not been surprised to find that Darlene's father was a drunken loudmouth, her mother a tart and Darlene pretty much like her mother.

Nevertheless, blinded by love, Danny had married Darlene and was now the proud father of two children: a boy and a girl, seven and six respectively. While Danny had never been one for talking much, it was becoming increasingly evident from his unease at the very mention of Darlene's name that he was troubled by secret doubts which he could not articulate. The marriage, Ricketts suspected, was on the rocks and Danny didn't want to even think about it.

No such problem, however, with the big black sergeant, Andrew Winston, formerly of Barbados, who was sitting beside Danny, looking twice his size, and crafting poetry in his notebook, as he usually did to pass the time. In fact, since the Falklands campaign, Andrew had become something of a celebrity within the Regiment, having had his first book of poems published by a small company based in London's Notting Hill Gate, and even receiving a good review in the highly respected magazine *Orbit*. When most of the book's print-run was remaindered, Andrew bought the books himself, and sold them off cheaply, personally signed, either to his friends in the Regiment or, more often, to their wives, who clearly were deeply interested in six-foot, handsome, black poets.

As the poems were about Andrew's experiences with the Regiment, he had also sent copies of the book to the Imperial War Museum. When the curator wrote back, thanking him for his contribution and assuring him that the three signed copies would be placed in the museum's library, Andrew was so thrilled that he rushed straight out and married his latest girlfriend, a beauty from his home town in Barbados. Now he too was a father – in his case, of three girls – and he appeared to have no complaints.

'I used to spend so much time chasing nooky,' he explained to Ricketts, 'that I didn't have any left for my poetry. Now I've got it on tap every night and I'm much more creative. Marriage has its good points, Sarge.'

In the intervening years, Ricketts had been

promoted to sergeant-major, Andrew to corporal and then sergeant, while Jock McGregor, Paddy Clarke and the reticent Danny had become corporals. Geordie Butler and Taff Burgess, however, although experienced soldiers, had repeatedly been denied promotion because of their many drunken misdemeanours. Also because, as Ricketts suspected, they simply didn't want responsibility and *preferred* being troopers.

As for Ricketts, now nearing 40, he was increasingly fond of the comforts of home, appreciating his wife Maggie more than ever, and taking a greater interest in his two daughters. It still surprised him that they were now virtually adults: Anna, 19, was working as a hairdresser in Hereford, while Julia, a year younger, was preparing to take her A levels and hoping to go to art school. Though he was proud of them, they made him feel his age.

Now, thinking about his family, and surrounded by his men in the cramped, clamorous hold of the Hercules, Ricketts was forced to countenance the fact that the battle for Kuwait might be his last active engagement with the Regiment. In future, while still being involved, he was more likely to be in the background, planning and orchestrating ops, rather than taking part in them. For that reason, he was looking forward to this campaign with even more enthusiasm than usual. It marked a specific stage in his life, and a very important one. After this he would settle down.

'How much longer to go?' Andrew asked no one in particular, suffering from a creative block and just needing someone to talk to.

'About twenty minutes,' Ricketts replied. 'We're already descending.'

'Thank Christ,' Andrew burst out. 'I can't stand these damned flights. You can burn me or freeze me or shoot me, man, but keep me out of these transports. I can't bear being cooped up.'

'You're going to be cooped up when we land,' Paddy gloated. 'In a fucking OP in the fucking desert – hot by day, cold by night. How's that grab you, Sergeant?'

'I don't mind,' Andrew replied. 'I'm a man who likes his privacy. Just stick me in a hole in the ground and let me live with myself. Since I'm the only man here worth talking to, I'd rather talk to myself.'

'You might find yourself talking to an Iraqi trying to cut your black throat.'

'Lord have mercy, hallelujah, I is ready and waitin'. Ever since that Saddam Hussein pissed on Kuwait City I's bin dyin' to come to the rescue. It's part of my imperialist nature. My noble English blood, brothers!'

As the customary repartee – bullshit, as they always called it – poured from the other troopers, Ricketts thought of the march of events that had followed Saddam's invasion. When the news broke, Ricketts had been sceptical about Saddam's remaining in Kuwait City, assuming it to be a bluff designed to get him his way in other matters. Since then, however, Saddam had stuck to his guns. Because of his intransigence, the UN had imposed economic sanctions and a trade ban on Iraq; President Bush had 'drawn a line in the sand' and sent thousands of troops to Saudi Arabia; 12 Arab states, along with Britain and France, had done the same; over 100,000 refugees had crossed into Jordan; Saddam had used British hostages as a 'human shield', paraded others on television, and then declared Kuwait Iraq's nineteenth province and released the hostages as a political gesture; and the UN Security Council had voted for the use of force against Iraq if it did not withdraw from Kuwait by 15 January.

By 22 December, shortly after the UN General Assembly had condemned Iraq for violating human rights in Kuwait, Saddam had vowed that he would never give up Kuwait and threatened to use atomic and chemical weapons if attacked. As he was still showing no signs of relenting, war was almost certainly on the cards.

''Scuse me for asking, boss,' Geordie said to Major Hailsham, 'but is it true we're not the first to be flown in?'

'I don't know what you're talking about,' Major Hailsham replied. He had been promoted shortly after his return from the Falklands, when Major Parkinson was transferred to another unit. With his sardonic sense of humour and excellent operational record, he was a popular commanding officer of the squadron.

'You don't?'

'No, Trooper, I don't. If any other members of the Regiment have been inserted, I wasn't informed.' Mike Hailsham was still a handsome schoolboy with a wicked grin. 'But since I'm only the CO of *this* benighted squadron, they wouldn't even *think* to inform me, would they?'

'I guess that's right, boss,' Geordie responded, deadpan. 'We'll all have to accept that.'

In truth they all knew, and were envious of the fact, that other members of the Regiment had been working undercover in Iraq since a few days before the invasion, having flown incognito, in 'civvies', on British Airways flight 149 from London to Delhi, with a fuelling stop in Kuwait. Finding themselves in the middle of Saddam's invasion, which had begun in the middle of that same morning – slightly earlier than anticipated by the 'green slime', the Intelligence Corps – the SAS men had melted away, dispersing in two directions, some to send back information from behind Iraqi lines, others to do the same from Kuwait itself, where they would now be hiding in a succession of 'safe' houses and operating under the very noses of the Iraqis. Naturally, their presence in Kuwait was unofficial and therefore remained resolutely unacknowledged.

'We're coming in to land.' Hailsham observed needlessly as the overloaded Hercules began its shuddering descent. 'Check your kit and prepare to disembark. I want no delays.'

'Aye, aye, boss,' Ricketts said, then bawled the same order along the hold of the aircraft.

Cumbersome at the best of times, though always reliable, the Hercules shuddered even more as it descended, groaning and squealing as if about to fall apart. Eventually it bounced heavily onto the runway, bellowed, shook violently and rattled as it taxied along the tarmac, before finally groaning to a halt.

Letting out a united cheer, the men unsnapped their safety belts and stood up in a tangle of colliding weapons and bergens. After a lot of noise from outside, the transport's rear ramp fell down, letting light pour in, and the men clattered down onto the sunlit, sweltering tarmac of Riyadh airport.

It was not the end of the SAS men's long journey. Lined up along the runway of the airport were RAF Tornado F-3 air-defence aircraft which had arrived four months ago, shortly after the fall of Kuwait, flying in from the massive Dhahran air-base. There were also a dozen RAF CH-47 Chinook helicopters of 7 Squadron's Special Forces Flight.

The Regiment's recently acquired, state-of-the-art desert warfare weaponry, including Thorn-EMI 5kg hand-held thermal imagers, Magellan satellite navigation aids – SATNAV GPS, or Global Positioning Systems – laser designators and other equipment, was unloaded from the Hercules and transferred to the Chinooks. When the transfer was over, the men, who had been milling about on the tarmac, stretching their legs and breathing in deeply the warm, fresh air, also boarded the helicopters and were flown on to Al Jubail, an immense, modern port on Saudi Arabia's east coast, some four hundred miles from Riyadh and about five hundred from Kuwait City. They emerged from the Chinooks a couple of hours later, glad to be back on solid ground.

Though originally built as a centre for oil and light industry, Al Jubail had never been developed properly and was now being used fully for the first time as a receiving port for the Allied equipment and supplies being brought in on more than a hundred ships, mostly from European ports, but also from Cyprus, Liberia and Panama. While some of the British servicemen in transit, mainly those of the Queen's Royal Irish Hussars and the 7th Armoured Brigade, were billeted in huts and sheds originally intended for the industrial workers, most were housed in the enormous, constantly growing 'Tent City' located in the port area and already equipped with camp-beds, showers, chemical toilets and a field kitchen run by the Americans.

'Home sweet home!' Sergeant Andrew Winston said, dumping his bergen on the floor beside a camp-bed in the sweltering late-afternoon heat of the space allocated to the Regiment for the duration of its stay in Al Jubail.

'Having just come down from the trees,' Geordie replied, 'you'd be used to living out in the open. That's one up to you, Sarge.'

'You don't like it, Geordie? Too hot for you, is it?'

'You could obviously do with sweating off a few pounds,' Geordie replied, tugging experimentally at the ropes of his lean-to tent to check that they were tight, 'but me, I'm as slim as a man can go, so I don't need melting down in this fucking heat.'

'I'm relieved,' Taff Burgess said, laying his M16 out carefully on his camp-bed and gazing out over the rows of tents divided by paths that led in one direction to the port and in the other to the airstrip, other accommodations and the guarded compounds containing the armoured transport and tanks. Hundreds of thousands of troops, British, American and French, crowded the spaces between the tents, eating, drinking, writing letters, taking open-air showers and going in and out of chemical latrines. Their constant movement and the ever-present desert wind created drifting clouds of sand and dust that made them look ghostlike in the shimmering light.

'I wouldn't fancy being in one of those huts in this fucking heat,' Taff said. 'It must be like a Turkish bath in there. At least we can breathe out here.'

'All *I'm* breathin' is dust,' replied Jock. 'That and bloody sand. I've got sand in my boots, in my eyes, in my mouth, and even up the eye of my fucking dick. This place is just like Oman.'

'You're too old to remember Oman,' Paddy ribbed him, stretched out languidly on his camp-bed, hands folded beneath his head, acting really cool in the sweltering heat. 'Relax, boys, you're gonna have a good time here. Compared to what's to come, it's probably Paradise.'

'I doubt that,' Geordie said.

He was right. Their accommodations were close to the Royal Corps of Transport's Force Maintenance Area, or FMA, and the constant noise, combined with the heat, made for irritable days and sleepless nights. Since they were there for five days, waiting for the rest of their equipment to be brought in by ship, the lack of sleep was no joke. To make matters worse, they were ordered to take NAP tablets, which were meant to reduce the damaging effects of gas in the event of a chemical attack, but also gave everyone diarrhoea.

'My shit comes out like piss,' Paddy informed the others. 'And I hear these tablets also contain a lot of bromide, so say goodbye to your sex life.'

Already running non-stop to the latrines, they felt even worse after the biological vaccinations against whooping cough, which they received at the same time and which knocked most of them out for twenty-four hours.

'Say goodbye to your fucking sanity,' Jock said groggily, as the others moaned and groaned on their camp-beds. 'Christ, I feel dizzy!'

Scarcely recovered, they were nevertheless made to spend a large part of each day on the Jerboa Range of the training ground at Al Fadhili, inland from Al Jubail, where they shot at targets and markers while being bellowed and spat at by the aggressive camels of passing Bedouin.

'Those bastards on camels are straight out of *Lawrence of Arabia*,' Geordie announced to all within earshot. 'A fucking good film, that was.'

'I never wanted to be in the movies,' Andrew replied, 'and those camels stink. What the hell are we *doing* here?'

'Waiting for the rest of our equipment, coming in with the Navy. Need I say more?'

'Fucking Navy!' Taff spat.

21

Soon sickened by the repetitive, useless training, which they had done many times before, they were all pleased when, on the fifth day, the despised Navy finally arrived at the port with their missing supplies.

By this time, with over half a million Coalition troops and the greatest air force ever assembled in history clogging Al Jubail, the space being used by the SAS was desperately needed. The Regiment was therefore hurriedly packed up and driven back to the airstrip. From there, Hercules transports flew the relieved men to a forward operating base, or FOB, located at a Saudi airport in the desert, a day's drive from the border of western Iraq.

'We operate from here,' Major Hailsham told the men the minute they stepped off the planes into another sea of flapping tents on a flat, barren plain. 'Welcome to hell.'

It wasn't quite hell, but it was certainly no paradise. The FOB was a dense throng of lean-to tents divided by roads filled with brightly painted 'Pink Panther' Land Rovers, Honda motorcycles, Challenger tanks, and other armoured vehicles and trucks, many of which were being used to support the tents and their camouflaged netting. On all sides of the makeshift camp there was nothing but desert, stretching nine hundred miles from the Red Sea to Kuwait and the Gulf, southwards to the Arabian Sea beyond Oman – more than a million square miles in all. It was a very big area to cover. Also, it was surprisingly cold, especially at night.

The first thing the SAS men learnt was that they could not phone home, their mail would be censored and normal radio transmissions were restricted. And, of course, they could not drink alcohol – not even here in the desert, for the Bedouin still often passed the camp on their camels. Similarly, the men had to respect Muslim customs and not flaunt their Western habits or religious preferences, except in the privacy of their tents.

'Should this make you resent the fact that we're here to defend the Kuwaitis,' Hailsham said, 'I would remind you that we have our own interests at heart. In fact, we're here to safeguard Arabian oil, which furnishes over two-thirds of the world's needs, including ours. To lose it to Saddam would have devastating consequences for the West, including Great Britain. I'd also remind you that there are approximately thirty thousand expatriates in Saudi Arabia who need our protection. To give them that, we need the trust of the Bedouin. Please don't forget it.'

In their view, the men were not compensated for such restrictions by being treated like lords. On the contrary, their living conditions were basic, with portable showers, chemical toilets and meals consisting mainly of sausages and baked beans, sometimes curry with rice, spooned up from mess-tins as quickly as possible to stop sand or dust from getting on it, then washed down with hot tea.

The freezing nights were long – about eleven hours of darkness – and the men, stretched out beside their tanks and armoured vehicles or huddled up in their slit trenches, could do little to pass the time other than listen to the restricted programmes of Forces Broadcasting or study the brilliant stars over the flat, featureless, seemingly endless black desert.

From the BBC they learned that back in England Wing-Commander David Farquhar had lost secret documents and a laptop computer containing an outline version of the American war plan. The fact that this news was conveyed by the BBC even before it was known officially to the Coalition Forces in the Gulf caused much sardonic mirth among the men. They also learnt that the Prime Minister, Margaret Thatcher, had been replaced by John Major, whom many thought would not be as supportive of them as had been the Iron Lady.

'Not *my* cup of tea,' Major Hailsham said, summing up the general feeling among the men, 'but at least she always stuck by her guns. She also stuck up for the Special Forces. I don't know that John Major will. This could be a bad blow to us.'

'We'll survive,' Sergeant-Major Ricketts replied.

For the SAS, the first five months of the crisis had been a time of intense frustration. As Britain's leading exponents of desert warfare, they were, by January, the only Regiment without a certain role in any war with Iraq, even though an FOB had been established in the Gulf since August, with D and G Squadrons carrying out intensive exercises in the desolate area of the Rub Al Khali, or the Empty Quarter, testing men and equipment. At that stage, their primary function was supposed to be the rescue of the hostages being used as a human shield by Saddam; but with the release of the hostages in the second week of December, that function had become redundant and left them with no clearly defined role.

'At the moment,' Hailsham explained to Ricketts,

'with the cooperation of the American Special Operations Central Command, we're working hand in glove with the 5th Special Forces Group, the Amphibious Sea Air Land, or SEAL, units, the US Air Force special force and the Psychological Operations and Civil Aid or, to be brief, Psyops and Civaid. Also, since it's perfectly clear that the outcome of any war with Saddam Hussein will be determined by air power, we're boning up on the use of lasers for target designation with the Tornado and similar bombers. Front-line reconnaissance, however, is still under the control of the 5th Special Forces Group and US Marine Corps recon specialists. This isn't raising the spirits of the men to any great heights.'

'Presumably we need the permission of our imposing US Commander-in-Chief, Norman Schwarzkopf, to take a more active role,' said Ricketts.

'Unfortunately, yes – though I have it on the best of authority that General Sir Peter de la Billière, our former SAS commander and now commander of the British forces here in Saudi Arabia, is putting in a good word for us.'

'I should bloody hope so,' Ricketts replied.

'Apart from that we're just twiddling our thumbs.'

'There are worse vices, boss.'

Hailsham grinned. 'Anyway, it's bound to happen soon and I think we should consider our course of action. My view is that we should revert to the kind of campaign David Stirling ran during World War Two – deep-penetration, hit-and-run raids behind enemy lines, destroying their planes on the ground, attacking their lines of communication, ambushing their patrols and causing general disruption and mayhem.'

'In armed Land Rovers.'

'Right. The Pink Panthers. In and out in clouds of dust with all guns firing. Personally, I'd love it.'

'Then let's hope we get to do it,' Ricketts said. 'Come on, boss, let's go for chow.'

They were just about to leave the tent when the telephone rang.

2

'I've called you together,' Major Hailsham addressed the troopers assembled outside his lean-to on the edge of the city of tents spread across the desert plain, 'to tell you that plans for the liberation of Kuwait are already well advanced and the operation's been codenamed "Desert Storm".'

When the men burst into applause and cheering, it hit Hailsham just how frustrated they had been during the past few days, not knowing exactly why they were here and fed up with the repetitive lessons on survival in the desert or the use of the latest high-tech equipment. While this FOB was busy and noisy all day, with helicopters constantly taking off and landing, aircraft roaring overhead and Challenger tanks and armoured vehicles being put through their paces, the activity was purely of a time-filling nature, albeit masquerading as practice. Meanwhile, the 'Pink Panther' Land Rovers and motorcycles were sitting idly outside the tents. What Hailsham's men wanted, he now realized, was more positive action and a clearly defined reason for being here. Now at last they were getting it.

'The basic plan,' Hailsham continued when the men had quietened down, 'is for battleships of the US Navy to bombard the Iraqi coastal positions and offshore islands of Kuwait while US Marines make an amphibious landing from the Gulf. At the same time, Arab elements of the Coalition forces will head overland, straight for Kuwait. Meanwhile, US Marine Corps will be engaging the Iraqis due north of them. The Syrians and Egyptians will push to the north, make a right-handed swing, and come into Kuwait City from the west – hopefully, if things go as planned – meeting up with the Coalition Arab forces already there. No Western forces will enter the capital until it's been cleared by Islamic troops.'

'Very decent of us,' Geordie said sarcastically.

'Very sensible of us,' Ricketts pointed out. 'It shows that this war is for the Kuwaitis and we're simply supporting them.'

'Correct,' Hailsham said. 'The city must be liberated by Muslim forces to avoid accusations of exploitation or desecration by Christians. We'll follow them in.'

'So what's the state of play at the moment?' Sergeant Andrew Winston asked. 'Are we ready to move?'

'Not quite. As our heavy tank units haven't arrived yet, all that stands between Saddam's five thousand-odd tanks and the oil riches of Saudi Arabia are a few thousand US paratroopers and Marines . . .' Jeers and farting noises from the SAS troops interrupted Hailsham, who went on, '. . . around twenty-four US Army AH-64A Apache attack helicopters, a few hundred Coalition aircraft, US special Forces Troops . . .' – more derisory remarks and noises from the SAS troopers. – '. . . And, of course, us.' Loud cheering. 'However, while thousands more Coalition troops – British, American and French – are being flown and shipped in every day, the Gulf is filling up with aircraft carriers and their F-18 Hornet fighters, F-14 Tomcat attack fighters, A-6E Intruder bombers, and KA-6d tanker jets for mid-air refuelling. By the time the UN deadline for Saddam's withdrawal is reached, the greatest army in history will have been assembled in Saudi Arabia and will be ready to move.'

'What's our new role,' Danny 'Baby Face'

Porter asked solemnly, 'now that all the hostages have been released?'

'A good question, Corporal. As you're doubtless aware by now, on 2 December Saddam Hussein test-fired three ballistic missiles – similar to the Soviet-built Scuds – over four hundred miles of Iraqi territory, provocatively aiming them in the direction of Israel. It's our belief that if the battle for Kuwait begins – which it will if Saddam ignores the Coalition's demand for withdrawal by the fifteenth of this month – he'll deliberately fire on Israel in order to lure it into the war.'

'So?' Paddy Clarke said. 'We can do with all the help we can get and the Israelis are sharp.'

'I agree about the Israelis, but in this particular theatre of operations we simply can't afford to have them taking part. In fact, their intervention would be an absolute disaster, losing us the Arab members of the Coalition and maybe even turning them against us. Our new task, then, is to help prevent Saddam attacking Israel.'

'And how do we do that?' Jock McGregor asked.

'By locating and destroying the Scud bunkers, trailer-erector launchers, mobile units and support systems hidden deep in Iraqi territory.'

'Can't they be located by satellite?' Andrew Winston asked. 'I've heard that the Yanks have two orbiting spacecraft that can sweep the launch areas with infrared detectors every 12 seconds.'

'They're not all that brilliant,' Sergeant-Major Ricketts pointed out. 'In fact, they even failed to spot Saddam's so-called supergun at Jabe Hamryn, north of Baghdad. That barrel was 170 feet long and sticking into the sky like a big dick – yet the satellites missed it!'

'Ricketts is right,' Major Hailsham said. 'Aerial reconnaissance can be flawed. The recent Scud test shot, from a base near Basra, was in the final stages of its flight before a US satellite detected the flare from its rocket motor. The satellites, it seems, can only pick them up when they're in flight – and that's often too late. Also, the Iraqis are switching off their Squat Eye guidance radar systems, which further reduces our chances of finding them – so we still need good old-fashioned eyeball recces.'

'From OPs.'

'Yes, Corporal Porter, that's the idea.'

'How many Scuds do they have?' Danny asked, as solemn as ever.

'Present estimates vary from four hundred to a thousand missiles on thirty to thirty-six sites and maybe two hundred mobile launchers.'

Andrew gave a low whistle. 'That's a lot, boss.'

'No argument there, Sergeant.'

'So what happens when we locate bunkers or mobile launchers?'

'Either we call in air power or we relay the info to Intelligence HQ in Riyadh. Patriot surface-to-air missiles will then be alerted automatically to the Scud's course and speed – a process that only takes a few minutes.'

'Our parameters?'

'As of this moment, we're the only ones allowed to cross the line ahead of other ground forces.' This caused whistles of approval and sporadic clapping, which tailed off when Hailsham waved his hand for silence. 'We have a secondary reason for being allowed to go in ahead. The Coalition is greatly concerned about Iraq's chemical-warfare capability. At the moment we know very little about the types of chemical agents Saddam has in his arsenal. We *do* know he has mustard and nerve gas and is likely to arm his Scuds with them. So one of our jobs may be to infiltrate the contaminated areas and collect samples of the agents being used.

The samples will then be flown back to Porton Down for analysis and, hopefully, the creation of an antidote.'

'I don't like the sound of *that*,' Andrew said. 'I don't like them chemicals, man.'

'Nor do I, Sergeant.'

'How do we insert?' Danny asked.

'The Regiment will be broken up into two sets of mobile teams: one for deep-penetration ops in Iraq; the other for hit-and-run raids in the desert, using Land Rovers – just like they did in Africa during World War Two.'

'Sounds like fun,' Geordie said. 'I'll buy that, boss.'

'Me, too,' agreed Jock. 'Are you going to throw in some motorbikes?'

'Yes,' Hailsham said.

'I haven't been in a Pink Panther since Oman,' Andrew said, glancing back over his shoulder at the brightly painted Land Rovers and motorcycles on the dusty tracks between the lean-to tents. 'Look at 'em! As pretty as a picture.' He turned back to grin at Major Hailsham. 'Count me in, boss.'

'I have your name and number, Sergeant Winston.'

'When do we move out?' asked Taff Burgess.

'We have to be gone by the night of the twenty-second. If Saddam doesn't withdraw from Kuwait on the fifteenth, hostilities will begin on the twenty-ninth. That gives us seven days to do as much damage as possible before Desert Storm commences.'

While talking to the men, Hailsham frequently had to shout against the noise of the RAF Chinooks that were taking off and landing in billowing clouds of sand on the nearby airstrip. Even noisier were the Tornado F-3 air-defence planes roaring frequently overhead, going to or returning from practice flights out in the desert. Also churning up clouds of sand and creating a lot of noise were the Challenger tanks being put through their paces on the sands surrounding the camp. This was a large, busy FOB.

'What are the negatives?' Andrew asked.

'Local beliefs, sand and water.'

'That's not too clear, boss.'

'As you know, the men here call the desert the GAFA, or "Great Arabian Fuck All".' The explanation copped a few knowing laughs. 'It's amusing, but accurate,' Hailsham said when the laughter had died down. 'Out there, where we'll be going, the desert appears to be empty of every-thing except sand and gravel. That appearance,

35

however, is deceptive. Even the most barren stretch probably belongs to somebody and will be highly valued as grazing for the camels still maintained here by the Saudis, particularly those of high rank. As it is with their religion, so it is with their property: we have to be careful not to give offence.'

'And the other problems?'

'Too much sand and too little water,' Hailsham replied. 'Sand ingestion gives us severe mechanical problems. Even with filters, the life of helicopter engines is reduced to about a tenth of normal usage. The power-packs of the Challenger tanks are failing so often that 7th Armoured Brigade's desert training had to be curtailed. Other supply vehicles that were perfectly fine in Europe, when loaded here sink into the sand. And container trucks are particularly useless here. In fact, we've had to borrow a lot of M453 tracked vehicles from the Yanks. We'll be using them in conjunction with wheeled vehicles for staged resupply journeys. A further problem is that the desert is mostly flat, featureless terrain, which makes direction-finding difficult for the supply trucks. They can also get bogged down in the sand, thus becoming exposed.'

None of the men showed too much concern at that.

'Water?' Danny asked.

'It normally comes from the desalination plant at Al Jubail, but if we miss the REME supply columns, or if we're out on patrol, we'll have to drink the fossil water from the prehistoric aquifers beneath the desert floor. Of course the sappers will also be prospecting the best sites for artesian wells, but they have to negotiate with local landowners, who aren't always keen.'

'I'd rather drink my own piss,' big Andrew said. 'It won't be the first time.'

'As it is with the flight crewmen,' Hailsham continued when the laughter had died down, 'you'll all be given approximately £800 worth of gold, to help you if you're caught or find yourselves cut off and faced with non-friendly civilians who want their palms greased. You'll also be carrying a chit written in Arabic, promising that Her Majesty's Government will pay the sum of £5000 to anyone who returns you safely to friendly territory or persons. If nothing else, I trust that makes you feel important.'

'I'm important enough without that,' said Andrew without hesitation. 'You can look me up in the Imperial War Museum. I'm in there with the greats.'

'You do us all proud, Sergeant Winston. Any questions, men?'

'Yeah,' Paddy said. 'What do we do between now and the twenty-second?'

'We prepare,' Hailsham said.

The men dispersed and went their separate ways, most of them looking a lot happier than they had done for the past couple of days.

Ricketts put his thumb up in the air. 'Very good, boss.' Hailsham just grinned.

3

On 19 January, five days before the planned date, the Squadron was kitted out with weapons, survival equipment and battle clothes especially modified for desert conditions, before being flown from the FOB to a landing zone (LZ) somewhere deep in Iraq.

Since the briefing in early January, they had all undergone special training and weapons testing in the Empty Quarter, a vast, uninhabited region some distance from Al Jubail, with an emphasis on desert driving, survival in dust, sand, fierce heat and freezing cold, the protection of weapons from the same, and direction-finding by the moon and stars in case of compass failure. They were also trained in the use of laser designators for marking targets. All were looking forward to finishing the training and being airlifted to the LZ on the twenty-second.

They were therefore taken by surprise when, at 0001 hours Zulu – one minute past three local time, or one minute past midnight Greenwich Mean Time – on Thursday 17 January, two days after the deadline given for Saddam's withdrawal from Kuwait – which he ignored – eight US Apaches of the 101st Airborne Division, equipped with laser spot trackers and range-finders, attacked Iraqi radars with Hellfire missiles, rockets and 30mm cannon shells, destroying two command centres and their Soviet radars, Tall Spoon and King Rest, thereby creating a safe corridor for Allied aircraft.

Simultaneously, Tomahawk Cruise missiles from the Coalition aircraft-carriers in the Gulf rained down on Baghdad while British Tornadoes skimmed at low level across the desert at 800kph, also heading north for Baghdad. These were followed almost instantly by another wave of 'jammer' aircraft intent on suppressing enemy defences, top-cover fighters, more Tornado bombers, reconnaissance planes, AWACS early-warning, intelligence-gathering and target-identification aircraft, and the deadly, delta-winged F-117A Stealth fighter-bombers. The latter, invisible to enemy radar and often mistaken for UFOs, were likened by many to 'ghost' planes.

In no time at all, nocturnal Baghdad was illuminated by the greatest fireworks display in history and covered by an enormous umbrella of turbulent black smoke.

In the first 24 hours of this incredibly complex, computer-controlled war, over a thousand sorties were flown and over a hundred missiles launched against 158 targets, including communications centres and Scud launching sites, with as many as twelve combat aircraft being refuelled in-flight simultaneously by tankers stacked six deep in the air.

During the day, the first Allied casualty was the loss of a single Tornado. During the night of the seventeenth, however, from Iraqi airfields and secret bases in the west of the country, Saddam's military commanders unleashed a volley of eight Scud missiles at Israel. Two landed in Haifa and four in Tel Aviv. They were followed immediately by more Scud attacks on Riyadh, where the War Room and main communications of the Coalition effort were located.

Even as the citizens of Haifa, Tel Aviv and Riyadh were donning NBC suits, designed for use during nuclear, biological or chemical attack, or placing gas masks over their heads, Patriot anti-missile missiles were taking off with a

41

deafening cacophony. These were followed rapidly by an equally loud din overhead as the incoming Scuds were hit and exploded, filling the sky with great flashes of silvery light, mushrooms of black smoke and spectacular webs of crimson tracers and downward-curving streams of dazzling white, yellow and blood-red flame.

By the second day of the war, RAF aircrews were attempting to trap Iraqi aircraft hidden in hardened aircraft shelters, or HASs, by bombing the access tracks and taxiways leading from the shelters to the runways. At the same time, US giant B52s were carrying out round-the-clock, high-altitude attritional bombing raids designed to demoralize, exhaust and daze the Iraqi troops by denying them sleep, when not actually killing them.

By Day Three, however, it had become clear that the major threat to the Coalition was the Scuds, particularly those on mobile launchers.

'Which is where we come in,' Major Hailsham told his assembled troopers outside his tent in the FOB in Al Jubail. 'The difficulty in tracking mobile Scud launchers is complicated by Saddam's use of dummy rockets that look realistic from the air and contain fuel that explodes when hit by a bomb, thereby encouraging our pilots to report more strikes than they've actually made. They also use dummy mobile launchers with real crews and they, too, look genuine from the air.'

'You mean the crews of the dummy mobile launchers have to drive around the desert, deliberately trying to be spotted, in order to misdirect the fire from our aircraft?'

'Correct,' Hailsham said.

'Some job!' Geordie exclaimed. 'Rather them than me! Driving around just to be picked off by any passing aircraft and become another statistic on their kill counts. No, thanks. Not *my* cup of tea!'

'As if those Air Force bastards don't already come out with enough bullshit when they're doing their sums,' Andrew said, flashing his perfect teeth. 'The day I find an honest Air Force kill count I'll eat my own cock.'

'*If* you can find it,' Geordie said, which brought the house down.

OK, men, that's enough,' Hailsham admonished them, continuing when he had regained their attention: 'It's becoming clear that because of these dummy sites and launchers, the number of Scuds taken out by the aircrews is considerably less than at first anticipated. And as the real ones can't be seen from the air, eyeball recces and personal contact are needed. So, my good fellows, we're going to take them out ourselves, with particular emphasis on those within range of Israel, located in the desert round two Iraqi airfields known only as H2 and H3. So far, the Israelis are refusing to be drawn into the war. We therefore have to stop the Scud attacks on Israel before their patience wears out.'

'What's the terrain like around H2 and H3?' Ricketts asked.

'Fortunately a lot of it's less flat and open than most parts of the desert,' replied Hailsham, using his pointer to indicate the area on the map behind him. 'The demarcation line is between the British and US territories on the most distant of the three MSRs [military supply routes] running north-east from Baghdad to Amman. If the Americans operate mostly to the north of it, in the area they call Scud Boulevard, or the northern "Scud box", as they call it, and we keep to Scud Alley, south of the main road, there'll be no danger of us fighting each other accidentally. Our territory, Scud Alley, is the Jordanian lava plateau, a relatively high, hilly area with deep wadis that are often flash-flooded after storms. Loose rock instead of sand, though dense sandstorms are blown in from other areas. Lots of rain instead of burning sun. Freezing cold at night. In fact, it's more like the Falklands than it is like Oman, so you shouldn't find it too strange.'

'I remember the Falklands well,' Paddy said. 'Rain, hail and snow.'

'Right,' Jock concurred. 'OPs always flooded with water. Fucking wind every day. I thought this place would be a pleasant change – balmy nights, lots of sunshine.'

'You just want to look like me,' Andrew teased him. 'Suntanned and beautiful.'

'Spare me!' Jock retorted.

'That's enough,' said Hailsham, with a wave of his hand. 'Let's get back to the business in hand.'

'Yes, boss,' Geordie said, grinning mischievously at each of his mates in turn and cracking his knuckles.

'Good.' Glancing outside the lean-to tent, Hailsham saw the sun sinking towards the flat horizon, casting its crimson light on the white plain as darkness crept in. Helicopters and fighter planes were silhouetted in its huge, fiery eye like ink-black cut-outs suspended on invisible threads. From where he stood they looked beautiful. 'The Regiment will undertake three lines of attack,' he continued. 'Some teams will stake out static, covert road-watch patrols to report the movement of Scud traffic. Others will then vector F-15 strike aircraft onto the Scuds to destroy them.'

'What kind of teams?' asked Danny.

'Lurp teams – eight men. To be inserted by chopper at an LZ about 140 to 180 miles behind the enemy border, without any transport other than desert boots and a strong will.'

The 'Lurp' teams Hailsham referred to were LRRP, or long-range reconnaissance patrols.

'A strong will,' Andrew echoed with a devilish grin. 'That whittles it down to one man – me – and that isn't enough.'

'In parallel,' Hailsham said when the anticipated scorn had been poured on Andrew, 'there'll be fighting columns of up to a dozen well-armed Land Rovers carrying one and a half tons of war *matériel* each, manned by a half squadron of thirty men or more. We'll have four such columns. Their job will be to penetrate one of two major areas in the west, near the border with Jordan, from where the Scuds are launched. This "Scud box" is a well-defended area of desert of approximately 240 square miles, including the motorway linking Baghdad with Amman. Around twelve to fourteen mobile launchers are thought to be in or near the area.'

'Do we move by day or night?' Ricketts asked.

'It's not the Empty Quarter, so we'll mostly move by night. According to Intelligence, Bedouin come and go constantly. There's also a surprising amount of civilian traffic, much of it generated by fear of Western vengeance on Baghdad. Last but not least, because it's a critically important military zone, it's filled with Iraqi military personnel of all kinds, including Scud crews and the militia.'

'How do we insert?' said Andrew.

'Two of the OP patrols will go in on foot. Another will be lifted in by RAF Chinooks. The rest will drive in on stripped-down Land Rovers and motorbikes. We cross the border on the twentieth – tomorrow.'

'Who does what?' asked Danny.

'Allocation of duties is being drawn up right now and you'll all be informed within the hour. Any more questions?'

'No, boss,' was the general response.

'OK, men, go and have some chow. Get as much rest as possible. You'll get your allocations later. Departure time will be the afternoon or early evening. That's it. Class dismissed.' As the men turned away, heading for the mess tent, Hailsham indicated that Ricketts should remain. 'I have a special job for you,' he said. 'Pull up a chair, Sergeant-Major.'

Ricketts sat in a wooden chair on the other side of the trestle table Hailsham was using as a desk. The major placed two cups on the table and removed the cap from a vacuum flask. 'Tea?' he asked. When Ricketts nodded, he poured two cups of hot, white tea, then pushed one over to Ricketts. 'Sorry, Sergeant-Major, no sugar.' He glanced out over the sea of tents, now sinking back into a crimson twilight streaked with great shadows. After sipping some tea, he turned back to Ricketts. 'Before anyone goes anywhere,' he said, 'we have to cut Iraq's links with the outside world. They're in the shape of a complex web of communications towers known as microwave links, set up in the desert, danger-ously close to main roads and supply routes.'

'Should be easy to find,' Ricketts said, trying his hot tea.

'Not that easy, Sergeant-Major. The towers may be visible, but the fibre-optic cables are buried well below ground. So far, even the

US National Security Council's combined intelligence and scientific know-how hasn't been able to bug them or tap into them – let alone destroy them.'

Ricketts spread his hands in the air, indicating bewilderment. 'So how do we knock out Iraq's whole communications system? It's too widespread, boss.'

'We don't necessarily have to knock the whole system out,' Hailsham said. 'According to the green slime, it's the communications system coming out of Baghdad that controls Saddam's trigger-finger. Like the rest of the system, that network is a mixture of microwave link towers, in which telecom messages are transmitted short distances by air waves, and by fibre-optic cables buried in the ground and capable of carrying an enormous amount of data. We've received enough info from Intelligence to enable us to concentrate on the fibre-optic cables. Those lines carry Baghdad's orders to the Iraqi troops responsible for Scud operations. They also run Saddam Hussein's diplomatic traffic to Amman, Geneva, Paris and the UN, thus increasing his political credibility. It's our job to destroy that credibility as well as the Scuds – and we have to do it immediately.'

'You mean tonight?'

'Exactly. I want you to pick 40 of your most reliable men and have them ready to be airlifted before midnight. I'm coming with you. Our LZ is an area approximately sixty kilometres south of Baghdad, near the main road that leads to Basra. According to Intelligence, the highest density of Baghdad's fibre-optic cables are buried there and the ground is relatively easy to dig. We're going to dig down, remove a sample of cable for analysis, then blow up the rest – so we need a couple of demolition experts. Any questions, Ricketts?'

'No questions, boss.'

'I'm delighted to hear it. Have you finished your tea?'

'Yes.'

'Then go to it.'

Ricketts grinned, finished his tea, then stood up and left the tent. Heading back to his own lean-to, he was enthralled by the sight of so many tents on the dark plain, under the desert's starlit sky, but even more thrilled – indeed almost ecstatic – to be back in business at last.

It was what he and most of his mates lived for.

4

At approximately midnight, two of the RAF's CH-47 twin-blade Chinooks lifted Ricketts's chosen team of 40 men off the airstrip of the FOB and headed through the night sky for the LZ. The men, packed into the gloomy, noisy interior of the helicopter, were wearing the normal beige beret, but without its winged-dagger badge and now camouflaged under a *shemagh*, or veil, that could also be wrapped around the eyes and mouth to protect them from dust and sand. (The same kind of veil was used to camouflage the standard 7.62mm SLR, or self-loading rifle.) The standard-issue woollen pullover was woven in colours that would blend in with the desert floor and matched the colouring of the high-topped, lace-up desert boots.

'I feel like an A-rab,' Geordie said. 'What do I look like?'

'Real cute,' Paddy replied.

'I always knew you adored me.'

Most of the men were armed either with the ubiquitous semi-automatic SLR or with 30-round, semi- and fully automatic M16s and their many attachments, including bayonets, bipods for accuracy when firing from the prone position, telescopic sights, night-vision aids, and M203 40mm grenade-launchers. Some had Heckler & Koch MP5 30-round sub-machine-guns. A few had belt-fed L7A2 7.62mm general-purpose machine-guns, or GPMGs, capable of firing 800 rounds a minute to a range of up to 1400 metres. All had standard-issue Browning FN 9mm high-power handguns on their hips, capable of firing 13 rounds in a couple of seconds.

These weapons and their bulky ammunition belts, combined with the standard bergens and camouflaging, made the men look awkward and bulky, almost Neanderthal. However, those weapons were only part of their personal equipment, and other, heavier weapons were taking up what little space they had left between them.

In case they were approached by tanks during the operation, the men were also carrying heavy support weapons, including the 94mm light anti-tank weapon, or LAW 80, which fired a high-explosive anti-tank (HEAT) rocket and could be used on bunkers as well as armoured vehicles; the portable FIM-92A Stinger anti-aircraft missile system, capable of firing a heat-seeking missile 8000 metres and fitted with a friend or foe identification, or FFI, system; and two different mortars: the 51mm mortar, which, though carried and operated by one man, could launch an HE bomb to a range of 750 metres, and the larger, heavier 81mm mortar, which required three men to carry it, but could fire HE bombs 5660 metres at a rate of eight rounds per minute.

'Tell me, Alfie,' Andrew said, bored out of his mind, and deciding to have a bit of sport with Sergeant Alfred Lloyd, who was sitting beside him, 'how come you're almost as tall as me, but only half of my weight?'

'I'm taller than you, fella, by half an inch. I can tell when our eyes meet.'

A dour Leicester man and SAS demolition specialist who had formerly been a Royal Engineer, then an ammunition technician with the Royal Army Ordnance Corps, Lloyd had unkempt red hair, a beakish, broken nose, and a lean face veined by booze and scorched by the sun.

'I'm always willing to give a man the benefit

of the doubt,' Andrew said, 'so how come, since you're even *taller* than me, you only weigh half my size?'

'I've sabotaged ships, aircraft, every type of armoured vehicle, power stations, communications centres, supply depots, railways and roads. It required a lot of climbing and running, which is why I'm still slim.'

Alfie Lloyd was indeed still as thin as a rake, though now heavily burdened like the others and divided from big Andrew by the boxes packed with explosives, charges, detonator caps and the many other tools of his dangerous trade. Andrew stared at them sceptically.

'Those bloody explosives, man, are they safe?'

'Sure.'

'I've heard that explosives go off real easy.'

'Bullshit. Most explosives are safe unless they're deliberately set off. You can hammer TNT into powdered crystals and it still won't explode. That's why it can be delivered by parachute. No problem at all.'

'Mmmmm,' Andrew murmured, not totally convinced. 'So what exactly *is* explosive, man? Give it to me in simple words.'

Alfie thought for a while, wondering how to reply, not being a man of great eloquence and aware that Andrew was a poet, slick with his tongue. Finally he said, 'You tell me.'

Andrew nodded and beamed.

'A solid or liquid substance which, under the influence of a certain stimulus, such as an exploding detonator, is rapidly converted into another substance with accompanying high pressure, leading to the outburst of violence and noise known as an explosion. What say you, Sergeant?'

'Is that fucking Swahili?'

'I'm from Barbados,' Andrew replied, 'where they only speak English.'

'You could have fooled me,' Alfie said, shaking his head. 'I thought *I* spoke English!'

'They only *think* they speak English in Barbados,' Paddy Clarke said. 'All that molasses and rum goes to their heads and makes them think they're white men. We should hand Andrew over to a missionary for a little correction.'

'The Paddy from Liverpool has spoken,' Andrew intoned. 'Let us bow down and throw up.'

'Can it, the lot of you,' the RAF Loadmaster barked at them as he materialized from the gloom. He glanced through one of the portholes in the passenger hold and announced: 'We're coming in, if we're lucky, to the LZ, so prepare to offload.'

'Yes, mother!' Taff chimed in a high, school-boy's voice, though he quickly made a great show of checking his gear when the Loadmaster gave him a baleful stare.

'Hey, Moorcock' Paddy said, turning to the new man beside him, eager for a little sport. 'Where did you say you were located before you were badged?'

'The Welsh Guards,' Moorcock answered, giving his kit a great deal of attention.

'See any action?' Paddy asked him.

'A brief tour of Northern Ireland,' Moorcock said, sliding his arms awkwardly through the webbing of his bergen. 'Though I didn't see much there.'

'Know much about the Iraqis?'

'No.'

'They're fuckin' murderous bastards. Don't on any account let yourself be caught. There's things worse than death, kid.'

'What's that, Corporal?' Trooper Stone asked with a grin, being less impressionable than his friend. Although he, like Moorcock and Gillett, had only recently been badged and was serving his probationary period, he wasn't about to take any bullshit from the older hands. 'What's worse than death, then?'

'They'll pull your nails out,' Paddy said.

'They'll gang-bang you,' Jock added.

'They'll chop your cock off and make you eat it with couscous,' Geordie put in. 'Then they'll cut your eyeballs out and make you suck them until you go gaga.'

'Go fuck yourselves,' Trooper Stone said.

'Leave these poor probationers alone,' threatened Andrew, 'or I'll personally chop *your* cocks off and shove them, all shrivelled, up your arses, which will then need some wiping.'

'Thanks, Sergeant,' Trooper Moorcock said, tightening the straps on his bergen and looking serious while his two friends, Stone and Gillett, grinned at each other.

'We're touching down,' the Loadmaster said. 'Hold on to your balls, lads . . . Three, two, one, zero . . . *Touchdown!*'

The transport landed with a lot of bouncing, roaring and metallic shrieking, but otherwise no problems, on an LZ located about half a mile from the main road that ran one way to Basra, 40 miles the other way to Baghdad.

The men disembarked even before the two Chinooks' engines had gone into neutral, spilling out of the side into dense clouds of sand whipped up by the twin-bladed rotors. When the billowing sand had subsided, the first thing they saw was a fantastic display of fireworks illuminating the distant horizon: immense webs of red and purple anti-aircraft fire, silvery-white explosions, showers of crimson sparks and streams of phosphorus fireflies.

'Baghdad,' Hailsham explained to those nearest to him. 'The Allies are bombing the hell out of it. Rather them than us.'

As their eyes adjusted to moonlit darkness, they saw the nearest two microwave links, soaring high above the flat plain, about a quarter mile apart, but less than twenty yards from the road. Spreading out and keeping their weapons at the ready, the men hiked across the dusty, wind-blown plain until they reached a point equidistant between the two towers. From here, the road was dangerously close – a mere twenty-odd yards.

'It's pretty dark,' Ricketts said, glancing in every direction, 'so if anyone comes along the road, we should be OK if we stay low. We need sentries on point in both directions, with the men not being used for digging keeping guard in LUPs.'

'Right,' Hailsham said.

Ricketts gave his instructions by means of hand signals. With the Chinooks waiting on the ground a quarter of a mile away, their rotors turning quietly in neutral, the bulk of the men broke into four-man teams, then fanned out to form a circle of LUPs, or lying-up positions, from where they could keep their eyes on the road and defend the diggers and demolition team if anyone came along.

Meanwhile Hailsham and Ricketts accompanied Sergeant Lloyd as he checked the alignment between the two communications towers and gauged where the fibre-optic cable was running between them, hidden under the ground.

'This is it,' he said, waving his hand from left to right to indicate an invisible line between the two towers. He turned to the dozen troopers selected to dig. 'I want a series of four holes about twelve foot apart, each six foot long and as deep as you need to go to expose the cable. That should be about four feet. If you see any transport coming along that road, or if we call a warning to you, drop down into the hole you're digging and don't make a move until given clearance. OK, get going.'

The men laid down their weapons, removed

spades and shovels from their bergens, and proceeded to dig the holes as required. As they did so, they and the others – now stretched belly-down in LUPs on the dark ground, their weapons at the ready and covering the road in both directions – were able to watch the fantastic pyrotechnics of crimson anti-aircraft tracer fire and silvery bomb bursts over distant Baghdad, which was being bombed by wave after wave of British, American and Saudi jets, as well as Tomahawk Cruise missiles fired from ships in the Gulf, flying in at just under the speed of sound at heights of 50–250 feet, to cause more devastation and death.

'Wow!' Andrew whispered, looking at the lights over the distant city. 'That's just beautiful, man!'

'Beautiful from here,' Hailsham replied. 'Hell on earth if you're there.'

'You men,' Sergeant Lloyd said to two of his eight sappers, both of whom had various explosives, charges and timers dangling from their webbing. 'I want you to take out those towers, one to each man. Fix enough explosives to the base to make sure the whole caboodle topples over. Use electronic timers that can be fired from here by remote control. Don't make any mistakes. When this lot goes up, those towers have to go up at the same time. Understood?'

'Yes, boss,' the men nodded.

Then they headed off in opposite directions, towards the tower each had selected, the explosives on their webbing bouncing up and down as they ran.

'You see that?' Geordie whispered to Trooper Gillett, having decided to pass the time by winding him up. 'Those explosives are liable to go off any second, taking us out with him.'

'Aw, come off it, Geordie!'

'No, kid, it's true! I'd be pissing in my pants if I was you. He'll blow up any minute now.'

'That's bullshit, Geordie,' Trooper Stone retorted. 'We all heard what Sergeant Lloyd said in the plane – explosives don't blow up easily.'

'Besides,' Trooper Gillett added, 'that sapper's practically out of sight already. If the stupid bastard blows himself up, we're well out of range. Pull the other one, Geordie.'

'Shut up, you men,' Sergeant Lloyd said, glancing down at the men digging the holes, 'these men have to concentrate. If you've got nothing better to do, I can always hand you a shovel.'

'No, thanks,' Geordie said, edging away. 'I

have to go and stand out on point. Have a nice day!'

'Fucking nerd,' Sergeant Lloyd said.

The digging alone took forty-five minutes. During that time two vehicles, about half an hour apart, came along the road, heading away from Baghdad, their headlights cutting a swathe through the darkness but not picking out the men who were concealed in LUPs, guns at the ready, only twenty yards or so away. The first vehicle was a Mercedes saloon filled with white-robed Arabs; the second was a soft-topped army truck packed with Iraqi soldiers. Both passed by and disappeared into the night, their drivers and passengers, probably fleeing from the air attacks on Baghdad, not knowing how close to death they had come in what they thought was an empty, safe area.

About twenty minutes after the army truck had passed by, one of the men uncovered a fibre-optic cable.

'That's it,' Sergeant Lloyd said, glancing down into the hole as the trooper who had reached the first cable wiped sweat from his brow. 'I want that whole stretch of cable cleared, Trooper, so get back to your digging.'

'Right, Sarge,' the trooper said. He continued

his digging. When the length of cable running across the bottom of the hole was completely exposed, he jumped out to let Lloyd jump in. Ricketts glanced left and right, checking the road in both directions, but there was no sign of any more movement. Satisfied, he knelt beside the hole in which Lloyd, unpacking his boxes, was already at work.

'Cable!' a trooper called from the next hole.

'Me, too!' someone else called, to be followed by a third, then a fourth.

'Tell them to clear the whole length of cable,' Lloyd told Ricketts, 'then get out of the holes. My men will do the rest.'

'Right,' Ricketts said, then stood and went from hole to hole, passing on Lloyd's orders.

'I've reached mine,' a man in the fifth hole told him. 'There it is,' said a man in the sixth hole, looking down and pointing.

By the time Ricketts had passed on Lloyd's instructions, the first men had completely uncovered their cables and were clambering gratefully out of the holes to wipe the mud off their hands and have a drink of hot tea from a vacuum flask. As they did so, Lloyd's assistants, all former sappers, jumped down into the holes to fix explosive charges to the cables.

Major Hailsham was kneeling on the rim of Lloyd's hole, looking down as Lloyd worked, so Ricketts, just as interested, knelt beside him.

Even as Iraqi MiGs and Mirage F-1s flew overhead, heading away from the battered air-fields of a spectacularly illuminated Baghdad, Sergeant Lloyd and his men coolly continued what they were doing. With Hailsham and Ricketts looking on, Lloyd sliced through a cable and slipped a piece into his bergen, to be shipped back to England for examination. He then packed C3/C4 plastic explosive around and between the exposed cables, fixed it in place, and attached a non-electrical firing system with a time fuse connected to a blasting cap in a thin aluminium tube, which he embedded carefully in the explosive charge. To the blasting cap he attached a detonating cord of reinforced prima-cord – a small, high-explosive core protected by half a dozen layers of material – which in turn was taped together with two primers and a detonator fixed to a timing device. He glanced up at Hailsham.

'Give us twenty minutes to get back to the choppers,' Hailsham said. 'That's all we need.'

'The other five started after me,' Lloyd replied, 'so I'll add on ten minutes.'

'Right,' Hailsham said, then turned to Ricketts as Lloyd set his timer. 'Signal the men to break up the LUPs and head back to the choppers.'

'Right, boss.' Ricketts used hand signals to convey Hailsham's instructions. From where he was standing, he saw nothing but dark emptiness, but then the men started appearing, rising up from the flat earth, silhouetted either by stars or the fireworks display over distant Baghdad. After strapping their bergens to their shoulders and picking up their weapons, they lumbered like misshapen beasts back towards the Chinooks, whose rotors were still spinning, though silently, their engines in neutral.

As the men retreated from the area, being swallowed up in darkness, Lloyd and his other demolition specialists emerged one by one from their separate holes, wiping the mud from their hands. While they were packing up their equipment, the other sappers returned and reported that they had placed the explosives and remote-control timing devices on the soaring communications towers. Satisfied, Sergeant Lloyd nodded, then led them all across the windswept plain, hurrying after the others.

Hailsham and Ricketts brought up the rear, the latter keeping his eye on the road. He saw nothing and finally turned away, walking faster to catch up with his men. When they reached the Chinooks, hazy behind the dust clouds swirling under the rotors, they gathered together to look back at the stretch of earth between the two towers. When Ricketts saw Hailsham and Lloyd checking their watches, he did the same. The whole job had taken ninety minutes so far.

Ricketts felt the ground shaking beneath his feet, then saw a dark eruption far ahead, equi-distant between the silhouetted towers, where the holes had been dug in the ground. As the vibrations turned into a rumbling, the earth erupted in a dark crescent and then a black, expanding hillock. Then the rumbling became a thunderous explosion that created a gigantic mushroom cloud of smoke, dust, sand and showering gravel, billowing up from a bed of white and blue flames fringed by crimson sparks. The mushroom cloud rose higher, expanded in all directions and was blotting out the stars even as its tendrils coiled languorously back down to shower the desert floor with its deadly debris. As one tower, then the other, collapsed and disappeared in the billowing smoke, the roaring tapered off into a rumbling and eventually faded into silence.

'Let's go!' Hailsham bawled.

Reluctantly, the men turned their backs on the spectacle before them, filed back into the Chinooks and were lifted off the desert plain before Iraqi troops arrived at the scene of the explosion, which they surely would.

When his Chinook had ascended and was heading back to Saudi Arabia, Ricketts glanced back through a porthole and saw the immense mushroom cloud settling down over what looked like an enormous crater surrounded by charred, upturned earth. Where the two towers had stood, there was now just a mess of tangled metal, spreading out a great distance.

With communications from Baghdad cut, the real fight could start.

5

The men chosen for long-range reconnaissance patrols, or 'Lurps', were given light-strike vehicles, or LSVs, and Land Rover 90s, more commonly known in SAS circles as 'Pink Panthers' or 'dinkies'. Each Pink Panther was a mobile arsenal, carrying a Magellan satellite navigation system, two M203 grenade-launchers, LAW 80 94mm anti-tank missiles, a front-mounted 7.62-mm GPMG, a rear-mounted 0.5in Browning heavy machine-gun, as well as Stinger anti-aircraft missiles for use against Iraqi helicopter gunships. The commander and driver were each given a pair of Litton night-vision goggles. An armed trooper from the Mobility Group was to accompany each Pink Panther on a motorbike. Each team also carried a laser designator to be used for marking targets for the Allied aircraft, whose laser-guided bombs could then home in accurately on air-defence sites, bunkers, radar sites, command-and-control centres and military factories.

At approximately midnight on 22 January two RAF Chinooks lifted a squadron of SAS men and their LSVs and Pink Panthers deep into the desert of western Iraq, in the area known as Scud Alley.

Looking through a porthole just before landing, Ricketts saw some of the US HH-531J Pave Low and HH-60G Night Hawk helicopters just below and ahead. Equipped with special electronic and night-flying systems, they were extremely efficient as pathfinders. They were, however, also transporting Pink Panthers, LSVs and Honda motorbikes, all of which were slung in nets below them and seemed to be flying just above the desert plain. The others, which Ricketts could not see, were slung below the Chinooks.

Turning away from the porthole and glancing around the helicopter's long, narrow, dark hold, Ricketts saw the men preparing for the landing. Coming on this insertion straight after the previous night's raid on the communications towers near Baghdad, Ricketts and most of the men were particularly tired. And yet they were glad to be back in business, instead of wasting their time in so-called further training on the hot, dusty plains of the Empty Quarter.

With the appearance of their RAF Loadmaster, Ricketts knew they were about to land. This was confirmed when the Chinook slowed down, stopping moving forward, hovered briefly, then made its vertical descent. When the Loadmaster shouted over the din for the men to prepare to unload, they all checked their safety belts, equipment and weapons while firing off the usual bullshit.

The Chinook hovered for some time while its underslung loads – the Land Rovers, LSVs and motorbikes – were set down gently and released, but eventually it moved forward, away from the disengaged loads, and touched down on the desert floor further on. It bounced lightly a few times, then its roar subsided as its rotors, though still spinning, went into neutral. The loading ramp was opened, allowing moonlight to beam in as the men disembarked.

Once outside, Ricketts was shocked by the cold, fierce wind. Tying his *shemagh* across his face to protect his nose and mouth from the swirling sand, he noticed the other men were doing the same. With their veils and the camouflaging over their berets, they looked like Arab militiamen.

The sky was clear of clouds, but the sweeping sand obscured the stars and the horizon was barely visible through the murk. The dropped vehicles, still in their netting, were about a hundred yards further back and the other two Chinooks, each of which held 44 fully equipped troops, were about to land about the same distance away in the opposite direction.

The first helicopter touched down without trouble. When the second followed, luckily a good distance away, the ground erupted beneath it with a mighty roar, spewing soil, sand and smoke. The wheels in contact with the ground were blown off by the blast, burst into flames and shot like rapidly spinning balls of fire through the billowing black smoke. The Chinook crashed down on its rear end, then tilted sideways, its rotors still spinning, barely missing the ground. Where the wheels had been, the fuselage was torn open and the twisted metal was scorched.

'Damn!' Major Hailsham explained. 'They've landed on a minefield!' He started forward instinctively, without thinking, but Ricketts grabbed his elbow and pulled him back. 'You're right, boss – it's a bloody minefield. There's not a thing we can do.' Understanding what Ricketts meant,

Hailsham nodded, then looked back across the dark plain.

The Chinook was not on fire, but its underside was badly damaged and the fuselage was shuddering violently as the pilot, knowing the men could not disembark, tried to lift off. As the troopers pouring out of the other Chinook milled about, looking at the damaged chopper and then glancing cautiously at the ground near their feet, wondering if they too were on a minefield, the damaged, tilting Chinook roared and shook even more, its rotors spinning faster, creating great clouds of sand. Slowly, with metallic shrieks of protest, it righted itself and lifted off the ground.

As the Chinook rose awkwardly and noisily from the minefield, obscured in its own swirling curtains of sand, dust and debris, Jock McGregor, in charge of a crackling PRC 319 portable radio system, called out to Captain Hailsham: 'The captain says to tell you he can't land without wheels, so he wants permission to return to the FOB and take his chances on a landing there.'

'Permission granted!' Hailsham bellowed against the combined noise of the roaring Chinook and the howling wind. 'Wish him good luck.'

'Aye, aye, boss!' Jock called back, waving

his hand in acknowledgement. He conveyed Hailsham's message over the radio as the Chinook reached flight altitude, hovered for a moment, then laboriously headed back towards Saudi Arabia, leaving an immense cloud of sand to settle over the minefield.

Hailsham's hazel eyes turned above his fluttering light-brown *shemagh* to look directly at Ricketts. 'Damn!' he exclaimed softly. 'Forty-four men down already. Ah, well, let's get started.'

The rest of the men from Hailsham's Chinook had already surrounded the vehicles and equipment disengaged from the underslung loads and were removing the nets in which they had been carried. Hailsham and Ricketts joined them. Glancing across the desert, they saw that the men from the second Chinook were doing the same. Hailsham called Jock over and asked for the microphone for his PRC 319, which he used for a chat with the NCO commanding the other group. Satisfied that they were all right, he told them to keep their eyes peeled for any sign of land-mines elsewhere.

'The first thing we have to do,' he said to Ricketts, handing the mike back to Jock, 'is get rid of that damned minefield over there.'

He waited until the conveyance netting had been removed from the first Pink Panther and the satellite communications system fixed to the vehicle, then called HQ in Riyadh, giving his grid reference and asking for an AWACS command aircraft to fly over and detonate the whole minefield. Receiving an affirmative, he turned off the SATCOM system and watched his men as they removed the netting from the other vehicles, attached the separately packed equipment, and prepared the vehicles for use.

The Pink Panthers were painted in a desert camouflage scheme of sunset pink, earth brown and sandy yellow, which made them look a bit like cartoon or funfair cars. They were, however, highly sophisticated vehicles, with 3.5-litre V-8 petrol engines, five-speed gearboxes, alternating four- or five-wheel drive, with cabins stripped down to the hull and windscreens removed. They were also bristling with machine-guns and heavily laden with bergens, ammunition bandoliers, camping equipment and radios. Short-burst radio and SATCOM antennae were fixed to the sides, jutting up in the air, high above the multidirectional barrels of the guns. A SATNAV Global Positioning System (GPS) receiver was mounted on the vehicle – though it could also be carried by hand – and a sun compass, also used for navigation, was mounted horizontally on the front. Smoke dischargers were fitted front and rear, detachable searchlights were positioned on each side, camouflage netting was rolled across the bonnet and there were extra storage racks for food, water, fuel, spare parts, more weapons, ammunition and the tools required for the construction of OPs, or observation posts.

The LSVs, based on the dune-buggies widely used on American beaches, were virtually no more than tubular-steel frames in roll cages – no roof, body panels or windscreen – with two seats in the middle, fat, low-pressure tyres on each corner and a powerful engine. But although their payload capacity was limited, they carried LAW 80 anti-tank rockets and man-portable MILAN guided-missile firing posts, which made them ideal for hit-and-run raids on enemy targets.

The motorbikes, one to accompany each Land Rover, were Honda production machines, used as outriders, mainly for forward-observation purposes in terrain impassable to the other vehicles. They were driven mostly by daring young cowboys armed with an M16 slung across the back and a Browning 9mm high-power handgun in a holster at the hip.

A sudden, staccato series of mechanical coughs and roaring reminded Hailsham and Ricketts of the troopers disgorged from the second Chinook. Looking sideways, they saw that they were starting up their Pink Panthers, LSVs and motorbikes even as the Chinook was lifting off in a swirling cloud of sand and gravel. That cloud swallowed the men below, but they soon burst out of it, driving their assorted, brightly coloured vehicles across the flat plain to encircle Hailsham's group and skid to a halt, churning up more sand and dust. Meanwhile the Chinook behind Hailsham and Ricketts also took off, soon joining the other in the sky, where they hovered close together for a moment, like giant copulating beetles, before heading back to the border.

When the men around Hailsham had settled down, he climbed up on the back of his chosen Land Rover and called them in around him for his final briefing.

'First,' he said, 'I want to remind you that following Iraq's launch of Scud missiles against Israel, destroying their mobile launchers has become our number one priority. We're here because conventional aerial reconnaissance methods are too slow to keep track of the highly mobile missiles, so improvised methods have to be adapted to put the Scuds out of business. This area is a Scud box known as Scud Alley. It's about 240 square miles – including the motorway linking Baghdad with Amman. For that reason, it's very well defended and we have to be on our toes.'

'Does that mean we only move by night?' Danny Porter asked.

'This is no Empty Quarter. In short, it's damned dangerous. So, yes, we move only by night.'

Andrew had been studying his map and now he looked up. 'How many mobile launchers in this particular area?'

'Around twelve to fourteen – and we're going to find them.'

'What happens when we do?'

'The USAF and US Navy have put heavily armed F-15Es, F-16 Fighting Falcons, A-10s and A-6E Intruders on round-the-clock patrols over the Scud boxes, both north, where their men are, and south, where we are. However, the pilots need precise targeting information before they can launch attacks. We've been sent in here as mobile teams to put eyes on the ground. For this purpose we'll set up covert OPs to cover key roads. When Scud convoys are spotted, we'll either mark the target with our laser designators or pass the grid reference on to an E-3 AWACS command aircraft, using our SATCOM systems.'

'We just roam freely?' Geordie asked.

'Strictly within the area marked for your own team on the maps. Two Land Rovers, one LSV and one Honda to each patrol. We break up right now. We keep in touch with each other with short-burst transmissions on the PRC 319s. We rendezvous for resupplies at midnight five days from now – in Wadi Tubal, also marked on your maps. If anyone has any problems getting back, he's to contact the others by radio. Any questions?'

'Yeah,' Paddy Clarke said, putting up his hand like a schoolboy. 'What the hell are we doing with American LSVs instead of just the Pink Panthers? The fucking things only have a range of 200 kilometres against a dinkie's 650. Bloody useless, boss, if you ask me.'

'It's a trial run,' Hailsham explained. 'The LSVs are particularly popular with the US Special Forces, including those operating in the northern Scud box. I agree that they're small and have a much shorter range, but they're also extremely powerful and can go where the Land Rovers can't. Also, their relatively quiet engines and reduced radar and infrared signatures make them pretty difficult to find or hit. The American Delta Force strongly recommends them, so we're trying them out, with particular regard to their speed and mobility over difficult terrain. Any *more* questions?' When their shaking heads told him no, he said, 'Right, men, let's hit the road.'

After the Troop had been divided up into individual teams, the men climbed into their allocated vehicles and prepared to take off. Ricketts was commander of one of the Pink Panthers, sitting up front beside the driver, Danny Porter, with Geordie in the rear compartment as gunner, in charge of the 360-degree-traverse Browning 0.5in-calibre machine-gun. Andrew and Paddy were in the accompanying LSV and a young trooper, John 'Johnny Boy' Willoughby was on the Honda outrider, with his *shemagh* over his mouth and eyes, his M16 across his shoulders and his Browning at his hip.

With their veils, night-vision goggles and exposed facial skin camouflaged in blackening 'cam' cream, the men looked like brigands from a 'Mad Max' film.

Hailsham was just about to give the signal to move out when Jock, handling the SATCOM system in his Pink Panther, told him an RAF

Tornado was on its way to detonate the mine-field. In less than a minute they heard it overhead and Hailsham confirmed the grid readings to the pilot over the SATCOM.

'With all due respect, sir,' the pilot responded, his voice distorted by static, 'I think you should get the hell out of there before I drop my impressive load. You're a mite too close for comfort.'

'Thank you, Captain,' Hailsham replied, deadpan. 'I think I know what you mean. We'll be gone by the time you get here. Over and out.' Immediately, he gave the signal to move out, which was conveyed by his NCOs from one vehicle to another. Suddenly the desert's silence was split by the roaring of the Land Rovers, the lesser clamour of the LSVs and the harsh chatter of the motorbikes as they revved up. Hailsham's Pink Panther left first, heading deeper into the desert, and as the other vehicles followed him, one after the other, they churned up an enormous cloud of sand and dust.

This was nothing compared to the cloud created by the exploding JP233 bombs of the Tornado when it swooped down five minutes later. By that time the SAS mobile patrols had gathered much further out on the plain, waiting to see the results of the air attack.

Even in the moonlight, the Tornado was an awesome vision, a beast of many limbs and appendages, beginning with its air-to-air refuelling probe and including massive, moveable 'swing' wings; a high fin with ESM, or electronic surveillance measure; underslung fuel tanks and alarm anti-radar missiles; plus underwing ECM, or electronic countermeasure, pods, and protruding TRB 199 twin engines. For all that, it was a monster of terrible beauty, gifted with terrain-following radar and a computerized cockpit that enabled it to fly in as low as fifty feet above the ground to drop its JP233 bombs.

The bombs, which included a series of cratering devices, drifted down from the aircraft by parachute and detonated just above the ground. That detonation propelled various charges deep into the ground, and when these exploded they heaved up the surface and created many large holes beneath it. The multiple, underground explosions caused a vast area of the desert floor to rumble and shake. Then it erupted in a spectacular, cataclysmic mushroom cloud of sand, dust, gravel, smoke and swirling tendrils of gaseous flame. The noise was deafening, the impact shattering, and the mushroom expanded to form a great canopy over the desert, blotting out the big moon and brilliant stars.

Only when the great mushroom cloud had started to collapse, falling back in upon itself, did the men in the Land Rovers, LSVs and motorbikes head off in the opposite direction, away from Saudi Arabia and deeper into Iraq, eventually going off in many different directions, cutting lines through the desert.

They were all on their own now.

6

The Scuds, genuine and false, had been reported as travelling along roads and tracks known as MSRs, or military supply routes. The SAS patrols had therefore each been given a preselected stretch of MSR to cover. Driving by night for an hour or so through the desert, with the Pink Panther and the LSV side by side, and the motorbike in the lead, Ricketts's group soon reached the area selected for their OP, located behind a ridge that offered a good view of the MSR below.

As they would be here for five days, they dug a large, deep, rectangular OP with one narrow end as the rest bay, the other, facing the MSR, for the observers and sentry, and a kit-well in the middle, holding weapons, ammunition, radio equipment, spare batteries, water cans and dry food. The OP was covered in canvas, which in turn was camouflaged with sand and gravel taken from the surrounding area, and the observation bay was screened by black hessian and contained a black-painted telescope on a tripod, as well as binoculars, night-vision aids, a camera, spare film, aerial photos previously taken by reconnaissance planes, codes and ciphers for radio transmissions, and logbooks and maps.

The weather in that area was exceptionally harsh, much colder than expected, and before the night was over they found themselves working in a dense cloud of freezing fog. By the time a blood-red sun rose over the flat horizon, bringing with it the heat, they all realized that they were in for extremes of hot and cold, with the accompanying threat of sunstroke or dehydration in the daylight, and hypothermia in the damp, freezing night.

Nevertheless the OP was completed just before full daylight came, with the spoil removed and scattered over the ground a good distance away. The vehicles were then covered in camouflage nets with hessian stitched in to keep out the sunlight.

Though they all had water bottles, the men knew the water would not last long, so while Danny and Geordie kept watch for enemy activity and the others sorted out the equipment in the OP, Jock expertly constructed a desert still.

After choosing the nearby spot where water would be most likely to collect, Jock dug a hole one metre deep and two metres wide, then filled it with vegetation soaked in his own urine. He placed a metal container in the centre, covered it with plastic sheeting with a rough undersurface, cut a hole in it and slid a drinking tube through the hole, leaving one end inside the container, the other extending out to the side. The sheeting was held down by stones placed around its circumference, with another couple of stones in the centre to depress the covering directly over the container. This simple device would provide up to a litre of drinking water every twenty-four hours by collecting the condensation that would form beneath the plastic and drip into the container.

'I'm not sure I can drink this,' Geordie said, 'knowing that the condensation was caused by your piss.'

'Right,' Paddy agreed. 'When we think of where that dick of yours has been, we want to know what your piss is like. These days a man can get AIDS just by breathing the air, so I think the water made from your condensation could be as deadly as cyanide.'

'You don't want to drink my water,' Jock replied, 'then *don't* drink my water. Who's inviting you, anyway?'

As for their own waste, the men excreted or urinated well away from the OP and either buried it or, in the latter case, let the ground soak it up.

'Personally,' Geordie said, 'I'm used to having a bog indoors, but Sergeant Winston, whose ancestors were not like yours and mine, probably thinks the cool breeze on his bare arse is a natural laxative.'

'At least it comes out of my arse,' Andrew replied without a pause, 'whereas with you, being a miraculous being, it comes out the top end.'

'Complete with lots of hot air,' Paddy added. 'Known as farting and wind.'

'In Newcastle they think that's civilized conversation,' 'Johnny Boy' Willoughby butted in, getting the measure of the company he was keeping and revelling in it. 'But up there they would, wouldn't they?'

'Amen to that,' Andrew said.

When everything was completed and they had settled down to their surveillance – some on guard, some on watch, Hailsham and Ricketts planning their raids on the likely Scud bunkers marked on their maps – Hailsham decided to send the half-crazy young Johnny Boy off on his Honda for eyeball reconnaissance of certain areas.

'You will also report on the movements of any military traffic across the desert or along the MSRs,' Hailsham said. 'Do you think you can do that, Trooper?'

'Yes, boss!' Johnny Boy snapped. Blond-haired, blue-eyed and handsome, he had nerves of steel and was as good as Niki Lauda on his motorbike, though more reckless. 'Scud bunkers, mobile units and any other military traffic on the desert or along the MSRs – you want it, you've got it, boss.'

'No derring-do,' Ricketts warned him. 'No personally favoured adventures. You stay out of sight where it's possible to do so, and you don't fire a shot unless fired upon. Is that understood?'

'Yes, boss! Absolutely!'

'We've heard stories about you, Trooper.'

'Fame at last, boss! What stories?'

'Reckless behaviour,' Hailsham told him. 'Courting danger for the hell of it. An irresistible impulse to be seen by the enemy and try to play cat-and-mouse with them. Any truth in it, Trooper?'

'Bloody scandalous, boss. Careless tongues and idle gossip. Since I'm usually out there on my own, how would anyone know that? No, boss, I'm A1 on this.'

'You have the benefit of the doubt,' Ricketts said, 'so don't let us down, Trooper. On your way and good luck.'

'Aye, aye, boss,' Johnny Boy said.

He left wearing his camouflaged SAS beret without the winged-dagger badge, his *shemagh* to cover his mouth and nose, and tinted spectacles to protect his eyes. An M16 rifle was slung across his back, a Browning 9mm high-power handgun sat on his hip, a leather-cased Fairburn-Sykes commando knife had been slipped down the inside of one of his desert boots, and he had carrier bags on either side of his motorbike. Taking off in a cloud of sand, he soon became a mere cloud in the distance and eventually disappeared.

As the desert was vast and relatively featureless, Johnny Boy would navigate generally with the sun compass mounted horizontally on the handlebars of his motorbike. For more precise positioning, particularly when calling in enemy positions to the OP, he would rely on the portable GPS receiver he had brought along in one of the carrier bags. By comparing coded signals from various satellites in fixed orbits around the earth, the GPS could calculate its position to within fifteen metres, but its complex electronics could fail, which is why the less accurate, though more reliable sun compass was always carried as well.

Using short-burst transmissions on the PRC 319, Ricketts was able to keep in touch with the other patrols, first learning that they were all OK and in their OP positions, then gradually building up a coherent picture of what they were doing and finding. Some had broken the rule of not travelling during the day and already taken out Scud bunkers and mobile launchers, either by calling down air strikes or, in the case of mobile launchers, doing it themselves before the launchers moved on.

'It was too damned frustrating,' Hailsham informed Ricketts by radio, 'to see the mobile launchers passing by untouched or the bunkers right in front of us, undefended. Time's too short for considerations of safety. We've got to take them all out.'

By the time Johnny Boy returned, in the late afternoon to beat the descending darkness, Ricketts and his men had seen a lot of military traffic passing both ways on the MSR below the ridge, though nothing that looked like a genuine Scud launcher. What they *did* see on the MSR were mobile Scud decoys, constructed in East Germany, complete with their own crews, only there to draw the fire of Coalition aircraft and encourage the pilots to submit false 'kill' reports.

'When I think I'm having it rough,' Jock said, 'I'll bless the fates for not making me do *that* job. What a way to go!'

'Better than getting cancer,' Paddy replied. 'Even better than AIDS. One little shell, a big bang, and it's all over before you even know it. I'd *kill* for that fucking job!'

When Johnny Boy got back – 'in time for supper', as he put it – he told them that the Scud mobile launchers were avoiding the MSRs and instead using old dirt tracks to cross the desert and evade the AWACS aircraft.

'I found two separate bunkers,' he told them, wolfing down his cold food and water. 'I've marked their positions on my maps. They're the same as the Iraqi hardened aircraft shelters: pyramid-shaped and flat-roofed, with sliding steel doors, half buried in heaped-up earth and sand to make them blend in with the desert. The mobile Scud launchers are huge, raised up on the backs of wheeled platforms towed by trucks. They're usually accompanied by a truck filled with armed troops, but they'd be pretty easy to take out. Just slam them with Stingers or MILANs while raking the troops with GPMGs. Piece of piss, boss.'

Carefully covering up the OP, Ricketts and the rest went out that same night in the Pink Panthers and LSVs, led by Johnny Boy on his Honda. First, he led them to the two bunkers, located about fifteen miles apart. The exact locations of the bunkers were then relayed by SATCOM to HQ in Riyadh. Those messages were relayed in turn to the US Tactical Aircraft Control Centre, from there to an AWACS aircraft, and thence to an F-15E already in the air on nocturnal combat patrol.

While the F-15E was en route to the bunker, Ricketts and his team illuminated the target with large, camera-like laser designators mounted on tripods. Having done this, they used the cover of darkness to quietly plant small, disposable transmitters around the bunker, jamming its communications and preventing it from radar-tracking the incoming attack plane.

At both locations the aircraft arrived within

half an hour of the original SATCOM message being relayed.

When the plane released its GBU-15 laser-guided bombs just ahead of the grid location received from the men on the ground, the bombs, homing in on the intense spot of light 'painted' on the bunkers by the designators, were directed with pinpoint accuracy through their open doors or, in the second case, an open window.

Blown to hell from inside, the bunkers belched flame, smoke and debris before collapsing in billowing clouds of sand and dust. Ricketts and his men then approached the site by foot, checking that the launchers had been taken out and that the members of the Scud teams were dead. The answer in both cases, at both locations, was brutally affirmative.

By the second day, after another grim night in the OP, with worsening weather, including alternating bouts of sleet, snow, hail and frost, Ricketts and his men, taking note of Hailsham's changed attitude and sharing his frustration, were patrolling the whole area in daylight and coming across many mobile Scud units. Soon learning that it took fifteen minutes or more for an aircraft to arrive on target and that often, in the case of a mobile launcher, this was too late, they began taking matters into their own hands. Rather than see a Scud escape, they blew it to hell with their Stinger or MILAN anti-tank missiles while massacring the accompanying troops with relentless fire from their machine-guns, M16s and SLRs.

Such attacks were made either from the weapons mounted on parked, camouflaged vehicles or from the LSV as it raced towards the convoy, its MILAN firing on the move. Even as the MILAN shells were tearing into the Scud launcher, causing it to explode with a mighty roar, the LSV would be swerving sideways and haring alongside the convoy, followed by the Pink Panther, thus enabling the GPMGs and small arms of Ricketts, Jock and Paddy – Andrew was driving the LSV, Danny the Pink Panther – to rake the surprised Iraqi troops with murderous fire.

Usually Johnny Boy would accompany the LSV and Pink Panther on their daring run around the Scud convoy, recklessly guiding his Honda with one hand while firing his Browning pistol with the other, rarely getting off his 13 shots without taking out at least a few Iraqis. Then the Pink Panther, LSV and motorbike would race away in churning clouds of sand even before the debris from the exploding Scud launcher had stopped raining down upon the dazed, dead or dying enemy soldiers. It was a dance of death on bullet-riddled desert sands, conducted with ruthless efficiency.

Over the next three days, encouraged by success, Ricketts and his men started going for the weak spots in Saddam's whole communications system, hitting microwave relay towers and communications bunkers, blowing them up where they were located, either along the MSRs or by the highway that ran between Baghdad and Amman. What they could not destroy with their Stingers, MILANs or plastic explosives, they smashed with sledgehammers.

The appalling weather was worsening, and despite their heavily padded jerkins and cloaks, the men were suffering even more from sleet, hail, frost and occasional snow. Two or three times during the night they had to light fires beneath their Land Rovers to prevent the diesel fuel from freezing. By the fourth night, fog and sand storms were added to their problems, so they were greatly relieved when, on the fifth day, they were able to pack up their gear, fill in their OPs and drive back to be resupplied, debriefed and reunited with the other patrols at the Wadi Tubal rendezvous, still inside Iraq.

The SAS ran its own supply column overland. This consisted of ten four-ton trucks crewed by badged SAS soldiers and REME mechanics, escorted by teams drawn from B Squadron in six armed Land Rovers. The caravan was led by an eccentric captain who informed Major Hailsham that his attacks on the Scud launchers had been successful, driving them further and further into the Iraqi hinterland, all but out of range of Israel and Saudi Arabia.

'The danger of Israel entering the war has receded,' the captain said, 'so you're now free to look for a wider variety of targets. The green slime has suggested radar sites, petroleum refineries, storage tanks and ammunition depots. Go to it, Major.'

When Hailsham conveyed this information to his Lurp teams, they celebrated their success by decorating their vehicles with stencilled silhouettes of individual kills, in the shape of Scud launchers and communications towers.

Over the next five days a mobile workshop was kept busy as more SAS columns came in from the Scud box. Entire engines were replaced, tyres, brakes and suspension were checked, weapons were stripped and serviced, and lost kit was replaced. Then Hailsham called his men together for another briefing.

'Having sussed from our raids that we're in the area,' he said, 'the Iraqis are bound to try hunting us down. So life in Scud Alley is going to be more dangerous from now on.'

Having given his men this grim warning, he then issued new orders, which naturally involved even deeper penetration of Scud Alley.

'We leave tomorrow,' he told them.

7

The plan was to position road-watch patrols overlooking the three MSRs that ran from the crowded Euphrates Valley up a vast desert slope to the Jordanian hills in the west. These were foot patrols. RAF Chinooks put down the three separate SAS groups – known as Road Watch North, Centre and South – about twenty miles apart on a north-south axis.

The most isolated of the teams inserted, Road Watch North, was dropped in the middle of the night in rocky terrain swept by a howling, freezing wind and pouring rain – not quite what they had expected in the desert. Though they unloaded their bergens and weapons as quickly as possible, they were still drenched even before the helicopter took off again and they could huddle in the nearest shelter available, near the head of a dry, dead-end wadi about fifteen feet deep. The wind was so strong, it practically drowned out the clamour of the departing chopper.

'Christ!' Taff exclaimed as he dropped his bergen to the ground between his raised knees and wrapped his arms around his shivering body. 'This is worse than the Falklands!'

'Yeah, right,' Geordie replied, wiping rain from his eyes and checking the waterproof wrapping around the PRC 319 radio system. 'I thought it was supposed to be a fucking desert.'

'It *is* desert,' Andrew said, glancing about him in bewilderment. 'It's just not *hot* desert. There's a lot of rock and gravel in this area and the weather's shit-awful.'

'Lots of rain, sleet and snow,' Ricketts explained. 'You'll get no suntan here.' Raising his head to peer over the rim of the wadi, squinting against the driving rain, he saw only flat terrain with the dark outline of a ridge a few hundred yards away, outlined against a black sky. No moon or stars out there. The wind was howling across the flat land, driving the rain before it. 'It looks like hell on earth out there. We couldn't have picked a worse night.'

'I want to go home already,' Andrew said. 'Where's the nearest friendly territory?'

'About a hundred and eighty-odd miles away.'

'I'll stay here,' Andrew said.

Geordie laughed sardonically as he unwrapped the covering of netting and hessian required for the OP. 'We'll fucking stay here all right. There's nowhere else to go. So we might as well put a roof over our heads and keep the rain out before this wadi turns into a swamp.' Even as he spoke, he received an incoming transmission signal on the PRC 319. After switching on the receiver and listening to the message, he handed the microphone to Ricketts. 'Road Watch South,' he explained.

Through an inordinate amount of static created by the storm, Ricketts just about heard the voice of Major Hailsham, who had insisted on being the commander of the road watch nearest the Saudi border. Now he was explaining over the radio that he had decided to go back to the FOB.

'The terrain of this LZ's completely feature-less,' he said, 'and much too exposed to be useful. If we stay here, we'll be sitting ducks for the Iraqis, so I'm calling the chopper back. Road Watch Centre might be having similar problems. How's it with you?'

'It's too early to say,' Ricketts responded. 'The combination of storm and darkness makes it difficult to see, so we'll stay here at least until the morning.'

'Read you, Sergeant-Major. Good luck. Over and out.'

'He's got good sense,' Geordie said when Ricketts had handed the microphone back.

'That's why he's an officer,' Andrew said, 'and you're still a mere trooper. Come on, guys, let's sort out this OP before we're all washed away.'

'Good idea,' Danny said.

Mercifully, the rain passed on a few minutes later and the howling wind gradually settled down to an eerie moan. While not a great comfort, this made it easier for the men to construct the OP with a camouflaged roof of netting, waterproof canvas, hessian and sand, as well as plastic sheeting to cover the waterlogged bottom of the wadi. It was long, narrow, cold and damp, but it was enough to be going on with, at least until morning broke.

What happened tomorrow would depend entirely on what they found when they could see the terrain. Right now, cold and damp, with the wind howling eerily, Ricketts, thinking of Hailsham's departure, was suffering an unaccustomed feeling of isolation.

That disquiet was increased when, shortly after

the completion of the OP, he received another radio message, this time from the commander of Road Watch Centre, stating that his LZ was on flat, moon-like terrain where concealment was virtually impossible.

'We're bugging out,' he said. 'Making a tactical withdrawal. As a parting shot, however, I'm going to call down an A10 air strike on the two enemy mobile radar systems I can see from right here. I'll keep you informed of events right up to the moment we actually leave. Over and out.'

The A10s duly arrived and were lined up on the target when the commander of Road Watch Centre realized that his LZ was being mistaken for the target. Immediately, he sent a radio signal to tactical HQ but the signal was not received. According to the next message received by Ricketts, the air attack destroyed the Iraqi radar and only narrowly missed the troopers who had called it up.

Ricketts and his men witnessed the air strike from ten miles away: another spectacular light show of crimson tracers, silvery explosions and fire-spewing missiles illuminating the night sky, accompanied by the distant thunder of explosions. When it ended, Ricketts received another message from the commander, saying they had nearly been bombed by their own planes, but at least the Iraqi positions had been destroyed. The commander then confirmed that his team was bugging out, making a hasty, controlled exit from the LZ by foot.

Ricketts wished him well, then cut communications, realizing with foreboding that his group, Road Watch North, was now completely on its own, 187 miles from friendly territory.

That thought chilled him as much as did the biting wind and the dark, damp earth around him.

Huddled up in their OP, the patrol spent a miserable first night, supposedly watching for the movement of Scud launchers along the nearby MSR, but in fact unable to see anything beyond a hundred yards or so. The weather remained bitterly cold, with temperatures well below freezing throughout the night, accompanied by gusts of driving wind, rain, sleet and snow. Ricketts was only too aware that it was weather similar to that which had often killed soldiers and civilians on the SAS training ground of Brecon Beacons.

Raising his head again, just before the break of dawn, he checked that the desert immediately around them was indeed flat rock, rising gently to a ridge about two hundred yards to the north.

It was. In the fading darkness he could see the ridge more clearly, outlined against a sky now showing patches of stars, with what appeared to be an angular rock formation on its low summit. The OP itself was located in a wadi running along the crest of a hill that fell away behind them and to the side. The terrain in front of them was flat for about four hundred yards, and then it, too, started falling away to the plain below. That plain was criss-crossed by the parallel lines of the MSRs about five miles away. All in all, it was a mountainous, rocky area, splashed here and there with white patches of snow, ice and frost. The wind blew all the time.

Eventually, to his despair, even before the dawn broke properly, Ricketts realized that what had appeared to be a rock formation was actually two Iraqi S60 anti-aircraft gun positions on top of the ridge overlooking his OP.

'Shit!' he hissed involuntarily.

'What's that, boss?' Andrew asked, removing the binoculars from his eyes after scanning the MSRs on the low desert plain to the west.

Ricketts said nothing. He merely pointed at the nearby ridge with his index finger.

'Oh, man!' Andrew sighed when he saw the Iraqi gun positions. 'We is in bad trouble, man!'

One by one the other men in the OP, some of whom had been sleeping, turned their heads to look up at the ridge and murmur their own version of despair.

There was no way to get out of the OP without being seen.

'We're trapped here,' Ricketts said.

'Christ!' Taff burst out, gazing up at the ridge with disbelief in his sleepless, bloodshot eyes. 'What the hell do we do?'

Ricketts wasn't sure, but he had to say something. 'We'll just have to sit tight and hope to hell something turns up.'

'What might that be, boss?'

As Danny rarely spoke, the question was well worth considering. But no immediate answer came to Ricketts. 'I don't know. I only know we can't move. Let's just do as much as we can while we're here. For a start, take notes on those anti-aircraft gun emplacements, then the movements of enemy aircraft or any activity on the ground, including those distant MSRs. What's happening there, Andrew?'

'Whoever picked this location for an OP,' Andrew replied, speaking with his binoculars to his eyes, 'ought to be hung, drawn and quartered – the slower the better. Those MSRs are a good five miles away and covered in fog. I can't see shit, boss.'

'The fog will disappear as the sun rises. Keep looking, Sergeant.'

A grey dawn led into an interminable day whose monotony was only broken for the individual men by a period on watch, a turn at domestic chores, sleep, then another period of watch. Even with the sunlight, the temperature scarcely rose above freezing point. Added to this torture was the boredom, relieved only by the military traffic passing along the distant MSR or the passage of aircraft, both Coalition and Iraqi, on their way to and from Baghdad or Basra. Notes on all these movements were duly recorded, but the men still felt trapped.

To make matters worse, radio transmissions to HQ were less than perfect. 'On HF,' Geordie informed Ricketts, 'I'm losing words and sometimes whole sentences. It's not helpful, boss.' Nevertheless, by the end of the first day Geordie had heard enough on high-frequency transmissions to be able to inform Ricketts that there was no news of the missing members of Road Watch Centre, who had bugged out of their LZ on foot. By now, Ricketts thought, they were either dead, wounded, captured or committing daring acts of espionage. It was best not to dwell on it.

Occasionally they heard sounds of human activity – a dog barking, goatherds calling to each other only a hundred yards away – sounds telling them that neither they nor the Iraqi soldiers on the ridge were completely alone in this vast, inhospitable wilderness.

Ricketts was still racking his brains over how to get out of this trap when, at sunset, with the mist again creeping over the flat, gravelly earth in front of the OP, the goatherds materialized over the crest of the slope 300 yards away. They were wearing the customary headcloth, the *keffia*, draped over their head and shoulders, and the *dish-disha*, a plain, one-piece shirt reaching from the throat to the feet. Their feet were in leather thongs. Urging the goats ahead of them with the aid of gnarled sticks and a couple of undernourished dogs, they were coming directly towards the OP. Ricketts counted four men.

Immediately, without a word, the SAS troopers placed themselves in firing positions along the OP, some of them aiming at the goatherds, others preparing to fire on the ridge should their position be given away to the gun crews. Luckily the dogs cut alongside the advancing goats, raced around in front of them and turned them back the way they had come.

'Thank Christ for that,' Taff whispered.

Ricketts, however, was certain that one of the goatherds, who had turned away with the goats but then turned back to stare quizzically at the raised earth around the OP, had actually seen it.

Whether or not he would tell someone later on remained to be seen. For the moment, he simply turned away and, as the evening descended, followed his animals and fellow goatherds down the far slope.

Ricketts heaved a sigh of relief.

'Close one,' Andrew said.

Another interminable evening and a hellishly cold, damp night had to be endured. The men could neither leave the OP to relieve themselves nor take a chance on leaving the OP altogether, in case the goatherd, who had possibly seen them, informed on them, in which case the Iraqi soldiers on the ridge would be waiting to ambush them.

When no movement on the part of the Iraqis was made by noon the second day, Ricketts resolved to try to bluff his way out. He was confirmed in this decision when the Arabs returned with their animals and the goatherd he suspected of having seen the OP looked only briefly in its direction. If the man had seen the OP – and Ricketts thought he had – he might be friendly to the Coalition forces. Either that, or he was wrongly assuming that the OP was part of the military operation being conducted by the Iraqi soldiers on the ridge. As either way the goats were going to reach the OP, thus exposing the position, Ricketts decided to try his bluff.

'Put on your *shemaghs*,' he instructed his men, 'and keep your mouths shut. I can speak a little Arabic, so let me do the talking.'

When he and the other men had put on their veils to hide their faces, Ricketts stood up in full view and tried waving in a friendly way at the Iraqi goatherds. Even if they turned out to be unfriendly, it was possible that with the *shemaghs* covering the berets and faces of the SAS troopers, the goatherds would mistake them for Iraqi troops and either ignore their presence or let them march off.

However, even as Ricketts was waving, the goatherds, looking uneasy, went off to the side again, disappearing down the rocky, frost-covered slope. At that moment a self-sustaining Iraqi unit with its command vehicle and tracked carriers arrived, braking to a halt about three hundred yards away.

As Ricketts ducked low, hardly believing what was happening, the canvas covers were whipped off the trucks and a battery of low-level anti-aircraft guns was revealed. The men in the trucks jumped out. Some of them made a camp-fire and started boiling soup or tea. Others made their way up to the ridge, to talk to the men in the gun emplacements.

Obviously the site chosen for the SAS OP was one that had also been chosen by the Iraqis as part of their rapidly growing air-defence network.

'Jesus Christ,' Andrew whispered, 'I think I'm having a bad dream!'

'I wish you were,' Ricketts replied. Determined to keep his wits together, he immediately sent a short-burst message over the SATCOM system, stating that an enemy triple-A gun was in position immediately north of the LZ. The terse reply was that the close proximity of the Iraqis made relief, resupply or rescue by air impossible, for to call down fire on the enemy would be to virtually attract the same to their own position. Unfortunately, they would have to sit tight and hope that the Iraqis would disappear, sooner or later.

'Fucking terrific,' Geordie said, replacing the microphone. 'We could be here for ever.'

'Even if we get out,' Taff asked, 'where the hell could we go?'

'Let's try taking them out,' Danny urged, itching for action. 'We've got nothing to lose.'

'Only our lives,' Ricketts replied. 'I say we sit tight, wait for that mobile unit to leave, then take our chances on getting out under cover of darkness, when the men on the ridge may not see us.'

'They may not leave for days,' Andrew said. 'They're settling in over there.'

'Let's wait, Andrew. Let's see.'

Unable to leave, they had to piss and shit in the OP, favouring the far end of the wadi, which eased neither the humiliation nor the stench. They were also running short of food and water. After another night huddled up in the cold, damp, narrow OP, fearful of sleeping in case the Iraqis came their way, they were not only close to serious exhaustion, but also in danger of contracting hypothermia.

'I say we get up and run,' Andrew suggested. 'Take our chances out there. We can't stay here much longer, boss.'

'Right,' Danny agreed, his finger itchy on the

trigger. 'Even if we don't have a chance, we can take some of them out with us.'

'No,' Ricketts replied. 'The men in that mobile unit packed up their plates and saucers this morning, so I think they'll leave soon. If they do, we'll stay here until this evening, then move out under cover of darkness.'

'Fucking right,' Geordie said.

Unfortunately their luck ran out. About noon that day, the third day, they saw the goatherd being driven in a jeep to the mobile unit and being deposited in front of an Iraqi officer. After words were exchanged, the Iraqi officer slapped the goatherd's face, threw him to the ground, kicked him viciously and then stared in the direction of the OP.

'Shit!' Ricketts exclaimed. 'The goatherd's told them about us.'

The OP was filled with the metallic clatter of weapons being brought into position as the Iraqi officer and some soldiers from the mobile group clambered hurriedly into a jeep and drove towards the OP.

Andrew opened fire with his GPMG, firing a sustained burst that peppered the jeep with noisily ricocheting 7.62mm bullets, bursting its front tyres and hitting the driver, who shook like a rag doll and released the steering wheel as his grey tunic was splashed with red. The men on either side of Andrew also opened fire as the jeep skidded sideways, exposing the men in the rear to a hail of bullets from the M16s and SLRs. The Iraqis were throwing their hands up and crying out with pain even as the rear tyres burst and the jeep rolled onto its side. When Andrew fired a burst into its petrol tank, it burst into flames. The men still alive, or simply wounded by the hail of bullets, screamed hideously as they were incinerated in the pyre of the blazing jeep.

At that moment a mortar shell exploded just in front of the OP, creating a thunderous din and a fountain of spewing earth that rained back down on Ricketts and his men.

'They're shooting at us from the gun emplacements on the ridge!' Danny shouted as another mortar shell exploded, filling the air with smoke and flying gravel, followed immediately by the stitching effects of machine-gun fire from the mobile unit 300 yards away.

'Get in touch with HQ!' Ricketts bawled to Geordie. 'Tell them we're bugging out and need covering fire!'

'I'm trying,' Geordie called back, 'but I'm not

getting through! The reception keeps fading in and out! We've got faulty transmission!'

Ricketts glanced out of the OP as the smoke from the mortar explosions drifted away and gave him a clear view once more. The exploded jeep was still blazing, but the men inside it were now silent, blackened, smouldering corpses. Beyond them, the remaining Iraqis of the mobile unit were passing weapons to one another in preparation for an assault on the OP. Another mortar shell exploded, fired from the distant ridge. This one landed even closer to the OP, making the ground shake, practically deafening the men, filling the air with acrid smoke and obscuring the view again.

'Stow your survival gear in your bergens,' Ricketts instructed his men, 'and let's get the hell out of here. We're in for a very long march, so don't take anything heavy.'

'I'm taking my GPMG,' Andrew insisted.

'You're a big boy,' Ricketts said with a grin, 'and you're the one who'll be carrying it. OK, let's bug out!'

The men clambered, heavily laden, out of the OP and made their way downhill as the first fusillade of fire came from the remaining Iraqi soldiers. Using any fold in the ground available, Ricketts's men fired back as they moved off.

Surprised, the Iraqis paused, then started shooting with renewed vigour with their small arms. As they did so, the soldiers behind them, on the trailer-truck, used the triple-A anti-aircraft guns on a low trajectory, thus converting the heavy-calibre guns into deadly infantry-support weapons.

Mere seconds after the last SAS trooper, Danny Porter, had clambered out of the OP and raced to catch up with the others, the gun crews on the ridge finally got an accurate calibration and two mortar shells blew the empty OP apart.

As the Iraqi troops advanced through the swirling smoke and raining gravel, bullets from their small arms stitched the ground around the SAS men, noisily ricocheting off rocks and sending stones flying in all directions. At the same time, shells from the triple-A anti-aircraft guns, as well as the mortars on the ridge, made the ground behind them erupt in a series of deafening explosions that spewed earth, gravel, sand and pieces of razor-sharp, burning shrapnel.

Ricketts felt himself being picked up in a roaring maelstrom, his breath sucked from scorched lungs, before he was whipped over once or twice and smashed back down to earth. His head was filled with a whistling sound and white light seared the darkness, but he managed to spit sand from his mouth and open his eyes again. He was flat on his back with smoke drifting above him. When he rolled over and pushed himself up on hands and knees, most of the contents of his bergen fell out, clattering noisily on the frosted gravel beneath him.

'A piece of shrapnel slashed your bergen,' Danny explained, grabbing Ricketts under the shoulder and helping him back to his feet, 'but you look OK, Sarge.'

'That shrapnel also damaged my radio,' Geordie said. 'Now it's completely fucking useless. You ask me, boss, I think we should ditch the bergens anyway. We've got a long walk ahead and the bergens are too heavy to carry.'

His ears still ringing, Ricketts glanced back the way he had come. Having reached the smouldering OP on the crest of the hill, the Iraqi troops were advancing around it and coming on down, firing their small arms on the march. The triple-A anti-aircraft guns had finally stopped firing, but the mortar on the ridge was still in action, its shells coming closer.

'OK,' Ricketts said. 'We're outnumbered and

outgunned. We'll have to leg it out of here. Ditch the bergens, radio and everything else except your weapons, water bottles and spare ammo. Keep what food you have left and your personal rescue beacons. Let's be quick about it. Andrew, keep those bastards away from us until we bug out.'

'Right, boss. Will do.' An impressively big man, Andrew handled the GPMG as if it was a lightweight toy. Instead of fixing it to the tripod – he didn't have the time anyway – he spread his strong legs, crooked the heavy weapon in one arm, and fired from the hip, his whole body shaking with the recoil as he moved the barrel left and right to spray in a broad arc. The noise was atrocious, but the burst of fire was deadly, bowling over many of the Iraqis and making the others scatter, throw themselves to the ground or race back up the hill to take cover in the still smouldering OP.

As the rest of the SAS troopers divested themselves of their bergens, taking only the bare essentials, they joined Andrew in keeping the Iraqis pinned down, by firing with their small arms. When the last of them had ditched his bergen and was ready to leave, they walked away backwards, firing from the hip for as long as required. Once out of range of the Iraqi gunfire, they turned away, spreading farther apart, and ran as fast as they could across the flat plain sweeping out from the bottom of the hill to the distant horizon.

The Iraqis, they knew, would follow cautiously. But follow they certainly would.

8

A few hours after legging it out of the OP, the men stopped for a rest in another hilly, rocky area that had emerged out of the flat plain just as a hazy-white sun was sinking over the darkening horizon. Just as it became completely dark, they saw the headlights of several vehicles following them.

'They're still on our tail,' Ricketts said, 'and won't stop till they catch us.'

'The night at least offers us some protection,' Andrew observed, 'so I say we keep moving, boss.'

Danny glanced around him, seeing nothing but a vast, flat plain with low hills in the distance. 'Which direction?' he asked.

Ricketts checked his map by the light of a pencil torch. 'Urbanized Iraq is to the east, so that way offers only certain capture. Westward is Jordan, a non-combatant ally of Saddam Hussein. As they've already handed over a downed American pilot to the Iraqis, I don't think they'll treat us any better.' He glanced up from the map and gazed south at the lights of the Iraqi troop trucks following them. 'That's south, so obviously we can't go there. Which leaves north. Or, more accurately, north-west and the frontier with Syria – a member of the anti-Iraqi coalition. We might be OK there.'

'*If* we get there,' Geordie said. 'It's a hell of a hike.'

'Any other ideas?' Andrew asked.

'Nope,' Geordie replied.

'Then north-west it is.' Andrew also glanced at the lights advancing far to the south. 'And I say we go now.'

'Let's try to shake those bastards off our tail,' Ricketts said. 'First, by going south, then a short leg to the west, then on a northerly heading, which will eventually lead us back to the north-westerly stretch of the MSR. If we follow that, while keeping clear of it, we should reach the border.'

Andrew flashed his perfect teeth in a broad grin. 'If any of you have prayers say them now, before you run out of breath.'

'Very funny, Sergeant,' Geordie said. 'We're all in fits. Can we walk and not talk?'

'Read you loud and clear, Geordie.'

'OK,' Ricketts said, 'let's go.'

Steering by compass, and with the help of their SATNAV global positioning system, they started off again, finding it easier without the heavy bergens, but not thrilled by the sight of that endless plain running out to the low hills on the horizon. The vehicles behind them had stopped moving, as they could see by the lights, which probably meant that the Iraqis had disembarked to search that particular area. It was a good sign. They would have to do that a lot. Which, in turn, would give the SAS troopers on foot the possibility of staying well ahead.

Without even thinking about it, they had fallen into file formation, with Danny well out front, taking the 'point' as lead scout and constantly checking what lay ahead through the infrared night-sight of his rifle. The others were strung out behind him, a good distance apart, maintaining irregular spaces between them to avoid unnecessary, or too many, casualties if attacked.

Marching behind Danny, Ricketts, as PC, was second in line, with Geordie, as signaller, though now without his radio, and Taff bringing up the rear as 'Tail-end Charlie'. While this was undoubtedly the safest method for this kind of march, it did not allow for conversation or any other time-passing activities, which in turn made them even more conscious of the distance, and therefore more tired.

Contributing to the latter problem was the fact that although they were blessedly free of their heavy bergens, they were still burdened with personal kit belts laden with basic survival gear, items of first aid, water bottles, emergency rations, spare ammunition, and smoke and fragmentation grenades. These alone made for a weight that would have broken most men's back on a hike such as this. Last but not least was the mentally exhausting need for constant vigilance, particularly with regard to minefields, which could have been anywhere and would, if they existed, be particularly hard to see in this wind-blown darkness.

The wind, both chilling and eerie, constantly blew sand and dust across the plain, covering up small rocks that could trip them, wadis into which they might inadvertently fall, and, worst of all, obscuring any minefields that might be there.

Should they come across a minefield, Danny,

out front on point, would almost certainly be the first to 'beat the clock'. He knew that, but he didn't give a damn – he always wanted to be first into the fray. Though remarkably youthful and still called 'Baby Face', Danny continued to be widely viewed by the other troopers as a natural soldier and killer. Out on point, the most dangerous place, was where he belonged.

After marching the men southwards for two and a half hours, or about twelve miles, Ricketts checked their location with his hand-held SATNAV GPS, then led them west for another six miles. This took them from flat desert to more rocky terrain, where the moonlight glinted on patches of ice and the wind whipped up snowflakes.

Feeling protected by the hills, they stopped for a break at the end of the twelve-mile stretch, some drinking the last of their water, others nibbling on barely edible dried food. Occasionally aircraft flew overhead, but in the darkness they could not make out if they were friend or foe. The wind howled constantly, blowing sand and dust around them, and the cold was eating at their bones, sinking in, taking hold.

'I feel exhausted already,' Taff said, 'and we

haven't even come very far. I don't know what's wrong with me.'

'Cold and lack of food,' Andrew said. 'More the cold than the food. The cold makes you feel tired.'

'I think my feet are blistered,' Geordie said, 'but I can't even feel them. Fucking numb, they are.'

'Better your feet than your cock,' Andrew said.

'That's numb as well.'

'Oh, boy, you is in trouble! Now you've nothing to pull on. Me? When I start feeling exhausted, I just pull on my big dong and think of England. That keeps me going.'

'It keeps you coming,' Geordie corrected him.

'I never cream my jeans,' Andrew retorted. 'I think it's bad manners.'

'Hey, Moorcock!' Geordie said, again moved by the impulse to stir a little shit with the probationers. 'Do you think it's bad manners to cream your jeans or do you stick to pyjamas?'

Trooper Moorcock, even though visibly exhausted, blushed a deep, virginal crimson. 'Gee, Geordie . . . I mean . . . Hey, come on, I don't have to . . . What I mean,' he said, struggling for an answer, 'is that I don't . . . I just *don't*.'

'Low sperm count?' Andrew asked.

'What?'

'Never mind.'

'He wouldn't know it if he had it in his hand,' Geordie said with a big grin. 'That's innocence for you.'

'Leave him alone,' Trooper Stone said, starting to understand this ritual. 'You guys are just trying to embarrass him. Now me, I have a high sperm count and it's in my hand quite a lot.'

'It's good for the complexion,' Taff managed, though his voice sounded shaky. 'At least that's what my women say.'

'What women?' Geordie asked. 'I've never seen you with a woman. That's why you're always wiping the sperm count off your fingers when you think we're not looking.'

'What does that mean?' Trooper Gillett asked, exhausted, confused and uneasy, wondering what the next hour would bring and starting to dread it.

'He's a bachelor,' Andrew explained. 'He doesn't have it on tap. When he wants it, he either buys an expensive meal for some tart or saves costs by going to bed with *Playboy*. His fingers often get tired though.'

'You filthy bastard,' Taff croaked.

'I'm not a bastard,' Andrew replied.

'I never know what you blokes are talking about,' Trooper Moorcock said, sounding strained, glancing down at his feet, and shivering helplessly. 'Why don't you talk English?'

'Those bastards are still coming after us,' Taff said, sounding breathless and hoarse.

When they looked back, across the immense, dark plain, they saw those familiar lights in the distance, on the move again.

'Come on,' Ricketts urged. 'Let's get going.'

They changed direction once more, this time onto a northerly heading, marching as quickly as they could, which was not as quick as before, trying to put more distance between themselves and the Iraqis behind them.

The moaning wind grew in strength, and snow began to fall. Frost was breaking under their desert boots and freezing their feet. The wind was biting and blew sand around them. Though they all had veils over their faces and tinted glasses protecting their eyes, the mixture of cutting sand and freezing snow was a further menace that had to be accepted.

The march seemed interminable and was thoroughly debilitating, a murderous combination of howling wind, freezing snow, biting sand, loneliness and the constant, exhausting need to beware of minefields, all the while keeping an eye on the Iraqis still in hot pursuit. The lights were right there behind them, advancing slowly but surely, still in the distance only because the Iraqi soldiers were constantly criss-crossing the desert, leaving no stone unturned. They were, however, gradually gaining distance and closing the gap.

As all the SAS men knew that they would, if captured, be treated with more than the usual harshness, they were given further impetus to keep moving, though the toll was now telling. Twice Taff tripped and fell, which was an indication of lack of attention brought on by exhaustion. This knowledge made Ricketts more uneasy.

By the time they got back to the MSR it was midnight. Already they had walked for seven hours and covered some forty miles. While the men had another short break, squatting on the windswept sand and drinking the last of their water, Ricketts surveyed the MSR through his night-vision binoculars. At one point, he noticed, it was one or two miles wide, a dangerously flat, open stretch, with dozens of tracks side by side, spread out across the desert. On rechecking, however, he realized that the MSR had made a sweeping curve not shown on the map and that their escape route now lay across that series of Iraqi-controlled, parallel desert tracks.

'That's pretty fucking hairy,' Geordie observed. 'It's wide-open out there.'

'Right,' Andrew agreed. 'And once we start crossing, we'll be completely exposed, with the likelihood of Iraqi military convoys coming along. Bloody dangerous, boss.'

'We've no choice,' Ricketts said. 'Either we take that chance or we sit here and let those bastards on our tail catch up with us. One advantage is that this damned wind that's been driving us mad is sweeping the sand and snow across the MSR, sometimes obscuring it. That should give us at least some protection. Also, the terrain at the far side is hilly, so if we can manage to get that far without being caught, we'll have more cover than we have here. Still, you're right, it could be hairy. It's a collective decision, men, but I say we keep going.'

The men automatically looked back at the lights of the trucks on their tail, then across the parallel tracks of the MSR, placed a good distance apart on another flat, featureless desert plain along which Iraqi military traffic was known to travel. It was a choice between a rock and a hard place, and all of them knew it.

'What about you, Taff?' Ricketts asked, nervous about his condition.

'Don't ask me,' Taff replied without the slightest trace of irony. 'I'm too exhausted to even think about it. To be honest, I'm not sure I can make it. I'm sorry. That's how I feel.'

'He's exhausted,' Danny said. 'There's no question about it. It's probably due to the cold more than the march, but either way he's in bad shape.'

'I say we take his kit and weapons off him,' the nervous, but decent, Trooper Moorcock suggested, 'and put him behind Danny in the file formation. That way we can watch him.'

'Can I take it from those statements,' Ricketts asked, 'that you're all in favour of going on?'

'Yes, boss.'

'Me, too,' Geordie said.

'Fucked if I'm going to stay here and have my fingernails pulled out by Iraqi pliers,' Andrew added sardonically. 'Let's do it, boss.'

'What about you men?' Ricketts asked the probationers, troopers Moorcock, Gillett and Stone.

'I'm with you,' Stone said.

'Me, too,' Gillett said.

Moorcock stared at his two friends, glanced at the others one by one, stared across the dark plain at the advancing lights of the Iraqi trucks, then turned back to Ricketts and nodded his agreement.

'Right,' Ricketts said. 'Divide Taff's kit and weapons between you and let's bug out of here.'

The men did as they were told, relieving the grateful Taff of his burden, then Danny headed off, Taff fell in behind him and the others took their places one by one, well apart in the standard file formation, following Danny down the slope to the desert plain and the wind-blown tracks of the MSR.

Still protecting their rear, Ricketts glanced back over his shoulder just before starting down the rocky slope. The lights of the Iraqi trucks were now dangerously close and the trucks were clearly picking up speed. Obviously the soldiers had realized that their quarry was not on the plain and that the MSR would have to be crossed. There was not much time left.

Ricketts hurried down the slope, following the others. Once out of the protection of the rocks, they were exposed to the full force of the wind and the fiercely swirling, stinging sand

and freezing snow. The blowing sand gave them cover, obscuring the bright stars, but was so dense that they had to close up, in case they lost sight of one another.

By the time they reached the MSR, or at least its first track, they were half blinded by the sand, frozen numb by the snow and not sure if they were heading in the right direction.

Danny looked left and right, checking the track's alignment, then raised his right hand and waved them on, stepping out in the lead. As they crossed the MSR, going from one track to the next, with sometimes a quarter of a mile between them, the sound of gunfire exploded behind them and bullets whipped past.

'They're right behind us!' Ricketts bawled.

Danny glanced back over his shoulder just as Ricketts turned away and fired his SLR at the headlamps beaming dimly through the gloom from approximately the first track of the MSR. One of the lights blinked out, obviously damaged by Ricketts's gunfire, but the others were moving inexorably forward, though mercifully at a snail's pace, because the sweeping sand and snow were blinding the drivers. Ricketts fired a second burst and another set of lights blinked out, but a fusillade of return fire from the trucks made sand and snow spurt viciously from the flat ground about him.

'Spread out and keep going!' Ricketts bawled.

'Give me a weapon!' Taff cried out to Danny.

'No!' Danny said. 'Run!'

He hared off across the next track, almost disappearing in the murk, and was followed by Taff and the others. Ricketts, protecting their rear, hurled a phosphorus grenade at the approaching lights, then dropped to one knee and continued firing. He was soon joined by Moorcock, Stone and Gillett, all firing as well.

The grenade exploded with a shocking roar, filling the darkness with an immense fountain of white flames, streaming fireflies of silvery phosphorus, swirling black smoke and billowing clouds of sand. The deafening roar of the explosion was followed by the screams of the wounded.

Geordie joined Ricketts and the other three, firing his M16 in rapid bursts, even as Danny reached the far side of the MSR and turned back to see what was happening. He saw Geordie drop to one knee beside Ricketts, both in the firing position and erratically illuminated in the silvery light of the explosion, just before the raining sand and swirling smoke obscured them completely.

Taff and Andrew burst out of the murk as Ricketts and Geordie disappeared.

'Let's get into the hills,' Danny said, 'and hope they catch up. That's what Ricketts wanted.'

'Yeah, let's go,' Andrew growled.

Another grenade exploded behind them, followed by gunfire from both sides, and the silvery flames and fireflies created by phosphorus briefly illuminated the stormy darkness as Andrew, Danny and Taff climbed up into the relative safety of the hills.

Once in the shelter of the lower slopes, surrounded by rocky outcroppings, they sat down and waited. But although the moving lights showed that the Iraqi trucks had turned back, there was no sign of the other SAS men. The fierce wind was blowing the sand and snow across an empty MSR.

'Shit!' Andrew hissed.

9

When a bitterly cold, wet dawn came, Andrew, Danny and Taff were laid up in shallow 'scrapes' within a circular sangar, or improvised wall, constructed from the loose rocks found about them. The sangar was positioned halfway up the slope overlooking the MSR. Protected from view by the low wall of the sangar, which blended in with its surroundings, they spent the whole miserable day watching Iraqi militiamen and reservists combing the flat plains below, obviously still looking for them. The Iraqi trucks had returned just after dawn, when the storm had abated, and were parked between two tracks of the MSR, near where Ricketts, Geordie and the others had last been seen. There was no sign of the latter and the wind-blown sand had covered up their tracks completely.

'Either they've been captured,' Andrew said,

'or they somehow managed to get off and leg out by a different route. If they don't turn up by nightfall, we'll do the same.'

'Get captured or leg out?' Taff asked, attempting some levity even though he felt as bad as he looked, which was truly dreadful.

'Leg out,' Andrew confirmed. He then looked carefully at Taff. 'Are you OK?'

'I'll survive,' Taff said.

Andrew glanced down the hill. 'I left my GPMG down there,' he said to Danny, 'when you told us to run. Even *I* couldn't carry that on the run. Now I feel naked.'

'You've still got your M16,' Danny replied, 'and that's all you'll want if we're to march all the way to the Syrian border.'

'I don't think I'll make that,' Taff said, looking serious. 'I feel nauseous and absolutely drained. Bloody awful, in fact. Why don't we try an aircrew beacon?'

'We will,' Andrew said, still glancing down the hill to the MSR, where the Iraqi troops were climbing back onto their trucks. 'They seem to have given up down there. If they have, if they leave, we'll try signalling with the beacon and hope to God that something turns up.'

At noon the Iraqis were still searching the area

below, so Andrew, Danny and Taff nibbled at the last of the high-calorie rations in their individual escape belts, checked their location with the aid of the belt's small-scale map and button compass, and decided between them what way to go when the Iraqis departed.

This they did not do until late afternoon, but finally they drove off, heading back across the MSR, the way they had come. Eventually they became no more than a puff of dust in the distant flatlands.

When the Iraqis had disappeared completely, Andrew unclipped the surface-to-air rescue beacon, or SARBE, from his kit belt. It was actually a small radio used for emergency communications between an aircraft and a party on the ground by means of a repeated, coded signal. Though they are mostly used by aircrew in case of crashes, the SAS carried them in the event of the loss of the bigger, more powerful PRC 319 radio. As they had lost that, as well as their SATCOM GPS, when they lost Ricketts and Geordie, Andrew was glad he had had the sense the bring his SARBE along instead of dumping it with his bergen. Using it, he sent a distress signal out and prayed that an AWACS aircraft would pick it up and attempt a rescue.

By sunset, this had still not happened. Ironically, just before the sun sank, an American F-15E flew overhead, but failed to see them and, as there were Iraqis in the area, sometimes along the MSR, Andrew did not dare send up a flare. The plane flew on, ignoring them.

'Damn!' Taff exclaimed hoarsely. 'There goes our last chance for today. That means at least another night in the open. I don't think I can stand it.'

'Not sitting up here, freezing our arses,' Andrew said, 'but we don't have to do that. We have to move out just to keep warm, and it's best to travel by night. When darkness falls, we should disappear.'

'I wonder what happened to Ricketts and Geordie.'

'Don't think about it,' Danny advised.

At nightfall, with Ricketts and Geordie still missing, the trio decided to push on again. After filling in their scrapes and breaking up the sangar, spreading the stones carelessly about to hide all trace of their presence, they started off and kept going until they reached high ground. This was well away from the constantly populated MSR and, with its hills and wadis, offered more protection from the elements, as well as from any Iraqis still hunting them.

Sitting on the high ground, Danny looked down through the night-sight mounted on his rifle. Scanning the flat plains, he could see for at least five miles, but there was no sign of the missing men. In the end, he decided to move on, away from the dangers of the MSR.

Still using a button compass and the small-scale map from Andrew's escape belt, they continued marching for another four hours, on a north-easterly bearing, over flat rock. By 0500 hours, just as Danny was starting to worry that they would be caught in the open when dawn broke, they came across a small tank berm with walls of soil six feet high and deep tank tracks leading away from it.

'Shelter at last,' Andrew whispered. 'We can catch some sleep here. I'll nod off like a baby. So will you, Taff.'

He was particularly concerned about Taff, who had developed a bad cough – which could, incidentally, give away their position – and was pale and visibly shaking with exhaustion. His weakness, Andrew suspected, was a by-product of the cold and damp, as well as the long march with no decent food and minimal drink.

'Yes,' Taff said, so hoarse he could hardly speak properly. 'That's all I need . . . Sleep . . . I need sleep . . . *All* of us . . . Sleep.'

'I'll keep watch,' Danny said. 'We'll take four-hour turns.'

'You and I will take turns,' Andrew corrected him, 'and let Taff rest up.'

'Fair enough,' Danny said.

Andrew and Taff lay head-to-toe in one of the ditches of the berm while Danny lay belly-down on its rim, his SLR in the firing position, his night-sight giving him an eerie blue view of the landscape in darkness.

Andrew fell asleep almost immediately, but Taff, who needed it more, was too exhausted to sleep either deeply or for long, and tossed and turned restlessly for hours, muttering under his breath. When he actually dropped off for short periods, he groaned aloud with bad dreams.

That groaning, like his coughing, could get them all in trouble, so Danny was doubly alert as he kept his long watch.

At least we're reasonably safe here, he thought.

He was wrong. When the dawn light came up, he saw an enemy position, including what looked like a hut or a box-like vehicle, with radio aerials sprouting from it, no more than 600 yards away.

Shocked, Danny slid back into the ditch and placed his hand over the groaning Taff's mouth. When Taff opened panicked eyes, Danny placed his hand on his forehead to keep his head down and was worried by how hot it was.

'Quiet, Taff!' he whispered. 'Don't say a word!'

The sound of his voice awakened Andrew, who jerked around, instantly alert, even as the fear in Taff's eyes was replaced with a dazed look. Danny removed his hand, then let the other slide away from Taff's mouth.

'There's an Iraqi position over there,' he said. 'About 600 yards. We're pinned down again.'

'Oh, no!' Andrew whispered. 'I don't believe this shit!' He rolled over onto his belly and slid up the muddy side of the ditch to gaze across the flat, frosty earth at the Iraqi position. 'Shit!' he muttered softly when he saw it. 'Jesus Christ! Can a man's luck get worse?' He rolled onto his side to look at Danny. 'We're fucked again, Baby Face. We're gonna have to stay here all day and slip out tonight.'

'Right,' Danny said.

They were indeed forced to stay all day in the ditch. Snow began to fall again. As the blizzard continued, the ditch filled with water and they lay there, unable to move, soaked and frozen. There was little water left in the bottles and all their rations were gone, except for two packets of biscuits still in Danny's escape belt. Everything else – all their kit, high-calorie rations and spare heavy-duty clothes – had gone with the bergens.

By sunset, after twelve hours prostrate in icy water, they were so chilled that they had no feeling in their hands or feet, even though the former were in fur-lined leather gloves. The cold had also penetrated their joints, knees and backs, making them so crippled that when they were preparing to leave, they could scarcely pick up their weapons. They had to put their heads down through the slings, then straighten up and let the guns just dangle.

'I've never felt so fucking awful in my life,' Andrew whispered, 'but I think I can make it. What about you two?'

'I'm OK,' Danny replied. 'I'm pretty stiff, but I think I'll loosen up when we get moving. What about you, Taff?'

Taff just stared at him. He seemed not to have heard. Sitting on the edge of the ditch, he looked like a statue. The snow was still falling.

Reaching over, Danny shook him by the shoulder. 'Hey, Taff, are you OK?'

'What?'

'I said, are you OK?'

'Yes, I guess so.'

'Come on, then, let's go.'

Taff could hardly move. They had to straighten him up first and practically push him out of the ditch. When they set off, heading away from the enemy position, protected by darkness and blanketed by falling snow, he kept falling behind. And when they waited for him to catch up, he soon fell behind again. His breathing, Danny noticed, was irregular and his gaze unfocused. At one point, when he fell behind and Danny went back to fetch him, he found him sitting, slumped over, on a low, snow-covered rock, breathing painfully and holding up his hands.

'Look,' he said, 'my hands have gone black. Why should that be?'

'You're wearing black leather gloves, Taff.'

'Am I?' Taff examined the gloves on his hands with delirious eyes. 'No, I'm not,' he said. 'My hands have turned black. Don't *lie* to me, Danny.'

'Just kidding,' Danny said. He didn't know what else to say. 'They've turned black with cold,' he finally lied, feeling guilty. 'Just put them back in your pockets and they'll soon be OK again.'

'Yes,' Taff said. 'Good thinking.' Placing his gloved hands in the pockets of his jacket, he stood up again. 'You lied to me,' he said.

'Sorry, Taff.' Danny led him up to Andrew, who was shivering in the falling snow. The sergeant studied Taff, then glanced searchingly at Danny, but made no actual comment. 'Taff's hands have turned black with cold,' Danny said, deliberately and loudly, for Taff's benefit, 'and since we're looking after his weapons, I told him to put his hands in his pockets.'

'Right,' Andrew replied. 'Understood.'

'They're warmer now,' Taff informed him.

'Good,' Andrew said. 'Let's move on, men.'

They marched for another hour, but the blizzard was getting worse. Taff coughed a lot and talked to himself and kept falling behind. Aware that he was gradually losing his senses due to hypothermia, Danny tried to keep Taff's thoughts focused and his legs moving by saying how good it would be when they got back to Hereford, to the base and their comfortable bashas, to warm pubs and good bitter.

'I don't know anybody in Hereford,' Taff said, sounding annoyed. 'I come from Wales. From . . .' He tried to think of the name, failed to recall it, stopped walking to give it more thought, then started walking again. 'None of your fucking business,' he mumbled with tears in his rheumy eyes. 'Fucking cold! Who are . . .?' Suddenly, he glanced sideways, at an invisible person beside him. 'What are *you* doing here? Who asked you to come here?' The stranger did not answer and Taff looked more confused. 'What time is it? Where are we? I'm cold. Who won the Derby?'

When he didn't speak his teeth chattered, so he spoke a lot. As long as he spoke he kept walking. When he tried to think he stopped walking. His lips had turned blue, his face a ghastly yellow. Some tears had actually frozen on his cheeks and made his skin look like glass. He was coughing and shivering.

Andrew and Danny stuck with him, going back for him, dragging him on, but eventually they started suffering from cold and exhaustion themselves. Convinced that he, too, could feel hypothermia setting in, Andrew feared that they would not last the night. Yet he kept going, forcing himself to concentrate, still checking their bearings with a pocket light and button compass, determined to get as far as possible before the dawn broke again.

'Escape and evasion,' he whispered. 'Escape and evasion. That's all you've got to remember.

Keep going, boss.' He was talking to himself, but not in delirium like Taff. Instead, he was coaxing himself to go on by parroting a well-known maxim from the Combat and Survival phase of Continuation Training and recalling what that training involved – concealment, route selection, the laying of false trails, living off the land, moving carefully. It was all coming back to him. 'Always carry your escape belt,' he whispered. 'Don't despair. Never give up. Come on, boss, keep going.'

Danny, who heard every word he said, knew just why he was saying it.

By now they were on very high ground, being swept by sleet and driving snow, crossing dangerous patches of ice with bare rock between. The stars were bright, framed in patches between dark clouds, and at times they were just like the ice glinting under their frozen desert boots.

Danny stopped to gaze down at the ice. When he looked up, Taff had disappeared.

'Shit,' Danny whispered, 'I'm tired of this.'

'What?' Andrew asked, also stopping.

'Taff has fallen behind again,' Danny said.

'Go get him,' Andrew said quietly. 'We can't leave him out there.'

'I know,' Danny replied.

He made his way back, easily tracing their uncovered footsteps in the thick snow, expecting to find Taff in a minute or two, but not doing so. When he finally found him, a good twenty minutes back, he was sitting against a rock face, practically covered in snow, his eyes closed, his blue lips frozen in the grimace of death.

Danny checked carefully, ensuring that Taff was dead, and knew at once that there was no doubt about it. Brought down by hypothermia and exhaustion, Taff had finally given in.

Danny said nothing. There was nothing to say. He waited until his friend was buried completely by the snow, then he went back to join Andrew and give him the news.

Andrew just nodded, too cold to speak. Then they pressed ahead, into the swirling snow.

10

If the road-watch teams were relying on concealment as their best ally, the mobile fighting columns led by Major Hailsham, with the expert help of Sergeants Jock McGregor and Paddy Clarke, were anything but covert. Each column consisted of about a dozen four-wheel-drive vehicles – the Land Rovers dubbed Pink Panthers, and light-strike vehicles, or LSVs – plus motorcycle outriders such as the flamboyant young trooper 'Johnny Boy' Willoughby, who could fire his Browning 9mm high-power handgun with one hand while driving his Honda with the other. Though the bikers were notoriously flamboyant in word and deed, they merely summed up the general nature of Hailsham's mobile fighting columns, which were not only overt, but extremely daring and, some would say, reckless.

The columns' Pink Panthers had proven their worth in the first raids into the Scud box a few weeks before. The American LSVs, while they tended to break down too easily, were gradually becoming valued for their speed and 'invisibility' in hit-and-run raids, though certain SAS officers harboured reservations.

'I felt like Buffalo Bill,' was Jock's assessment. 'Just riding in there with all guns blazing. Fucking fantastic, boss!'

'I know you found them exciting,' Major Hailsham replied calmly. 'You thought you were in a dodgem car in a funfair in Glasgow. Fast they may be, Sergeant, and wonderful to handle, but they *do* have a terribly small fuel tank and also tend to break down.'

'Bullshit,' said Marlon 'Red' Polanski, the US Army Master-Sergeant recently attached to the SAS from 1st Special Forces Group. 'Those little babies are in a class of their own. We've only had complaints from the SAS. You guys are spoiled rotten.'

'We're British,' Hailsham said, as if that explained everything.

'What the hell does *that* mean?' Red responded. 'You need more than the rest of us?'

'Certain standards, dear boy. High expectations.

We're not into mass-produced toys produced to warm a child's heart.'

'Beg your pardon, boss?' Jock said.

'No offence meant, Jock. I merely mean that the LSV, so beloved of the Delta Force, does not necessarily excite the SAS, nor even meet all of its requirements.'

They were drinking in a tent in Wadi Tubal. Not allowed alcohol in this Muslim country, they were making do with tonic water with ice and lemon. But as this tasted like an alcoholic drink, they were all feeling high.

'Goddammit,' Red said, 'I just don't believe this garbage. You go into the goddam desert, you raid Iraqi mobile units like Indians attacking a wagon train – in out and like whirling dervishes, always highly successful – and you do it in our LSVs and *still* complain they're no good. You must be outa your mind!'

'I didn't say they were *no* good,' Hailsham replied. 'I merely said they had faults.'

'Not as good as the old Pink Panther, right?'

'Exactly, my dear Master-Sergeant.'

Polanski grinned at the grinning Jock, then looked back at Hailsham. 'Does that mean you're not using them again?'

'No, Master-Sergeant. Surely that's why you're

here. To bear witness to how we use your little toys and offer advice.'

'I guess that's right, Major.'

'So when we next go out into the desert, we'll be taking the LSVs and you, our good-natured American friend, will be coming with us.'

'Terrific,' Red said. 'So, tell me, Major, how are your road watch teams doing?'

'Not too good at all.'

'They don't have our LSVs.'

'They don't have *any* transport, Master-Sergeant, which is why they are suffering so.' Hailsham waved his hand to take in the vast, barren plains stretching out on all sides of the tents of Wadi Tubal. 'They are somewhere out there, beyond that far horizon, legging it, doing God knows what, either surviving or failing. We will know in due course.'

Red shook his fine American head in confusion or disbelief. 'Goddammit,' he said, 'you Brits are so goddam cool. I can't figure you guys.'

'There's nothing to figure,' Hailsham said. 'We merely live by a simple rule.'

'What's that?'

'Who dares wins.'

While the road-watch teams were engaged in Scud

Alley, their movements unknown, Hailsham's mobile fighting columns, after being replenished and serviced by badged SAS soldiers and REME mechanics (or REMFs – rear-echelon motherfuckers) at the Wadi Tubal rendezvous, 87 miles inside Iraq, penetrated once more into the western wilderness.

Where initially their penetration had been limited to 25 miles because of fears that Israel would respond to the battering of Tel Aviv with a full-scale invasion of the same objectives as those allocated to the SAS and the USAF, the former's successful raids against the Scud bunkers and mobile launchers had removed that threat, leaving them free to roam where they wished and pick a broader range of targets. This they could do in an area of approximately 240 square miles, including the motorway linking Baghdad with the Jordanian capital, Amman. It was a critically important military area filled with an incongruous mixture of heavily armed Iraqi soldiers on mechanized transport and impassive robed Bedouin on camels.

In addition to their normal arsenal of devastating weapons, all of the Pink Panthers now had anti-aircraft and anti-tank missile carriers with, fore and aft, protective 360-degree-traverse

Browning 0.5in-calibre machine-guns. Most of the weapons were fitted with thermal imaging sights, and the drivers, including the men on the motorcycles, wore night-vision goggles.

The Pink Panthers looked even more exotic than before as the men had since added their personally stencilled silhouettes of 'kills', including Scud launchers and communications towers, to their already colourful paintwork.

'I don't envy you guys if the Iraqis catch you,' Red Polanski informed Major Hailsham as they studied the stencilled silhouettes. 'You're practically begging to get the sons of bitches mad.'

'No offence meant,' Hailsham replied. 'They're just a few little doodles.'

'Fucking A,' Red replied. 'A few little Van Goghs. All set to be framed and hung up in Saddam Hussein's bedroom. You guys get caught with those things on your cars and you'll be in *bad* shit. You'll learn how controversial art can be when it has the wrong audience. We're not talking art criticism here – we're talking dragons and dungeons.'

'My men don't play games,' Hailsham said.

Racing across the vast, flat plains, their wheels churning up clouds of dust, the Pink Panthers and LSVs were accompanied by the bikers, with

Johnny Boy right out in front, a *shemagh* veiling his face, tinted glasses protecting his eyes and an unofficial vivid-red scarf billowing out behind him. As usual, he had an M16 strapped across his back, a Browning 9mm pistol at his hip and a leather-encased Fairburn-Sykes commando knife slipped into one of his high-topped desert boots. Together with his *shemagh*, trailing scarf, tinted glasses and blackened face, his weapons made him look bizarrely heroic.

'If that kid's as good as he looks,' Red said to Jock, who was expertly driving their Pink Panther, 'he'll be pretty impressive.'

'He is,' Jock replied. 'What about you, Master-Sergeant?'

'I'm not as young as that kid,' Red replied, 'but I do OK, I guess. Not bad for an old man.' In fact, with two tours of Vietnam, a Purple Heart, a Bronze Star, and three years of covert activity with the élite Delta Force behind him, including service in Grenada and Panama, Red was a 'soldier's soldier', and certainly looked the part – sixteen stone of solid muscle, still handsome for his age, and deeply tanned by the sun of many countries. 'You ever see that movie, *Apocalypse Now*?' he asked.

'Yeah,' Jock said, glancing distractedly at

the fleet of Pink Panthers, LSVs and Honda motorbikes racing across the desert in a long line, their wheels churning up a cloud of sand about a quarter of a mile long. 'Bloody terrific.'

'You remember that scene where the officer says with real regret, "Someday this war's gonna end"?'

'Yes, boss, I do. Robert Duvall. A great actor. Him and his yellow scarf.'

'Well, Sergeant, that's what I've felt every day of this war. Someday – in this case, very soon – this war's gonna end . . . and I'm gonna regret it. That's a terrible truth.'

'It's the nature of the beast,' Jock replied. 'That's why we're all here.'

As the mobile columns made their way across the desert, the men going without lunch as morning became afternoon, RAF reconnaissance GR-1A Tornadoes from the airfield at Tabuk, in the far north-west, flew constantly overhead, heading for Baghdad, where they would use radar techniques to drop 1000lb bombs from 20,000 feet with pinpoint accuracy. Also seen frequently were heavily armed F-15s, F-16 Fighting Falcons, A-10s and A-6E Intruders on round-the-clock patrols – both north, where the Delta Force were operating, and south, where the SAS columns were heading.

Throughout their long journey to the location chosen for their laager, or fortified position, the men in the columns came in contact with no enemy transports or tanks, though they did see more than one caravan of Bedouin, in fluttering robes and astride camels burdened with carpets and bags filled with wares. The Bedouin watched the extraordinary columns of Pink Panthers, LSVs and motorbikes with interest, but did not seem unduly surprised.

'They have their own, unique lives to lead,' Hailsham explained to his driver, Paddy, 'and probably think we're as insubstantial as the wind – here today, gone tomorrow. When we're gone, the desert will still be here – and so will the Bedouin.'

'I feel weird when I see them,' Paddy replied. 'As if I'm living a history book.'

'I know what you mean, Sergeant.' Hailsham waved his hand to take in the other Pink Panthers, LSVs and motorbikes spread out across the desert, roaring and churning up great clouds of sand as they made tracks through the flat plain. 'Here we are in our armoured transport, with all these technological marvels, and there they are travelling by camel as if time has stood still. That's what makes it seem strange.'

The columns kept going, as if racing one another, not stopping for food or rest, to reach their destination before sunset. That destination was merely a convenient gathering place, a base, an Empty Quarter to be used as a jumping-off point for their many patrols outward in all directions.

Once there, in their Empty Quarter, a small holding force made a base, then the various groups broke up and went off in different directions to form a series of OPs and laagers across a broad front, though close enough to be able to reach one another other if help was required.

By last light, Hailsham's group had formed themselves into a half-squadron laager – a temporary fortified position of Pink Panthers and LSVs in the shape of a wagon-wheel – and were settling down for the night, with some men taking turns to sleep and stand guard.

By sunrise, though the main laager was still in position as a temporary, camouflaged base camp, the various Pink Panther and LSV crews were taking turns at prowling about the open expanse of flat, stony desert between Karbala, south-east of Baghdad, and Nukhaib, about sixty miles from the Saudi border.

There was no cover in this area. It was mostly flat, sandy desert with little sun and too much wind, appreciated only by the frequently seen Bedouin. The Iraqi militia were not spotted so often, though they certainly crossed the desert roads in soft-topped trucks and tanks. For this reason, Hailsham's men made a point of peering into culverts under main roads to check whether they concealed Scuds or other mobile units. If that happened to be the case, they took the Iraqi troops out with a withering hail of unexpected gunfire, then destroyed the Scuds or mobile big guns with plastic explosives or, failing that, with their trusty sledgehammers.

Passing Bedouin often witnessed them doing this, but showed no sign of curiosity, let alone outrage.

The ways in which the SAS men waged their mobile desert war were many and diverse. They blew up passing enemy trucks with their M19s, which could hurl small but potent 40mm armour-piercing grenades more than a thousand metres. They also blew up bridges and communications towers with a variety of explosives, including TNT, Semtex and C3/C4 plastic explosive. They illuminated entry points to enemy targets with large, tripod-mounted designators to enable the laser-guided GBU-15 and Paveway II bombs of the Allied aircraft to hit home with devastating accuracy.

Often dressed as Arabs and speaking Arabic, sometimes even riding camels, they moved dangerously close to enemy bases and establishments, even infiltrating their towns and villages, to bring back important information on armaments factories, oil refineries, communications and transportation systems, radar sites and command and control centres. This information was relayed via the SATCOM equipment on their backpacks to HQ in Riyadh, which passed it on to the AWACS aircraft on the prowl for fresh targets.

'Without us,' Paddy said, 'those fucking pilots wouldn't know shite from shinola. We're their eyes and their ears.'

'I'm sure they appreciate that,' Major Hailsham replied distractedly, gazing across the vast expanse of the desert and wondering where his missing road-watch team was.

'I hope so,' Paddy said. 'Fucking pilots!'

Even more dangerously, the SAS patrols would drive close to enemy airstrips, camouflage the

Pink Panthers, LSVs and motorbikes, go the rest of the distance by foot, locate the supply dumps, usually located near the edge of the base, and contaminate the aircraft fuel under the very noses of the Iraqi guards.

Johnny Boy often did this by himself – in unusual ways.

'I drive around the airstrip on my Honda,' the trooper informed US Master-Sergeant Red Polanski, whom he admired and was admired by, 'in full view of the Iraqi shitheads on guard. I'm wearing my *shemagh* and my face is painted brown, so when I wave like I'm just having fun, they think I'm a local nut. I do this until last light, when the lazy shits are half asleep, then I circle around to where the supply dumps are located and get off the bike. If no one's there, I go in – just cut the barbed wire with shears – and go about doing what I have to do. That's all there is to it.'

'And if someone's there?' Red asked, always keen to know every detail.

'I have a good piss in the sand, unconcerned, just another A-rab, and when the guard turns away, which he often does in disgust, I slip up behind him with my neat commando knife, slit his brown throat and enter via the gate as if I own the joint. I then contaminate their petrol – sorry, Red, their gasoline – and walk out and dawdle back here on my Honda.'

'Hold on!' said Red, always looking for a weak spot. 'If the fuckers find a dead guard by the tanks they're gonna know something's up.'

'Too true,' Johnny Boy replied, enjoying the challenge, thrilled to win. 'And for that very reason, when I have to silence a guard . . .'

'A typical Brit euphemism for something really nasty,' Red interrupted. 'I love it, kid. It's so cool!'

'When I have to silence a guard,' Johnny Boy continued, 'which will let them know it's sabotage, I deliberately tape an explosive charge to the petrol tanks. When they find it, they think they've been smart and know what I was up to. They remove the explosive charge and never think to examine their fucking petrol. Thus, for the next month or two, they have nothing but trouble with their aircraft, tanks and troop trucks – which is more valuable to us than simply blowing up the supplies. A good job well done, right?'

'Right,' Red replied admiringly.

Apart from their ambushes and acts of sabotage, the SAS men collected intelligence on enemy command and control centres, bunkers, and

SOLDIER A: SAS

nuclear, chemical, and biological weapons, as well as troop and aircraft movements. They also snatched enemy soldiers and either interrogated them or handed them over to the green slime, the Intelligence Corps to be given a hard time.

Sometimes, when specifically asked to find a prisoner for urgent interrogation, they would be compelled to take considerable chances. One method was to make a daring attack on a passing truck or column by racing up in their speedy light-strike vehicles, firing and throwing grenades while on the move, then hauling a surprised soldier into the LSV and roaring off in a protective cloud of sand caused by the explosions. Another was to sneak up on an enemy camp under cover of darkness and simply abduct one of the guards, silencing the other guards, if necessary, by slitting their throats.

These approaches, however, only produced prisoners of lowly rank, most of whom could impart little information. For more valuable prisoners they had to be more daring, which sometimes involved high-risk raids into the heart of passing convoys. In such raids, SAS troopers would hurl grenades and fire their small arms as the Pink Panther carrying them raced boldly between selected Iraqi vehicles to cut out the one containing officers. While the other Pink Panthers formed a buffer between the first Land Rover and the Iraqi column, SAS troopers in an LSV, often led by Red Polanski, would speed alongside the isolated officers' vehicle, shoot all of its occupants except one, abduct the survivor at gunpoint and then race away to safety, protected by the guns and grenades of the other Pink Panthers and LSVs. The latter would then also make their escape, using the smoke dischargers on the rear of their vehicles to create a protective screen behind them.

'I've got to hand it to you Brits,' Red Polanski said admiringly, 'you sure as hell know how to shake out. I've never seen anything like these goddam raids – and I've seen a lot. That kid on the motorbike, those guys in the Pink Panthers – dammit, even myself in the LSVs – like red Indians attacking a stagecoach in a Hollywood movie. Who said the British were inhibited? Not out here, they aren't!'

'You're too kind,' Major Hailsham said.

'Don't tell me it was nothing.'

'It was nothing,' Major Hailsham said. 'We're just doing our job.'

'Stop being so goddam humble. I hate Brit

humility. What you guys are doing in this desert is unprecedented. You're way out on your own, man.'

'I'm sure the men would be pleased to hear that.'

'So I'll tell 'em.'

'Please don't. The SAS encourages humility as well as humour, so I don't want you swelling their heads. Your Delta Force might need its ego stroked, but the SAS doesn't.'

'That's a crock of shit, Major.'

'It's a fact of life, Master-Sergeant.'

'Jesus, you guys are so cool you make sweat look like ice cubes.'

'Rather nice in the gin and tonic.'

'Which we can't drink in this damn country. Tell me, Major, have you had any news from your missing road-watch team?'

'Alas, no,' Hailsham said.

Increasingly, as the war continued and the Coalition forces advanced, Hailsham's men were coming across many Iraqi wounded abandoned by their comrades in battle, plus deserters only too glad to be captured. The finding of 'quality' prisoners for interrogation was therefore becoming a lot easier. In fact, over the first few weeks such Iraqis became an embarrassment, even a liability, to the SAS, as they required food, first aid, a place to stay and generally looking after.

'A bullet in the head and a grave in the sand,' Paddy suggested as a practical means of solving the problem. 'It's what they'd do to us.'

'Damn right,' said Red.

'Wrong,' Hailsham informed him. 'We can neither break the Geneva Convention nor give the Arabs of either side an excuse to call us imperialist barbarians. We must therefore treat all our prisoners with respect, consideration and kindness.'

'British pragmatism at its best,' Red commented with a wicked grin. 'There's even a sound reason for your so-called moderation. It sure as hell ain't straight from the heart.'

'Hearts are easily broken,' Hailsham said, 'and we can't afford breakage. More tea, Master-Sergeant?'

Often the individual Pink Panther and LSV teams would stay away from their temporary base, or laager, for more than a night or day, in which case they would construct their own camouflaged lying-up position, or LUP, and use it for sleep or short-term breaks. At such times Hailsham would luxuriate in the silence, in the grandeur of the desert sky, and recall earlier SAS tasks, which some, more romantically inclined, might describe as adventures.

In particular, he recalled the Falklands war, when he had first come to know his then revered superior, Major Parkinson, now with the Queen's Regiment, Sergeant-Major Ricketts, then a sergeant, and all the others now missing on that road watch.

Major Hailsham, then a captain, had been renowned for his sardonic tongue, but now, though his tongue remained acerbic, he was filled with concern.

There had been no radio call from the road watch team. No SARBE beacon. No communication via SATCOM. Helicopters sent over the area had found no trace of them. They had literally vanished. Now, even running his own successful campaign in the desert, Major Hailsham could not help but worry. Where the hell were they?

The night before Hailsham's columns were due to regroup and drive back to the Wadi Tubal rendezvous for resupply and debriefing, four Iraqi artillerymen, attempting to avoid a strike by a US A-10, drove off the road and across the desert – straight into the sentry position of Hailsham's half-squadron laager.

Without thinking twice, the SAS troopers

keeping watch in the semicircle of Pink Panthers poured Browning machine-gun fire into the oncoming vehicle, killing three of the Iraqis, one of whom virtually somersaulted out of the car and thumped onto the desert floor. The survivor, shaking visibly, climbed down with his hands raised and was instantly escorted to Major Hailsham, who spoke fluent Arabic.

Questioning the frightened young soldier, Hailsham learnt that he was the commander of his gun battery and a mine of information about the activities of the Iraqis in the area. The value of his intelligence was greatly increased when the prisoner produced the military maps that his men had been carrying. These described, to a trained eye, the detailed deployment of all the enemy brigades in western Iraq.

Realizing immediately that his work here was finished, Hailsham relayed the information back to the Tactical Air Coordination Centre, then ordered his men to destroy their LUPs, break up the laager, hide all evidence of their stay in this place and prepare to drive back to Wadi Tubal.

Even as they were leaving, heading into the setting sun, Allied bombers were striking the positions marked on the Iraqis maps and relayed to the TACC by Major Hailsham.

Had it not been for his missing road-watch team, Hailsham would have been pleased.

11

Andrew and Danny walked all night. Just before dawn they came off the high ground, down a slight gradient, and ended up in a shallow wadi, only three feet deep. There they lay, cuddled together for warmth. Normally in such circumstances they would have been hot-bedding, or sharing a sleeping bag between them, but since those had gone with the bergens, they just lay close together for the warmth that would prevent hypothermia.

As SAS troopers never discussed the dead, or those who 'beat the clock', neither said anything about Taff's death, though both were deeply grieved by it.

'Real cosy,' Andrew said, trying to lighten their load a little.

'Shut up,' Danny replied. 'I don't need your jokes.'

'Gee whiz, you're so sexy.'

'Shut up!'

'I's just all in a dizzy, little darlin', to have you so close.'

'One more word and I'm moving away from here.

'My lips are sealed tight.'

Andrew chuckled, but said no more after that. In truth he was too cold, his teeth practically chattering. If he, a fleshy man, felt that way, he knew that Danny felt worse.

It was a long, miserable night and Andrew hardly slept. He was now too exhausted to sleep properly, which only made matters worse. His thoughts were slipping and sliding, shifting in and out of gear. One minute he was thinking of his wife and children back in London, the next he was wondering how the hell to get out of this mess.

They still had rifles and hand-grenades, but everything else was gone. Even the high-calorie rations in their escape belts were finished and now they were starving. Left in the escape belts were the small-scale map and button compass, pocket knife, fishing line and hooks, hexamine fuel blocks and matches, but they were unlikely to catch any fish here, nor any other kind of food that could be gutted and cooked over a fire.

In fact here, in this freezing, wind-blown desert terrain, they dared not even light a fire, for fear that the smoke would give away their presence to the Iraqis. So they were in bad shape, gradually freezing, slowly starving, and if a miracle did not occur tomorrow they would be in worse trouble.

Unable to sleep, Andrew turned to look at Danny and realized that although he was nearly thirty, he still looked like a kid. He was rightly called 'Baby Face', and had the shyness to match, yet he also had the instincts of a killer and scared the hell out of everyone.

Danny had always baffled Andrew. He was like the late Hollywood actor Audie Murphy. Before becoming a film star, Audie Murphy had been the most decorated GI of World War Two, having killed an extraordinary number of German soldiers. Yet he was every bit as shy as his baby face made him seem. Always wanting to be a soldier, Andrew, when a schoolboy, had been particularly impressed by Audie Murphy playing himself in a film about his war years. In that movie, *To Hell and Back*, Murphy had looked like a kid and killed like a machine.

Danny had always impressed Andrew for the same reason. He was a baby-faced, shy, killing machine who rarely made a mistake. All his mistakes, as Ricketts had pointed out, were in his personal life.

This got Andrew thinking about Ricketts and the others. Where the hell were they? Had they managed to escape from the MSR? And if so, where had they gone and what were they doing? Indeed, were they even still alive?

Big Andrew shuddered at the thought that they might have been captured by the Iraqis. The green slime had confirmed that activities against the Scuds had badly frightened the Iraqis and made them embark on a determined hunt for SAS troops. If they caught any they would not treat them kindly – and the Iraqis, as Kuwait had taught the world, were quick to use torture.

That possibility lodged in Andrew's exhausted thoughts and took wildly exaggerated, haunting shapes, making him even less inclined to surrender to sleep.

He did, however, drop off for short periods, but his feverish thoughts and the constantly howling wind did not permit much sleep. Mercifully, the sky cleared and the sun rose in a clear blue sky that was not exactly hot, but warm enough to begin drying their sodden clothes and thawing their frozen limbs.

Looking around him, Andrew saw only the wadi, more rocky, hilly, frosty terrain on all sides, and a brooding, cloud-filled sky. Though the snow had stopped falling, the wind was still harsh and moaning like the voices of the damned.

'What do we do now?' Danny asked.

'We keep going,' Andrew replied. 'The march will warm us up. Also, we've got to find food and drink. But first I'm going to check my damn feet. They both hurt like hell.'

While a slightly refreshed Danny kept watch, Andrew pulled off his wet desert boots with great difficulty to find that his feet were swollen and badly blistered.

'Shit,' he said, 'this isn't going to help me.' He tried wrapping them in bandages from his kit belt, but his feet were so swollen that he could not get them back into the boots with the bandages on. Setting the bandages aside, he removed the small knife and matches from his escape belt, sterilized the knife by holding it in the flame of a match, then gritted his teeth and proceeded to lance the blisters one by one. It took quite a bit of time and hurt like the devil. It hurt even more when he swabbed the raw wounds with TCP. Thinking at one point that he was going to faint from pain, he nevertheless managed to complete the job. He then smeared two separate short strips of bandage with antiseptic cream, placed them once around his feet, providing only one extra, thin layer, and managed by so doing to get his soaked, filthy desert boots back on. His heart was racing from fighting the pain, but it was fading now.

Rolling around until he was lying on his belly beside Danny, he took hold of his SLR and gazed to the front. An Arab appeared at the bottom of the wadi with a big herd of goats.

'Damn!' Danny murmured, sliding his M16 into the firing position and flipping the sight up.

'Hold on,' Andrew cautioned him, placing his big hand on Danny's frail wrist. 'What are you doing?'

'I'm going to take that bastard out,' Danny said.

'Why?'

'Because he's coming right towards us, you bloody fool, and he'll soon be on top of us.'

'So what? He's just a goatherd.'

'An *Iraqi* goatherd,' Danny corrected him.

'He's a civilian,' Andrew insisted. 'You can't shoot a civilian.'

'Just watch me,' Danny said, taking aim along the sight and sliding his itchy finger to the trigger.

'He's a Bedu,' Andrew tried. 'The Bedouin are reported to be friendly to our cause, so he might actually help us.'

'I'm taking no chances.'

'He could help us,' Andrew said.

'He could turn us in,' Danny replied.

'Why the fuck would he care about that? He's not a soldier – he tends goats – and if we offer him some of our gold, he's not likely to say no. That gold would be a fortune to a guy like him.'

'Sorry, Andrew – no way.' Danny was still aiming along the sight, but now sliding his finger over the trigger.

'Look,' Andrew said more desperately, squeezing Danny's wrist, slyly trying to coax his finger off the trigger, 'he's a Bedu, which could mean he's friendly. He's also poor, which could mean he's greedy. Let's wave the gold under his nose and see what he says. He gets the gold if he takes us to the border. Come on, Danny, let's try it.'

By now, the goatherd, wearing a turban, an ancient coat of dark tweed, a long, tattered scarf and a pair of thongs, was sitting on a rock and idly watching his flock milling about at the end of the wadi.

Danny studied him through the sight, then slowly, reluctantly, withdrew his itchy finger from the trigger. 'Just go and ask him where we are,' he said. 'No more than that. I don't trust the bastard.'

'Sure,' Andrew said. 'Right.' Leaving his SLR on the ground, he stood up, waved his hand in a friendly manner and called out a greeting in Arabic. Surprised, the old goatherd looked up, but otherwise made no move. Still speaking fluent Arabic, which he had been taught at the Hereford and Army School of Languages, Andrew told the goatherd not to worry, explained who he was, and asked if he could come and talk to him. Not moving from where he was sitting, the man nodded agreement.

After glancing down at Danny and indicating with a wave of his hand that he should do nothing for the moment, Andrew walked along the wadi to speak to the goatherd. When he reached him, he saw that he was very old, with a thin, weather-beaten, good-humoured face. After exchanging a formal greeting, Andrew asked the old man if he spoke English.

'No,' the old man said in Arabic. 'I'm sorry.'

'It's me who should apologize,' Andrew replied, speaking the same language, 'because my Arabic is so poor.'

'It is a pleasure to find a foreigner who speaks it at all,' the goatherd said. 'What are you doing here?'

Andrew explained the situation, then asked the old man if they were far from the Syrian border.

'No,' the Arab said, shaking his head and pointing north-west. 'It is not very far. About ten kilometres in that direction.'

'Can you take us there?'

The Arab shook his head again. 'I am sorry,' he said, 'but I cannot afford to lose my goats. They are my sole livelihood.'

From his kit belt Andrew produced the pouch containing approximately £800 in small gold pieces, as well as the chit stating in Arabic that Her Majesty's Government would pay the sum of £5000 to anyone returning the bearer to friendly territory. He handed the old man the chit, waited until he had read it, then took hold of the Arab's wrist, turned his hand over and poured some gold pieces into it.

'You can have the rest,' he said, 'when you

deliver me and my friend to friendly people over the border. Will you do it?'

Smiling, the old Arab dropped the gold pieces, one by one, into the side pocket of his tweed coat. Then he stood up and nodded. 'Yes,' he said. 'Go, fetch your friend.'

Andrew returned to Danny and said, 'Hand me that SLR, mate. We're on our way home.'

Sitting upright, Danny passed the SLR to Andrew. 'No, thanks,' he said.

'What?'

'I'm not going,' Danny said.

'What the fuck do you mean, you're not going? This old guy is going to take us to the border. He's friendly *and* greedy.'

'If you believe him, go with him,' Danny said, 'but I'm not going with you.'

'For fuck's sake, Danny, he's OK!'

'I'm not trusting any Arab,' Danny said, 'and I don't think you should.'

'OK,' Andrew said. 'You believe what you want, but I'm going with him. Besides, the Iraqi search parties are closing in and we double our chances of evasion by splitting up.'

'We also reduce each other's odds on individual survival,' Danny replied. 'Bear that in mind, Sergeant.'

'I could order you to come for your own good,' Andrew said.

'You could, but you won't. That's not the way we do things.'

'Shit, Danny . . .'

'It's OK, Andrew, you go. I'd just rather not join you.'

'Too bad,' Andrew said.

'Your choice, Sarge. Have a safe trip.'

'Same to you, mate.' Andrew nodded, grinned, then went to join the goatherd, who was already walking away from his animals and clambering out of the wadi. Andrew glanced back at Danny, who looked frail and terribly alone. As if sensing Andrew's unhappiness, Danny suddenly waved and called out to him. Andrew stopped. 'What?'

'If anything happens to me and you survive, write a poem about me.'

'I will, mate, I promise. It'll be there in the Imperial War Museum for your children to read.'

'Right. Good luck, Sarge.'

'Same to you, Trooper.' Instantly feeling a lot better, Andrew waved again, then turned away and followed the Arab out of the wadi.

'How long did you say it was?' he asked when they had walked for five minutes.

'About ten kilometres,' the Arab replied. 'It will not take too long.'

In fact, it took less time than Andrew had anticipated. They walked for about twenty minutes, crossing some more rocky terrain with low hills on either side and a wedge-shaped stretch of desert in the distance, muddy brown in weak sunlight. Andrew checked his button compass, making sure they were heading north-west, and when he saw that they were he relaxed and looked up again.

At that moment, the Arab fled – surprisingly fast for an old man – shouting out that the man behind him was a British soldier.

Directly ahead of the Arab was a laager of soft-topped trucks, mobile anti-aircraft gun units, and heavily armed Iraqi militiamen, all staring at Andrew.

'Shit!' Andrew exclaimed, shocked, betrayed, momentarily frozen.

Regaining his senses, he turned and ran the other way, heading for the protection of the rocky outcroppings nearby. He heard shouting in Arabic, followed by firing rifles, and glanced over his shoulder to see the soldiers aiming at him, even as bullets kicked up dirt around him and ricocheted off the stones.

The militiamen ran towards Andrew and he stopped to return their fire. He managed to get off a short burst before he was hit. 'Shit!' he cried out again – the one word he could think of – then he felt his leg bursting with pain and giving way beneath him. He kept firing as he fell, his bullets whining into the sky, then collapsed onto hard stone and dust as the Iraqis surrounded him.

Excited, almost hysterical, they kicked him repeatedly, bent down and punched him, hammered him with their rifle butts, then grabbed him by the shoulders and hair and brutally hauled him across sharp, cutting stones to the vehicles of their laager.

When they dragged him between two trucks, into their camp, his real suffering began.

12

Major Hailsham and his men approached the elaborately camouflaged fixed missile site at night, guided to it by Trooper Willoughby. Parking the Pink Panthers and LSVs a good half mile away, they completed most of the journey by foot, then dropped to the ground and crawled on their bellies the final hundred metres or so, eventually taking up positions in a depression in the desert floor, forming a front a quarter of a mile long, just south of the site.

Hailsham studied the target through binoculars, using night-vision goggles. This missile site was the real thing, not an expensively built decoy. In the cold blue light of the goggles, he saw a missile-launching area, adjoining command posts, guidance systems, two separate radar areas, supply dumps and early-warning stations with automated sensors on high observation towers – all behind steel fences covered in barbed wire and patrolled by armed guards.

Right now, as he could clearly see from the activity in front of a concrete bunker and command post, a salvo of Scuds were being prepared for a multiple launch, possibly aimed at Israel. According to Intelligence, Saddam Hussein was still hoping to draw Israel into the war with another, unexpected Scud attack from a fixed missile site within range of that country. The green slime had therefore obtained the approximate location of the site and ordered Hailsham to find the exact location and take out the site. Now here he was with most of his squadron, lying belly-down in a useful hollow in the desert floor, looking up at a sky containing a full moon and brilliant stars. There was no wind tonight.

'I don't think we can take it ourselves,' he said.

'Neither do I,' said US Master-Sergeant Red Polanksi, likewise lying belly-down in the sand close to Hailsham. 'It's too widespread. There are too many troops. We wouldn't get in and out in time.'

'Let's blow a few fences, boss,' Johnny Boy

said from the other side of Hailsham. 'Take a few down with the MILAN and then race in and back out in the dinkies.'

'You're just spoiling for a fight,' Paddy Clarke said. 'This is all the Boy Scouts to you.'

'The Boy Scouts are from your day,' Johnny Boy retorted. 'They're not part of my background. So what do you say, boss?'

Hailsham shook his head. 'I say no. As our American friend noted, it's too widespread, there are too many troops and we'd never get in and out in time.'

'I'd be in and out like a whirling dervish,' the reckless trooper said, 'throwing grenades left and right.'

'Grenades wouldn't be enough,' Paddy objected. 'Even the MILAN wouldn't do it. We need heavier fire-power, but we wouldn't have the time to set it up. There's too much to be taken out in there and it's spread far and wide.'

'Correct,' Red said. 'What we need is air support. We'll have to call in a US strike force.'

'I thought you'd say that,' Hailsham said.

Red grinned. 'Sure. Why not? We need to flatten that goddam place – and for that we need really heavy air power within reach of this area. I suggest you let me call up a flight of the latest

F-15Es, or Strike Eagles, of the 336th Tactical Fighter Squadron.'

'What's so special about them?' asked Johnny Boy, always keen to learn from his older, more experienced, American hero.

'They're special all right,' Red answered, equally keen to advise his admirable, and admiring, young British protégé. 'Single-seat, 1600mph motherfuckers designed to attack ground targets using the Lantirn system.'

'The *what*?'

'Lantirn – with an "i". Low altitude navigation and targeting infrared for night. It's carried in two pods – one for navigation, the other for laser-targeting – both linked to the pilot's electronic helmet visor, which magnifies the target fifteenfold.'

'Sounds like Star Wars stuff,' Johnny Boy said, clearly intrigued.

'It is, kid. Short of firing laser beams as weapons, the Lantirn system is the ultimate in Star Wars technology, achieving better than ninety per cent accuracy and capable of dropping bombs within ten metres of the target on the first pass.' He turned to Hailsham. 'Believe me, Major, you couldn't do better.'

Hailsham thought about it for a moment.

Putting the binoculars back to his eyes, he studied the target once more. Removing the binoculars and night-vision goggles, he rubbed his tired eyes.

'What about the automatic early-warning sensors on those observation towers?'

Red sighed. 'The Strike Eagles'll be preceded by an EA-6B Prowler. Its avionic system includes five pods containing jamming transmitters. They fire streams of radio waves and electrons on seven different frequencies. The Prowler's wingtips pick up the target's radar waves and feed them into a computer that gives the frequency info needed for the jamming. One Prowler's enough to jam all the radars on that missile site. Once they're jammed, we can pinpoint the targets with our laser pistols.' When Johnny Boy whistled with admiration, Red grinned triumphantly. 'Should I get on the SATCOM?'

'The wonders of science,' Hailsham said. 'Yes, get on the SATCOM.'

As Red was relaying his request and grid references back to Saudi Arabia via the SATCOM system in the charge of Paddy Clarke, Hailsham crawled along his line of widely spaced men, stopping at the ones with portable laser designators to tell them which targets he wanted pinpointed once the Prowler had passed over and jammed the enemy radar. On the way back he stopped to have a few words with the men on the GPMGs and mortars, telling them not to use them unless fired at. By the time he returned to Master-Sergeant Polanski, the American had finished his transmission and was holding his thumb up.

'They'll be here in no time at all, Major. Just sit back and relax.'

'Thank you for the suggestion, Master-Sergeant. I might just do that.'

Reaching his original position, Hailsham rolled onto his stomach and again examined the missile site through his binoculars. In the eerie blue glow of his night-vision goggles, he saw that the Scuds, just recently wheeled out of the hangars on their mobile platforms, were being raised to an elevation suitable for long-range firing. Many armed guards and engineers were gathering around them.

'I think we got here just in time,' he said to Red. 'It looks like they plan to launch those things later tonight, or perhaps tomorrow at dawn. Another surprise attack.'

'More of a surprise,' Red said, 'since the Israelis think the Scud attacks have ended. Wouldn't *they* get a shock!'

185

'Let's hope they won't,' Hailsham said.

'You can depend on the good old US of A. Those planes will be here in no time.'

'I live by faith,' Hailsham said.

Red rolled over and grinned at Johnny Boy, who was lying on his back with his hands behind his head and his long legs crossed. The kid was only 24 and looked as cocky as they come, but as Red had already found out, he had nerves of steel, initiative and a lot of guts. Red liked the Brits generally, but Johnny Boy really amused him. He was like Red had been when he first joined the Marines – bright, straightforward, easily bored, in desperate need of adventure and excitement, willing to take chances for it. When he looked at the trooper, Red was looking deep in the mirror.

'Hey, kid,' he said.

'Yes, Red, what is it?'

'How long have you been in the Army?'

'You mean the Regiment? The SAS?'

'No, I mean the Army – in total.'

'Three years in the Army – one with the SAS.'

'What made you join?'

'Come on, Red, you know that. What the fuck made *you* join?'

Red laughed and slapped the kid's shoulder.

'Kid,' he said, 'you got no respect. That's court-martial language. But you're right, we both know why. Fun and games, right?'

'That sums it up, Red.'

'Some soldiers have better motives, kid.'

'Each to his own, Red.'

'You been in Belfast or Antrim?'

'Both,' Johnny Boy replied. 'Don't tell me you disapprove, Red. I hate American Irishmen.'

'What did you do over there, kid?'

'Not much that I enjoyed. I didn't have a motorbike then, and it rained all the time. Also, it was full of people like Sergeant Clarke, if you know what I mean.'

'Hey, knock it off!' Paddy said.

'Sorry, Sarge,' the trooper replied. 'I thought all Irishmen had wax in their unwashed ears and that you wouldn't hear me.'

'I heard you all right. It's hard to ignore someone farting. One more verbal fart like that and your handsome mug'll look like a pomegranate. That's blood-red, for your info.'

'Hear you loud and clear, Sergeant.'

'Stop interrupting,' Red said to Paddy. 'I'm trying to talk to the kid, here. Where do you come from, Johnny Boy? I mean, where were you born and raised?'

'England.'

'I *know* that, kid! Where?'

'The only place worth living in that country.'

'You mean London?'

'Right. Crouch End. That's in North London, Red. It's near Finsbury Park, where a lot of Sambos and Paddies have their beds, but I didn't mind that.'

'Johnny Boy!' Paddy exclaimed.

'Sorry, Paddy,' Johnny Boy said. 'A mere slip of the tongue in the night. I need my sleep, don't you know.'

'Are you working-class, kid?' asked the American.

'Sergeant *Clarke* is working-class . . .'

'Fuck you, Trooper!'

'. . . but I'm middle-class, English, and proud of it. My dad's an interior decorator . . .'

'He means a painter and decorator,' Paddy clarified helpfully.

'. . . and my mother runs the wallpaper shop and does my Dad's accounts. They're pretty decent, my parents.'

'So why did you join the Army?' Red asked, always eager for facts.

'Because my home life, though decent, was

fart-boring and I couldn't find work. So here I am, Red.'

'You're a good kid,' Red said, thinking of his own kids back at home and feeling a little emotional. 'You're a bit on the wild side, I reckon, but otherwise you're OK.'

'Thanks, Red, so are you. Not bad for a Yank.'

'Read you loud and clear, kid.'

The bullshit continued for another thirty minutes or so until it was interrupted by Major Hailsham, who quietly said, 'There's the plane.'

The Prowler was high overhead, its lights shining like two stars, its grey underside laden with five pods that made it look like a great pregnant bird. It came no lower, not needing to risk low altitude, but it flew directly over the missile site, then turned around to come back again. Hailsham picked up his binoculars and studied the missile site. The guards in the observation towers were pointing up at the Prowler. Yet they were unconcerned. It was too high up for an attack plane. The guards watched it as it circled back over the site and then returned to where it had come from. When they saw that it was definitely leaving, they relaxed again.

'Is that it?' Hailsham asked.

Red was back on the SATCOM, just finishing his transmission. He faced Hailsham and stuck his thumb up in the air. 'That's it,' he said. 'The Iraqi radar is jammed. The Strike Eagles were flying in just behind it and are practically here. Start painting your targets.'

Johnny Boy removed his hands from behind his head, uncrossed his long legs, sat up and turned to the front. 'I've got to see this,' he said.

Using the PRC 319, Hailsham contacted the groups with the portable laser designators and told them to illuminate their selected targets for the incoming aircraft. Within minutes the various designators had 'warmed' or 'painted' their targets with a spot of intense light that could be picked up by the aircraft and would enable their missiles and bombs to be directed to the targets with incredible accuracy.

The flight of Strike Eagles arrived within minutes and came in low and fast, looking less fat-bellied than the Prowler, but more terrifying, with high twin fins, F100-PW-220 turbofan Pratt & Whitney jets, and a payload of AIM-9L Sidewinders, AIM-74 Sparrows and M61A1 20mm rotary cannons. Sweeping down and across the desert with awesome precision, one after the other, creating a godalmighty roar, they released two missiles at a time, raked the site with their cannons, levelled out and were ascending even before their missiles had struck home. Hitting their targets with shocking violence, the missiles made the ground erupt, spewing earth, sand and smoke, the latter streaked with yellow flames, and blowing the buildings apart with a cataclysmic, deafening fury.

The command posts were blown apart, the great radar bowls buckled, the supply dumps burst into flames, and the observation towers, also torn apart by the cannons, eventually collapsed, with men hurtling down, screaming, through the falling debris. Other men suffered worse, set ablaze and burning alive, running to and fro like balls of fire while their world exploded around them.

The Strike Eagles flew away, practically disappeared, returned, came back down with missiles searing and cannons thundering, then shot away again. The steel fences melted. Another building went up in flames. More burning men were screaming in the smoke that billowed up, black as oil, like heavy curtains, to meet the cascading sand. The Strike Eagles made a final run, getting rid of their payloads, and the devastation, as spectacular as it was hideous, was finally complete.

When the Strike Eagles saluted and flew away, back to base, the once widely spread, heavily guarded missile complex had been reduced to a grim pile of blazing, smoking rubble piled up around a few skeletal buildings, smouldering corpses and some shocked, dazed survivors.

'Let's bug out,' Hailsham said. He stood up and used hand signals to notify the other men. The hand signals were passed along the long line and the men started moving out.

A great mushroom cloud of exploded sand and smoke was spreading over the blazing, smouldering ruins of the missile site as Hailsham gratefully turned his back to it.

'Impressive, right?' Red asked with a broad, boyish grin.

'Oh, yes,' Major Hailsham said.

'Brilliant!' Johnny Boy exclaimed excitedly. 'Like a fucking great light show. Knocked 'em for six, Red!'

'We hit it right on the nose, kid.'

The stench of scorched flesh and burning fuel was being carried on the breeze as the squadron legged it back across the desert floor to the vehicles parked half a mile away. Hailsham stood up in his Pink Panther, beside his driver, Paddy Clarke, about to give the hand signal, when a column of sand obscuring the stars to the west drew his attention.

'What . . .?'

'Fucking Iraqis!' Johnny Boy exclaimed as his Honda motorbike roared into life. 'Let's get the hell out of here.'

Hailsham dropped his hand, clearly illuminated in the moonlight, as Paddy switched on the ignition and revved up the engine. The other vehicles did the same, one driver hearing the other, then they all raced away from the missile site with a discordant roaring.

The wheels of their vehicles churned up more sand, advertising their whereabouts.

Johnny Boy cut away from the column and headed directly towards the advancing Iraqi trucks.

Red looked on in disbelief as the LSV he was in, driven by an SAS Trooper, raced on ahead.

'What the fuck's he doing?' he asked the driver.

'Just causing some aggro,' the driver said, not fazed in the slightest.

Johnny Boy roared straight at the advancing Iraqi trucks on his motorbike, his headlamp turned off, and unholstered his Browning with one hand while holding the handlebars with the other.

He kept racing towards the column, hardly noticed in the darkness, and then turned sharp right, cutting across the oncoming trucks, and emptied his 13 rounds into the lights and windscreens he passed. Some of the lights went out. He heard glass shattering. One of the trucks careered sideways and crashed into another as Johnny Boy turned left, letting the Iraqi trucks pass him, and circled to come back up their rear.

Holstering his hand gun, he unclipped a phosphorus grenade. He let go of the handlebars, unpinned the grenade before the handlebars started shaking, then grabbed them again with his free hand and lobbed the grenade straight into the rear of the truck in front of him.

He again turned sharply to the right and was roaring away, out of range, when the grenade exploded in the back of the truck, in the very laps of the troops, blowing the canvas covering off and causing jagged fingers of white flame and streams of phosphorus fireflies to fan out through the darkness as the flying canvas burst into flames and fell smoking to earth.

The truck veered sideways and, as the first had done, smashed into another one.

Johnny Boy was already racing back to his own column when the Iraqis in the remaining trucks opened fire with their small arms. The bullets, which were not aimed at him, as he was well out to the side and still practically invisible, whistled dangerously close to him as he turned in and headed back to his mates.

'Nice one, Johnny!' he whispered.

Hailsham saw the colliding trucks, the grenade explosion and burning canvas, but also saw that the other trucks were still in pursuit. Not wanting a long chase, as this limited the use of fire-power, he used hand signals, which were passed from one vehicle to another, to tell the men to form the Pink Panthers and LSVs into a circular laager. They did so and then unwrapped their arsenal of GPMGs, MILANs, Stingers, 60mm LAWs, 81mm mortars and small arms just as Johnny Boy came roaring out of the moonlit plain and skidded to a halt between Major Hailsham and US Master-Sergeant Polanski.

The trooper swung his leg off the motorbike, propped it up on its support, unslung his M16 from his shoulder and went to join Red, who was crouched down behind his LSV, about to take aim with his own M16.

'I caused a bit of confusion out there,' Johnny Boy said, trying not to sound too proud.

'It's a pity you didn't stop 'em,' Red said. 'Here they come, kid.'

The Iraqi trucks, all lights blazing, came out of an immense cloud of sand created by their own wheels. They stopped within rifle range, disgorging their troops, just as Hailsham dropped his right hand and the SAS opened fire. The GPMGs roared relentlessly as the MILANs, Stingers, LAWs and mortars backblasted, sending their bombs raining down on the Iraqi trucks with devastating results. More shooting flames and boiling smoke. At least two trucks exploded. The Iraqi troops ran left and right, escaping the explosions, spreading out to return the fire, as the SAS opened up with their small arms and caused more devastation. More Iraqis screamed and fell, but the others remained courageous, spreading out and setting up their own mortars in the midst of that withering fire. Their mortars spewed flame and smoke and then the first shells exploded.

Hailsham was deafened, then covered in showering sand. When his ears cleared and his vision returned, he looked up from where he lay and saw a blackened shell hole in the ground just in front of Red's LSV, positioned beside Hailsham's Pink Panther. Red and Johnny

Boy were OK, still behind the LSV, but the front of the vehicle had been badly damaged and its tyres had burst into flames. Sand was raining down everywhere. Dense smoke obscured the view. Hailsham clambered back to his feet, saw his damaged SLR, unholstered his Browning and walked up to Red. The American and the young trooper were firing their M16s. Hailsham was about to say something – he didn't know quite what – when a wave of nausea assailed him and he had to sit down again.

'Are you OK, boss?' Paddy asked. 'That exploding mortar shell knocked you for six.'

'A little dizzy,' Hailsham said. 'What's happening, Paddy?'

'We've held them back, boss, but they're a stubborn bunch of bastards. They're digging in there. We've knocked out all their trucks and taken out a lot of men, but the ones left aren't going to let us go. You've got to admire them, boss.'

'This is no time for admiration, Paddy. Do you think we can hold here?'

'Well . . .'

'No,' Red said, crawling up on his hands and knees, though with his M16 held in one hand and his lips grimly set. 'We may have knocked out their trucks and downed a lot of their men, but one of those left still has a radio and is using it right now. You know what that means, Major? More Iraqi troops nearby. I say we shoot and scoot, Major, before the others get here. We won't stand a prayer otherwise.'

'OK, gentlemen, let's go.'

Hailsham's head had cleared and he stood up again. 'Relay the message to everyone,' he said to Paddy. 'Tell them we're bugging out. Tell them not to wait for further orders – they're to take off right now. They all know where the FOB is and they've got to get back under their own steam. OK, let's get to it.'

Paddy rushed around the laager, passing on Hailsham's message, as Hailsham clambered into his Pink Panther, smacking an ear to clear it, even as more Iraqi mortar shells exploded nearby.

'What about me?' Red said, ducking as exploding sand spewed over him. 'My LSV's in the wrecker's yard.'

'Come with me,' Johnny Boy offered. 'On the back of my bike. Have yourself an adventure.'

Red glanced at Hailsham.

'Why not?' Hailsham said. 'Most of the Pink Panthers, including mine, are full up – and Willoughby's reliable.'

'Hi, ho!' Red said. He climbed up on the motorbike behind Johnny Boy, just as Paddy returned from the far side of the laager. Paddy took the driving seat of the Pink Panther and looked directly at Hailsham.

'Yes, boss?'

'Yes,' Hailsham said.

Paddy put his foot down and the Pink Panther roared into life, shooting out from the circular laager and cutting a track through the sand. The other vehicles did the same, breaking away one by one, following Hailsham across the flat plain, away from the Iraqis. As the latter had no working trucks left, since most were in flames, they could only offer a fusillade of small-arms fire that did little damage.

One final Iraqi mortar shell, however, fired by the bloody fingers of a wounded militiaman, looped down to the rear of the Pink Panthers and LSVs that were making their escape across the desert. It exploded just as Johnny Boy was roaring past on his motorbike with Red Polanski sitting on the back, a great smile on his sunburnt face.

The explosion lifted the bike up in the air and flipped it into a spin that sent Johnny Boy and the American in opposite directions before they crashed down again.

Hailsham didn't know they were gone until it was too late.

'We can't turn back now,' he said when he realized they were missing. 'Let's just pray that they make it.'

13

Ricketts made it. When the Iraqi trucks advanced across the dark MSR, with the militiamen fanning out between them and firing on the march, he, Geordie and the other three troopers, Gillett, Moorcock and Stone, were saved by the curtain of swirling sand and smoke created by the phosphorus grenades. Down on one knee, in the firing position, with Geordie beside him and the troopers spread out behind them, returning the fire of the Iraqis, Ricketts saw the headlights of the advancing trucks blink out, shattered by bullets, as the smoke and sand from the explosions of the phosphorus grenades formed a spectacular curtain that temporarily obscured the view for both sides.

'Let's shoot and scoot,' he said to Geordie, 'while those bastards can't see us.'

'Right,' Geordie said. 'Got ya.'

'We head south along this MSR for about five hundred metres, but spreading out at different angles, then turn left and head straight for those hills behind us, spreading out again to hit the bottom of the hills at five different locations. When we get approximately three hundred metres up the hill, we'll all move in the direction required to meet the others. It's not exactly a precise rendezvous, but it's all I can offer. OK?'

'OK, boss.' Geordie turned back and relayed this information to the other three, even as they continued pouring fire into the smokescreen separating them from the advancing Iraqis. Each man stopped firing just long enough for Geordie to impart his message. 'Right, boss,' each trooper said in turn, then started firing again. When the last man had confirmed he understood, Geordie nodded at Ricketts.

'Shoot and scoot!' Ricketts bawled, rising to his feet and firing from the hip. '*Shoot and scoot!*'

In an SOP, or standard operating procedure, originally designed for jungle warfare, the five men immediately made a tactical withdrawal that involved splitting up and taking different routes to their emergency rendezvous while returning a heavy barrage of fire for as long as possible, thus confusing the enemy, who would think the fire was coming from all directions. In this case, they were aided immeasurably by the curtain of falling sand and swirling smoke, which must have made their separate, relentless bursts of gunfire appear to the Iraqis lost in the sand and smoke to be coming from more men than there were.

For Ricketts and the others the tactic worked, confusing the Iraqis long enough to let them race southward along the MSR, protected by the billowing smoke and sand, firing as they ran, before turning back and heading straight for the hills where, Ricketts knew, Andrew, Danny and Taff had already gone.

Briefly parted from the others as they all took different routes toward the hills, Ricketts reached the lower slopes just as the smoke was clearing from the MSR and some Iraqi troops, bolder than the others, raced in his direction.

Ricketts dropped to one knee, resting his M16 on the ground, and pulled a grenade from his ammo belt as he jumped up again. It was another phosphorus grenade, designed to do maximum damage, but even before it had completed its downward arc, he had followed it with a smoke grenade.

The grenades went off one after the other, even

as Ricketts was picking up his M16 and hurrying up the lower slopes of the frosted hills. The first explosion was spectacular, erupting between the Iraqi troops, blowing some into the air, and tearing the darkness with fingers of silvery light and showering phosphorus fireflies. The second exploded a second later, less spectacular but just as effective, creating a choking smokescreen that completely blinded those not wounded or killed by the first. By the time the smoke cleared, exposing the dead and wounded to the other Iraqis, Ricketts was well up the lower slopes of the hill and out of their sight.

They gave up the chase after that. Ricketts saw them from the hill. They were milling about on the smoky MSR, checking their dead and wounded. As Ricketts, smiling, started backtracking to meet up with the others, the Iraqis were picking up their casualties and putting them in the trucks. By the time Ricketts had reached Geordie and his three troopers, the Iraqi trucks were driving away, back across the MSR, gradually becoming lost in the cloud of dust churned up by their wheels.

'They haven't forgotten us,' Ricketts said when he met up with the Geordie and his men, all having made it safely to the hill. 'They have our location and they'll probably send choppers or planes. We better move out immediately.'

'What about Andrew, Danny and Taff?'

'No one saw them on the way here?'

The other three shook their heads.

'Then we have to forget them. We can't comb these hills for them. Either they made it or they didn't. If they did, they should be well on their way by now, striking out on their own.'

Ricketts looked at the other three men, the recently badged probationers, and asked, 'What about you men? Are you OK?'

'Sure, boss,' Trooper Stone, always the coolest of the three, said with a wide, cocky grin.

'I'm fine, too,' Gillett said. 'I had a few moments back there on the MSR, but I think I'm OK now.'

'Moorcock?'

'No problems.'

'Are you sure?'

'I think so. I mean, I'm feeling pretty tired and sometimes a bit confused, but I guess one is caused by the other . . .'

'It is.'

'. . . and apart from that, I think I can make it.'

'Were you frightened back there?'

Moorcock looked a little embarrassed. 'Well . . . yes, I was frightened. Why not admit it? Yes, boss, I was.'

'Good,' Ricketts said. 'That means you're not dead yet. What about you two back there? Were you frightened as well? Don't be scared to admit it.'

'Not me,' Stone said. 'I swear to God, I wasn't frightened. Maybe a little bit *nervous*, but not actually frightened.'

'Being nervous helps,' Ricketts said. 'What about you, Gillett?'

'I thought I was shitting my trousers, but I managed to hold it in.'

'Your probationary period's over,' Ricketts said. 'You men have all earned your winged badge. OK, let's march.'

The first day was long and arduous, with snow and sleet dogging the group, as well as search helicopters sent over the MSRs by the few Iraqis who had survived the previous battle. It was early morning by the time they crossed the low hills, but by the late afternoon, having to lie low repeatedly to let the choppers fly over, they had only covered about three miles.

The night was better, bringing some respite

from the search parties, and they managed to cover another twelve miles or so before first light. Unable to build a proper LUP, since the required equipment had been discarded, they rested in scrapes until noon, then struck out again.

There were fewer helicopters by then, but there were more ground troops, not only combing the area for them, but also on the look out for the troops of the élite Delta Force, the American equivalent of the SAS, who were known to be working inside Iraq's second main Scud reserve – the northern Scud box, known as Scud Boulevard, located along the border with Syria.

'That's where we're going,' Ricketts explained, checking his small-scale map and button compass. 'To a place called Al Qaim, near the Syrian border. We should find friendly forces there.'

They were relatively lucky for most of the journey, making good progress over three nights and two days, but the nearer they came to the northern Scud box, the more populated was the area, with the many intersecting roads, long used for trading between the locals and those across the frontier, becoming increasingly busy. Ignoring the war going on in their midst, the locals, dressed in the traditional *keffia* and *dish-disha*, carrying their wares on makeshift rucksacks on their backs, on rickety old carts hauled by donkeys, or on camels, often with vicious dogs snapping around them, went about their unchanging business as if all was normal.

In this area the Iraqis, fearful of attack from the northern Scud box or invasion from the border, were particularly nervous and opened fire on anyone not instantly recognizable as a local trader. Ricketts and his men were therefore not surprised to often find dead civilians on the roads and in the fields, or by the banks of the Euphrates river, their corpses torn to shreds by the local wild life and covered with bloated, frantic flies.

'Cor, what a pong!' Geordie said, holding his nose as they passed one such corpse. Geordie was in file behind Ricketts, but temporarily caught up with him by hurrying to get away from the stench. 'Those fucking Iraqis should get rid of these poor buggers, not just leave 'em as food for wild dogs and flies. Just leavin' 'em could cause an epidemic worse than fucking AIDS.'

'You've had AIDS, Geordie?'

'Don't come it, Sergeant-Major. You get that fucking disease, you don't survive it, from what I've been told.'

'From experienced friends, right?'

'No, Ricketts – wrong. There's no bleedin'

poofters in *my* circle, so don't try it on. I just read about it in the papers, is all. I've come no closer to the fucking disease than that, so don't suggest otherwise.'

'Just a thought,' Ricketts said. He was just amusing himself, passing the time, trying to find some distraction from the pain of his blistered feet, his exhaustion, his hunger and his thirst, during this last leg of the journey to Al Qaim. The remaining high-calorie food in their escape belts was gone, the water had gone even sooner, and now they were all beginning to suffer from the lack of replenishment. Thank God, they would reach the border town in a matter of hours.

'Let's take a break,' he said. It was nearing last light and he wanted to make the final leg of the journey by night. Relieved, the men settled down in a semicircle, Ricketts and Geordie sitting together, and the three troopers lying on their backs to stretch their legs and rest up.

'Tell me, Ricketts,' Geordie said, 'what did you do before you joined the Army?'

'I was a toolpusher – first on the North Sea oil rigs, then in the oilfields in the Gulf.

'So you know this area already!'

'Not *this* area,' Ricketts said, 'but I knew Kuwait as it was about fifteen years ago.'

'You had a good time?'

'I had my wife and kids with me, which certainly helped a lot, but you couldn't do any boozing and there wasn't too much else to keep you busy. I was glad to get home.'

'What do you think of the A-rabs?'

'I respect them. They can be volatile and cruel, but they're also proud, good-humoured and generous. We could learn a lot from them.'

'You joined the Army when you returned from the Gulf?'

'More or less. I got a job as a salesman for the oil company, couldn't stand it, became pretty bored with middle-class life and decided I'd rather fight in Belfast than sleep soundly at night. I joined up, served my time in Northern Ireland, then applied for the SAS. I've never regretted it.'

'Yeah, everyone knows you love it, Ricketts. So what will you do when this show's over and they give you a desk job? I mean, at your age they're not likely to let you go on active service again.'

'No, they won't. I think this is the last time.' Ricketts shrugged, expressing regret and resignation. 'I don't think I could stand a desk job – not even with the Regiment – so I guess I'll take early retirement and sign on with a security firm. Even that would be better than pushing a pen.'

'You could become a mercenary.'

'I don't approve of them.'

'Then become a military instructor for Third World countries. They're always looking for experienced former soldiers and anyone with your track record would be a gift to them.'

'That's a thought,' Ricketts said. 'But I think I'm at an age where my wife's going to expect me home a bit more, so I'll probably end up as a security guard.'

'You could do worse,' Geordie said.

Ricketts glanced over his shoulder and saw that the sun was sinking, casting last light on the horizon and, he hoped, on the border. 'OK, men,' he said. 'Let's strike out again.'

Wearily, the men climbed to their feet and fell without thinking into file formation, with Geordie out front on point, troopers Gillett, Moorcock and Stone in the middle, and Ricketts bringing up the rear. They progressed without incident for another two hours, then stopped for another break and to let Ricketts check his small-scale map with the aid of a pencil torch.

'According to this map,' he said with a deep surge of pleasurable anticipation, 'we're only six miles from Al Qaim. I therefore suggest that we get up and go before what energy we have left deserts us. If we stay here too long we'll become too lethargic to move. So let's move right now and get it over with.'

'I'll second that,' Geordie said.

When the three troopers agreed, all keen to get to safety, they climbed to their feet, picked up their weapons, and started across the dark field, away from the Euphrates, toward the lights shining from what they hoped were friendly houses in the distance.

They had only been walking five minutes when the first shots rang out.

'*Shake out*!' Ricketts bawled and they all threw themselves to the ground as bullets whipped over their heads to ricochet off the rocks behind them. They were returning the enemy fire from a belly-down position even before they actually saw the Iraqi troops approaching from the front, spreading out, silhouetted by the lights around Al Qaim, firing on the move.

There were a lot of them, Ricketts noticed, as he fired his SLR. Far too many to be dealt with. The only way forward was to go back and circle around. Ricketts stopped firing and waved his right hand to draw the attention of the others, all of whom were firing their M16s and SLRs at the mass of shadowy figures zigzagging towards them.

'We meet between those palm trees,' Ricketts shouted above the shocking din. 'Right there by the river. OK? *Shoot and scoot!*'

They all jumped to their feet and ran sideways, towards the river, spreading out and firing their weapons on the move. Some Iraqis fell, but the others kept moving, shouting warnings to one another as they fired.

Trooper Moorcock was ahead of Ricketts, zigzagging like the Iraqis, firing on the move, but then he suddenly jerked back, his beret flying off his head, followed by pieces of splintered bone from the back of his skull as his weapon sailed out of his upraised hands and he crashed onto his back. He was already dead when Ricketts leaned over him to check, so Ricketts jumped up and continued running, holding his SLR against his waist and firing on the run.

He heard the sound of a mortar firing and tried to shout a warning. The shell exploded between Geordie and Stone before he could do so. Geordie managed to keep running, but Stone was less lucky, being picked up by the blast and turned over and slammed down again.

He had been crossing the field diagonally, heading away from Ricketts, intending to confuse the Iraqis as part of the SOP of shoot and scoot, so now he was too far away for Ricketts to help him. However, as Ricketts kept running, he saw Stone standing up again, holding onto his wounded elbow and limping towards Gillett, who was rushing over to give him covering fire. Unable to walk – clearly wounded in the foot or leg as well as in his elbow – Stone collapsed again. Gillett was standing between him and the Iraqis, keeping up a protective hail of gunfire with his M16, as Ricketts plunged into the shade of the palm trees by the river-bank.

Looking back, he saw Gillett dropping his gun and raising his hands above his head. The Iraqis surrounded him, forced him onto his belly, aimed their weapons at him and Stone, but did not fire at them. Instead, a few stood guard while the others spread out again and advanced towards the river, this time not firing.

'*Ricketts*!'

Looking along the river-bank, Ricketts saw Geordie hurrying towards him, at the crouch and still holding his SLR. When he reached Ricketts, he straightened up and stared across the dark, moonlit field at the advancing Iraqis.

'They're obviously well-disciplined militia-men,' he said, 'so Gillett and Stone might be OK. What the hell do *we* do?'

Ricketts studied the advancing Iraqis, then stared over the river. The water was icy, about 400 yards wide, flooding the banks and flowing quickly.

'The only escape route left is north,' he said. 'That means crossing the river.'

'Are you fucking joking?' Geordie asked. 'That river's in flood. The current's too strong. It'll sweep us away.'

'We have to take that chance, Geordie. Either we do that or we stay here. Do we toss or decide?'

Geordie studied the river with growing trepidation. 'Did you ever see that movie, *Butch Cassidy and the Sundance Kid*?'

'Yes,' Ricketts replied.

'Who's Butch and who's Sundance?' Geordie asked.

'Let's find out,' Ricketts said.

After hurriedly discarding their weapons, kit belt and desert boots, they walked to the flooded bank and tentatively dipped their toes in to check the temperature and strength of the current. The water was ice-cold and the current was fierce.

They gazed at one another, momentarily undecided, then glanced back over their shoulders to
see that the Iraqis were still advancing and would
soon be at the line of palm trees, practically on
top of them.

'Fuck it,' Geordie said. Then he took a deep
breath and plunged in, followed by Ricketts.

The shock of the icy water took Ricketts's
breath away and momentarily blotted out all
thought. It was even colder than he'd expected,
already numbing much of his body, and he
realized that if he was in it too long, he'd
freeze to death before he reached the far bank.
That bank was far away and the current was
very strong, having already swept Geordie off
course and now doing to same to Ricketts, no
matter how hard he struggled to swim against it.
Nevertheless, he kept going, no longer having a
choice, and was spurred to greater efforts when
gunshots rang out and the water spurted up near
him where many bullets were striking it.

Ricketts went under and stayed down as
long as possible, though the total darkness,
fiercely tugging current and lack of feeling in
his chilled limbs was disorienting and filled
him with the fear that he was making no
progress at all, or might even be swimming

towards the bottom rather than across to the far side.

Though normally possessing nerves of steel, he experienced a fleeting panic of the kind he had not known since childhood. It made him burst through the surface, where he soon saw that he was in another area, well away from the palm trees where the Iraqis had been firing, and out in the middle of the river.

Geordie, he noticed when his eyes had cleared of water, was still swimming as well, though much slower, now slightly behind, and a good way upstream.

Ricketts kept swimming, fighting against the fierce current, making headway, but with agonizing slowness, being swept along even as he managed to inch forward, closer to the far bank. Now he felt numb all over, except for darting pains in his feet, and was scarcely able to move his hands when he dipped them in the water.

His lungs were on fire. He was breathing in spasms. The river roared and splashed, pummelled him and froze him, but he fought vigorously against it, swimming, always swimming, and at last reached the far bank.

Scrambling halfway out, Ricketts was swept sideways and almost fell, but hurled himself forward again, hitting the bank with a soft thud and sinking into the mud. Rolling over and kicking himself backwards, he kept going until all of him was free of the rushing water. Relieved, he rolled over onto his belly, retching and gasping for breath for some time.

When eventually he looked up, he saw Geordie a lot further along the bank, also lying face down, but barely moving. Though dripping wet and shivering with cold, Ricketts clambered to his feet, almost toppled over with dizziness, recovered and made his way carefully along the muddy, slippery bank to where Geordie was lying, wet and covered with mud. Ricketts shook him gently by the shoulder, calling his name.

Geordie rolled over. He was breathing with shocking harshness and stared up with dazed eyes.

'Did we make it?'

'Yes, Geordie, we made it.'

'I'm not sure that I did.' He tried to sit up but failed, hardly getting his shoulders off the ground, so Ricketts knelt beside him and helped him into a sitting position. 'Fuck,' Geordie gasped, 'I feel awful. I can hardly breathe. My heart's racing. I can't feel a thing.'

'You'll be OK in a minute or two, Geordie. Just take your time.'

Geordie just nodded, trying to control his raucous breathing, shivering even more than Ricketts had done, as if out of control. Looking along the bank, Ricketts saw a ruined mud hut just beyond it, surrounded by a few scraggy palm trees, illuminated by moonlight.

'That house looks uninhabited,' Ricketts said. 'Let me help you over there. At least we'll be out of this wind and can stay there until we dry out. Do you think you can make it?'

'With your help,' Geordie gasped.

Ricketts slipped an arm around Geordie's back, sliding it up under his armpits to give him leverage. Even with such assistance, Geordie could hardly stand and Ricketts had to practically carry him all the way, from the rushing river and fierce, freezing wind to the relative shelter of the palm trees around the mud hut. The hut was falling down and had only half a roof, but the walls would offer protection from the wind. Ricketts helped Geordie inside. The floor was covered with rubble and rubbish, but at least it was dry. Ricketts managed to clear a space of sharp-edged debris and laid Geordie down.

'OK?'

Geordie nodded, though he looked and sounded awful. His face was a ghastly, deathly white and his breathing was anguished. His lips and hands had turned blue.

'We're only a mile or two from the border,' Ricketts told him. 'I think we've made it, Geordie.'

Geordie closed his eyes and tried to catch his breath. 'Cold,' he managed to croak eventually. 'Can't feel anything . . . Hurting, too . . . where it's not cold . . . Need to be warm.'

'I know,' Ricketts said, 'but we can't light a fire. If we do, the smoke will give us away. We'll just have to dry out.'

'Not dry,' Geordie murmured. 'Wet and cold . . . Feeling sick and . . .' He choked and then coughed up more water and what looked like blood. 'Fuck you, Andrew, I'm OK.'

'I'm not Andrew,' Ricketts informed him, suddenly realizing that Geordie was very ill. 'I'm Ricketts – Sergeant-Major Ricketts. Try to stay awake, Geordie.'

'Sleep . . . Good idea . . . Need sleep to wake up . . . You keep watch, Baby Face . . .' He coughed again and spat more blood. 'Mum? Is that you, Dad? Why's it so dark in here? I won't do it. *I won't!*'

He soon started rambling, becoming inco-
herent, the words spilling out in a torrent of
recollection and hallucination. He was icy to
the touch, obviously dying from hypothermia,
and eventually, as Ricketts had feared, he sank
into a coma.

Ricketts didn't have a thing to cover him up
with when he went to find help. The man he left
lying in that rubble was a shivering wreck.

Across the rocky field, looking away from
the river, Ricketts saw the lights of another
dwelling. After hurrying across to it, through the
striations of dawn's pale light, he peered through
the window and saw that it was inhabited by
an Arab family. The children were still sleeping,
while their parents were squatting on woven mats
on the floor and eating what looked like boiled
rice or couscous from an earthenware bowl. An
older man, wearing traditional dress, was seated
in a chair near the wall, reading a book by the
light of a flickering oil lamp. Forced to take a
chance, Ricketts hurried back to the front of the
house and knocked on the door. It was opened
by the older man, who looked at him with dull
curiosity, but no sign of fear.

Speaking crude Arabic, Ricketts explained who
he was and that he had a sick man in the nearby

mud hut. 'We just want to cross the border,' he said, 'but we need some kind of transport, for which we can pay well. Will you help us?'

The old man glanced over his shoulder, obviously focusing on the mud hut, then nodded and said, as best Ricketts could understand: 'My neighbour has a truck you can hire. He lives a few hundred metres away. You go back and look after your friend while I fetch the truck.'

'My friend is very cold,' Ricketts told him. 'Can you lend me a blanket?'

The old man nodded, disappeared inside, then stepped out again, holding a thick blanket. 'Here,' he said. 'Now go. I will soon return with the truck.'

When Ricketts thanked him, he turned away and hurried along the mud track that led to the next house, visible through the early-morning mist, about 500 yards further on. Ricketts stepped off the track and hurried back across the field, towards the river, until he came to the broken-down hut.

When Ricketts hurried inside with the blanket, he found that Geordie had died. Shocked and grieving, he knelt beside his friend. After closing his eyes, he covered him up with the blanket. He then sat in the rubble, drained by an awful numbness, staring blindly at a patch of cloudy-grey sky that was framed by the hole of broken bricks in the opposite wall.

Ricketts sat there for a long time, exhausted, almost broken, until the sound of the approaching truck jerked him out of his reverie. After glancing down at the blanket, as if expecting to find Geordie alive, he stood up and went to the broken wall and looked across the rocky field.

It was not a farmer's truck that he saw.

It was a truck filled with heavily armed Iraqi troops.

'Bastard!' he exploded, then turned away, hurried across the room, glanced one last time at his dead friend, and clambered over the broken wall at the back, out of the hut.

Ricketts ran for it, bullets whistled past his head. Reaching a hill, he dropped low and rolled down it as more bullets whipped through the air above him and whined into the empty sky.

He picked himself up and kept running, heading for Syria.

14

Danny Porter struck out on his own, determined not to be captured. When he heard the sounds of shooting from a long way beyond the wadi, shortly after Andrew had left with the Arab goat-herd, he knew that Andrew had been betrayed and was now either dead or in captivity. He also knew that the Iraqis would suspect the presence of other British troopers and intensify the search for them. Since those British troopers came down to one man, himself, he had no doubts that he was in for a hard time.

Leaving the wadi, Danny walked on a pre-arranged bearing, due north, aiming for the Euphrates. It was thirty-six hours since he had drunk and he badly needed water, but only fifteen minutes after leaving the wadi, he saw an Iraqi troop truck behind him, heading for the spot where he had lain up. Realizing that the Arab goatherd had informed the Iraqis of his presence, he started walking even faster, trying to forget his hunger and thirst, forcing himself to keep moving.

Alone now and feeling it, he walked for the rest of that day and night, his third on the run. Iraqi search helicopters often flew overhead, repeatedly forcing him to lie low. He had to do the same to avoid passing army trucks, all filled with troops and bristling with weapons.

Next day the sky was clear and the snow had stopped falling, which made Danny's march a little easier. But Iraqi helicopters were still searching the area and many bands of heavily armed militiamen were assiduously combing the windswept hills and valleys for him. Put off by the sight of them, he constructed a simple lying-up position and laid up for the rest of that day, only breaking the LUP down, erasing all traces of his presence, and moving on again, when last light had come.

After another nine-hour march, in the early hours of the morning, he saw the Euphrates through his night-sight. It was in a flat plain below him, a winding strip of muddy water, with palms trees and houses scattered along its banks. He also saw a small village surrounded by irrigated fields and more scattered palm trees.

As dogs were barking from the houses, he made his way down to the river's edge with great caution. Stepping into the water, he sank to his waist in soft mud and had to drag himself out. After lying belly-down to get his breath back, he sat up again and filled his water bottles.

Soaked and muddy, he laid up for the day in a dry wadi system close to the village. His morale was at a low ebb, but he remembered the disciplines of Continuation Training and managed to perk himself up a little. Though filthy, the water was drinkable and helped to quench his thirst. He finished the last of the biscuits taken from his escape belt, then tried to prepare himself for what he knew would be severe hunger pangs.

However, Danny's feet were in a bad way. He had lost most of his toenails and his blisters were suppurating. As the blisters were on the soles of his feet, they made walking an agonizing endurance test. With his adrenalin still running strongly, he did not feel particularly tired. In any case, when he tried to sleep, the air was so cold that every ten minutes or so he woke up shuddering violently.

Still in darkness, he moved off again, following the murky Euphrates, from which he was able to obtain enough water to survive. Also, by staying in the valley he avoided exposure to the pitiless windchill that had killed Taff Burgess and threatened him and Andrew with hypothermia. He was, however, in a populated area, thus running a greater risk of discovery. He minimized this by avoiding all human habitation.

Again, Danny tried to summon assistance with his SARBE rescue beacon, but without success. Probably, he reasoned, it was not precise enough to enable the SAS search helicopters to locate him. As he also knew full well, the intense Iraqi activity in the area and the widespread AA gun batteries raised the odds against a successful pick-up.

In fact, throughout his lengthy, arduous march Danny was constantly seeing Iraqi troops on the move or civilians walking about in large groups, obviously as organized search parties. To make matters worse, they were out mostly during the night when, as the Iraqis knew, he would be travelling. Because of this, he advanced at a snail's pace, being forced to repeatedly stop, scan the area through his night-sight, stop again, backtrack, watch, wait, and eventually move on, treading with care.

It made demands on his patience. He endured it either by focusing intently on his SAS training or by thinking about other things, notably home. Though taking confidence and pride from being an SAS soldier, and from his capacity for survival, Danny had always lacked such virtues in his personal life and now knew that he had been more than naïve in falling for the first girl who had showed an interest in him and letting vanity blind him to the fact that they lived in separate worlds. His wife Darlene was attractive, but she liked a good time, and now, even though they had two children, she was fooling around a lot. Danny knew this was true because his mates had told him so and his father and mother, always keen to support him, had confirmed the depressing fact.

While able to make a soldier's 'kill' as casually as slicing bread, Danny, who sliced throats instead of loaves, was otherwise too sentimental for his own good. He could not, therefore, bear the thought that his children – like him, born and bred in Kingswinford, in the West Midlands – were being brought up by a mother who liked a lively night life and spent more time away from home than in it. He knew this because his parents had told him so and were, reportedly, spending more nights with the children than Darlene could count or even remember.

'We're too old for this,' Danny's father had

complained in a phone call to the Paludrine Club in Hereford. 'So you better come home and sort her out. She's a right boozy tart, that one.'

Danny hadn't sorted her out because he didn't know how to start. He just wanted to be with the Regiment, sorting out any enemy they cared to give him, which he knew he could do well.

Now, filling time, fighting isolation and silence, embarked on a long march that could mean life or death, he reflected long and hard on his domestic problems, but decided that such thoughts were negative and possibly dangerous. He would focus, instead, on staying alive and getting home in one piece.

In the early hours of the fifth day he found another LUP, this time on a cliff face over 600 feet high. From there he could look out over the river to an Arab village located on the far bank, where the people were walking about peacefully and life seemed to be normal. For most of the day he watched men fishing in the river, pains in his stomach, saliva in his throat, constantly, obsessively thinking of how hungry he was. By last light he was practically starving and glad to move on.

That night he found himself between the river and a motorway, in a corridor which varied in width from one mile to six. As the wadi systems coming down towards the river demanded continual descents and climbs, he tried to save energy by keeping out of them and instead walking parallel with the road, which he knew was dangerous.

Indeed, shortly after taking to the side of the road, he heard the drone of a vehicle coming up behind him. Dropping immediately to the ground and looking back through his night-sight, he saw a black dot on the motorway, growing bigger each second. When it passed him, he was surprised to see that it was one of the increasingly rare mobile Scuds, its missile on the back of a noisy wheeled platform, its green tarpaulin flapping. Still not forgetting his rigorous training, Danny dutifully made a note of the time and place.

To his despair, however, he was informed by a nearby motorway sign that he was 50 kilometres further from the border than he had anticipated. This meant that he had at least one more full day and two nights on the march.

After marching for another hour, when last light was approaching, the only place he could find to 'basha down' was a rubbish-strewn culvert passing under the motorway embankment.

Six feet high and nearly ten wide, it was relatively safe, reasonably dry and protected him against the night's cold wind.

Early the next morning, soon after daybreak, he heard the jingle of bells – a familiar sound by now – as a herd of goats was ushered through the tunnel on its way to pasture.

'Shit!' he whispered, then hurried out of the culvert to hide in a nearby ditch, where he remained until the man and his goats had passed.

Knowing that the goatherd would eventually return, Danny crawled along a wadi, going to ground each time a car came down the road. Most of the cars were military troop trucks or jeeps, though some were battered old heaps driven by local workers and a few were chauffeur-driven Mercedes filled with wealthy Arabs.

After crawling along the wadi for about six miles, tearing his army trousers and cutting his hands and knees, which left a trail of blood behind him, Danny found a hole in the ground and lay there for the rest of the day. Yet another miserable day.

Moving out again that night, he found that the terrain consisted of small hills covered with scrubby thorn bushes and complex wadi systems that made him feel he was scrambling up and down through endless quarries. Exhausting though this was, dehydration was becoming a more serious problem. This was not helped by the fact that he had to keep away from the river, where most of the houses had vicious dogs whose noisy barking would give away his presence.

Finally reaching the end of the series of wadis, he headed due west and had an easier time until stopped by the barbed-wire fence of a heavily guarded military establishment.

Suddenly, an air-raid siren wailed. Thinking he had been seen, Danny immediately went to ground and searched the darkness ahead with his night-sight. He saw a number of AA gun positions, with tall towers that looked like radio masts on the high ground behind them. A surprising number of armed patrols were walking about, with a lot of the men scanning the sky as the siren continued its demented wailing.

Realizing that he had stumbled on a highly sensitive Iraqi signals command post about to be attacked by Allied aircraft, Danny stood up and hurried away, running at the crouch, weaving left and right, and praying to God that the facility was not being protected by minefields.

It was impossible to check this as the ground was in darkness and the air raid had already begun, with French Jaguars dropping their bombs from high in the night sky, well out of range of the pounding Iraqi guns. The explosions were catastrophic, shaking the ground beneath his feet, illuminating the darkness with rapidly flickering, silvery light and filling the air with crimson sparks and phosphorus fireflies.

Danny dropped to the ground, letting the shock waves pass away, then jumped out and started running again. He repeated this process over and over again until, after what seemed like an eternity, the air raid ended and the Jaguars disappeared.

Looking back, Danny saw that the main facility was now much further behind him, with many of its buildings on fire, some of the fencing blown away, other parts scorched and buckled, and a pall of smoke covering all. Nevertheless, as he now realized, that fenced-in area was only one part of the facility and the rest of it was scattered far and wide, over a broad expanse of land filled with wadis and ditches, criss-crossed by a web of roads and dirt tracks.

Luckily, there were no minefields, though Danny spent most of that night trying to extricate himself from the grounds of the military complex which, since the bombing raid, had been filled with patrolling foot soldiers, roaring troop-trucks, and heavily guarded mobile gun batteries.

Eventually, feeling exhausted and in a state of disorientation, he came to a road junction, where he found himself stuck between a three-man vehicle-control point and a fixed AA gun site. Unable to go forward, but determined not to turn back, he crawled into a culvert beneath the road, scraping his already bloody knees and losing more blood.

The culvert was filled with foul-smelling rubbish that almost made him retch. His feet, as well as his raw knees, had become extremely painful, with many cuts and ulcerated blisters. As it was pitch dark in the culvert, he could do little about this and instead, as the night progressed and the silence wrapped itself around him, he was tormented with hunger, thirst and cold.

At first light he moved on, circling around the vehicle-control point and the gun batteries, feeling increasingly weak and dizzy, aware that he was losing his sense of balance and might not last much longer. This, he dimly realized, was due to dehydration, which would kill him if he failed to find water. Miraculously, just as he saw another vehicle-control point and was about to collapse at the mere sight of it, he came across a small stream flowing over white stones of surprising brightness. Filled with gratitude and relief, he dropped to his hands and knees, then shoved his whole face into the freezing water and greedily drank it.

Just as quickly jerking upright with revulsion, he spat the water out. It was foul. Even worse, it was burning his mouth and tongue. Forcing spittle into his mouth to rid himself of the bitter, acid taste, he spat again, though could not stop shivering with weakness, shock and growing nausea. Already, that single, brief taste of the water had scorched and blistered his mouth, making his tongue swell up dangerously, threatening to choke him.

Glancing down into the water, at the surprisingly pure white stones below, he realized they had been burnt clean by the same substance that was searing his mouth. Chemical waste. Recognizing the fact, Danny went into a spasm of repeated vomiting, which only ended when there was nothing left to throw up. Now, with his belly empty and his swollen tongue threatening to choke him, he knew that he was on his last legs and could not last much longer. However, recalling all he had been taught in the Combat and Survival Phase of Continuation Training, he refused to give in to despair and instead crawled into another culvert, where he lay up all day, trying to regain his strength and conquer his hunger and thirst by force of will.

To an extent, he succeeded, and once the darkness fell he walked past the vehicle-control point in dead ground, where he could not be seen. But he was barely past it when flashing in the sky far behind him indicated that the facility was being bombed again by the Allies. This time, he could not have run even if he had had to – though luckily there was no need. The facility was now a long way behind him, with the sounds of the air raid mercifully distant and muffled. Eventually darkness reclaimed the sky and the silence returned.

Danny, though unsteady on his feet, resolutely kept walking. Suddenly, in the dark night, he came upon barbed-wire fencing that appeared to run for miles on both sides of him. Assuming he had reached the border, he climbed over the barbed wire where wooden stakes had been driven through it for support. The pain was excruciating, particularly when the barbed wire tore his already bleeding knees and hands, but he gritted his teeth and endured, sweating profusely, until he could drop down to the other side.

Lights were shining in the distance, but by now he was so weak and confused he was starting to hear voices in his head.

'*It'll be there in the Imperial War Museum for your children to read,*' Andrew said distinctly.

Shocked, Danny glanced about him, but there was no sign of Andrew. Then he remembered that he was marching all alone and that Andrew had either been killed or captured.

'*The men in that mobile unit packed up their plates and saucers this morning,*' Ricketts said, loud and clear, '*and I think they'll be leaving soon.*'

Danny glanced around again, but Ricketts was nowhere in sight.

'*We need a loaf of bread,*' Darlene said. '*Can you go out and get one, luv?*'

'Yes, Darlene,' Danny replied to the bitter wind.

As he walked towards the distant lights, which he hoped were friendly houses, he collapsed twice and each time became unconscious. The second time, he fell flat on his face and saw, when he recovered and examined himself in his hand mirror, that he had broken his formerly perfect nose.

'Very nice,' he said to the mirror. 'Now you look more mature.'

During moments of lucidity, Danny realized that he was in serious trouble and was likely to collapse for good if he did not find drinkable water soon. At first light, badly depleted, afraid that collapse was imminent, he sat with his back against the wall of a wadi and distinctly heard his mates calling to him.

'*Hey, Baby Face*!' Jock called.

'*Quick, Danny*!' yelled Paddy. '*Get your arse over here*!'

What Danny could *see*, however, about 200 yards away, was an isolated goatherd's shack. Two hundred yards was not far, but to him it seemed miles.

'Damn it, Danny,' he said aloud, but with difficulty because his tongue was so swollen, 'don't give up now. You've come this far, go the rest of the mile. Stand up, Danny. Start walking.'

That was enough to get him started. It even brought his senses back. He remembered to break down his rifle into its component parts to show that he was not a combatant. Carrying the pieces in a small sack, he managed to walk as far as the goatherd's shack, where he found a woman outside, kneeling by an open fire boiling soup in a pan as children played happily around her. She looked up, unsurprised, when Danny stopped before her and coughed into his clenched fist.

'Hello,' he said in his basic Arabic. 'Sorry to trouble you, but could you tell me exactly where I am?'

Registering from his appearance and imperfect Arabic that he was a Coalition soldier, the woman smiled and waved to the other side of the barbed-wire fence, where Danny saw a border post with an Iraqi flag fluttering on its watch-tower. The woman spoke to him in Arabic, then, seeing that he didn't understand, pointed to the watch-tower and said, 'Iraq!' She then pointed to the ground at her feet and said, 'Syria. *Syria!*'

Realizing that he had made it, after marching for six days and seven nights, and covering a total of 117 miles, Danny raised his hand in a weak gesture of gratitude, then collapsed.

15

Arriving safely in Syria at separate locations and different times, Ricketts and Danny were handed over to the Coalition forces and flown immediately to Tabuk in the northern desert of Saudi Arabia, then from there back to the SAS FOB located 87 miles inside Iraq.

Reunited with a relieved Major Hailsham in his lean-to in the FOB, the three men shared their regrets over the deaths of Geordie and Moorcock, then speculated briefly on what had happened to those gone missing – specifically the much-loved Sergeant Andrew Winston, the lesser known, relatively new troopers Gillett and Stone, and, of course, the redoubtable biker, Trooper Johnny Boy Willoughby, and the American Special Forces Master-Sergeant Red Polanski. Knowing that they were either dead or imprisoned, possibly even being tortured, and that nothing could be done to help them, the three men in the lean-to became embarrassed and hastily changed the subject.

'You might like to know, Danny,' Major Hailsham said, 'that the reason we couldn't respond to your SARBE beacon is that according to Intelligence the Iraqis alerted nearly two thousand troops when you escaped. Those, along with extensive helicopter and aircraft recces, made picking you up, let alone finding you, virtually impossible. In fact, they even alerted civilians along the river-bank to look out for you and any others like you.'

'Yes,' Danny replied, 'I sussed that. That's why I was constantly encountering troops on the move or civilians walking about the whole night, from last to first light. That's why it took me so long.'

'You were lucky you got here at all,' Hailsham said. 'That was a record-breaking march by any standards, and you did it through the heart of enemy territory and came out in one piece. That's some achievement, Corporal.'

'Thanks, boss.'

'And all you suffered was a broken nose,' Ricketts said. 'It makes you look more mature.'

'Thank *you*, Sergeant-Major!'

Ricketts and Hailsham grinned.

'How did you actually get back to safety?' Hailsham asked. 'Some Syrian woman, did you say? Any hanky-panky?'

Danny blushed and looked terribly serious. 'No, boss,' he said. 'I collapsed from exhaustion, hunger and relief when that Syrian woman told me I'd crossed the border. While I was still unconscious, the woman's husband put me on a bed of straw in the barn for the animals. He left me there until I recovered. I slept there until I was ready to leave.'

'Sleeping with the animals,' Hailsham said. 'As close to nature as a man can possibly get. And then?'

'When I regained consciousness, the woman built up my strength with a daily diet of soup and bread. When I was fit enough to walk, she took me to the nearest town, where a fat Syrian official handed me over to the police. When I showed them my letter of reward for safe transfer, they tore it up, threw me in a filthy cell and beat the shit out of me – just for fun, I think.'

'Absolutely disgraceful,' Hailsham said.

'No argument there, boss.'

'And so?'

'Having got that little bit of aggro out of

their systems, they drove me away in a battered Mercedes, passing a sign pointing to Baghdad. When I commented on this, the bastards had another bit of sport by saying that's where they were taking me – to hand me over to Saddam's secret police. Luckily, they were just joking. In fact, they drove me to a Saudi border town, where I was handed over to the British Embassy. The toffs in the Embassy, who seemed embarrassed by my presence, got me on that American plane flying in to Tabuk. I guess you know all the rest.'

'No saucy scandals, then?' Hailsham still looked hopeful.

'Sorry, boss. Can't help you there.'

'We're glad to have you back all the same,' Hailsham said in his most soothing manner. 'You were quite lucky, Danny.'

'Yes, boss, I was.'

'So was I,' Ricketts said. 'A lot luckier than those other poor sods, caught by the Iraqis.'

Realizing, by the sudden silence, that he had got back onto an unwelcome subject, Ricketts glanced out of Hailsham's camouflaged lean-to at the many tanks, trucks, mobile gunnery units, Land Rovers, LSVs and motorbikes spread between the other tents in the setting sun. The sight of them sent a powerful surge of pride through him. Suddenly ashamed, however, of the pleasure he was feeling when the others might be in bad trouble, even dead, he coughed into his fist, returned his gaze to Hailsham, and asked, 'How are things going with the war?'

'It's practically over,' Hailsham said. 'The air strikes have severely damaged Saddam's airfields and disrupted his command and control structure. We've broken his communications links to the front. Ninety per cent of Iraq's internal communications have been knocked out and the transportation of fuel severely disrupted. Damage to ammunition storage dumps has been slight so far, but the long-term supply of missiles has been seriously interrupted and the production of chemical-warfare stocks hit hard. The national electricity grid has been shut down. The Scuds have been pursued into the wilds of Iraq, well out of harm's way – at least out of range of Israel – and our own raids have spread panic and confusion throughout the Iraqi army, which has, according to the green slime, mistaken our small numbers for a regiment of about ten thousand men.'

'And the ground war?'

'It's well under way. Two major invasion forces

crossed the border simultaneously at 0400 hours the day before yesterday. In the east, elements of the 1st and 2nd US Marine Divisions broke through the minefields into Kuwait and fought their way due north towards Kuwait City. At the same time, in the far west, elements of the American 18 Corps, with French reinforcements, made a wide sweep across the desert. The Americans eventually severed Highway 8, which runs from Basra to Baghdad, thereby trapping the Republican Guard divisions. While they were doing that, the French were securing the western flank of the advance.'

'Neat,' Ricketts said.

'The third part of the invasion,' Hailsham continued, 'was the airborne attack by the 101st Assault Division – the Screaming Eagles – who shipped two thousand men in three hundred helicopters to establish an FOB well inside Iraq, striking at the severed Highway 8. Meanwhile, in the east, the US Navy was shelling the coast and the 1st US Cavalry Division were continuing their artillery raids and reconnaissance patrols in the area of Wadi at Batin. By G plus one, the day after the start of the ground war, the British 7th Armoured Brigade, spearheaded by the Queen's Royal Hussars and fourteen hundred Challenger tanks, was advancing into Iraq along the sixteen lanes opened up by the 1st Mechanized Infantry Division. Right now, even as we talk, and while the Iraqis are inexplicably continuing to focus their attention on their southern front, the Americans in the north-west are cutting the highway to Baghdad, the Arab forces in the east are advancing on Kuwait, the Egyptians are taking large numbers of prisoners, and 18 Corps is advancing towards the Republican Guard divisions in the far north-east. Already nearly ten thousand prisoners had been captured and hundreds more are waving white flags. You got back just in time.'

'For what? What are we slated for?'

Before Hailsham could answer, a familiar, insolent voice cracked like a whip: '*Sir*! Trooper John Willoughby reporting for duty, *sir*!'

Looking around in surprise, Ricketts, Danny and Major Hailsham saw Johnny Boy snapping to attention and clipping a theatrically smart salute, even though his beret was missing and his desert clothing covered in blood and filth. He had a broad, cheeky grin on his handsome face.

'Johnny Boy!' Danny cried out in surprise.

'Jesus!' Ricketts murmured.

'Well, I'll be damned,' Hailsham said. 'Please

give me, an explanation, Trooper, for your recent absence.'

''Scuse me, boss,' Johnny Boy said, 'but Trooper Willoughby is absolutely shagged and begs permission to sit.'

'Place your arse on a chair, Trooper Willoughby, then make your report.'

Still grinning cockily, Johnny Boy took one of the folding chairs at the table, wiped some dust off his bloody, filthy clothes, swept his blonde hair back from his forehead with an elegant hand movement, then nodded, as if congratulating himself.

'Well, sir . . .' he began.

'Where's Master-Sergeant Polanski?' Hailsham interjected.

'In the hospital at Riyadh,' the trooper answered, 'waiting to be shipped back to the States. He has a hole in his side and it hurts like hell, but he's going to be OK. Some guy, that old Red!'

'We all knew you adored him,' Hailsham responded drily. 'Now go back to the beginning, dear boy.'

'Yes, boss.' Johnny Boy leant forward comfortably in his seat like a born storyteller. 'Well, boss, when we were following you on the Honda, a mortar shell took us out and we found ourselves lying on the desert floor with the Iraqis steaming right at us.'

'That's when we lost you,' Hailsham said.

'Yes, boss, that was it. I picked my face out of the sand and saw you racing away . . .'

'Go on,' Hailsham said.

'Well,' Johnny Boy continued, polishing each word like a gem, 'I was pretty bruised from the fall and old Red seemed unconscious, which may be why the Iraqis neither killed us nor beat the shit out of us. Instead, most of them chased you lot while one truck stayed behind to pick us up. I pretended to be unconscious – at least *almost* unconscious – you know? Moaning and groaning with eyes closed – and since Red apparently was that way, they must have thought we were harmless . . .'

'How unimaginative,' Hailsham interjected softly.

'. . . so they threw us into the back of a soft-topped truck, on the floor, surrounded by half a dozen exhausted militiamen.'

Johnny Boy straightened up, drawing out the silence for effect, then beamed and leant forward again to continue his story.

'Of course, we didn't have any weapons. At least that's what the poor sods thought. But I still had my commando knife tucked down my boot and the daft bastards didn't see that. The truck had turned around and was heading back the way it had come when old Red groaned and opened his eyes and then gave me the wink. One of the Iraqis kicked his arse and he groaned again and closed his eyes, acting as if he was half-dead and pretty well out of it. But I knew he wasn't. So, when the Iraqis started gibbering among themselves, having an argument about something, I slipped out my knife and slammed it into the boot right by my hand – right through the guy's foot.'

'Very good,' Hailsham murmured.

'He came off his seat screaming, dropping his Kalashnikov right on top of me, and I grabbed it and was sitting up and firing before the others knew what was happening. I did the six of them and the driver – shot him through the back of the neck. The truck went out of control and raced on across the desert, which conveniently was flat, and finally slowed down of its own accord, then stopped altogether. Old Red helped me throw the stiffs out, including the driver, then I got behind the wheel and we drove off – not after you, in case we ran into the ones following you, but

45 degrees the other way, hoping to circle back towards you.'

'Obviously you didn't make it,' Hailsham said.

Johnny Boy sighed melodramatically. 'No, sir. We drove for about two hours and then – would you believe it? – we were attacked by an American F-15E, using Sidewinder missiles and cannon fire. We dived out of the truck just before it was hit, but Polanski didn't manage to run away as fast as me and so received a piece of flying debris in his gut when the truck blew apart.'

'He's *older* than you,' Hailsham remarked.

'Yes, boss, that's true.'

'We must practise humility,' Hailsham told him. 'So what happened next?'

'That piece of burning-hot, sharp metal punched a hole right though him, just missing his stomach, though still losing him an awful lot of blood.' The trooper shook his head in disbelieving recollection. 'Can you guess what old John Wayne did then?'

'I'm sure you'll inform us,' Rickett said.

'With no more than a field dressing and morphine to keep him going, he walked with me for two days and nights, constantly cursing his wound but not letting it bring him down, and boasting that this was the kind of A1 endurance number that only the supermen of his Yankee Delta Force could pull off.'

'I can imagine,' Hailsham said wearily.

'Then, on the third day,' Johnny Boy went on, oblivious to Hailsham's gentle irony, 'we came across an Iraqi border post, near Saudi Arabia. It only had a few guards inside and one truck outside. Having taken a couple of hand-grenades off the Iraqis I'd killed, I sneaked up on the border post at last light, mailed them a couple of grenades in through the window, and ran like hell back to where Red, though still bleeding profusely, was keeping me covered with the Kalashnikov we'd stolen from the Iraqis who'd captured us. The border post went up in smoke and all the guards inside were killed. We took the truck parked near the gate and drove to the border. When we got there, we ditched the truck and weapons and crossed over on foot, with old Red, now bleeding worse than ever, not stopping once. We found ourselves in Scud Boulevard and the Yanks – some guys from Red's Delta Force – came out of nowhere to pick us up. They choppered us back to Riyadh, rushed Red to the medics, and shoved me onto a passing Chinook to get me back here. So here I am, boss.'

The trooper sat back in his chair and beamed at them all. However, the praise he was so clearly expecting failed to materialize.

'About bloody time,' Hailsham said instead. 'Now let's get back to business.'

While Johnny Boy was looking distinctly hard done by, Hailsham, trying to hide his grin, turned back to Ricketts.

'As I was saying, Sergeant-Major, we're going back into Iraq. While the advance is continuing, there's still lots for us to do – espionage, ambush, disruption, confusion, and general hit-and-run raids against communications towers and the remaining Scuds. We won't be short of work.'

'Where is it this time?' Ricketts asked.

'We're going back to Scud Alley.'

16

For the next five days, as the war wound down to a close, Hailsham's men roamed and struck with growing confidence at an enemy increasingly demoralized. Their favourite hunting ground was Wadi Amiq, also known as Wadi Amij, running west between two main roads from the Euphrates to the town of Ar Rutbah – part of the area known as Scud Alley.

Having no specific targets, but determined to cause as much disruption and confusion as poss-ible with hit-and-run raids on anything crossing their path, the men spent the first day roaming the terrain with the aid of their Magellan satellite navigation systems, prepared to take on anything they could find.

They found nothing at all. On the second day, however, when cruising across the desert at noon, they spotted a mobile Iraqi convoy of fourteen vehicles, including Scud transporter-erectors and escorts for defence against attack by tanks and aircraft. Parked alongside the trail, the convoy was under camouflage, but clearly preparing to move off again. As it did so, Hailsham followed, calling an air strike while on the move.

Thirty minutes later four F-15s arrived to attack the column one after another with Sidewinder missiles. As usual, the explosions were spectacularly ferocious, creating great mushrooms of spiralling sand and flying debris of all kinds. But when the sand had settled down it was clear that only one of the four strikes had hit the target, leaving a solitary transporter-erector in ruins in an immense, blackened shell hole. When the four strike aircraft flew off to return to base, the rest of the Iraqi column remained untouched.

'Bloody Air Force!' Johnny Boy said in disgust. 'They couldn't hit a barn door if you took them by the hand and led them up to it.'

'The wonders of technology,' Ricketts added. 'We didn't paint the targets with our designators and there's the sorry result – practically nothing.'

'It's back to good, old-fashioned ground warfare,' Hailsham said. 'Let's try the MILANs.'

With the LSVs bringing up the rear, Hailsham led his Pink Panther Land Rovers forward to a location within range, and within sight, of the enemy column. There the men quickly uncovered their MILAN anti-tank guided missile units, one to each Pink Panther. At 765mm in length, weighing 27.68kg, and with a bulky launcher-guidance unit, periscopic optical sight, missile tube with folding wings, wide exit point for 6.66kg shells, and an exceptionally sturdy tripod, the MILAN was an impressive piece of equipment to have mounted on the back of a Land Rover.

Experts one and all, the troopers in the Pink Panthers picked separate targets in the column, then aimed and fired almost simultaneously. The sound of the combined backblasts was impressive, with smoke spewing from both ends of the MILANs. Less than ten seconds later an Iraqi transporter-erector and three trucks exploded, virtually at the same time.

'So much for the Air Force!' Danny said, glancing at Ricketts and offering a rare smile. 'Let the bastards beat that!'

But even before the smoke of the explosions had cleared, the Iraqi triple-A machine guns mounted on wheeled transports hit back with a continuous barrage of fire, causing bullets to ricochet off the Pink Panthers with a harsh metallic drumming while the sand was stitched in jagged lines about them.

Realizing that he was outgunned, Hailsham ordered the Pink Panthers to make a tactical withdrawal, out of range of the Iraqi machine-guns. Then he called on US air power again.

This time, when the F-15s swept down, they struck more accurately, making strikes along most of the column, causing the few remaining trucks and one transporter-erector to race away from billowing black smoke and flames toward the sun-streaked horizon.

While heading back to base, Hailsham's column was attacked by an A-10 pilot who obviously mistook the Land Rovers and LSVs, moving almost bumper to bumper, for a single long Iraqi vehicle, perhaps a mobile Scud launcher. Coming in low, the pilot raked the column with his cannons, causing two of the Land Rovers to explode while the others scattered quickly, churning up clouds of sand, to avoid suffering a similar fate.

'Stupid bloody Air Force!' Johnny Boy exploded, shaking his free fist at the departing aircraft as he roared past Captain Hailsham's Land Rover on his green Honda. 'Are you all fucking blind?'

'I don't blame him,' Captain Hailsham said,

standing up in his Pink Panther and clearing the sand from his eyes with a delicate, probing finger. 'I'm beginning to wonder myself. OK, driver, take us back to the others.'

Regrouping after the attack, the men in the remaining vehicles were relieved to find that the occupants of the two damaged Pink Panthers had managed to jump out before their petrol tanks exploded. Dividing the men among the remaining vehicles, they left the damaged Land Rovers smouldering in the sand and headed back across the barren desert.

Less than an hour later they came over a low hill to find themselves facing a heavily defended Iraqi observation tower. They had barely seen it when a barrage of gunfire from a whole troop of Iraqi militiamen caused them to urgently spread out in different directions and circle back to the top of the ridge, which gave some protection.

While some of them jumped out of the vehicles to give covering fire from behind the Pink Panthers, others put down a heavy barrage with the vehicles' 7.62 GPMGs or rear-mounted 0.5in Browning heavy machine-guns.

Even from where he was kneeling at the back of a Pink Panther, leaning out repeatedly to fire his SLR, Ricketts could see the sand boiling around the Iraqis as the rapid fire of the machine-guns tore at the ground around them, between them and below them. Some of them fell over, cut down by the hail of bullets, but the others, clearly seasoned troopers, merely slipped back into the shadow of the observation tower and released another barrage of gunfire from there.

This caused sand to spew up around the SAS men, as well as ricocheting dangerously off the Pink Panthers and LSVs.

'If those bastards hit my bike,' Johnny Boy said, obviously frustrated at not being able to do much other than hide behind the Pink Panther, 'I think I'll go apeshit.'

'Those Iraqis are well hidden in the shadows of that tower,' Ricketts said, 'while we're out here in the open like sitting ducks. I say we stop worrying about the militiamen and take the tower out instead.'

'Good thinking,' Hailsham replied. Twisting around to glance back along the line of Pink Panthers, he said: 'Go down the line, Willoughby, and tell the men with the LAWs and mortars to keep striking at the base of that tower. I want them to bring it down.'

'Yes, boss,' the trooper said with a cocky schoolboy's grin. 'I'm on my way, boss.'

'You stay here,' Ricketts said. 'I'll go instead. I want to make sure they do this properly. OK, boss?'

'Fine,' Hailsham said.

'Can't I come with you?' Johnny Boy begged.

'OK,' Ricketts said. He crawled down the line until he reached the Pink Panthers run by the team with the 60mm light anti-tank weapon, or LAW – a single-shot rocket firing a 66mm warhead capable of penetrating tanks and aircraft at 300 metres. When he told the LAW team what he wanted, one of them removed the protective caps from each end of the launcher, then extended the tube containing the rocket to its full length of 90cm. The folding sight popped up automatically. The second man held the launcher on his shoulder and looked along the sight. Ricketts gave him the target, but told him to wait for his signal. He then crawled over to the mortar team crouched behind the adjoining Pink Panther.

The L16 ML 81mm mortar has an adjustable bipod supporting the tube that holds the sighting mechanism. With a range of over five kilometres, it is usually fired at a target identified by a forward observer; but in this case the compass bearing would be ignored in favour of guesswork, using the calibrated dial sight for aiming. When

Ricketts told the mortar team what he wanted, one of the men adjusted the bipod to give the nearest correct angle for the estimated range, then waited for Ricketts to signal.

Having given both teams estimated measurements for the two front supports of the observation tower, where sand was still spitting wildly from the relentless SAS fire, Ricketts raised and then lowered his right hand.

The LAW and the mortar fired at the same time. After a few seconds – though it seemed longer than that – two simultaneous explosions erupted on either side of the base of the tower, just missing it, but killing some of the Iraqi soldiers firing out of its shadow.

'Fuck,' one of the LAW team said. 'Too short.'

'Not by much,' his partner said. 'We just need about five more degrees elevation and we should hit it right on the nose.'

'Go to it,' Ricketts said. 'When you get the proper range and actually hit the base of the tower, keep shelling the exact same spot until you blow it away. If the mortar team does the same to the other side, the whole caboose should fall down.'

'Right on top of those fucking militiamen,' Johnny Boy enthused.

'You've got it,' Ricketts replied.

The Iraqi response to the shelling was an extended burst of machine-gun fire from the observation post on top of the tower and a more violent barrage from the militiamen hidden in the shadows beneath it. Safe behind their Pink Panthers, the LAW and mortar teams reloaded their weapons, raised the elevation a few degrees, and fired off another simultaneous round. This time the explosions appeared to be right on target, but when the swirling smoke and spewing sand finally cleared away, it was evident that the shells had again fallen short, though dispatching more militiamen in the process.

'Third time lucky,' one of the LAW men said.

'No question, mate,' his partner replied.

They were correct. The third set of simultaneous explosions erupted right under the crisscrossing steel supports of the tower, blackening and buckling them slightly, as well as killing more Iraqi troops.

'That's it,' Ricketts said. 'You're dead on target. Now keep pouring those shells on exactly the same spot and you should be able to bring that bastard down.'

'It's as good as done,' the LAW man said.

Though the Iraqis were still managing to keep

up enough fire-power to cause devastation to the ground around the SAS troop, with bullets ricocheting off the vehicles and making the sand explode in jagged, snake-like lines about them, the repeated shelling by the LAW and 81mm mortar, combined with the relentless small-arms fire of the rest of the squadron, soon turned the base of the observation tower into an inferno of spitting, swirling sand and smoke. That the Iraqis still managed to return the fire at all was amazing, since it seemed they must surely choke to death, if not actually dying in the hail of bullets. Yet they did courageously return the fire, albeit with diminishing ferocity, while the supports of the tower behind them buckled more with each explosion, smouldered, turned blacker, and the structure itself began to tilt forward at a dangerous angle.

Though the machine-gunner high up in the observation post kept firing, some of the observers started clambering down the ladder, clearly frightened that the tower was going to topple.

It did so before any of the fleeing men reached the ground. As two final explosions smashed through the buckled lower supports, the tower tilted forward still further, the ladder snapped free and the men scrambling down it screamed as they fell off and plunged up to fifty feet to the ground. The tower was now leaning even more, with its support girders buckling and breaking, and the militiamen on the ground started running as it finally crashed down.

With the Iraqi troops on the ground coming out into the open, many were either killed in the withering hail of fire from the SAS or died when the enormous tower crushed them under tons of crumpling, shrieking metal. Its collapse shook the desert floor and created a mushroom cloud of sand that obscured the men screaming and dying in a tangle of steel.

Even before the spiralling sand had subsided, Johnny Boy was back on his Honda, driving with one hand, brandishing his Browning pistol in the other, leading the Pink Panthers and LSVs towards the few Iraqis who had miraculously escaped and were trying to take cover behind the wreckage. The trooper ignored the bullets whining past his head, though he weaved left and right to make himself more difficult to hit and eventually swept out and in again, coming up behind his victims to pick them off one by one as he roared past.

Meanwhile the Pink Panthers and LSVs continued advancing from the front, but spread out to form two semicircles that encompassed the wreckage. The men fired on the move, keeping up a relentless barrage, not stopping until the handful of remaining Iraqis, now dazed and terrified, threw down their weapons and waved their *shemaghs* like flags, in surrender.

Captain Hailsham used a hand signal to indicate 'Cease fire'.

The sudden silence was eerie, as was the sight of the surviving militiamen raising their hands in the ruins, ghostlike in the swirling dust and smoke, covered in dust themselves, surrounded by a multitude of dead, some shot, others crushed by the girders, which, now littering the desert floor and obscured by drifting dust, formed an immense, hideous sarcophagus of steel.

After accepting the surrender of the ten surviving Iraqis, Hailsham divided them between the Pink Panthers and drove them back to base, where a soft-topped truck with armed escort drove them on to the FOB. From there they would be taken to one of the growing number of Allied POW camps.

Having disposed of the prisoners, Hailsham let his men have a good night's rest, then led them back into the desert for another day of hit-and-run raids.

Locating another, less heavily defended Iraqi observation post, they engaged in another firefight, killing two Iraqis and taking half a dozen prisoners. That was Day Two.

During Day Three they called in an air strike against a large radar complex built around a microwave communications tower. The complex was pulverized and the tower collapsed into the dust, leaving nothing but debris on the smoke-wreathed plain and another bunch of prisoners to be looked after.

On Day Four, as the increasingly successful column of Pink Panthers and LSVs made its way back toward the Saudi border, they were attacked by another troop of Iraqis. This time, however, the Iraqis had the advantage, being strung out along, and partially hidden by, an irregular ridge that blocked the path of the SAS column.

The ambush opened with simultaneous mortar explosions that tore up the ground between the Pink Panthers and LSVs. One of the latter was picked up by an explosion and slewed to the side, cutting a groove through the ground and hurling up sand behind it, before rolling over and coming to rest upside down, throwing its occupants clear. One of the unfortunate crew remained where he was lying, limbs akimbo, splashed with blood, but the other stood up and was immediately flung onto his back by a savage burst of machine-gun fire.

Even as the shot trooper spasmed violently and died, the other SAS vehicles were breaking off in opposite directions, weaving between the explosions and the spitting, bullet-riddled sand, to circle back and form a defensive laager further away from the ridge. Once in semicircular formation, the men jumped out of the vehicles, taking cover behind them, in some instances dragging down the heavy GPMGs in order to mount them on tripods on the desert floor and give the Iraqis as good as they were getting.

'Get those mortars set up!' Hailsham bawled, practically rolling backwards out of his Pink Panther to fall to the sand and pick himself up again. 'I want that whole ridge blown to hell. Corporal Clarke,' he said to Paddy, who was already firing his SLR, 'I want you to take some men and bug out south of here, then circle west and come back under cover of that slight incline to our right to do as much damage as you can manage from that angle. Take a GPMG.'

'Right, boss,' Paddy said.

The ground roared and erupted at the other side of the Pink Panther, showering Hailsham and those around him.

'Corporal McGregor,' Hailsham called to Jock, who was firing bursts from his M16, 'I want you to do the same, but circle east until you're parallel with Paddy. I want your team to take a GPMG as well.'

'Right, boss. Will do.'

'Get going, then.' As Paddy and Jock crawled away, trying to avoid the spitting bullets and mortar explosions, Hailsham glanced at Danny, also firing his SLR, then turned to Ricketts, saying, 'Well, we certainly walked into this one. How on earth do we get out?'

Casting his gaze beyond the overturned LSV and the two lifeless SAS troopers spread-eagled near it, Ricketts saw that the irregular ridge was rendering the Iraqis practically invisible. Their mortars were set up slightly down the slope behind the ridge and most of the men using small arms were lying behind the ledge of the rim, only raising their heads above it long enough to fire and duck down again. It was indeed possible that Jock and Paddy would be able to pick some off from the side, but most of them would still be out of sight, firing with impunity unless taken out by SAS mortars.

As if to help Hailsham and Ricketts with their sombre deliberations, the SAS mortar teams started firing from just behind them, lobbing their shells high in order to let them fall behind the ridge. This they did, churning up spirals of sand that rose above the ridge, hopefully signifying that damage had been inflicted on the Iraqis, though that could not be verified.

Ricketts glanced east and west to see Jock and Paddy, each trailing a three-man team and GPMG, circling around from far behind to come up on either side of the laager and lay down a two-pronged barrage.

'I can't see us going forward,' Ricketts said, 'because there's no way of advancing up that ridge without insupportable losses.'

'I agree,' Hailsham said. 'On the other hand, if we head back the way we came, they'll just up roots and follow us. By then, we'll be deep in their territory and ripe for the picking.'

'Call in an air strike,' Danny suggested, 'and let them do the work for us.'

'We're too close,' Hailsham told him. 'Any air strike is going to strike us, so let's leave them out of it.'

'We can go back further,' Danny said.

'They'll pick us off like flies,' Ricketts reminded him, 'the minute we climb up into the dinkies.'

'Which gets us back where we started,' Hailsham said. 'Right here. Still trapped.'

At that moment, the GPMG of Jock's team started roaring, the bullets making the sand dance in a jagged line that first exploded just below the ridge and then followed an erratic, oblique course up to its rim, where the bullets whined off harmlessly into thin air.

Less than a minute later the other GPMG did the same, with similar results. Both teams were rewarded when mortar shells from somewhere behind the ridge whistled down and exploded dangerously close to them, showering the men and their useless GPMGs with sand, soil and gravel.

Shortly after those mortar shells had been followed by others, coming closer all the time, Jock used his PRC 319 to contact Hailsham and inform him that he still could not see a thing beyond the ridge, even though he was clearly a sitting duck for the Iraqi mortar teams behind it.

When Paddy called in with the same message, Hailsham told both teams to bug out.

At that moment an Iraqi mortar shell hit a Pink Panther, filling the air with flying debris that caused almost as much damage as the blast itself. When the smoke had cleared away and those nearby had regained their hearing – namely, Hailsham, Ricketts and Danny – they saw one SAS trooper pinned lifeless beneath the smouldering remains of the vehicle, another lying in a pool of blood with his neck almost severed by a piece of jagged metal, and a third, though still alive, badly peppered by shrapnel and groaning, semi-conscious, in terrible pain.

'Let's *all* bug out,' Captain Hailsham said. 'We have no other option. We'll shoot and scoot, and hope for the best. After that, it's each man for himself. What do you say?'

'Shoot and scoot,' Ricketts confirmed.

'Have that wounded man picked up and placed in my Pink Panther,' Hailsham told Danny. 'Then pass the word around the laager that we're going to shoot and scoot, meeting back at the FOB in our own time. We go at my signal.'

'Right, boss,' Danny said. He scurried off at the crouch as more mortar shells exploded, showering all of them yet again.

Glancing in both directions, Ricketts saw Jock and Paddy coming back in with their teams, crouched low and weaving, with the ground erupting behind them and sand spitting viciously between them. Miraculously, they all managed to get back into the laager without being hit.

Just as they arrived back, two troopers heaved the wounded man, now on a makeshift stretcher, up into the rear of Hailsham's Pink Panther and Danny took his place in the adjoining vehicle, preparing to drive Ricketts out.

Johnny Boy was swinging his leg over the Honda and already revving it up.

'Fucking A,' he said. 'Right!'

Captain Hailsham raised his hand high in the air, held it there for a moment, then dropped it, bawling: '*Shoot and scoot*!'

The Pink Panthers and LSVs roared into life, revving up, as Johnny Boy shot ahead in a cloud of churning sand, this time gripping the handlebars firmly. Racing up towards the ridge with Iraqi bullets whining about him, he was followed almost instantly by the Pink Panthers and LSVs, their troopers already firing at the ridge with their small arms and GPMGs. The crest of the ridge was torn apart by the syncopated barrage of gunfire.

Suddenly Johnny Boy sailed into the air, leaving behind his motorbike, which exploded in mid-air, and flinging his arms wide as he somersaulted and crashed back down again.

He was dead and they all knew it, so no one stopped for him. Instead they swerved around him and raced on up the slope to reach the top of the ridge, mangle some stunned Iraqis, then bounce and swerve down the other side in dense clouds of swirling sand.

One LSV hit the ground nose-first. It somersaulted and crashed, throwing one trooper out, crushing the other, and exploding when its fuel tank burst and bullets set it on fire. The trooper flung clear, as he was peppered by Iraqi bullets, was mercifully already dead from a broken neck.

The rest raced down the other side, bursting out of the trap, and then spread out, heading off in different directions, to confuse the Iraqis.

Captain Hailsham saw the wide open spaces and could hardly believe it. Ricketts saw the same – the vast sweep of the empty desert – but then he heard a dreadful roaring, felt the hot breath of the beast, and was picked up and hurled through a shocking, unreal, searing silence.

He returned to a recognizable world of clamour and pain.

The sky was above him, mortar shells were

exploding around him, and Danny, whose perfect features had earlier been marred by a broken nose, was leaning over him and trying to talk to him through a roaring shower of earth.

'. . . OK?' Danny bawled.

Ricketts shook his head. He had meant to say 'No' but he couldn't speak.

'Can you get up?' Danny asked.

'No,' Ricketts managed to croak, suddenly visualizing his wife and two daughters back in England, and swelling up with love for them. 'Don't think I can move at all.'

'Shit,' Danny said. Another shell exploded nearby. Bullets were making the sand spit all around him as his eyes filled with tears. 'Damn it, Ricketts, just . . .'

'What happened, Danny?'

'A mortar shell fell too close. We were tipped over, Ricketts, flung out, just before we got clear away.'

'The others?'

'Most of them made it, but they're long gone by now.'

'Get going, Danny. No need to stay with me.'

'The Pink Panther's fit for the wrecker's yard. I'm trapped here with you, boss.'

'Start running.'

'No.'

'That's an order.'

'I can't hear it.'

'I thought you were a tough nut, a killer – so why don't you run?'

'Go fuck yourself, Ricketts.' Danny glanced back over his shoulder, up the slope, towards the ridge, and saw a bunch of Iraqis coming down, their weapons aimed at him. 'Too late,' he said, turning back to Ricketts. 'They're calling our number right now and you know what they'll do, boss.'

He reached down, removed his Browning from its holster, held Ricketts's head up, then put the barrel of the gun to his temple.

'You *know* what they'll do, boss. There's no Geneva Convention here. Say the word and I'll finish it. It'll be a lot quicker.'

Ricketts, though still in bad pain, grinned wryly at Danny's suggestion. 'No,' he replied, prepared to get a bullet in the head in combat but not about to invite it in the ritual all SAS wives dreaded. 'I'm not joining the Exit Club just yet. Now get up and run, Danny.'

Danny sighed and turned away from Ricketts

to aim his handgun at the Iraqis. 'No, Sergeant-Major. I've never run in my life. Let's see who gets the most. Start counting, boss.'

'You mad bastard,' Ricketts said.

The Iraqis all fired at once. Ricketts raised his head as the ground erupted around Danny. The baby-faced corporal convulsed, his clothing torn to shreds, blood bursting from bullet holes, and then was picked up and punched back by the fusillade of gunfire, to land with a thud close to Ricketts.

'Danny!' Ricketts screamed. He managed to roll over and touch his friend's shoulder just before the enemy gunfire reached him too, brutally, irrevocably blotting out his whole world.

17

On 26 February 1991, a mere hundred hours after the land war had begun, but nearly seven months after the start of the Iraqi invasion, a defeated Iraq announced that it was withdrawing from Kuwait. Within hours, in a Baghdad Radio broadcast, Saddam Hussein renounced his claims on that country. Subsequently, Allied Marines entered Kuwait City in the wake of the victorious Kuwaiti and Saudi armies.

The capital had already been infiltrated by the Boat Group of the SAS, which had been tasked with spreading confusion and chaos among the Iraqi troops based there. Working closely with the US Navy's SEALS on a programme of disinformation, the SBS had managed to convince the Iraqis that the US Marines were poised to storm the city's shoreline. It had also sabotaged Iraqi bases and set up OPs to call in air strikes and gunfire from the Allied battleships anchored in the Gulf.

Last but not least, it was SAS troops who had captured the British Embassy in Kuwait in the final hours of the war. They abseiled onto the roof from a Sea King helicopter used explosives to blow off the doors, cleared the rooms with stun grenades, and checked that the building was free of booby-traps. Ambassador Michael Weston was then able to return and replace the tattered Union Jack with a new one.

Even after the loss of Sergeant-Major Ricketts, whose body was already being flown back to Hereford, Major Hailsham had insisted that his remaining men should be allowed to fight all the way back to Kuwait. During that long march they did little fighting, but instead found themselves collecting more and more Iraqi prisoners, most of whom were in pitiful condition and all too keen to surrender by advancing with hands raised or even lying belly-down in the sand and waiting to be picked up. By that stage, the Allied camps for Iraqi prisoners were growing bigger every day and being looked after by the infantry battalions of the Coldstream Guards, the Royal Highland Fusiliers and the King's Own Scottish Borderers. Passing them in his Pink

Panther, now battered and filthy, Hailsham was reminded of grainy old newsreels of the packed POW camps in Europe during World War Two. Though the most high-tech war in history had just been fought, some things never changed.

Like many of the liberators, Major Hailsham, meeting up with some of his other SAS troops in liberated Kuwait, was shocked by what he found there. As Saddam Hussein had ordered his retreating troops to blow up the city's landmarks, most of its most beautiful and important buildings, including the Emir's residence, the Dasman Palace, were either in ruins or seriously damaged. The beaches and streets of the city were cluttered with munitions that continued to take the lives of many innocent children. A grisly search of the city's morgues, basements and houses used by the Iraqi forces turned up hideous evidence of the widespread use of torture against Kuwaiti citizens, including electrocution and mutilation.

Heightening the hellish atmosphere, the pall of smoke that covered the city had turned the sky a nightmarish, constant black, rendered even more frightening by the oily smoke pouring in from the six hundred or so oil wells cruelly set ablaze by the Iraqis. All around Kuwait City, under that stark black sky, the burning oil wells had created a fearsome wall of fire.

After Saddam's generals officially surrendered in a tent in the sand, the Iraqis started handing over Coalition POWs. While the captured British, American, Saudi and Kuwaiti airmen were welcomed off a Red Cross plane at Riyadh amid a blaze of media attention, two SAS men, troopers Stone and Gillett – the former wounded, the latter badly bruised – were quietly led away from the aircraft by the rear cargo door.

Some hours later, ten other prisoners, including the British Tornado pilot John Peters, who had been paraded so shamelessly on television by the Iraqis shortly after being captured, were also released.

While the widely publicized Peters was shaking hands with British diplomats at the Jordanian border, another man released with him was spirited away from the scene as if he had never existed. That man was SAS Sergeant Andrew Winston.

How did you manage to stay sane in captivity?' Andrew was asked by Major Hailsham when safely back in the barracks in Hereford, England, and having a booze-up in the Paludrine Club with

Hailsham, Jock, Paddy and the recently blooded troopers Stone and Gillett, both of whom, like Andrew, had survived their period of brutal captivity.

Though every man present in the bar was fully aware of the fact that the SAS had suffered dreadful losses in Iraq, it was a Regimental tradition not to discuss the dead, or those who had failed to 'beat the clock', and so the names of their own deceased – Sergeant-Major Phil Ricketts, Sergeant Danny Porter and Trooper John Willoughby – while on everyone's mind, had not actually been mentioned.

The names of those who had died had already been inscribed on plaques fixed to the base of the Regimental clock tower, at the SAS HQ, Stirling Lines. Tribute had thus been paid, and now everyone in the bar was determined to return to his normal, self-protective routine of bullshit and banter.

'How did I stay sane?' Andrew repeated mockingly, determined to make light of his heavy burden as he waved his lined notebook. 'Piece of piss. I just created some poems in my head, based on my experiences with my captors, then wrote them down in this little book on the plane coming back. That's what kept *me* sane, boss.'

'More bullshit,' Paddy said.

'More hot air,' Jock added.

'We'll have to compare notes,' Stone suggested in his dry, ironic way.

'I didn't know you wrote poetry,' Gillett said. 'Gee, that's really surprised me. When can we read them?'

'Ah, those,' big Andrew replied, flashing his perfect teeth in a teasing smile and doing a neat, theatrical double-take, 'they're tales for another day.'

SOLDIER B: SAS

HEROES OF THE SOUTH ATLANTIC

PRELUDE

Phil Ricketts was having another nightmare based on fact. He was reliving with dreadful clarity that moment the previous year when, in a shit-hole of a housing estate in Andersonstown, West Belfast, Lampton had made his mistake and copped it.

They had moved out at dawn for a carefully planned house assault after being informed by the 'green slime', the Intelligence Corps, that a couple of IRA men were being hidden in the estate and preparing to snipe at a British Army foot patrol. As Ricketts sat between his mates in the cramped rear of the armoured 'pig' taking them along the Falls Road, secure in his assault waistcoat, checking his Heckler & Koch MP5 and adjusting his gas mask, he glanced out the back and was reminded again of just how much he detested being in Northern Ireland. This wasn't a real war with an enemy to respect, but rather, a

1

dirty game of hide and seek, a demeaning police action, a bloody skirmish against faceless killers, mean-faced adolescents, hate-filled children and contemptuous housewives. Christ, Ricketts loathed it.

He was filled with this loathing as the pig took him through the mean streets of Belfast in dawn's grey light – past terraced houses with doors and windows bricked up, pubs barricaded with concrete blocks, even off-licences and other shops protected by coils of barbed wire – but he managed to swallow his bile when the pig neared the estate and Sergeant Lampton, Ricketts's best friend, started counting off the distance to the leap: 'Two hundred metres . . . one hundred . . . fifty metres . . . *Go! Go! Go!*'

The armoured vehicle screeched to a halt, its rear doors burst open, and the men leapt out one by one, carrying their weapons in the 'Belfast cradle', then raced across the debris-strewn lawns in front of the bleak rows of flats, still wreathed in the early-morning mist.

Such actions were so fast, they were over before you knew it. Ricketts raced ahead with Lampton, across the grass, into the block and along the litter-strewn walkway as someone shouted a warning – a child's voice, loud and high-pitched – and a door slammed shut just above. Up a spiral of steps, along a covered balcony, boots clattering on the concrete, making a hell of a racket, then Lampton was at the door in front of Ricketts, taking aim with the Remington 870 pump-action shotgun. The noise was ear-splitting, echoing under the walkway's low roof, as the wood around the Yale lock exploded and the door was kicked open. Lampton dropped to his knees, lowering the shotgun, taking aim with his 9 mm Browning handgun as Ricketts rushed into the room, his Heckler at the ready, bawling for the bastards to surrender even as he hurled in a stun grenade.

The grenade exploded, cracking the walls and ceiling, but when its flash had faded away an empty room was revealed. Cursing, Ricketts and the others explored the whole flat, tearing down the curtains, kicking over tables and chairs, ensuring that no one was hiding anywhere, then covering each other as they backed out again, swearing in frustration.

'Let's try the flats next door!' 'Gumboot' Gillis bawled, his voice distorted eerily by the gas mask. 'The fuckers on either side!'

But before they could do so other doors opened and housewives stepped out, still wearing their nightdresses, curlers in their hair, swearing just like the SAS men and bending over to drum metal bin lids on the brick walls and concrete floor of the walkway. The noise was deafening, growing louder every second, as more women emerged to do the same, followed by children. Their shrieked obscenities added dramatically to the bedlam until, as Ricketts knew would eventually happen, the first bottle was thrown.

'Whores!' Gumboot exclaimed when the bottle shattered near his feet. 'And mind those little cunts with 'em!'

'Damn!' Lampton said, glancing up and down the walkway, then over the concrete wall, the shotgun in one hand, the Browning in the other, but briefly forgetting all he had been taught and failing to watch his own back. 'Let's get the hell out of here.'

That was his first and last mistake.

A ragged, gaunt-faced adolescent had followed them up the stairs and now emerged from the stairwell with his pistol aimed right at Lampton. He fired three times, in rapid succession, and Lampton was thrown back, bouncing against the concrete wall, as the kid disappeared again. Lampton dropped both his weapons and quivered epileptically, blood bursting from his gas mask, and was falling as Ricketts raced to the stairs, bawling, 'Christ! Pick him up and let's go!' He chased after the assassin, bottles bursting around him, the drumming bin lids and shrieked obscenities resounding insanely in his head as he plunged into the dangerous darkness of the stairwell without thinking. Then . . .

Ricketts, as he often did these days, was groaning and punching at thin air as he awoke from his nightmare. He soon realized that in fact he had been woken up by a mate, SAS Corporal Paddy Clarke, who was excitedly jabbing his finger at the TV in the barracks, saying, 'Sit up, Ricketts!' Everyone called him by his surname, or 'Sarge'. 'Look! A bunch of Royal Marines have been forced to surrender in . . .'

Gumboot started his weekend leave with a quick fuck with some bint he'd picked up in King's Cross. As he sweated on her passive body, propping himself up on his outspread hands, he was thinking about how the break-up of his marriage had reduced him to this.

Of course, he knew what had caused it – the good old SAS. His wife, Linda, had been torn between fear of what could befall him and anger at his going away so often. What she had hated, Gumboot loved – both the danger and the travelling – so what happened had to happen eventually – and finally did. Linda turned to another man, shacked up with him, and when Gumboot returned from Belfast, where Lampton had bought it, his wife and kids were missing from his home in Barnstaple, Devon, though a note had been left on the kitchen table, kindly telling him why.

Linda had been having an affair with a local farmer, James Brody, and had decided to move in with him 'for the sake of the children'. She wanted a husband at home, Linda had written in her neat hand, preferably one not slated to be killed or, worse, crippled for life. Sorry, Gumboot, goodbye.

Bloody slag, Gumboot thought with satisfying vindictiveness, as he laboured on the whore stretched out below him. They're all the same, if you ask me. He knew that wasn't true, but it made him feel good saying it – just as it had made him feel good when, in a drunken stupor, he had gone to Brody's imposing farmhouse, called him to the door, beat the shit out of him while Linda howled in protest, and then returned for another bout in the local pub. He had drunk a lot after that, mooning about his empty home, and was delighted to be called back to the Regiment and posted to Belfast.

Most of the men hated Belfast, but Gumboot had found his salvation there. Even the banshee wails of contemptuous Falls Road hags had helped to distract him from his sorrows. He had loved being in bandit country, away from Devon and Linda's betrayal – loved it even after Lampton bought it with three shots to the head. Blood all over the fucking place. Lampton dragged out by his ankles, down the stairs of the housing estate as Ricketts, his best friend, released a howl of grief and rage, then raced on ahead to find the killer.

No such luck. That estate was a labyrinth. The kid with the gun was protected by the housewives and 'dickers' – the gangs of kids who monitored the movements of the security forces and passed on the word. Ricketts had been distraught. Lots of nightmares after that. But Gumboot, though angry at Lampton's death, still liked it in Belfast.

Fighting was better than sex or booze, though few would admit it. In fact, this whore was pretty good and Gumboot was almost there, which prompted him to think of other things and delay his climax.

Sex was fine, but not enough. He needed to be back with the Regiment. Even when not engaged in a specific operation, he preferred it at the SAS 'basha' in Hereford, cut off from the normal world. A basha is the place where an SAS man is based at any given time – whether it be his barracks or a makeshift shelter erected in action.

Gumboot lived for the SAS. Life with so-called 'normal' people was boring and offered no satisfaction. Gumboot liked his bit of action, the danger and excitement, the thunder of the guns and the reek of cordite, and so he constantly yearned to be overseas, risking life and limb.

Even right now, as he climaxed, Gumboot was yearning for that. He groaned, convulsed and then relaxed. The tart patted his spine in a friendly manner, then glanced at her watch.

'You've still got twenty minutes,' she informed him.

'I'm amazed,' Gumboot said.

Rolling off her, he lit a cigarette and thoughtfully blew a couple of smoke rings. Then, realizing that he had nothing more to say to the woman, he switched on the radio beside the bed.

'. . . islands,' a BBC newsreader was announcing grimly, 'were invaded earlier today by . . .'

'Fucking great,' Gumboot muttered.

Corporal 'Jock' McGregor and troopers 'Taff' Burgess and Andrew Winston were having their regular Friday-night piss-up in their favourite pub in Redhill, Hereford, not far from the 'Kremlin' – the Intelligence Section – and their barracks. Jock was short, lean and red-faced, Taff was of medium height, broad-chested and pale-faced, and Andrew, who towered over his two mates, was as black as pitch.

Well into his third pint, Jock was staring up at Andrew, thinking what a big bastard he was, and recalling that if anyone called him 'Andy' they were asking for trouble. Born in Brixton, to a white man from the area and a black mother from Barbados, Andrew felt at home in England, but even more so with the Regiment. After transferring to the SAS from the Royal Engineers, he had soon become renowned for his pride and fierce temper. He was also widely respected for the bravery and skill he had shown during the SAS strikes against rebel strongholds on Defa and Shershitti, in Oman, in the mid-1970s.

Taff was a big man too, though not as tall as Andrew, and his smile, when he wasn't annoyed, was as sweet as a child's. On the other hand, when he was riled, he'd take the whole room apart without thinking twice. A good trooper, though, always reliable in a tight spot, and like Andrew one with plenty of experience of the kind that mattered most. Not bad for a Welshman.

'Now me,' Jock was saying, although it was not what he was thinking, 'I say that while it's nice to have a wee break, a long break is misery. Men like us, we're not cut out for all this peace. What we need is some action.'

'Oman,' Andrew said, nodding vigorously, deep in thought. 'Damn it, man, I loved it there. That desert was livin' poetry, boys, and that's what I'm into.'

'He even writes it,' Taff said, wiping his lips with the back of his hand and grinning slyly. 'I think it's a lot of shite he writes, but it keeps him from mischief.'

Jock and Andrew laughed. It was true enough, after all. Inside Andrew's huge, badly scarred body a fine poet was struggling to get out. Even natural killers like Andrew, thought Jock, have their sensitive side.

'I just do it for fun,' Andrew explained. 'They're poems about the Regiment. Some day I'm gonna put them in a book and give the book to the Imperial War Museum. Then I'll die happy.'

Human nature, Jock thought, studying his friend's ebony face and huge body. There's a tender wee soul hidden somewhere in there. Though at times, like when you're on an op with him, you'd never believe it, so savage the bastard turns.

'I'll die happy,' Jock said, 'if they just find us something proper to do, instead of more pointless field exercises. I don't mind a "sickener" occasionally, but now we're just killing time.'

'Right,' Taff said, swigging his extra-strength beer, licking his ever-thirsty lips. 'They pull us out of bloody Belfast, leaving only ten behind, and now they don't know what to do except keep us busy with bullshit. That's the only point of those bloody exercises – it's just keepin' us busy.'

'Also keeping us fit,' Jock said, automatically stretching himself, recalling the endless repeats of Sickeners One and Two – the four-mile runs, cross-graining the Brecons – running from summit to summit across the Brecon Beacons – setting up primitive base camps on the same freezing hills, the horrors of the entrail ditch, lengthy swims in OGs – olive-green battle dress – weapons and explosives training, map-reading, language and initiative tests, parachute jumps, combat and survival, escape and evasion – in fact, endless repeats of everything they had endured during Initial Selection and its subsequent five months of murderous tests – all just because they had no war to fight and had to be kept on form.

Jock didn't mind doing it for a purpose, but he hated time-filling. He didn't have a wife and kids – nor did Taff or Andrew – so like them, he wanted to be somewhere else, putting his training to good use.

'It was because of Lampton,' Andrew said, gazing around the busy bar, taking in the country-squire types and thinking what sheltered lives they led, insulated from the real world by inherited status and wealth, removed from questions of black and white, the crude realities of blood and bone. 'If he hadn't dropped his guard and copped it, we'd all be there still.'

That quietened them all a moment. They didn't normally discuss the dead – those who had failed to 'beat the clock.' Andrew realized that he'd said the wrong thing and felt bad about it. Embarrassed, he gazed around the bar again, reflecting that some of those privileged-looking old codgers had possibly fought in the last war, or in Malaysia or Aden, and might even be connected to the Regiment, which could explain why they lived here. You never knew if someone was in or not, so you shouldn't pass judgement.

'Look,' Taff said, squinting up through clouds

12

of cigarette and cigar smoke at the TV angled over the busy bar. 'It's a special broadcast,' he said. 'Something about an invasion . . .'

'Is that *British* troops we're seeing with their hands up?' Jock interrupted, watching the grainy newsreel images on the box. 'Where the hell is that?'

'Something about Argentina,' Andrew replied. 'Not quite there, but nearby.'

'I love her,' Danny Porter said without the slightest trace of guile, 'and I want to marry her and protect her always. I'm here to ask your permission.'

Danny was holding Darlene's hand in the tiny living-room in the small house in Kingswinford, West Midlands, bravely facing her mother and father. Mrs Dankworth was a fading peroxide blonde with a wicked sense of humour and too great a love of men, including Danny. However, her husband, Vince, was further advanced in his state of not entirely natural decay, with unshaven jowls and a beer belly, a face scarred slightly by a broken bottle in a pub fight. He also had a tendency to feel superior to most folk.

Vince Dankworth's sneer was presently reserved for the way in which Danny shamelessly held

Darlene's hand and kept smiling encouragingly at her, which hardly squared with the little berk's timid nature. He thought that Danny was a little berk because, although he was in the Army, he rarely talked about it and invariably mumbled evasively when he did. Vince was an ageing rocker and constant fan of Gene Vincent, after whose wife, Darlene, the subject of one of Vincent's great rock-'n'-roll laments, Vince had emotionally named his own daughter. In fact, Vince had originally been called Victor, which just about says it all.

Yeah, Gene Vincent! Now there was a real rocker. A gaunt, acned face, black leather pants and jacket, his leg in a brace which he pounded against the floor as he sneered and leered at the audience, before hitting the road again and smashing up some more motel rooms. The first really rebellious rocker, a bona fide original – not like that preening pretender Elvis Presley with his big, dark, girlish eyelashes and smarmy love songs.

Yes, Vince admired wild men – the 'bona fides', as he called them – and so could hardly accept that young Danny, who seemed so shy, even slightly effeminate, could actually be in the Army, let alone in the so-called Special Air Service.

Special for what?

Danny was 22, though he looked about 18. For this very reason, when Vince asked him what he had done in the Army in Northern Ireland and Danny merely shrugged shyly, mumbling something about 'not much', Vince completely believed him.

He would never have believed, on the other hand, that the shy young man sitting modestly in front of him had the instincts of a born killer and was renowned in the SAS for the number of times he had fearlessly practised the 'double tap' against known terrorists in Belfast. This involved entering incognito some of the most dangerous areas of the city to discharge thirteen rounds from his Browning high-power handgun in under three seconds, at close range, into his victim's body, then making his escape in a car parked nearby before witnesses had time to gather their wits.

Danny's ruthlessness was breathtaking, even to more seasoned members of the Regiment, but since such assassinations could not be sanctioned by the authorities, let alone recognized, he never received commendations and certainly never discussed his work with the Regiment. He would only say he was in the 'Army', mumbling uncomfortably when he did so, thus encouraging the former Ted and fan of greasy Gene Vincent to suspect that his daughter's baby-faced boyfriend was some kind of poofter.

Now the baby-faced, whispering poofter was asking Vince for his daughter's hand in marriage. Well, what could you say?

'Right,' Vince said magnanimously. 'I guess that's it, then. You want to marry Darlene – OK then, I won't stand in yer way. Me and Darlene's mum, we married young as well, so I guess we can't say no.'

He smirked at Darlene's bottle-blonde mum as she pursed her lips in a sensual 'O', blowing a couple of smoke rings, her bosom rising and falling impressively under a tight, low-cut blouse.

'Dead right,' she replied.

'Thank you, Mr and Mrs Dankworth,' Danny said. 'I won't let Darlene down. God, I'm so pleased. Thank you.'

'Yeah, yeah,' good old Vince said impatiently. 'Hey, love, you'll soon have a son-in-law. That should turn you grey!'

It wasn't the kind of house where you uncorked champagne, so Danny took Darlene out for a beer and a game of pool in the local pool hall, a right den of iniquity, to which he had been introduced by Vince.

'Paul Newman and Jackie Gleason,' Vince had said. 'That movie, *The Hustler*. A fucking master-piece, kid. A work of art. A real man's game, is pool.'

Danny, though not yet a man in Vince's eyes, had learnt the game quickly, but was careful never to beat his girlfriend's dad. With his dreamy baby face hiding the instincts of a killer, Danny knew exactly what he wanted – and what he wanted was Darlene.

'You probably think I'm pretty coarse playing pool,' Darlene said as they walked along slummy streets to the pool hall. 'But a lot of me workmates play it as well. It's the real gear around here.'

Darlene was a switchboard operator for British Telecom, and her workmates, as Danny had noticed, could be a bit on the free side. Danny, who had his innocent side, thought this was real neat.

'It's a good game,' he told Darlene reassuringly. 'It sharpens the reflexes.'

'Oh, you don't need *those* sharpened,' Darlene said with a surprisingly coarse chuckle. 'Your reflexes are *wonderful*!'

Danny blushed brightly with embarrassment and pride, which made Darlene love him all the more.

'God,' she said, 'you're so *sweet*.'

Which made him blush all the more.

Once in the pool hall, they ordered a pint of beer each and while waiting for a vacant table discussed when they should marry. As Danny was between ops with his Regiment, and therefore based in the camp in Hereford rather than in Belfast, they agreed that they should do it as soon as possible.

'I can't wait any longer,' Darlene said. 'Oh, I do love you, Danny.'

When Danny studied Darlene's sweet, moon-shaped face, bright-green eyes and jet-black hair, a lump always came to his throat. Now, with Willy Nelson singing 'Always On My Mind' coming from the radio perched high on one wall, that lump returned to his throat and filled him up with emotion.

'I love you, too,' he said.

He wasn't a man of many words, but Darlene didn't mind. She responded to his tender, loving nature and was touched by his reticence.

'That table's free,' Danny told her.

Though only five feet two, Darlene had a perfect body and long legs. She liked to show off in tight sweaters and jeans – to 'wind 'em up', as her mother had always taught her. When playing pool, which involved certain contortions, Darlene was a sight to behold.

Perhaps for this reason, a player at the next table, another member of the great unwashed – a ring through his nose, with another dangling from one ear, hairy chest bared in a leather waistcoat above black leather pants and tatty high-heeled boots decorated with skull and crossbones – eventually put his head back, blew a stream of cigarette smoke, and sneered to his mates, 'With tits like *that* bouncing on the velvet, how can she lose, guys?'

The sudden silence that followed was like an explosion, freezing everyone momentarily, as Danny spun his pool cue over, slid his grip to the narrow tip and brought the handle down like a club on the sneering git's skull.

As the lout howled and grabbed his head, pouring blood, looking dazed, Danny moved in without thinking to karate-chop him twice in the guts. The guy jack-knifed dramatically, making a strangling sound, and was vomiting even as Danny jumped back and again used his hand like a guillotine. This one chopped smartly at his exposed nape, for he was leaning forward, and he was face down on the floor in his own puke before he knew what was happening.

Danny knew he was doing wrong – using his skills for personal reasons – but his killer instincts were overwhelming, so great was his rage. He raised his right boot, about to break the bastard's neck, but Darlene cried out 'No!' and pulled him away, leaving his victim free to continue spewing on the floorboards.

'Shit, man!' someone whispered in fearful admiration. Then Stevie Wonder, who was singing 'That Girl', was cut off in mid-sentence.

'This is a special announcement,' the radio announcer said. 'Today, 2 April, 1982, a garrison of British Royal Marines guarding Port Stanley, capital of the Falkland Islands, was forced to surrender to . . .'

'The Falkland Islands?' Danny broke in, instantly distracted, no longer angry, and oblivious to the groaning man on the floor. 'Where's the Falkland Islands, Darlene?'

It was just another day for Major Richard Parkinson. As usual, he awoke at six in the morning and slipped quietly out of bed, letting his wife, Jane, get a little more sleep. Leaving the bedroom, Parkinson took the stairs up to his large converted loft, where he stripped off his pyjamas, put on a pair of shorts and proceeded to do 75 press-ups.

Though proud that at forty-four he could still do that many, Parkinson didn't stop there. Rising from the floor, his whipcord body slick with sweat, and then standing on tiptoe to grab the chin-up bar he had inserted between two cross-beams, he began his usual fifty pull-ups.

Most men half his age could not have managed this with such ease, but Parkinson, though a little out of breath, was otherwise still in fine shape when he finished. After a few more exercises – touching his toes and lifting weights – he went downstairs, into the bathroom, stripped off his shorts and stepped into the shower, where he switched the water from hot to icy cold. Cleansed and invigorated, he dressed in his freshly pressed OGs, complete with medals and winged-dagger badge, then sauntered into the country-style kitchen, located at the back of the house overlooking a well-kept lawn and garden and offering a panoramic view of the countryside. From here you could see the rooftops of Hereford and the spire of the church.

When not overseas or at the Duke of York's Barracks, in London's King's Road, Parkinson treated his wife to tea in bed every morning. He did this now, waking her up gently, running the fingers of his free hand through her hair as he set the cup and saucer on the cabinet beside the bed. Jane glanced up, smiling sleepily, then rolled away from him. The daughter of Lieutenant-Colonel Michael Lovelock – formerly of the Durham Light Infantry, then the SAS, a much-decorated veteran of Malaya and Oman, now in command of the Counter Revolutionary Warfare (CRW) Wing responsible for Northern Ireland – she was used to the demands of the Regiment and accepted her husband's unwavering routine as perfectly normal.

Parkinson returned the smile, but to the back of his wife's head, knowing that she would snatch a few more minutes of sleep, yet instinctively wake up before the tea was cold. After gently squeezing her shoulder, which made her purr like a cat, he turned and left the bedroom, automatically glancing into the other two bedrooms, where his children, now both married, had once slept and played. Reminded of his age, but certainly not feeling it, he returned to the kitchen to have breakfast and a quick scan of *The Times*.

His breakfast was frugal: orange juice, one boiled egg with brown toast, then a cup of black coffee. Parkinson did not believe in overeating; nor did he smoke or drink.

Opening his newspaper, he read that yesterday Argentina had invaded the Falkland Islands, overwhelming the single company of Royal Marines guarding the capital, Port Stanley. An emergency session of Parliament had been called – the first Saturday sitting since the Suez crisis – and the Prime Minister, Margaret Thatcher, was scheduled to make a statement detailing Britain's response to the invasion.

Parkinson immediately picked up the telephone and called his Commanding Officer, Lieutenant-Colonel Michael Pryce-Jones, at Stirling Lines, the home and heart of the SAS.

'I've just read the morning paper,' he said. 'It sounds serious, boss.'

'Quite serious, old chap,' Pryce-Jones replied, making no attempt to hide his delight at the prospect of war. 'In fact, *damned* serious. A bunch of bloody Argies trying to steal a British territory and we're supposed to sit back and take it? Not likely, I say!'

'Mrs Thatcher won't let them,' Parkinson replied. 'We all know what she's like. She'll insist that it's her duty to defend and preserve British sovereignty, no matter how small the territory involved. I think we're in for some action.'

'Damned right, we are. A task force of 40 warships, including the aircraft-carriers *Invincible* and *Hermes*, with 1000 commandos, is already being assembled, though the fleet hasn't yet been given orders to sail. The usual political posturing will have to be endured first, thus wasting valuable time, but war with Argentina is inevitable. By tonight, the United Nations Security Council will almost certainly be compelled to demand a cessation of hostilities and an immediate withdrawal of the Argentinian invasion force. Then there'll be negotiations. But cheering crowds are already gathering outside the presidential palace in Buenos Aires to celebrate the recapture of the so-called Malvinas, so it's unlikely that General Galtieri – he's the head of the military junta – will voluntarily back down. War it will have to be – and we'll be part of it. You'd better get in here.'

Parkinson hurried out of the house, climbed into his car and drove off at high speed, heading for Stirling Lines.

1

'I don't think I have to tell you men why you've been called back to camp on three hours' notice,' Major Parkinson said to his men on Sunday morning, 4 April, 1982, as he stood beside Captain Michael 'Mike' Hailsham of the Mountain Troop and Captain Laurence E. Grenville of the Special Boat Squadron (SBS), in the briefing room of the 'Kremlin', the SAS intelligence section at Stirling Lines, in Redhill, Hereford. 'Suffice to say that since its forced surrender to the Argentinians in Port Stanley on Friday, the unfortunate company of Royal Marines has been further humiliated by being forced to lie face down on the ground to be photographed for propaganda purposes. That's why you've all been called back. We can't let the bloody Argies get away with that, let alone their damned invasion of the Falkland Islands.'

'So why are we still sitting here?' Sergeant Ricketts asked.

'Right, boss,' Corporal Jock McGregor added. 'Our arses are freezing on these chairs while the Navy goes gung-ho.'

'True,' Major Parkinson said calmly, immune to their expected sarcasm, since the SAS not only used the informal 'boss' instead of 'sir', but also encouraged free thinking and initiative. 'A Royal Navy Task Force is set to sail from Portsmouth for the Falklands tomorrow. That task force will include frigates, destroyers, troop carriers, landing ships and supply vessels. Its two aircraft-carriers, HMS *Invincible* and HMS *Hermes*, will be crammed with Harrier jump-jets and helicopters, as well as with Royal Marines and Paratroops. Although she carries mainly Sea Harriers, HMS *Hermes* also has Sea King HC4s of 846 Naval Air Squadron, equipped to land the commandos with whom they normally train. At the same time, other ships will be leaving Plymouth to link up with yet more forces from Gibraltar. All in all, it will be Britain's greatest display of Naval strength since Suez.'

'But not including us,' Taff Burgess complained, grinning laconically at his fellow SAS troopers.

'Right,' Sergeant Ricketts snapped, not grinning at all. 'I've heard that the Royal Marines' special Boat Squadron have already asked for two divers – one a former Marine – to complete a team flying to Ascension Island, where they hope to join a British submarine in the South Atlantic.'

'*We've* heard, also,' SBS Captain Grenville said in his familiar terse way, 'that two members of G Squadron joined 2 SB Section at RAF Lyneham.'

'Yet there are still no movement orders for this Squadron,' Trooper Burgess said. 'What's going on, boss?'

Major Parkinson smiled. 'Oh, ye of little faith. In fact, earlier this morning our OC called the senior officer in command of the Falklands operation – Brigadier Julian Thompson, Commander of 3 Commando Brigade, Royal Marines . . .'

'Now on seventy-two hours' notice to sail for the South Atlantic,' Ricketts interjected sarcastically.

'. . . and insisted that he include us in the Task Force. He was informed by the brigadier that Naval and Royal Marine staffs are working around the clock to arrange the embarkation of the men and war stores needed to spearhead any reconquest of the islands. This operation has been code-named "Corporate" and we'll be part of it.'

'How?' Trooper Andrew Winston asked, rubbing his hand against his cheek and displaying an unwavering gaze that could make grown men tremble.

'Oh, dear, you trust us so little!' said the formerly renowned mountaineer and still dashingly handsome Captain Hailsham of the Mountain Troop.

Major Parkinson let the derisive laughter die away, then said in a graver tone: 'The Task Force has been gathered together to show the world, and particularly Argentina, that Britain is serious about the fate of the so-called Malvinas. It will therefore be leaving to military music and a lot of patriotic flag-waving, in full view of the assembled international media.' He paused for emphasis, before adding: 'But we'll be leaving as well. We will simply go quietly – flying out tomorrow.'

This time his men whistled and applauded, obviously pleased. Parkinson raised his hands to silence them. When they had calmed down, one of them, Trooper Danny 'Baby Face' Porter, put his hand up and asked: 'Do we have anything on the Falklands, boss?'

Major Parkinson nodded to Captain Hailsham, who said: 'Yesterday the Kremlin's staff gathered together all the information they could find

28

about the islands in the MOD map-room – most of it from the British Antarctic Survey's HQ in Cambridge and other, more confidential sources. You'll find those reports in the folders on the desks in front of you. Make sure you know the details off by heart before we fly out.'

'Are there any contingency plans in SAS files or elsewhere for a recovery of the Falklands, if necessary?' the astute Ricketts asked.

'No,' Hailsham said bluntly. 'All of the long-term planners who considered it felt it would be next to impossible to sustain such a campaign.'

'How come?'

Hailsham nodded to Captain Grenville, who was in constant contact with SBS intelligence. 'The nearest feasible base from which to launch an amphibious assault is the very Ascension Island you've just mentioned,' Grenville said. 'That's nearly 7000 kilometres from the UK ports and airfields. As for Port Stanley itself, it's a further 6250 kilometres from Ascension – and there's only open ocean, apart from Ascension, between the UK and the Falklands.'

'That may be a problem for desk-bound planners,' Ricketts said. 'It's not a problem for us.'

'Correct,' Parkinson said briskly, proud to hear such a remark from one of his men and eager to jump back into the briefing. 'So tomorrow, 5 April, a small advance party from this squadron – the 80 men gathered together here – commanded by Major Cedric Delves, will fly out to Ascension Island to take part in the highly secret Task Force 317.9 – being formed to recapture South Georgia.'

A general murmur of approval spread around the briefing room, only silenced when Trooper Winston asked: 'Who divides and rules?'

'The work of all special forces, including the Special Air Service and the Special Boat Squadron, is to be coordinated through a command cell in Rear-Admiral Woodward's HMS *Hermes*, the flagship of the Royal Navy Task Force. I'll be aboard with some of you men.'

'Do you think there's going to be conflict, boss?'

'Not immediately,' Major Parkinson said. 'You'll fly out to Ascension and familiarize yourselves with local conditions as best you can.'

'What does that mean?'

'Ascension is a small island that can hardly sustain its civilian population of a thousand,' Captain Grenville explained. 'For this reason, the Royal Navy is going to severely limit the numbers of commandos and other forces who can be ashore at any one time. The opportunities for further training will therefore be limited.'

'Any more questions?' Major Parkinson asked when the silence stretched on too long.

'Yeah,' Trooper Gumboot Gillis said, licking his lips and grinning like a mischievous schoolboy. 'Apart from its thousand head of human sheep, what else is on Ascension Island?'

'A British telecommunications centre, a US airbase, a US space-research centre, and a US gin-palace called the Volcano Club. That should see *you* right, Trooper. Any more questions?'

They all had a good laugh at that, but no hands went up.

'Then I suggest you all return to your bashas, open those reports, and ensure that you've memorized them by tomorrow. You'll be kitted out in the morning. Thank you, gentlemen.'

Major Parkinson and his two captains stepped away from the blackboard as the 80 soldiers pushed back their chairs and started to file out of the briefing room, most looking happy.

2

The selected members of D Squadron flew out of England on C-130 Hercules transport aircraft specially converted to flight-refuelling tankers. With their passenger and carrier holds containing long-range fuel tanks, the aircraft were short on breathing space, as well as noisy and bumpy, making for a long, uncomfortable flight that put no one in a good mood.

After landing on Ascension Island, the 80 men were driven in Bedfords from Wideawake airfield, located in featureless, wind-blown terrain, to be billeted in an equally desolate, disused school surrounded by flatlands of volcanic rock. There they made up their bashas, then attended the first of what would be many boring briefings from the 'green slime'. The Intelligence Corps staff informed them that no war had yet broken out and they would therefore be spending their days on the island undergoing limited, special training for the Falklands. This news was greeted with a universal groan of frustration.

'Christ, what a hell-hole,' Jock said that first evening as he drank beer with his mates in the Volcano Club, the American bar on Wideawake airfield, its windows giving a view of the rows of aircraft outside, including Vulcan bombers, Victor tankers, Starlifters, Nimrod recce planes and their own cumbersome Hercules transports. 'It's no more than a lump of scraggy rock in the middle of the bleedin' South Atlantic. What the hell are we doing here?'

'This is the nearest base for an amphibious assault on South Georgia,' big Andrew explained. '*That's* why we're here, mate.'

'And not alone either,' Taff said, sitting beside Baby Face Porter. 'Just look around you.'

He was referring to the other men in the packed, smoky bar, representing M Company, 42 Commando, Royal Marines, the RAF, the Royal Naval Aircraft Servicing Unit, Royal Engineers, and other members of the British Forces Support Unit. Though no more than a volcanic dust heap, nine miles across at its widest, the island had a BBC relay station, a 10,000-foot runway built by NASA, a satellite tracking station and a firing range. Now being used as a staging post for the Task Force, it was receiving an average of six Hercules flights a day, as well as a constant stream of men and equipment ferried in from the fleet anchored out at sea. As there was not enough accommodation for the personnel arriving daily, the men were forced to spend most of their time aboard ship, only being ferried to the island when it was their turn for weapons testing on the firing range, craft drills on the beach, other forms of training, or work. A lot of those men were here now, filling up the formerly quiet Volcano Club.

'Fuck 'em,' Gumboot said, polishing off the last of his inch-thick steak in garlic butter and washing it down with another mouthful of beer. 'Them Argie bastards made British RMs lie face down on the ground. I say crash a couple of Hercules into the fucking runway at Port Stanley. Two C-130s filled with our men. We'd have the Argies running like scared rabbits before we were out of the planes.'

'If you got that far,' Ricketts said. 'Rumour has it the airfield is ringed with 7000 Argentinian troops and an anti-aircraft battalion equipped with ground-to-air missiles. The C-130s, not fast at the best of times, would be sitting ducks.'

'Right,' baby-faced Danny put in, nodding emphatically. 'We would not beat the clock, my friend.'

'Well, when are we going to *do* something?'

'When the diplomats fail, as they will. Only then will we move.'

'Jesus Christ!' Gumboot exploded.

The special training began the next day and covered a wide variety of situations. Though the eighty-odd troops were already sweating in the tropical heat of Ascension Island, they were compelled to wear outfits suitable to the Arctic conditions of their eventual destination.

'The Falklands are notable for cold weather and wind,' Sergeant Ricketts explained as the men prepared. 'The two together can result in windchill, which can freeze exposed flesh in minutes. So you have to get used to operating in this gear, whether or not you like it.'

The 'gear' to which he referred was windproof and waterproof clothing which covered the whole body and was based on the so-called 'layer system', whereby layers of clothing are added or taken away depending on the temperature and level of activity. If moisture is trapped inside garments, sweat cools very quickly in the Arctic and the wearer starts freezing. Most of the

Arctic battle gear was therefore made from Gore-tex, which keeps heat in but allows moisture to escape.

Other items of kit distributed to the Regiment that first morning included mittens, face masks, ski boots, snow shoes and skis. Nevertheless, even kitted out like this, the kind of training the Regiment could do was fairly limited. Wearing their bulky Gore-tex weatherproof jackets, wool sweaters, Royal Marine camouflage trousers and heavy boots in the heat of Ascension Island was a distinctly uncomfortable way of undergoing so-called 'special training'. As for the training itself, given that the Arctic climate of the Falklands had to be simulated in a very different environment, very little new, relevant training could be managed. They tested their weapons on the firing range, rehearsed in canoes and Gemini inflatable assault boats in the shallow waters just off the beach, and practised abseiling from noisily hovering Wessex helicopters. But most of it was fairly basic stuff and all too familiar.

'We're just wanking here,' Gumboot said, summarizing the widespread feeling of frustration. 'Just passing time. Those Navy choppers are cross-decking troops every day, so they can be shipped on to the Falklands – it's just us being left here. I'm gonna go mad with fucking boredom if they don't move us on soon. Completely out of my mind.'

'Right on,' young Danny said, looking yearningly at all the ships anchored out at sea. 'I know what you mean.'

Pretty soon, just to keep the men busy, the instructors were resorting to the well-known torments of Continuation-and-Cross Training, including four-man patrol tactics, signalling, first aid, demolition, hand-to-hand combat and general combat survival. While most of it was of obvious use, it had all been done before, and after a few days the men were sick of it. To make matters worse, the Navy had placed many restrictions on what could be done on the island. This further displeased the members of the Regiment.

'I'll tell you one thing,' Corporal Paddy Clarke said two days later in the Volcano Club. 'I'm fucking tired of playing amateur soldiers every morning on this bit of volcanic rock – just learning the terrain and repeating the lessons of Sickener One. Then listening to the green slime givin' their boring lectures every bloody afternoon. Bullshit, bullshit and more bullshit. If we have to retrain, let's do it properly – not all this basic REMF stuff.'

REMFs was the SAS term for the boys at the back – the 'rear-echelon motherfuckers'.

'It's the Navy's fault,' Baby Face said. He was yearning for Darlene and looking lovelorn. 'As the Head Shed said at the briefing back in the Kremlin, the Navy's limiting the numbers of troops who can be ashore at any time – and that limits our training. It's always the Navy.'

'Right on,' Gumboot said. 'It's always the Navy's fault. They're just tryin' to take advantage. Those bastards want to keep us trapped here while they get all the glory.'

'No glory to be had,' big Taff Burgess pointed out mildly. 'At least, not so far. The politicians are still farting around while we sit here sweating.'

'Besides,' Ricketts added, 'it's not just the Navy. It's this damned terrain. We can't train you properly in this place because we've nothing to work with – no snow, no ice crevasses, no mud. Here we only have featureless terrain and sea, which is not much use to us.'

They all knew what he meant. The main key to survival in an Arctic environment is to get out of the wind and defeat the cold. For this reason, all SAS troopers routinely receive training in the construction of shelters such as snow holes, snow caves and igloos, as well as instruction in ski techniques and navigation in Arctic conditions. Special training in those areas was clearly impossible on Ascension Island, where the ground was too hard to simulate snow holes and too flat to construct dry ski runs.

'At least we've done some weapons training,' Ricketts said. 'Thanks for small mercies.'

In fact the only special weapons training they had done was in how to keep their weapons in working order in the dismal weather of the Falklands. Because in extremely cold conditions lubricants thicken, causing jams and sluggish action, all unnecessary lubricants had to be removed, with only the surfaces of the bolt being lubricated, and the rest left dry. Similarly, ammunition had to be cleaned of all oil and condensation. This required a little learning, but not much, so the men were soon bored again.

'Small mercies?' Jock said. '*What* fucking small mercies? I'm going mad doing nothing on this hell-hole while the task force sails on to the Falklands. I don't think it's right.'

'It's the Navy,' Gumboot said, returning to their favourite punchbag. 'Those bastards sail on to the Falklands while we jerk off back here.'

'I wouldn't mind,' Paddy said, 'if there was something to do here.' He lit a cigarette, puffing smoke. 'But there's nothing but this miserable bloody club and a lot of rocks and the sea. It's like being in prison.'

'Not quite, lads,' big Andrew said philosophically as he twisted a piece of paper into a tight ball and dropped it into his half-pint glass of Drambuie. 'Just take a look at this place. Here we are, in the South Atlantic Ocean, on what's essentially a piece of volcanic rock, only discovered on Ascension Day in 1501. There's poetry in this primitive place, man. Sheer visual poetry.'

'He's talkin' shite again,' Jock said, shaking his head in despair. 'He'll soon set it to music.'

A few of the lads laughed, but Andrew remained unfazed. He swirled the Drambuie in his glass, letting it thoroughly soak the crumpled piece of paper floating on top. 'Where's your sense of military history?' he challenged them, staring at each in turn. 'Did you know that this place was uninhabited until the British established a garrison when Napoleon was sent to St Helena in 1815? That makes a line of history from Napoleon to us, sitting right here. I think that's kind of magical.'

'Where's St Helena?' Jock asked. 'The other side of the island?'

'Seven hundred and fifty miles south-east of

here,' Andrew explained with a studied display of patience. 'A mere drop in the ocean. And to there – we're practically sitting in his ghostly lap – the great Napoleon was exiled. Now I think that's real magical, man – and magic is poetry.'

'I'm gonna puke,' Gumboot said.

'Don't blame you,' Jock agreed.

'I salute the great fellow-soldier,' Andrew said gravely. Then he flicked his lighter, set fire to the ball of paper in the Drambuie, put the flaming concoction to his lips and swallowed it.

It was the kind of sport the Regiment enjoyed and Andrew's mates all applauded. When he had finished his drink, the ball of paper was still on fire. He put his lips over the glass and appeared to suck up the flame. When he put the glass down, the fire was out. The men clapped and cheered again.

'Anyway,' Ricketts said when the noise had subsided, 'I think Parkinson should get on the blower and try to stir up some action.'

'Talk of the devil,' Paddy said, indicating the door with a nod of his head as Major Parkinson entered the bar and walked straight to their table.

'Evening, chaps,' he said. 'Sitting here moaning and groaning, are you?' The men jeered and howled melodramatically, until Parkinson pulled up a chair and sat down with them. 'Contrary to what you bullshit artists think, our CO has been keen to get this squadron embarked. He's therefore pleased to inform you, through me, that today he received a request for an SAS troop, the whole of D Squadron, to sail in the Royal Fleet Auxiliary *Fort Austin* for a proper assignment.'

Reprieved at last, the men roared their approval.

Some twelve hours later, in the grey light of dawn, the men of the SAS Squadron were driven away from Wideawake airfield, past planes, helicopters, fork-lifts, supply trucks, advance-communications equipment and stockpiles of fuel, rations and medical supplies, to the nearby beach, where Gemini inflatables were waiting to take them out to the fleet of battleships that would carry them on to the South Atlantic.

3

The 22,890-ton RFA *Fort Austin* sailed under the Blue Ensign in company with the large destroyer HMS *Antrim* (6200 tons), the frigate *Plymouth* (2800 tons), and the large fleet tanker *Tidespring* (27,400 tons). Maintaining radio silence, the fleet soon left Ascension Island far behind to become surrounded by the deep swells and ominous grey waves of the forbidding South Atlantic.

Although normally unarmed, the *Fort Austin* was carrying improvised weaponry, including GPMGs, general-purpose machine-guns. It had also embarked four Lynx helicopters specially fitted for firing the Sea Skua missile, and it was loaded with 3500 tons of ammunition, stores and spares. With a length of 183.8 metres, a beam of 24.1 metres and a draught of 14.9 metres, she was an impressive sight, and, to the uninitiated, overwhelming inside.

Spending most of their days and nights in the dimly lit, sweltering hold, in tightly packed tiers of bunk beds and hammocks, surrounded by dangling equipment and clothes hanging from stanchions, in a tangle of bags, packs, bergens and weapons, with little to do except be patient, the SAS men passed the time by studying as much detail of the islands as they had been given by Intelligence, playing cards, writing letters in which they could not state their whereabouts, visiting the latrines out of boredom as well as need, and exchanging the usual banter and bullshit.

'Here comes young Danny, just back from the head, getting his lovely Darlene out of his system by having a good wank. How did it go, kid?'

'None of your business, Gumboot.'

'Shot a healthy wad, did you? Enough to last you till tomorrow? Me, I can do it ten times a day and it's still not enough. That's why women can't get enough of me – because I just keep on coming.'

'They can't get enough of you,' big Andrew corrected him, 'because you pay them too much. The whores of London have never had it so good – at least not since your missus ran off and sent you on the prowl around King's Cross. At least Danny here doesn't have to pay for it. He has youth on his side.'

'Hey, look, he's blushing! Danny's face has gone all red. If he had as much heat in his dick, we'd all be in trouble.'

'Shut up, Jock,' Ricketts said. 'You've got a mouth like a sewer. Go and pick on someone your age – another geriatric.'

'I'm the same age as Danny. He just *looks* younger than me. That's because I'm a man of broad experience and it shows in my face.'

'Dissipation,' Andrew said. 'Your mug certainly shows that. Now me, I'm often mistaken for Muhammad Ali. Black is beautiful, friends.'

When feeling trapped or claustrophobic in the crowded, noisy hold, a man could make his escape by touring the immense ship and observing the constant activity that went on in its other holds and on the flight deck. Most of this revolved around the transfer of stores and equipment, either to smaller ships alongside or by jackstay rigs or helicopters to HM ships. The noise both above and below decks was therefore considerable nearly all day, and sometimes went on through the night.

'Fucking Navy,' Jock said. 'You'd have to be mad to join it. I mean, trapped on this floating factory for weeks on end with only the sea all around you. You'd have to be psycho.'

'That's what *they* say about *us*,' Andrew replied, 'and maybe they're right.'

'They're just a bunch of poofters,' Gumboot said, leaning against the railing and spitting over the side to baptize the sea. 'We've all known that for years. That's why they like life aboard ship, packed cosily together in their bunks. Why *else* would they do it?'

'Three days we've been at sea already,' Taff said, ignoring Jock's base observation and instead watching another helicopter taking off with a roar, silhouetted by a pale, cloud-streaked sun as it created a wind that whipped their faces and pummelled their bodies. 'One more day and I'll go mad.'

'Won't we all?' Ricketts murmured.

Luckily, they managed to survive the next day – and on the fifth, 9 April, *Antrim*'s fleet linked up with the ice patrol ship the *Endurance* 1600 kilometres north of South Georgia, and, escorted by it, began closing in on the island.

'Thank God!' Danny exclaimed softly, again leaning on the railing and gazing hopefully at the distant, as yet featureless grey horizon. 'Now let's see some dry land.'

However, as approval for the operation had not yet been received from London, another ten days passed before Major Parkinson could announce its commencement.

'How are the men holding up?' he asked Sergeant Ricketts.

'Not bad, boss, but they're obviously getting a bit frustrated. There isn't much to do down there in the hold except listen to the hammering of the engines, play cards, write letters, trade bullshit and take the piss out of passing sailors.'

'But no trouble so far?'

'Not so far – but their remarks to the sailors are becoming more saucy by the day, so there could be some punch-ups in the near future. There's a lot of energy needs squandering down there, one way or the other.'

'We'd better distract them.'

'I think so, boss.'

'Let's keep them extra busy, Sergeant. Every minute of every day. Otherwise, I'm afraid you'll be right and they'll start popping sailors. Let's burn up all that healthy, excess energy before they release it another way.'

'Good thinking, boss,' Ricketts said.

Within each of the four Sabre Squadrons of the SAS – A, B, C and D – there are four kinds of 16-man specialist groups: Mountain Troops for mountain and Arctic warfare; Boat Troops for amphibious warfare; Mobility Troops for operations in Land Rovers and fast-attack vehicles, as well as on motorcycles; and Air Troops for freefall parachute operations. However, during their training, the men must serve with every group, to make them adaptable to any of the four main forms of warfare.

Given the nature of the Falklands, the SAS men on *Fort Austin* were divided into the two groups needed for this particular operation: the Mountain Troop, led by Captain Hailsham and including Sergeant Ricketts, Corporal Clarke and troopers Porter and Winston, which would be used for land-based reconnaissance and engagements; and the Boat Troop, led by Captain Grenville and including Corporal McGregor and troopers Burgess and Gillis, to be used for any required amphibious landings.

The first group was therefore kept as busy as possible with interminable lessons on the geography and topography of the Falklands; the second with similar lessons on the tides and waterways of the islands and with the constant checking of their Gemini inflatables and Klepper canoes.

Nevertheless, life aboard ship became increasingly dull and frustrating, leading to restlessness, moans and groans and even an occasional angry confrontation between SAS Troopers and the crew. Sergeant Ricketts was therefore relieved when at last they were called to the briefing room by an obviously pleased Major Parkinson.

'I've just been informed,' he told his frustrated SAS Troop, 'that our accompanying tanker, *Tidespring*, is carrying M Company of 42 Commando, Royal Marines – destined to be landed in South Georgia.'

There were murmurs and many wide-eyed glances among the men.

'This island,' Parkinson continued when they had settled down again, 'lies 1300 kilometres east-south-east of the Falklands and, as the main base of the British Antarctic Survey, is particularly important to Great Britain. Its recapture will therefore be a clear indication to the world in general and Argentina in particular that if necessary we Brits will fight to recapture any territory stolen from us.'

'About time!' Gumboot exclaimed.

'Bloody right,' Jock said emphatically.

'Let's get them up and running,' Taff Burgess added, smiling at the ceiling. 'Let's kick the shite out of them.'

The ensuing laughter and applause were

silenced when Ricketts, on the ball as always, asked: 'Who's in charge *this* time?'

'The second-in-command of 42 Commando, Major Guy Sheridan RM, will be in command of the landing forces, including us' – a few groans at this – 'and he'll work with our CO aboard the *Antrim* in planning the assault on the island.' This brought more cheers. 'In addition to us, Sheridan has 120 men of M Company and about twenty-five swimmer-canoeists of 2 SBS, Royal Marines. There's also a small detachment of Marines aboard the *Antrim* with M Company's Recce Troop, a mortar section and the company OC. In all, about 235 men.'

'How many Argentinians are holding the island?' Ricketts asked.

'We don't know for sure. Why? Are you worried?'

'No, boss, I'm not.'

'I didn't think so,' Parkinson said with a grin. 'Anyway, we've just received a signal . . .'

'I thought we were sailing in radio silence,' big Taff butted in.

'It was dropped from a maritime reconnaissance aircraft,' Parkinson explained. 'A signal authorizing us to carry out covert recces on South Georgia.' This sparked off more cheering.

'As part of this, plans are being drawn up for our Mountain Troop to land north of Leith, where the Argentinians have reportedly been collecting scrap from an old whaling station. And 2 SBS will land about the same time in Hounds Bay, south-east of the island's main settlement of Grytviken, and move up the coast in inflatable boats to establish observation posts, which can observe the settlement from across five kilometres of open water. That's it. Any questions?'

'When do we leave?' Andrew asked.

'The operation has already commenced. On your feet, bullshit artists. We're busy at last.'

4

Because South Georgia was out of range of land-based aircraft, D squadron transhipped by Wessex helicopter from *Fort Austin* to the ice patrol ship HMS *Endurance*, which would sail closer to the shore, enabling them to fly in to their landing zone.

Looking down on the South Atlantic, where a man could freeze to death in a couple of hours, Ricketts wasn't the only one to give a slight, involuntary shudder, no matter how fearless he might normally have been. He was glad, therefore, when a streak of crimson appeared in the alluvial, snot-grey sea, then took shape as the hull of the *Endurance*, also known as the 'Red Plum'. Though smaller than the *Fort Austin*, the *Endurance* was equipped with two Wasp helicopters. To facilitate their landing, a large hangar had been built abaft the ship's funnel, extending her poop deck to create a helicopter landing pad. It was onto this that the helicopter containing the SAS team landed, bobbing up and down, to and fro, above the treacherous, surging, shadowy waves, before settling at last on the solid but constantly swaying deck.

Once aboard the new ship, Major Parkinson held another briefing, this one solely for the 16 members of his Mountain Troop, which would be led by the young and handsome, but decidedly efficient, Captain Mike Hailsham, and including Sergeant Ricketts, Corporal Jock McGregor, Trooper Danny Baby Face Porter, and the massive Trooper Andrew Winston.

Captain Hailsham was standing beside Parkinson throughout the briefing, which took place in a large, committee-room-sized cabin located above the flight decks, with drenched portholes giving a distorted view of the featureless grey sea and sky outside.

'Right,' Major Parkinson began. 'To put you in the picture, the Special Boat Squadron has been given the task of reconnoitring Grytviken and King Edward's Point while the Mountain Troop, meaning you lot, under the command of Captain Hailsham here, will be landed on Fortuna Glacier, South Georgia, to establish observation posts for the gathering of intelligence on the Argentinian forces. This may not be as easy at it sounds, for reasons which Captain Hailsham will now explain.'

Parkinson stepped aside as Hailsham picked up his pointer and tapped it against the map pinned to the board. 'The Fortuna Glacier is a potential death-trap,' he said bluntly. 'Its five arms flow down into the South Atlantic and are veined with hundreds of deep fissures and pressure ridges. At the top of the glacier, where the weight of the ice pressures downwards, it's comparatively level, but there are also hundreds of mile-deep crevasses. These can swallow a man up to his waist – though if he's lucky, the bulk of his bergen will break his fall and his colleagues will then be able to drag him out.'

This drew snorts of derision from some of the men. 'Don't laugh,' Captain Hailsham admonished them. 'I'm not joking about this. That glacier is massive, filled with crevasses, and extremely dangerous. In good weather conditions the procedure I've just described will be adequate to the situation, enabling us to advance, albeit slowly. However, in sub-zero temperatures and gale-force winds, which we're likely to encounter, it's extremely hazardous. In fact, sudden gales, which come from the mountains and are then funnelled down valleys, can produce gusts of over 240 kilometres per hour. To make matters worse, the weather's unpredictable. What may appear as a window of clear weather can be closed in minutes by whirling snow storms, producing a blinding white-out. So believe me, that glacier is treacherous.'

'Luckily, Captain Hailsham has Himalayan experience,' Major Parkinson interjected. 'That, at least, is a help.'

'If it's that hazardous, why choose the glacier for an OP?' Ricketts asked, thinking it was a poor site for an observation post.

'I have to confess,' Parkinson replied, 'that 42 Commando's second-in-command, Major Guy Sheridan, advised against it. However, the importance of that high point overlooking Grytviken and Leith Harbour, combined with Captain Hailsham's experience as a civilian mountaineer, was enough to make us take a chance and attempt a landing on this difficult LZ. We were encouraged further when we found that this ship carries detailed charts and maps of the area, now pinned up behind me.'

Captain Hailsham tapped the drawings on the board with his pointer. 'These plans of the buildings on King Edward's Point were carefully traced from drawings. The buildings housed the British Antarctic Survey settlement before the Royal Marines were forced to surrender to the Argentinians. The same buildings now house the Argentinian HQ. They're located at the mouth of a cove a thousand metres from Grytviken. That's what we hope to observe from the OP on the Fortuna Glacier.' After a short silence, Hailsham asked: 'Any questions?'

There were no questions, so Ricketts said: 'Silence is consent. I say let's go now, boss.'

'I always take note of the wishes of my men,' Major Parkinson replied with a grin. 'OK, Cap'n, get going.'

Captain Hailsham enthusiastically left the cabin, followed by the others.

The men prepared themselves with their usual thoroughness. Arctic cold-weather kit was drawn from the *Endurance*'s stores, including Swedish civilian mountaineering boots, which they used instead of their normal-issue boots. Weapons were signed for and carefully checked, including SLR semi-automatic rifles with 20-round steel magazines; 7.62mm general-purpose machine-guns; a couple of Armalites with single-shot, breech-loaded, pump-action grenade-launchers; M202s with 66mm, trigger-mechanism incendiary rockets; Browning 9mm high-power handguns; and fragmentation, white-phosphorus, CS-gas and smoke grenades. The weapons were thoroughly checked, then the machine-guns, rifles and pistols were cleansed of unnecessary lubricants, to prevent them from seizing up on the freezing glacier.

Other equipment, apart from food and drink, included a couple of PRC 319 HF/VHF radio systems and an older Clansman high-frequency set, which could also be used as a Morse or CW, continuous-wave, transmitter. Also loaded onto the troop-carrying Wessex helicopters were four sledges, or *pulks*, which could be hauled by hand and would be used to transport the weapons and other equipment from the LZ to the summit of the glacier.

When this vital work was done, the men gathered on the landing pads of the ship and took their places in the two Royal Marine Wessex Mark 5 helicopters flown in for this op from the fleet oiler, the *Tidespring*, and the smaller Wessex Mark 3, from the RFA *Antrim*, to be flown by Lieutenant-Commander Randolph Pedler RN. At midday the helicopters took off and headed for

South Georgia, flying above a sludge-coloured sea, through a sky ominous with black clouds.

'It looks as welcoming as hell down there,' Trooper Winston observed, glancing over his shoulder, through the window. 'It's just not as warm.'

'Getting cold feet, are you?'

'My feet are fine, Gumboot. I'm merely casting my poetic eye over the scene and making a measured observation. That landscape's as white as your face. Feeling ill, are you?'

'Very funny,' Gumboot said. 'The company poet has just spoken. He's trying to hide the fact that he's got cold feet by changing the subject. We all know just how white *he'd* be looking if he wasn't so black.'

'Now that's real poetic, Gumboot.'

'Thanks, Andrew, you're too kind. When you come down out of the trees and learn to spell you can write me up in your notebook.'

'Ho, ho,' Andrew said. 'A shaft of wit from the white-faced wonder. They grow his kind like turnips in Devon, where the folks all chew straws.'

'I like Devon,' Baby Face Danny, said. 'I once took Darlene there. We stayed in a hotel at Paignton and had a wonderful time.'

'In separate rooms,' Paddy said.

'Having simultaneous wet dreams,' Gumboot added.

'You shouldn't make fun of young love,' Taff Burges rebuked them. 'I think it's cruel to do that.'

'I don't mind,' Danny said. 'I know they're just pulling my leg.'

'To keep him from pulling his dick,' Gumboot said, 'which he seems to do all the time these days.'

'That's true love,' Andrew said.

'I'd call it lust, but what's the difference?'

'Now we know why your missus ran off,' Andrew said, flashing his perfect teeth at Gumboot. 'You were too sensitive and sentimental for her, too romantic to live with.'

'Now *that's* cruel,' Gumboot said. 'That's hitting a man below the belt. I could reply in kind by making comments about your girlfriends, but since I know that it's little boys you like, I'll keep my trap shut.'

'Little boys like *me*, Gumboot.'

'Yes, Andrew, I know they do. They like your nice smile, your black skin, your poetry and the fact that you have a dong so tiny you can slip it in smoothly. Say no more – I'm outraged.'

'Scared shitless more like it.' Paddy's grin was wicked. 'I can tell by the colour of his gills that he has constipation.'

'Scared? *Me* scared? Who said that? Stand up and be counted!'

'I would if I could but I can't because my poor knees are knocking. Yeah, Andrew, you're absolutely right: it looks like all hell down there.'

The bantering, Ricketts knew, was not a cover for fear, but a healthy way of psyching themselves up for the work to be done. Now, having exhausted conversation and nearing the LZ, they fell into a contemplative silence, each secretly preparing in his own way for what was to come.

Ricketts studied them with pride and a great deal of admiration. Trooper Danny Porter, who was a baby-faced Audie Murphy with the same lethal instincts, looked grave and almost delicate beside the enormous bulk of Trooper Andrew Winston, who was scribbling down his thoughts, or poetry, in a notebook, as he often did just before an action. Corporal Paddy Clarke, born and bred in Liverpool, was tapping his left foot and soundlessly whistling as he checked his SLR semi-automatic rifle. Trooper Taff Burgess, a beefy Welshman with a dark-eyed, slightly childish face, was glancing distractedly about him and offering his usual dreamy smile. Corporal Jock McGregor was rolling his own ciggies, which he would smoke at a later date, and displaying not the slightest sign of concern. And Trooper Gumboot Gillis, the small, sinewy, ferret-faced, former Devon farm-worker, was distractedly scratching at his balls.

All of them, in their different ways, were exceptional soldiers – truly the best of the best, a hand-picked elite. Which is why, as Sergeant Ricketts also knew, they were in the SAS.

Unclipping his safety belt, Ricketts made his way to the front of the helicopter, where Captain Hailsham was strapped in beside the Mark 3 pilot, Lieutenant-Commander Randolph Pedler RN. Looking out, past Hailsham's head, Ricketts saw a charcoal-coloured, snow-streaked stretch of mountainous land on a grey horizon, growing larger each second.

'Is that South Georgia?' he asked.

'It sure is,' Lieutenant-Commander Pedler said. 'And it doesn't look good out there. We're hoping to reach the LZ 500 metres above sea level, but I think we've got snow. That won't make it easy.'

Pedler was right. Within minutes the mountains of the approaching island could be seen more clearly and were covered with falling snow.

'You'd better go back and strap yourself in,' Captain Hailsham warned Ricketts. 'We're in for a bumpy ride.'

'Right, boss,' Ricketts replied, then returned to the main cabin to strap himself in with the other troops.

Nearing the LZ, they were met by wind-driven snow that created a 'white-out' by making earth and sky indistinguishable. Nevertheless, with the aid of the Mark 3's computerized navigational system, Lieutenant-Commander Pedler led the other two helicopters on through the dangerous gorges of South Georgia until the sheer face of the Fortuna Glacier emerged eerily from a curtain of falling snow. There they hovered, then ascended and descended, trying to find a place to land, with the roaring helicopters being buffeted dangerously by the fierce, howling wind.

The first attempt to land was unsuccessful, so eventually Pedler and the others flew away to circle the glacier in the hope of finding a clear area. They weren't able to land until the third attempt, later that afternoon, when the wind was blowing at 50mph. It was like landing in hell.

When the troops disembarked from the helicopters, or 'helos' as the Navy called them, the fierce wind was driving fine particles of ice before it. These stung the men's eyes if they were not wearing goggles and, more dangerously, choked the mechanisms of their weapons.

As they unloaded their equipment and long, lightweight *pulks*, they were sheltered from the worst of the weather. Also, the hot exhaust fumes of the helicopters gave them a deceptive feeling of warmth. But when they lifted off, the 16 SAS troopers, being suddenly, brutally hit by the full force of those biting, 50mph winds, realized just what they were up against.

'Shit!' Paddy exclaimed, wiping snow from his Arctic hood and examining the weapons he was putting onto his *pulk*. 'They're not only choked up – they're frozen solid as well. Completely fucking useless.'

'Damn!' Captain Hailsham exclaimed softly, also checking the frozen weapons. 'During the helicopter flight the warm metal must have attracted a thin film of water. Exposed to this damned wind, it froze.'

'Great!' Andrew said, rolling his eyes, then squinting into the howling gale. 'Weapons like ice lollies. Let's just hope the bloody Argies don't show up until we get them thawed out again.'

'The Argies won't show up here,' Ricketts said.

'Still,' Captain Hailsham warned him, 'we have to get off this glacier before nightfall. 'If we don't, we're likely to freeze to death.'

'Right, boss,' Ricketts said, forced to shout against the raging wind, but finding it difficult because his lips were already becoming numb. 'We better get going then. I suggest we break the men up into four groups, each roped together, and go down the glacier in arrow formation. That way, we won't lose each other and can help each other out if there's trouble.'

'Right, Sergeant, let's do it.'

After splitting up into four patrols, one of which included Ricketts, Andrew, Danny, and Paddy, the men attached themselves to the *pulks* loaded with food and ammunition, roped themselves together in four separate groups, then advanced down the glacier in arrowhead formation, inhuman in their bulky Arctic suits and hoods, ghostlike in the mist and swirling snow.

One patrol had orders to watch Leith, one Stromness and one Husvik, four miles from the LZ. The fourth, led by Ricketts, had intended going down the opposite west slope to recce Fortuna Bay for boat and helicopter landing points. However, this was not to be. As the men edged slowly forward, the storm actually grew worse, with the wind howling louder and the snow thickening around them, reducing visibility to almost zero.

The ice surface of the glacier was covered with snow, which was gathering in the crevasses. The men could not always see the indentations in the snow, and within a few metres they came to a halt when young Danny became the first to cry out instinctively as he plunged through the snow-covered ice.

His fall was stopped by his bergen, his back-pack, straddling the fissure, leaving him buried from the waist down.

'Christ!' he cried, frantically waving his hands above his head. 'Get me outta here!'

'Don't move!' Ricketts called to him, tugging on the rope, meanwhile pulling himself forward to anchor Danny with his pickaxe and prevent him sinking deeper into the crevasse. Andrew and Paddy then did the same, hooking their pickaxes under Danny's armpits, then taking hold of his shoulders to pull him back up to solid ground.

Once Danny had shaken off the snow and ice, they all stepped over the crevasse, leaned into the wind and continued their advance down the white, gleaming side of the glacier. Then Paddy fell into another crevasse, compelling them to stop and start the rescue procedure all over again.

This occurred repeatedly, to one man after another. It was also happening to the other groups, whom Ricketts could see as shadowy, inhuman shapes in the snow storm, clearly struggling yet making little progress.

As the storm grew worse, their advance was reduced to a snail's pace. By nightfall, when already they were frozen and exhausted, they had managed to cover only about half a mile.

'I'm afraid Sheridan was right!' Captain Hailsham shouted to Ricketts. 'We're wasting our time here!'

Unable to do more in the relentless, continuing snow storm, the four patrols regrouped in the gathering gloom of the evening and attempted to make camp for the night. Seeking protection from the piercing cold, they found the least exposed part of the glacier, under a rock outcrop, and there tried to put up three-man tents. When these were whipped away by the violent gale, snapping like living things as they disappeared in the darkness, the men dug snow holes and attempted to sleep in 'bivvy bags' with their boots on. By midnight, however, hurricane force 11 winds were howling over the mountains, which not only prevented sleep, but also brought a real risk of hypothermia and frostbite. At this point, the experience of Captain Hailsham told him to give up.

'The troop will have to be withdrawn as soon as possible,' he informed Ricketts. 'Otherwise, the frostbite could become so acute that some of us might even lose our limbs. Get on that radio, Sergeant, and tell them to lift us out.'

Using the PRC 319 HF/VHF radio system, Ricketts did as he was told, and was soon in touch with HMS *Endurance*. He was informed that three Wessex helicopters would be despatched early the next morning, one from the *Antrim*, the other from HMS *Tidespring*, and that he was to send up a SARBE, or surface-to-air rescue beacon, when he saw them.

'We're freezing our balls off here,' Ricketts said, 'and it's getting worse every minute, so try getting to us as soon as possible. Over.'

'First light, on the nose,' he was informed. 'Over and out.'

'Fucking first light,' Paddy spluttered when informed that he would be spending the rest of the night on the glacier. 'They'll be too busy banging each other in their bunks to give us a thought. Typical fucking Navy! Just leave us to get hypothermia or frostbite, while they warm themselves by getting it up the rear end. I'm pissed off, I can tell you!'

'They can't fly in this storm in the dark,' Ricketts explained. 'It's as simple as that. Now get as deep down in those holes as you can go, lads. Don't let the cold get to you.'

'Right, boss,' Andrew replied. 'Think of your darling Darlene,' he then said to Danny, who was expertly digging in beside him. 'That should keep *you* warm, mate!'

'Aw, knock it off,' said Danny, embarrassed, before turning away and curling up in his bivvy bag. 'You're just trying to make me blush.'

'Some ladies like guys who blush,' Andrew replied, wriggling into his own bivvy bag as the snow fell on him. 'They'd drop their knickers at the very sight of a flushed male face.'

'You're so crude,' Danny complained.

'He wants you blushing,' Paddy said, ''cause when you do, we don't need the beacons. Your face glows in the dark.'

'OK,' Ricketts said when the laughter died down, 'that's enough of the bullshit. Now let's all get some shut-eye.'

'Yes, boss,' they replied.

The banter was a necessary antidote to the appalling conditions, for the ensuing night was hellish, with the hurricane force 11 wind not abating at all, and the snow and ice beating at them every second, instantly flaying them if they made the mistake of exposing a patch of skin to the elements. Sleep was impossible, or at least came in fits and starts, and by dawn, when a pale sun shone through, they were exhausted and numb.

The Navy pilots were as good as their word. Even before he heard them – since the wind was still roaring, the sweeping snow still hissing – Ricketts saw the three Wessex helicopters coming in to attempt a landing on the glacier and pick them up. Wriggling quickly out of his bivvy bag, he sent up a beacon as the rest of the group came back to life, smacking the snow off their hoods and gloves, then slapping themselves to get their circulation going.

'What a bloody disaster!' Paddy said. 'A complete waste of time!'

'Shut up, Trooper,' Ricketts barked at him while watching the green smoke of his chemical flare spreading through the still dark, cloudy and snow-streaked sky directly above.

Contacting the helo on the PRC 319, he learnt that the lead pilot in the Mark 3 was again

Lieutenant-Commander Pedler, who had brought them here, and that he had spotted them and was coming in for a landing. The Mark 3 duly descended through the raging blizzard, its rotors causing a more violent snowstorm as it nervously touched down. It was followed immediately by the other two helicopters.

'You're a sight for sore eyes,' Captain Hailsham shouted at Lieutenant-Commander Pedler.

'You can sing my praises later,' Pedler replied. 'For now, let's load up and take off. This damned storm's getting worse.'

As quickly as possible, given the appalling conditions, the men distributed their equipment to the three helicopters, then took their own places. Pedler's Mark 3 lifted off first, followed by the two Mark 5s, one of which was carrying Captain Hailsham, Ricketts, Paddy Clarke, young Danny and big Andrew.

'Good riddance,' the latter said, looking down on the gleaming, storm-swept glacier as the chopper ascended.

'The most useless bloody op I've ever been on,' Paddy said, wiping the melting snow from his face. 'A complete waste of time.'

'Shut it, troopers,' Ricketts admonished them, glancing through the window. 'No need for . . .'

He stopped in mid-sentence when he saw the other Mark 5 flying into a particularly fierce gust of snow, a virtual white-out, that appeared to be forcing it off course, then back down, nose first, to the ground. 'Oh, Christ!' Ricketts groaned as the Mark 5 wobbled widely, clearly fighting to right itself, then went down, crashing into the glacier in a mess of buckling skis, breaking rotors and flying glass, all of which was obscured in geysering snow.

The helicopter shuddered like a dying elephant as the snow fell on it.

'They went down!' Danny shouted involuntarily.

Even as the Mark 5 crashed, Ricketts heard Pedler's voice coming over the radio, saying that he was going to land again on a rescue mission.

'Message received,' the pilot up ahead said. 'We're coming down after you. Over and out.'

'Damned right, we are,' Andrew said.

Ricketts saw Pedler's Mark 3 turn back and descend, straight back into the blizzard, until it had practically disappeared in the swirling snow. The remaining Mark 5 followed suit, turning back to where they had come from, and soon it too was enveloped in a thick curtain of swirling snow.

It was virtually another white-out, with glacier

and sky indistinguishable, but then the snow thinned a little and Ricketts saw the Mark 3 landing, its spinning rotors sweeping up more snow and hurling it over the crashed aircraft, from which he could make out some figures emerging.

The wall of the glacier was now directly outside the window of the Mark 5, appearing to rise rapidly as the helicopter descended, then the rotors whipped up more snow as it settled down on its skis, bounced a little and stopped.

'Let's go!' Captain Hailsham called out.

Ricketts and his men all jumped out of the helicopter, intent on a rescue operation. But when they had disembarked and crossed to the Mark 3, positioned beside the crashed Mark 5, they found Pedler's men already helping the survivors into their own helo, all of them looking eerily unnatural in their bulky Arctic outfits, spectral in the blizzard.

An SAS corporal, a new man, was the only person injured of the seven aboard. Even though the pilot's cabin had been smashed to hell, the pilot was all right.

'Our helo can hold more men than yours,' Lieutenant-Commander Collins, the Royal Navy pilot of the Mark 5, reminded Lieutenant-Commander Pedler, 'so you take three, including the injured man, and we'll take the other four.'

'Right,' Pedler said. 'Thanks. Let's hope we get the hell out of here.'

'I recommend the ditching of everything but weapons and belt equipment. You could also lighten your helo by leaving some of its special equipment on the ground.'

'Good thinking. Let's do it. Fix it up, Cap'n.'

Hailsham called the men together to tell them what he wanted. When the men had done as they were told, discarding everything but weapons and belt equipment, and the Mark 3 had been stripped of some of its special equipment, which was hastily buried under the ice and snow, the men were distributed between the two operational helicopters and they took off again.

The Mark 5 had barely lifted off the ground when it flew into a white-out, was buffeted by a fierce wind and, with its heavy load, became the second to crash. Ricketts felt the helo shaking like a car with punctured tyres, then it tilted to one side, showing the ground directly below, and the pilot called out a warning just before it went down.

'Oh, Christ, not again!' young Danny cried out in disbelief.

'Hold on!' Ricketts bawled.

The rotor blades made contact first, snapping off and spinning away, then the skis buckled beneath the crashing fuselage, making the helo tilt further. The men inside were scattered like skittles, hurled against each other, and scrambled about on the floor of the passenger cabin, cursing loudly, as their weapons and other equipment were thrown about, clattering all around them.

The helo shuddered and shrieked, its metal buckling, glass breaking, then it quivered in the swirling snow and sank into impacted ice.

'Jesus Christ!' Andrew exploded, picking himself up and glancing at the mess all around him. 'I don't believe this shit, man.'

'All out!' Captain Hailsham bawled, as he and the pilot unbuckled their safety belts and turned back into the disordered passenger cabin.

'Not again!' Danny complained. 'I can't stand it out there.'

'Out!' Ricketts bawled. '*Out!*'

Amazingly, no one had been hurt and all of the men made their escape from the wreckage, dropping down onto the ice and snow, back into the raging storm and its fiercely swirling sleet.

Even before the last man had emerged, Pedler's helicopter became visible in the stormy sky as he courageously returned to the glacier, checking out their location.

'Is that radio working?' Captain Hailsham wanted to know.

'Yes, sir,' Ricketts said. 'I'm trying to get in touch with them right now. Zulu to Tiger, Zulu to Tiger. Can you hear me? Over.'

'Tiger to Zulu, Tiger to Zulu. I hear you loud and clear. We're short on fuel up here, so we can't land again. You'll have to hang in there until I get back to the *Antrim* and top up the tanks. What's the damage down there? Over.'

'Zulu to Tiger. Zulu to Tiger. The helo's a write-off, but no one's been hurt. We'll try to survive here as best we can, but you better be quick. It's below freezing here. Over.'

'Tiger to Zulu. Tiger to Zulu. I have your position and I'll be back. Over and out.'

Ricketts turned off his microphone as the helicopter high above turned away and headed back out to sea, soon disappearing beyond a broad bank of dense clouds and dark sky.

'I still don't believe this shit, man,' Andrew groaned. 'What a fucking disaster!'

'That Major Sheridan advised us against it,' Danny reminded them. 'He's probably smirking right now.'

'He won't be smirking, Trooper,' Ricketts said, 'so there's no need for that talk. What's done has been done, so let's just settle in here as best we can and wait for the helo. Let's not freeze to death here.'

'Sergeant Ricketts is right,' Captain Hailsham said. 'We run the risk of hypothermia or frost-bite, so let's take special care. Belt in and wrap up, men.'

This, Ricketts knew, would be the worst time for all of them – the time when the strongest man could break. First the failure of the mission, then a night of hellish cold, followed by two helicopter crashes in a row, now being trapped here again. The physical enemy was the cold, but the loss of morale could be more dangerous, particularly if it led to self-pity or a sense of despair.

However, this was exactly the kind of situation the SAS were trained for, both physically and psychologically, and Ricketts was pleased to see his 15 remaining men rising to the challenge by making themselves as comfortable as they could, with only one survival tent and hardly any kit, even as the snow continued falling and gradually buried them.

It was a long, grim day, with the blizzard unrelenting and the men, taking turns to keep warm in the single tent, gradually becoming covered in snow and merging into the landscape.

Pedler returned a few hours later, trying to find a landing place, but was defeated by the growing ferocity of the storm and had to go back to the ship. However, even later that day he courageously returned yet again, this time managing to land, and picked up the frozen, exhausted men.

Dangerously overloaded, the Mark 3 limped back to the *Antrim*, a red streak in the vast greyness, and dropped onto the swaying deck like a bloated fly too heavy to stay aloft. It was not a graceful touch-down, given the weight of the helicopter, but it was an exemplary display of skill and courage of the kind the SAS admired.

'Didn't even *see* an Argie,' Danny said wryly, trying to make light of the disaster. 'They must all be in England.'

That copped a few sour laughs.

5

'Let's face it, gentlemen,' the grim-faced OC of the Squadron said in the briefing room aboard the *Antrim*, now sailing for Stromness Bay, South Georgia, 'the whole Fortuna Glacier op was a total, humiliating disaster.'

'Sorry, boss,' Major Parkinson said, 'but I'm afraid I can't agree. The fact that two Naval helicopters crashed was due to the weather, not to our men. In fact our men showed exemplary courage, given what they endured.'

'Exemplary courage,' the OC replied drily, 'was also shown by the three Navy pilots, particularly Lieutenant-Commander Pedler. We can't take too much credit for that. Even worse, it was 42 Commando's second-in-command who warned us not to attempt it. Our mistake and humiliation, Major Parkinson. Let's admit it.'

'No, sir. The endurance displayed by our men

is already the talk of the whole fleet. In that sense, at least, it was a victory. I think we did well, sir.'

The OC grinned. 'Such loyalty!' Then he became serious again. 'Nevertheless, we can't let the matter rest here. We must have that reconnaissance. The recapture of South Georgia will be another turn of the screw as London tries to avoid the need for a full-scale assault on the Falkland Islands. Also, though it has no airfields, South Georgia represents a base much closer to the Falklands than Ascension Island – one where we can at least anchor our ships beyond the range of Argentinian fighter-bombers. If we can't manage an insertion by air, let's go in by sea.'

'I second that, boss,' said Boat Troop Captain Laurence E. Grenville. 'I believe we should launch our Gemini inflatables and try to set up OPs on the north-west of the island.'

'Naturally, you would,' Captain Hailsham said tersely.

'Well,' Grenville replied, 'the Fortuna Glacier is obviously out of the question, so we might as well try elsewhere, landing by sea.'

'I agree,' the OC said. 'We should try for Grass Island as a jump-off point to Leith and Stromness. If we can establish a couple of OPs there, we'll have compensated for the Fortuna

Glacier disaster. I suggest we take this action immediately – let's say this afternoon.'

'Right, sir,' Captain Grenville said, grinning impishly at Major Parkinson and Captain Hailsham. 'I'll get it organized right away.'

Hailsham grinned too, and held up his thumb, good-naturedly acknowledging Grenville's little *coup*. 'Who dares wins,' he said.

Grinning even more broadly, Grenville left the briefing room and made his way down through the many hatches and corridors of the swaying ship to the hold used for rest and mass briefings. There, he found Sergeant Ricketts, still exhausted from the previous day's ordeal, surrounded by the equally shattered members of the Mountain Troop and the still fresh, bantering Boat Troop.

'. . . and I maintain,' Danny was saying defensively, 'that . . .'

'Bullshit,' Gumboot interjected. 'No point blaming the bloody Navy. If you'd had men of calibre, like us, you'd have managed somehow.'

'Right,' Jock added. 'If they'd given the job to our Boat Troop, instead of you bullshit artists, we'd be sitting in an OP on that glacier right now – not thawing out our frozen dicks on this Navy brig.'

'The only bullshit artists here are the sods of the

Boat Troop,' big Andrew said, grinning at Danny, Paddy and Ricketts in turn, 'and right now the bullshit's flying like diarrhoea. You bastards can hardly row your fucking boats, let alone climb a glacier.'

Captain Grenville had been standing at the other side of the hatchway, just listening, amused, but he stepped forward when the good-humoured jeering and clapping of both sides had subsided. When he stepped into the recreation room, which the SAS were using as an all-purpose barracks, with bashas made up on the floor, the noise subsided even more.

'Sounds like bullshit from both sides,' Grenville said. 'At least you troopers are still awake. Anyway, if points are to be made, now's the time to make them. I've come to say we're going to try another insertion, this time by sea, in the hope of setting up an OP on Grass Island, about two miles from Leith. If you bullshit artists of the Boat Troop think you're better, now's your chance to prove it.'

After another outburst of hoots and catcalls, the former from the Boat Troop, the latter from the Mountain Troop, Ricketts, more serious than the others, asked: 'What are we supposed to be doing in the meantime?'

'You rest up and wait,' Grenville told him. 'Once we set up OPs, there's going to be a wide-scale assault on South Georgia. You'll all be involved in that.'

'Throwing snowballs,' Gumboot said, standing up with a wicked grin on his face. 'That's why you got in the Mountain Troop.'

The anticipated rejoinders flew thick and fast, until Captain Grenville silenced them all with his raised hand.

'OK, that's enough. I want all members of the Boat Troop to get kitted out immediately, then gather at the docking area. We're going to launch as soon as the Geminis are inflated. I'll see you down there in one hour. That's it, gentlemen. On your way.'

The members of the Boat Troop cheered and hurried out through the hatchway, leaving Ricketts and the rest of his exhausted team to thaw out and get some rest.

The docking area at the stern of the ship had been opened and was already being flooded when the men of the Boat Troop assembled near the launching bay. Kitted out with waterproof clothing and the usual array of weapons, the Boat Troop also carried special survival suits, life-jackets and

SARBE beacons, to facilitate the pick-ups and, if necessary, aid rescue from the sea.

The five Geminis to be used in the operation, already inflated and roped to the docking bay, were being lifted towards the men on the rising sea as it poured into the open stern to flood the bay area, rushing, roaring and spewing spray in every direction.

Seeing it from this vantage point, the sea appeared to slope up to the distant, stormy horizon, soaring and rolling dramatically in immense, shadowed waves that appeared to be about to swamp the ship, though they simply made it rise and fall as if made of cork. The sky was just as threatening, hanging low, filled with black clouds, and the wind that came rushing in to smack the men was icy and vicious.

'Looks like hell out there,' Grenville said. 'I think we're in for a rough time.'

'So let's go, boss,' urged Jock. 'We best go before nightfall.'

'Right, Corporal. Let's do it.'

The men embarked in the five Geminis, three to each boat, with Captain Grenville in charge of the lead craft, Gumboot, Taff and Jock sharing another. There were two large inflatables, powered by 40hp outboard motors, and three smaller versions, powered by 18hp motors, with the smaller ones roped to the larger ones – two to one, one to the other. When the docking ropes had been untied and the outboard motors turned on, the inflatables cruised out of the docking area, one after the other, and immediately were carried up and away on the giant swells of the windswept sea.

The immense waves picked the boats up, carried them through shrieking wind, above ravines of light-flecked darkness, then swept them back down into roaring, spinning tunnels formed by waves curling almost above them, threatening to swamp them. When low in the water, the waves pounded against the inflatables and washed over the men, pummelling them mercilessly and making a dreadful drumming sound against the rubber hulls. When raised on high, barrelling along the crest of the waves with the men glancing down what appeared to be dizzy depths of light and darkness, the outboard engines, coming clear of the water, shrieked and shook dementedly.

Within minutes the *Antrim*, which had been towering above them like a brightly lit skyscraper, receded into the stormy ocean, blending in with the grey haze where sea and sky merged, until little of it remained within view. Then it disappeared completely, leaving only the sea and sky, while the inflatables, rising and falling, plunging in and out of the water, shrieked and vibrated like wild things that could not be controlled.

In his smaller inflatable, roped to Captain Grenville's larger boat, Taff struggled with the rudder, trying to keep the boat close to the one ahead in case the rope snapped. It was a Herculean endeavour, requiring great physical strength, since the howling wind and raging, roaring water were relentlessly trying to hammer and tear it from his hand.

Jock McGregor and Taff Burgess were seated right in front of him, both leaning forward, heads bowed, stretched out over the strapped-down weapons and equipment. In charge of the waterproof PRC 319 radio, Jock was keeping in contact with Captain Grenville in the larger Gemini, which, a good distance ahead of them, kept disappearing in immense fountains of spray, then materializing again, often on the crest of giant waves. It seemed to float high above them, almost touching the black, tumultuous clouds, as if about to take wing.

'Christ, Taff!' Gumboot bawled back over his hunched shoulder. 'What the fuck are you doin' back there? This inflatable's like a bloody buckin' bronco! Keep control of that rudder!'

'Go screw yourself, Gumboot,' Taff shouted against the roaring wind. 'If I can't control this rudder, no one can – not in this bloody sea.'

'Excuses, excuses – always bloody excuses!'

'If I didn't have my hand on this rudder, I'd shove it right down your tonsils.'

'You and whose army?'

Jock knew that the banter was simply a healthy way of letting off steam at difficult times. All the same, their conversation was distracting and could cause him to miss something on the radio. Glancing up at the raging sea, observing the immense, curling waves and dark, boiling sky, he decided to tell them to shut up, to enable him to make a call to Captain Grenville in the Gemini ahead. Even now, this was being carried aloft on the crest of a wave, only to be swept down the other side, out of sight once more.

At that moment, the corporal in charge of the small boat roped to the other large Gemini cried over the radio: 'Damn it! Our outboard motor's cut out! It's not working, Captain!'

'We'll try to tow you,' said Captain Marsh of the other large Gemini, 'but in this kind of wind . . . Damn, the tow rope's already too taut. I don't think it'll hold.'

Glancing ahead and to the side, Jock saw the

rope that tied his own and another small inflatable to Captain Grenville's large Gemini. It was being given enough slack to hold because Taff, controlling the rudder, was also driving the outboard motor and trying to keep up with the boat ahead. However, with its engine dead, the other inflatable's tow rope had stretched as tight as it could go and looked to be on the point of snapping in two.

Jock felt he should warn them. His stomach heaved as, about to make the call, his own, smaller Gemini, roped to the one in front, followed its dizzying course up the next wave, then plunged down the other side, into barrelling darkness and the deafening roar of the churning sea.

When it emerged, the outboard motor had cut out.

'What the hell . . .?' Taff bawled, furiously working the rudder, glancing back over his shoulder at the silent mechanism, which was smashing in and out of the water, but flapping about loosely. 'Fucking hell!' he exclaimed. 'The bastard's practically been torn off by the waves. We've no engine left, Jock.'

'Jesus Christ! What else?' Jock pleaded, glancing back at the smashed motor, then across the boiling, roaring sea just as the rope of the third small craft, being towed by the other big Gemini, snapped in two, with the two halves whipping up in the air like giant, crazed snakes, only to be slapped back down by the howling wind. Set free, the small inflatable, its outboard motor dead, went spinning away from the larger craft, completely out of control, then disappeared beyond a series of high waves. It did not reappear.

'Shit!' Gumboot exclaimed, his flinty eyes scanning the sea, fearlessly taking in all that was happening. 'I think we're fucked, mates.'

He was not far wrong. Even as Taff fought with the rudder and Jock checked the location of the boat ahead, the lack of an engine let the surging waves sweep their boat violently to the west, snapping the tow rope.

'We're adrift! Gumboot bawled.

Taff struggled with the rudder, trying to turn towards Captain Grenville's Gemini, but the loss of an outboard motor defeated him, giving the sea dominion. The inflatable was swept up on a wave, careered down the other side, miraculously survived a spinning tunnel of roaring water, then rushed farther westward. Grenville's Gemini soon disappeared, moving on towards Stromness and now hidden by the surging waves, while Taff, exhausted, struggling with his useless rudder, was forced to give up and let the raging sea take them where it would.

It took them towards Antarctica.

Captain Grenville watched the second dinghy disappear beyond the turbulent horizon with a deep feeling of shock. Now he was left with only one dinghy in tow, while the other large Gemini had none. He had just lost two boats and six good men, with little hope of getting them back. He could scarcely believe it.

Glancing in one direction, he saw only the raging sea and its soul mate, the cloud-black sky; glancing ahead he saw the jagged hills of Grass Island emerging out of the storm. He looked out to sea again, desperately hoping to spot the lost boats, but he saw only huge waves, one falling and breaking on the other with a terrible roar.

Praying to God that the men in the lost boats would be all right, though holding out little hope, he turned back to his own men and said, 'All right, we're still here, practically there, so let's make our insertion. That beach is only half a mile away and we're going straight onto it.'

The storm abated a little as they headed for the shore, but about 400 yards out, when the white, frozen hills were visible through the mist, snow started falling on them, as if to make up for the lessening wind. The men huddled up in their waterproof outfits and prepared for the landing.

Luckily, the closer they came to the shore, the less the wind blew and the more settled the formerly raging sea became. Slowing down their outboard motors, the pilots of the two large Geminis inched carefully into shallow waters, then stopped and anchored, enabling the men to clamber out and wade to the shore, carrying their light M16s above their heads.

'Leave the rest of the equipment in the boats,' Captain Grenville ordered. 'We may not be stopping here.'

Leaving his exhausted men on the beach, within sight of the inflatables bobbing out in shallow water, Grenville held his M16 at the ready and hurried up the snow-covered hill directly ahead. Reaching the summit, he was able to look across the small island to Leith Harbour, only two miles away. Blocks of ice were floating in the water, but the storm had abated. Glancing around him, Grenville saw nothing but other hills covered with snow and ice; there was no sign of Argentinian troops. Looking out to sea, he could not even see the British fleet; nor was there any sign of the two missing dinghies – only what now looked like calmer sea under a dark, stormy sky, from which snow was falling steadily. Satisfied, he returned to the men resting on the snow-covered, pebbled shore.

'There's no storm between here and Leith Harbour,' he said, 'so I think we should move on to South Georgia and set up our OPs. Let's do it now, before the storm reaches here or a new one starts up. Do you men think you're up to it?'

'Do birds sing?' one of the men asked. 'Do men shit? Of *course* we're up to it, boss.'

'That's the spirit, lads. So, let's get going.'

They returned to the boats, started the outboard motors and cruised around the small, bleak island. They then set off across the two miles of ice-filled water, heading straight for South Georgia. The sky was low and ominous, but the storm did not return, and the darkness, which had fallen with great speed, offered protection from Argentinian observation posts. Cruising slowly, quietly, between drifting blocks of ice, they managed to reach Stromness Bay without seeing, or even hearing, Argentinian patrol boats. However, just as Grenville was beginning to feel more confident, thinking his troubles were behind him, the blocks of ice gave way to drifting packs of gleaming, sharp ice splinters which punctured the inflatables, one after the other in rapid succession, causing the air to hiss out of them.

'Christ!' Captain Grenville exclaimed softly, then regained his sense of humour and said, 'OK, lads, abandon ship! Take everything but the rats.'

They were now only about thirty yards from the shore, in shallow, ice-filled water, which allowed them to clamber out of the hissing, sinking inflatables, form a chain from the boats to the shore, and pass the equipment along the human chain before the assault boats, crumpling pitifully, sank for good. Now, no matter what happened, they had no means of returning to the Fleet, hidden beyond the horizon.

Encircled by mountains that hid them from the Argentinians in Grytviken, they hid under an outcrop of rock until they had dried all of the equipment, shucked off their lifebelts, and were ready to march on in pursuit of locations suitable for observation posts.

'Since we can't get back to the fleet,' Grenville said, 'we'll just have to avoid the Argies and stay here until the assault begins. Bearing in mind that it can't begin until the fleet receives our recces, it's up to us to do the best we can and send back as much intelligence as possible.'

'Not much else to do around here,' a corporal said sardonically, 'so we might as well do that.'

'No belly dancers,' a trooper said. 'No strippers. No pubs full of beer. A man has to do something.'

'Then let's go,' Grenville said.

After checking his map for two areas of high ground overlooking Leith Harbour and Stromness Bay – though not so obvious that the Argentinians would expect to find them there – Grenville broke the remaining members of his troop into two separate units, one to establish an observation post in the hills above Leith, the other, his own, to establish one above Stromness. He then marched his own team up to his selected vantage point overlooking both areas, where they settled down to building their OP.

Thirty years earlier both areas had been whaling stations, boasting hundreds of workers, but now they were virtually deserted and, viewed from the wind-whipped, moaning hills, they revealed themselves as no more than a few scattered lights in the night's chill, occasionally moonlit, darkness.

Though sited on high ground to provide the best possible view of enemy activities and enable transmission of information back to base, the OP had to be dug into the earth to screen it from enemy eyes. In this instance, Grenville remained on guard and radio watch while his three troopers, using spades and pickaxes, dug the hole in which they would stay until the assault came.

Because Grenville had no idea when the assault from the fleet would take place, he anticipated a long stay here and therefore had the men dig a rectangular layout, rather than the short-term star shape. The spoil from their digging was removed in bergens and sprinkled unobtrusively over the ground a good distance from the OP. Once this had been done, the hole was lined with plastic sheets and the troops put up a hessian screen, with a poncho and overhead camouflage net, supported by wooden stakes, iron pickets, and chicken wire, and including a camouflaged entry and exit hole. When this business was completed; the troopers, wearing face veils and thick leather gloves, settled down in the OP, taking turns as telescope observer and sentry, as well as in the rest bays, with their kit-well, including the weapons, piled up in the middle.

From the completed OP Grenville's signaller was able to establish communications with the *Antrim*, thus enabling Grenville to inform his OC about what had happened to him and the others. In return, he was informed that one of the missing boats had been found by helicopter and the crew returned safely to the fleet. The other missing boat, containing Corporal Jock McGregor and troopers Taff Burgess and Gumboot Gillis, was still missing, its occupants presumed drowned.

Disturbed by that news, Grenville tried not to show it and instead encouraged his men to settle down to the business of observing Argentinian movements from their OP.

The wind howled eerily all night. The snow covered them like a blanket. Before long, they were cramped, cold and uncomfortable, boots wet, limbs numbed by constricted blood. For most it would have been a night in hell, but Grenville and his men had been trained for this.

'Yesterday afternoon,' Major Parkinson informed the OC of the Squadron, in the company of Captain Hailsham and Sergeant Ricketts in the OC's private cabin aboard the *Antrim*, now anchored with the other ships far north of South Georgia, 'an Argentinian submarine was observed reconnoitring the coastline of the island, almost certainly looking for signs of British landings.'

'Did they see anything?'

'We don't think so.'

'But some of our men are safely ashore.'

'Correct. Captain Grenville managed to make it with three of the Geminis, two large and one small, after which he divided the men into two groups to set up well-hidden OPs in Leith and Stromness. We're now in radio contact.'

'What about the submarine?'

'The first good news is that while searching for it in his helo, Lieutenant-Commander Pedler spotted one of the missing SAS inflatables and lifted its three men to safety.'

'Which men?'

'Corporal Woodward and troopers Blakely and Powell.'

'What about the inflatable?'

'Corporal Woodward ensured that it would sink before letting himself be lifted up. Both Woodward and Pedler have confirmed that it sank before they left the area.'

'Excellent. Any sign of the second lost inflatable?'

'No, boss. Either it sank or it's been blown clear of the island, into the southern ocean.'

The OC just nodded, revealing little emotion. 'And the Argentinian submarine?'

'According to Argentinian radio signals monitored by the *Endurance* while she was anchored in Hound Bay, the submarine recently landed reinforcements on the island, bringing the Argentinian garrison strength up to about 140 men.'

'That's useful information, Major Parkinson, but not too encouraging.'

'Then let me encourage you, boss. Not long before dawn, Pedler's helo spotted the submarine on the surface as she sailed over the shallows of Cumberland Bay, heading out to look for the British fleet. He straddled her with two depth-charges. Soon afterwards, she was attacked by the *Endurance*'s Wasp and the Lynx from the destroyer HMS *Brilliant*. Those helicopters forced the submarine to run for King Edward's Point, with her conning tower damaged and listing after being hit by missiles.'

'That's good news, certainly. A real setback for the Argentinians. Let's hope the blighter sinks before it reaches King Edward's Point or at least is incapacitated when it gets there, which will set them back even more.' The OC sipped some coffee, put his cup down, then glanced at the map pinned on the wall, showing South Georgia and the surrounding area, with Leith Harbour, Stromness Bay and Grytviken clearly marked. 'Twenty-four hours ago,' he continued, 'just before our ships scattered north, Major Sheridan gave his final orders for an immediate landing to seize Leith and Stromness, even though our recces there are incomplete.'

'A bit early, I'd have thought,' Parkinson said.

'And what do *you* think, Sergeant?' the OC, grinning slyly, asked Ricketts. 'I want to hear from the lower ranks.'

'I think he's keen to get his men ashore.'

'Why would that be?'

'Probably because there's been pressure from London to take the islands quickly.'

'For what reason?'

'As a further indication of Britain's political resolve. I think it makes sense, boss.'

'It's good to know that the lower ranks are well informed. Yes, Sergeant, it makes sense.' The OC smiled again, then glanced at the map of South Georgia. 'With the *Tidespring* still replenishing her tanks, M Company is six hours or more away from the coast. A landing force will therefore have to be improvised if we're to exploit the Argentinians' setback. In fact this has already been arranged between me and Major Sheridan. We're forming a quick reaction force of three composite troops aboard this very ship. Major Parkinson will lead the Mountain and remaining Boat troops; 2 SBS and the recce sections of

42 Commando will form a second composite troop; and the third troop will be made up from commando mortar-men and the ship's Marines.'

'That only comes to about seventy-five men,' Major Parkinson said. 'Scarcely more than half the strength of the Argentinian garrison.'

'You think the odds are too great?' the OC asked.

'Who dares wins,' Ricketts said.

After three days in his OP overlooking Stromness, Captain Grenville was virtually buried in snow, feeling as miserable as his SAS troop looked, but refusing to give in to self-pity and resolutely sending back to the fleet every scrap of information he had picked up on the movements of the Argentinians, both on land and out at sea, including the frequent submarine patrols out of Leith Harbour. This information had come from a combination of radio interception and visual observation, the latter either from foot patrols which went dangerously close to the Argentinian bases, to spy on them at close quarters, or by using binoculars to scan the sea from the hills. Either way, it was meticulously recorded and radioed back to the fleet under the most uncomfortable, dangerous circumstances.

The men, though now buried in snow, smelling their own shit and piss, increasingly frozen and exhausted, would hold out to the bitter end.

Like his men, Grenville was able and willing to hold out as long as necessary, but during the early afternoon of that third grim day, with the snow still falling on him, he was finding it difficult because of his concern for the three men still missing: Corporal Jock McGregor and troopers Taff Burgess and Gumboot Gillis – good men all, now almost certainly drowned because of the weather. Given the nature of the Fortuna Glacier fiasco, the way in which the other men had been lost was dreadfully ironic.

Determined not to give in to morbid thoughts, and to uphold the precepts of the SAS by sticking it out as long as possible, Grenville gazed over the piled-up snow of his OP to observe Grass Island and, beyond it, the vast, grey, empty sea, now dimly, eerily lit by early afternoon's pale sun.

Suddenly a series of fiery flickerings illuminated the horizon. Then the distant roar of the fleet's big guns made the whole OP shake. The first shells exploded far below, sending smoke billowing up from the lower slopes of Leith Harbour and Stromness Bay.

The assault had begun.

6

With the thunder of the *Antrim*'s two 114mm guns pounding in their ears, Major Parkinson and his men, including Captain Hailsham and Sergeant Ricketts, all in full battle kit, filed into the helicopters clamped to the ship's landing pads. Taking his seat between big Andrew and Baby Face, Ricketts strapped himself in, then glanced out through the rain-streaked window as the ship swayed and tilted to one side. The sea, which was full of deep swells, seemed very far below him. When he looked in the other direction, back towards the ship, he saw the big guns jolting each time they fired, wreathing the whole deck in smoke.

The combined bedlam of the helicopters and the guns was like the end of the world and became even worse when, with more noise and much shuddering, the holding clamps were released and the helicopters lifted off the deck. They ascended vertically, hovered above the landing pad, moved sideways to hover right above the sea, then headed for shore.

'About time,' Danny said, clutching his high-velocity M16A2 assault rifle and instinctively running his fingers over his webbing and 30-round box magazines. 'I'm dead keen to go and take out those Argies.'

'We're not taking anyone out,' Ricketts said. 'We're just trying to scare them. We want their surrender.'

'They made Royal Marines lie belly-down on the ground,' Danny replied, with the dulcet tones of a choirboy. 'What we want is their balls.'

'I'll second that,' Paddy said.

Even as the helos headed for the shore, the big guns of the *Antrim* and the *Plymouth* were continuing to pound in a relentless onslaught that would ensure the landing area and Brown Mountain, which dominated it, were clear of Argentinians. Looking across that short stretch of mottled sea, Ricketts saw the billowing columns of smoke where the shells were exploding.

'What a fucking noise,' Paddy said. 'We should have plugged up our ears.'

'Those guns sound like music to me,' big

Andrew replied as he jotted down more words in his notebook. 'I take heart from that sound.'

'More poetry, is it?' Paddy asked. 'More shite for the Imperial War Museum?'

'The true artist is rarely appreciated in his own time,' Andrew said, closing the notebook and slipping it into one of the zipped pockets of his jacket. 'My day will come.'

The shore was now rushing at them, pebbled, streaked with snow, with the shells exploding further inland, on the hills of Brown Mountain. Ricketts glanced westward, beyond the other two helicopters, to where sea and sky met, thinking bitterly of how Taff, Jock and Gumboot had been lost. Either they had drowned or were still drifting helplessly towards the Antarctic, in which case they would almost certainly freeze to death, after suffering hypothermia and frostbite. A hell of a way to go.

When he looked down, he saw the shore whipping out of view, to give way to the inland hills and valleys, mostly barren and brown, though brightened here and there by snow and frost. The ground was rushing up at him.

'We're coming in!' Major Parkinson shouted from up front. 'Prepare for the landing!'

The men unclipped their safety belts and

stood awkwardly in a metallic jangle of rifles, hand-grenades, bayonets, ammunition belts and water bottles. Burdened with bergens, bulky in their Gore-tex jackets, they resembled strange, hunchbacked animals. The helo shuddered as it slowed down, hovering right above the ground. The door opened with a screech as it descended, letting the cold air come howling in.

Major Parkinson was at the opening, standing beside Captain Hailsham, a radio-telephone held up to his ear, his free hand firmly gripping a support as the wind beat wildly at him, threatening to suck him out and spin him away like a twig.

As they approached the ground, the rotors whipped up dirt and snow, made foliage dance and bend, creating a minor hurricane that shook the whole helo. 'Go! Go! Go!' Parkinson bawled – and the first man disappeared through the opening before the helicopter had touched down. It did so as the second man went out and the queue inched towards the door. The helo was still bouncing lightly on its landing skis as Ricketts followed the others out, landing safely on the snowy, frosted ground.

He fanned out with the men already advancing, leaning forward to escape the drag of the whirlwind created by the helo's spinning, roaring rotors. The men all had their weapons at the ready, but there was no sign of enemy troops – only that desolate, rolling landscape, blanketed in snow and frost, viewed hazily through a white-gauze curtain of loose snow whipped up by the spinning rotors.

'Let's go! Move out!'

They were on the lower slopes of Hestesletten, a high valley located about a mile south-east of the former British Antarctic Survey buildings on King Edward's Point and separated from it by Brown Mountain. The sea surrounded them on all sides, flat and featureless from the heights, but the Fleet was now clearly visible, with its aircraft-carriers, destroyers, frigates, tankers and supply ships spread out as far back as the horizon.

The guns of the *Antrim* and the *Plymouth* were still firing, laying down a barrage that would methodically move forward to within 800 yards of the enemy position, the aim being to demoralize them rather than cause physical damage – a further ploy in the diplomatic war to recapture the Falklands. Plumes of smoke were still billowing up from the other side of Brown Mountain as the shells fell relentlessly around King Edward's Point.

'That's it,' Paddy said. 'Pound the shite out of

the bastards. Make 'em blind, deaf and dumb before we get there. Give them all diarrhoea.'

'Shut up, Paddy,' Ricketts said without malice. 'Come on, men, let's move out!'

The helos were already taking off again, whipping up more soil, stones and loose snow, as the men fanned out and started uphill, burdened under their bergens and carrying an assortment of firepower, including Heckler & Koch MPA3 sub-machine-guns, M16A2 assault rifles, 7.62mm self-loading rifles, Browning 9mm high-power handguns, 81mm mortars, fragmentation, white-phosphorus and smoke grenades, plus all the ammunition required for them. Also taken along were laser rangefinders, thermal imagers for night viewing, a couple of radios and, in the heavily loaded bergens, food, drink, toiletries and first-aid kits.

As the guns roared out at sea and shells exploded on the far side of Brown Mountain, filling the air beyond the summit with billowing clouds of smoke that dispersed under sullen clouds, the men marched uphill with weapons at the ready.

'We're being followed by the other composite troops being landed by boat,' Major Parkinson explained with the suppressed glee of an ageing officer who was having his last fling. 'The plan is to meet at the British Antarctic Survey buildings on King Edward's Point, so let's fan out and head for that very place.'

'Sure thing, boss,' Ricketts said, glancing back over his shoulder, down the slopes of the mountain, to see half a dozen landing-craft cutting a swathe through the sea as they surged away from the fleet, heading for the shore, under the protection of Sea King heli-copters.

Glancing left and right, to where his men had fanned out along the frosty slopes of brown grass and stone, Ricketts saw the monolithic Trooper Andrew Winston – the only man who didn't appear dwarfed by his bergen and other equip-ment – striding fearlessly towards the crest of the mountain. Beside him, Baby Face Porter seemed very slight indeed, though he looked distinctly energetic, as he always did when properly engaged.

Proud of his men, Ricketts was also intrigued by them: touched by the poet hidden in Trooper Winston's huge body; just as he was amused by the gap between young Danny's naïvety when it came to his beloved Darlene, whom Ricketts thought was a tart, and his finely honed, assured killer's instincts when it came to warfare. 'Baby Face' indeed!

Then there was Corporal Paddy Clarke, who, barely educated and far from sophisticated, had never been known to make a mistake in action. He was one of the best of the SAS.

Ricketts studied them with pride, glad to be one of them, but inevitably they made him think of the men missing at sea – Gumboot Gillis and Taff Burgess, and Jock McGregor – and those thoughts, which were depressing, were also dangerously distracting and therefore had to be expunged ruthlessly from his mind, so that he could concentrate on the job at hand. The surrounding hills could be filled with Argentinian troops, so this was no time for mournful thoughts.

Out at sea, the big guns of the *Antrim* and the *Plymouth* were pounding away. More smoke was billowing up from beyond the summit of Brown Mountain, obviously rising from the explosions in the area of King Edward's Point and Grytviken, on the opposite side of the bay.

'Spread out even more!' Major Parkinson shouted, trying to make himself heard above the thunder of the big guns and the roar of the explosions. 'There could be mines in this area, so keep your eyes well peeled.'

They marched for another hour in a tense, watchful silence, relieved only by the booming of the guns out at sea and the explosions from the far side of the mountain. The hills they were crossing seemed devoid of all life, though the wind was constantly moving the sparse foliage, keeping the men on edge, aiming their weapons at anything that moved, ever ready to open fire.

When another hour had passed, Ricketts was practically yearning to engage the enemy, if only to find relief from this nerve-racking non-event of a march. Sometimes, when in action, he thought of his wife and children – as he was now doing occasionally – but mostly his thoughts drifted to previous engagements, the good and bad experiences they had given him – successful raids, disasters or the death of friends, like Lampton in Belfast. Such recollections were, at least, a way of staying focused on all the skills he had been taught, reminding him that the enemy could be all around him, watching him right now.

Glancing to his left, Ricketts saw the quick movement of tussocks of grass, followed by what appeared to be the rise and fall of a balaclava helmet. Without thinking twice, he called out a warning, dropped to his knees and let rip with a burst of gunfire from his M16A2. The noise was shocking, reverberating around the hills, and the tussocks of grass he had seen moving were torn apart by the bullets, exploding into the air.

A blood-curdling screeching was heard as the other men also opened fire. Ricketts jumped up and ran towards the enemy position, followed almost immediately by the other men. The inhuman sound continued, but no fire was returned as Ricketts and the others advanced, weapons at the ready, to where the remaining grass, now thrashing wildly, was soaked in fresh blood. They all studied the victim.

'Shit!' Andrew exclaimed.

'So *that's* what an Argie looks like!' Paddy said, grinning mockingly at Ricketts. 'Good one, Sarge!'

They had just shot an elephant seal, which was still screaming and writhing in agony in its own blood, its white ribs smashed and exposed through torn, flapping skin, its eyes wild with shock.

'Oh, God,' Ricketts said.

There was a sudden, short burst of fire from an M16 assault rifle and the seal shuddered violently, then was still.

Baby Face, who had fired the shots, stepped forward, gently kicked the seal with his boot, checking that it was dead, then stepped back again.

'Just putting it out of its misery,' he said, calmly checking his weapon. 'Only thing to do.'

'Yeah, right,' Paddy said after too long a silence.

'Let's move on,' Major Parkinson ordered, leading the way, now in sight of the summit of the hill and keen to get there. 'And if anything else moves, shoot it,' he added. 'We can't take chances, lads.'

In fact, though more than one elephant seal copped it by making a sudden movement and going down in a hail of bullets before the men finally reached the summit, no Argentinian troops were seen on the mountain range.

From the mountain's summit, through a curtain of smoke thrown up by the exploding shells of the fleet, they could see only what looked like a deserted settlement with white flags flying from several buildings – though the Argentinian flag still flew from its mast near the headquarters, formerly the British Antarctic Survey settlement, on King Edward's Point.

Most of the barrage had been laid down with air-burst shells, but other shells from the fleet had filled the hills above the rocky cove with ugly black holes. Nevertheless, the barrage had, as planned, been stopped before reaching the cove itself, leaving the white-walled, red-roofed buildings on King Edward's Point intact, as was the old whaling station of Grytviken on the opposite shore.

The Argentinian submarine damaged by AS 12 missiles had indeed managed to limp into harbour and was beached there, right in front of the untouched settlement.

'Those *are* white flags we're seeing, are they not?' Major Parkinson asked rhetorically.

'Yes, boss,' Captain Hailsham said. 'Looks like the big guns did the trick.'

'Let's find out,' Parkinson said. 'Signaller! Get in touch with Major Sheridan on the *Antrim*, then give me that phone.' The trooper in charge of the PRC 319 did as he had been told, then handed the telephone to Parkinson. When he had finished speaking to Major Sheridan, Parkinson handed the phone back and turned to Hailsham and Ricketts. 'Excellent. Sheridan's already been in contact through the *Antrim*'s radio with the Argentinian headquarters in the Survey buildings and they've confirmed that they're eager to surrender. However, they also warned that there are minefields laid in defence of their weapon pits.'

'Then I suggest we go in via the shore,' Captain Hailsham said. 'As their submarines have been moving in and out of there, we can assume they won't have mined that area.'

'Right.' Parkinson turned to Ricketts. 'Move the men down to the shore, Sergeant. Ensure that they don't get trigger-happy. If the Argies emerge with their hands up – as I think they will – let them come out in one piece.'

'Yes, boss. Will do.'

Ricketts called the men together and told them what was happening. 'So keep your fingers off the triggers,' he added, 'if they come out with their hands up.'

'Politics!' Paddy said in disgust, then spat on the ground.

'If I step on a mine going down there,' big Andrew said, 'I want you guys to take that settlement apart.'

'That's a *British* settlement,' Danny reminded him. 'That's why the fleet didn't shell it.'

'Very kind of them, I'm sure. I bet the Argies are real pleased. We lost at least three men out on that sea while those Argie bastards sat down there laughing.'

'Bullshit,' Ricketts said, staring up at Andrew's angry brown eyes. 'The fact that we lost three men at sea isn't an issue here. This isn't the bloody Boy Scouts, Trooper – it's the SAS – and any of you could cop it at any time, which is no cause for bitching. It's just part of the job.'

'Yes, boss.'

'Let's go.'

Led by Parkinson and Hailsham, they marched across hills pock-marked by scorched shell holes, high above the settlement, then went carefully downhill towards the shore, keeping their eyes peeled for buried mines. No mines went off, no one was hurt, and just as they reached the shore and were advancing on the tall radio towers in front of the settlement, Argentinian soldiers started emerging from the buildings, a few waving white flags, the others raising their hands in the air.

'Looks like you were right, boss,' Ricketts said.

'Yes,' Parkinson replied. 'Surrender it is.'

Even as some of the SAS troop fanned out to surround the Argentinians and keep them under cover, others entered the buildings to check for snipers and booby traps.

'Not too impressive, are they?' Paddy mused, studying the unshaven, frightened men coming out of the buildings with their hands raised. 'They look like a bunch of fucking schoolkids.'

'They're mostly conscripts,' Andrew explained. 'Not professional soldiers. Most of them didn't even want to fight this war. The poor sods were forced into it.'

'My heart bleeds for them,' Paddy said.

'Mine doesn't,' Danny said. 'You don't put Royal Marines on the ground and then take bleedin' photographs.'

'I shudder to think what this kid would be feeling,' Paddy said to Andrew, 'if those Royal Marines had been SAS troopers.'

'If they had been,' Andrew replied, indicating the prisoners with a nod of his head, 'these poor bastards wouldn't be alive right now. Danny Boy would have slaughtered them.'

'Yeah,' Paddy said, 'I believe he would have.'

Parkinson and Hailsham, carefully covered by Ricketts, Andrew, Paddy and Danny, advanced to meet the Argentinian captain walking cautiously towards them beside a corporal holding a makeshift, wind-blown white flag. The officer wasn't young and he carried himself with quiet dignity. When he reached Parkinson, his back stiffened and he saluted. Parkinson returned the salute.

'Captain Bicain,' the Argentinian said in good English, introducing himself. 'As Commander of this garrison, I wish to formally offer our surrender.'

'Thank you, Captain,' Parkinson replied. 'I accept your surrender on a temporary basis. The formal acceptance will take place tomorrow when more British troops, including my superiors, fly into Leith. In the meantime, we'll look after your men and treat you with respect.'

'Of course,' Captain Bicain said with some pride and a distinct touch of arrogance. 'Why not? We have only been performing our duty in this little gesture.'

'A little gesture?' Parkinson asked. 'This is a war!'

Captain Bicain smiled, shrugged, and shook his head in denial. 'A war? No, Captain, it was merely a gesture. *El gesto de las Malvinas* – the Falklands gesture. That's what we call it in Argentina, and that's what it is. This is no real war, Captain.'

'Call it what you will,' Parkinson replied, his cheeks reddening with anger, 'but please consider yourself a prisoner of war – as are all of your troops. For the time being, at least until the others arrive, we'll return you to your quarters and keep you under guard. Hopefully you'll be shipped out tomorrow.'

'Thank you,' Captain Bicain said, kicking his heels and saluting again. He was then marched away by Captain Hailsham and two SAS troopers, disappearing into the building from which he had just emerged as Parkinson's men surrounded the other, less proud Argentinians.

'A gesture!' Parkinson exclaimed in disgust. 'I suppose that will ease the national conscience – not war: a mere gesture. Pretty neat, yes?'

He was addressing Captain Grenville, who merely grinned. 'Come on, Captain,' Parkinson said, 'let's investigate this settlement thoroughly. Our job isn't finished yet.'

'Yes, boss, let's do that.'

They were just about to march off when a Lynx helicopter descended, whipping up a wind that beat wildly at them and filled the air with flying pebbles. It landed on the shore near the radio antennae.

Jock, Taff and Gumboot jumped out of the helicopter, whooping gleefully and raising their M16s above their heads. The rest of the troop, getting over their surprise, let out a mighty cheer.

'Drowned at sea?' Gumboot said, standing with Taff and Jock, surrounded by his mates, and studied mournfully by the defeated Argentinians. 'You gotta be joking, mate!'

'After being blown westward for a bit,' Taff explained, 'thinking we'd end up in Antarctica, we managed to wade ashore on the north coast of Stromness Bay, about four kilos from our intended landing point.'

'We've been there for the past three days,' Jock added, 'freezing our nuts off, but maintaining radio silence so as not to fuck up this operation. Then, when you lot landed, we sent out a SARBE radio signal and got picked up by the helo.'

'I know you lot were secretly *hoping* we'd copped it,' Gumboot said with a wide grin, 'but unfortunately for you, here we are, fit and rarin' to go.'

'And still good with the bullshit,' Ricketts said, grinning. 'OK, men, let's get back to work. I want all the Argentinian weapons collected and laid out here on the ground. Then search the Argies and bed them down for the night. We've no time to listen to Gumboot's tall tales. We've got a long wait ahead of us.'

Laughing, unable to hide their delight, the men either patted Gumboot, Taff and Jock on the back or more formally shook them by the hand, before going back to the job in hand.

The enemy weapons were collected and piled up in front of the HQ, the Argentinians were searched, locked up and kept under guard in the settlement buildings, and the SAS settled down to wait for the arrival of the men from the landing-craft.

Next morning, when the replacements had arrived, SAS and SBS teams flew into Leith and formally accepted the surrender of its garrison.

The Argentinian flag was lowered and the White Ensign was soon fluttering alongside the Union Jack, over Grytviken.

'South Georgia's been recaptured,' Major Parkinson announced proudly to his men. 'Now it's on to the Falklands.'

7

While D Squadron, under the temporary command of Captain Hailsham, were finishing off their task in South Georgia, Major Parkinson and Captain Grenville of the Boat Troop were flown out on a 772 Naval Air Squadron Wessex Mark 5 to join G Squadron on the fleet replenishment ship, the 22,890-ton Royal Fleet Auxiliary *Resource*.

The RFA *Resource* had a helicopter flight deck from which troopers could be flown to other ships, including HMS Hermes, now leading the naval battle group towards the Falklands. It was not unusual, therefore, that when the Wessex Mark 5 came in to land, other matt olive-drab helicopters were circling above, also waiting to land, while the Royal Naval Squadron ground crew and frantic flight-deck parties busily loaded the helos, either by hand or with jackstay rigs.

After disembarking onto the noisy, seemingly chaotic flight deck, high above the stormy sea, Parkinson and Grenville were met by Navy Chief Petty Officer Ken Brown who guided them through the ship's labyrinthine corridors and hatchways to the surprisingly large briefing room. There they partook of tea and sandwiches while Lieutenant-Commander Chris Holdfield of Naval Intelligence and Lieutenant-Colonel Adrian Granthorpe of SAS Intelligence, the much-maligned 'green slime', discussed their plans for the invasion of the Falkland Islands.

'How can we be sure that we won't reach an agreement with the Argentinians?' was Parkinson's first question. 'Now that we've recaptured South Georgia, they just might capitulate.'

'No, they won't,' Lieutenant-Colonel Granthorpe replied. 'They're now in too deep to back out with dignity. Neither the recapture of South Georgia nor any kind of diplomacy will be enough to get the Argentinians to voluntarily hand back the islands. We've checked this with Whitehall and they agree. It's just not going to happen.'

'I see,' Parkinson said, surprisingly guilty at how pleased he felt to know that conflict was coming. 'So what are you planning?'

'First, we use the whole fleet as a threat to

the occupation forces,' Lieutenant-Commander Holdfield informed him, 'then we put a landing force ashore.'

'Which is where we come in.'

'Correct,' Granthorpe said. 'However, before any landing can be made, we need to know the exact disposition of the Argentinian garrison's defences. So far we've assessed most of them to be dug in around Port Stanley, with the heaviest concentration facing south-west to prevent an advance along the road from Fitzroy. Unfortunately, that's about all we've managed to confirm so far.'

'No aerial or satellite pictures available?' Parkinson asked.

'None. And most of their defences are well camouflaged. For this reason, what we now require is good, old-fashioned, eyeball recces, for which we think the SAS and SBS are ideally suited.'

'Deep-penetration raids.'

'Exactly. These should cover not only the two main islands of East and West Falkland, but also some of the smaller islands around the coastline.'

'That's a lot of coastline,' Captain Grenville pointed out. 'Approximately '15,000 kilometres.'

'The SBS has spoken,' Granthorpe said with a smile. 'Was that an observation or a complaint?'

'Purely an observation.'

'I'm delighted to hear it.' Granthorpe turned to Major Parkinson. 'What are your problems?'

'The two main islands,' Parkinson replied, 'have a total area nearly equivalent to that of Wales, with a terrain like Dartmoor – windswept, rough pasture, no trees. However, there are many bogs and rock runs of slippery, moss-sided boulders, which in some runs are a metre or more across. To make matters worse, although the hills along the northern half of East Falkland rise to only 450 metres on Mount Kent, their climate is like that on English hills of twice that height. I think even the Special Forces will have a considerable problem in surviving in such conditions for lengthy periods of time – let alone doing so without being detected by the Argentinians.'

'This won't be made any easier,' Grenville added, 'by the fact that the Argentinians, at least according to our intelligence reports, are still in fighting spirit and have effective radio direction-finding equipment. They could use those to pick up our signals and locate the whereabouts of our OPs.'

'That's a chance you'll have to take,' Granthorpe replied. 'It's imperative that we reconnoitre all areas dominated by the enemy on East Falkland. We also have to maintain close observation of the garrisons on West Falkland.'

Lieutenant-Commander Holdfield jabbed his finger at the large map pinned to the board behind him. 'The latter lies 20 kilometres to the north, across Falkland Sound from the eastern island. Not too great a distance between them. In broad terms, therefore, the plan is to land on East Falkland sufficiently far from Port Stanley's airfield and large garrison, to enable a beachhead to be established before it can be heavily counter-attacked. From there, the main thrust of the attack will cross the mountains, where, as we believe, the Argentinians won't be expecting any major force. Once across these uplands, the back door to Stanley will be open.'

'Then let's kick it open,' Parkinson said. 'I'll arrange to fly my men out from South Georgia to the fleet and then land them from here.'

'Thank you, Major. Good luck.'

Chief Petty Officer Ken Brown led Parkinson and Grenville to the radio room, where with visibly mounting enthusiasm, Parkinson got in touch with South Georgia and issued instructions for the Squadron to be flown out. After receiving personal confirmation from Captain Hailsham, he switched off the microphone, turned to face Captain Grenville, and raised his thumb triumphantly. Grenville did the same, grinning lopsidedly, then he and Parkinson were led out of the radio cabin by Brown who, once he had them in the corridor, turned back to face them.

'So where do we make our HQ?' Parkinson asked him.

'Well, sir . . .' Chief Petty Officer Brown tried to hide a helpless grin by coughing into his fist. 'Actually, the only location I could find was the presently unused ladies' toilet?'

Parkinson stared steadily at him for a moment, then asked, as if deaf: 'Did you say the ladies' toilet?'

'Yes, sir,' Brown replied, now grinning openly. 'Sorry, but it's the only available room.' He spread his hands in the air in an expansive gesture. 'It's big, sir, believe me. Lots of space in there. We've already installed radios, and tables and chairs. Even a hot-drinks machine – soup, coffee and tea. If you need anything else, just ask. I think you'll be happy there.'

'You think this is funny, Petty Officer?'

'Absolutely not. No, sir!'

'Then get that grin off your face and take us to see it.'

'Of course. This way, sir.' Still grinning, the Chief Petty Officer led them through a hatchway, down a couple of flights of stairs, and through a dimly lit, smoke-filled hold filled with half-naked troops resting on tiers of bunks, in a tangle of clothing and equipment, to another corridor. The ladies' toilet was located at the end of it. 'This is it, sir,' Brown said, opening the door and waving them in.

Parkinson stepped in first, followed by Grenville and Brown, and thoughtfully studied the room. It was indeed surprisingly large, with a row of cubicles along one wall, a radio system resting on a bench against the opposite wall, a couple of portholes to one side, giving a view of the sea, and three folding tables, placed together in the middle, surrounded by hard chairs. A blackboard on a stand had been placed equidistant between the portholes, with a map of the Falkland Islands and tide charts already pinned to it.

Parkinson nodded. 'I'm impressed, Petty Officer. I think this should be sufficient unto our needs. So where do we sleep?'

'In cabins in the officers' quarters, sir. Back

where we came from. You'll find your name on the door and the key in the lock.'

'You have thieves aboard this ship, Petty Officer?'

'Nothing is perfect under the sun or moon. In truth, the odd item goes missing, sir.'

'The SAS don't steal from each other. Perhaps you should join us.'

'That's a very kind invitation, sir, but I'm not as young as I used to be.'

Parkinson smiled at that. 'Very good, Petty Officer. I'm sure we can find our way back to our cabins. Your responsibilities end here.'

'Thank you, sir. My pleasure.'

Still grinning, the Chief Petty Officer departed, leaving Parkinson and Grenville alone in the room. Now also both smiling, they studied the room, then faced one another.

'So, what do you really think?' Grenville asked.

'I think it's fine,' Parkinson said. 'If nothing else, it should feed a few fantasies. Let's go up on deck.'

Leaving the ladies' toilet and closing the door, they made their way back along the corridor, through the hold filled with troops, and back up a series of ladders to the helicopter flight deck, where other troops were being cross-decked and helos being loaded with the aid of bright-yellow jackstay rigs. Other ships, including destroyers and aircraft carriers, were spread across the stormy sea to form a great armada, with aircraft taking off and landing constantly, flying between the airborne helicopters with breathtaking precision.

'Modern warfare,' Parkinson said to Grenville, 'is truly spectacular.'

'They don't make movies like this any more,' Grenville replied. 'Their budgets won't wear it.'

'I'm going to miss it, Laurence.'

'Yes, boss, I'm sure you will.'

Gripping the wet railing, letting the beating spray soak his face, Parkinson surveyed the scene with a helpless feeling of loss, remembering that his time with the SAS would soon be up, putting an end to the most exciting and challenging days of his life.

Coming to the SAS, like his father-in-law, from the Durham Light Infantry, he had taken part in the assault on the Jebel Akhdar in Oman in 1959, when he was only 22; organized a series of cross-border raids in Borneo in 1964, served in Northern Ireland throughout the troubled 1970s, and even helped orchestrate the daring rescue during the Iranian Embassy siege of 1980. Those were adventures a man didn't easily forget.

A military man by inclination as well as upbringing, he had a restless personality, needed constant distraction and could imagine no life outside the Regiment. Yet at 44, age was catching up with him, his time with the Regiment was running out, and unless something unexpected turned up elsewhere, this would almost certainly be his last engagement. With luck, he might be given a desk job back in England, in the Intelligence Corps at Stirling Lines, but even that wasn't guaranteed – and other options were limited.

The thought of an administrative position, shuffling papers instead of men, endorsing plans instead of making them, filled Parkinson with immeasurable gloom. Nor was he thrilled by the notion of taking early retirement and tending the garden of his house in Hereford, attractive though it was.

Even at his age, he now realized, he was not a man cut out for a 'normal' life. So, as he gazed at the ships spread out on the stormy sea, at the roaring planes and helicopters, he accepted that he was where he belonged and would not enjoy leaving it. Thank God for this campaign.

'I think the use of four-man patrols,' Parkinson said to Captain Grenville, needing to distract himself from his thoughts, 'is the best way to recce East and West Falkland. Insert on both islands and disperse the groups in all directions, marching by night to predetermined locations for the individual observation posts. Staying as long as necessary. Radio silence to be maintained until they've done all they can do and need lifting out. With so many small groups scattered all over, the chances of being caught are much reduced and the amount of intelligence gathered should be greatly increased. Naturally, the assault will only begin when that intelligence is gathered and assessed.'

'I agree,' Grenville said.

'The Squadron arrives tomorrow morning. In the meantime, while we're waiting, we can study those maps in the ladies' toilet and select the best places for the OPs. Let's go back down, Laurence.'

'Might as well get started,' Grenville replied. 'No point standing up here all day.'

Parkinson could happily have stayed up there all day, watching the aircraft, helicopters, destroyers and carriers, but he knew that it would do him little good, apart from making him sadder. So, after taking one last, fond glance at the fleet, he sighed and followed Captain Grenville back into the ship, down into its labyrinth of hatchways and corridors and holds, past the hundreds of troops resting in tiers of steel bunks, smoking and reading and playing cards and writing letters, in dimly lit holds smelling of sweat and stale, smoke-filled air. They made their way through it all to the smaller, cleaner, much brighter ladies' toilet, where the SAS HQ was now formally located.

There, compelled to smile at their lot, they unpinned the maps on the blackboard, spread them out on the tables and proceeded to plan the Squadron's deep-penetration raids on East and West Falkland.

8

The least exciting, but most demanding and valuable, of all SAS operations is the setting up and maintaining of observation posts by four-man patrols for recces inside enemy territory.

Chosen as the Patrol Commander, or PC, on the Squadron's transfer from South Georgia to the *Resource*, Ricketts was allowed to select his own team. He chose three men with the required specialist skills for this particular job: Corporal Paddy Clarke, Trooper Danny Porter, and the big black poet, Trooper Andrew Winston.

Unable to conduct the normal rehearsal phase because they were aboard ship, Major Parkinson instead briefed his team with the aid of maps and aerial photos taken from previous aircraft reconnaissance flights. Ricketts was then given a day to prepare the patrol, make his own plan of operations based on the briefing and tell the other three what was expected of them. He then chose, and supervised the inspection of, the required equipment and weapons, ensuring that radios and batteries were working, ammunition was clean, grenades were primed, rations were drawn and water bottles were filled. The weapons, of which there were a considerable number and variety, were individually tested by being fired at the turbulent sea from the wind-blown deck of the ship.

When this was completed, the members of the patrol were flown in on two 845 Squadron Wessex Mark 5 helicopters, which carried them the 125 miles from the *Resource* to the LZ near the centre of East Falkland. The night flight took them over the misty north-west coast of the island, then through a high-ridged, moonlit valley that led to the uplands. Wearing his Passive Night Goggles, or PNGs, which enabled him to see in the dark, even if only in shades of dream-like blue, the pilot had no difficulty in landing them on the correct LZ. Nevertheless, he did not touch down for long.

Though the idea had been to land a long way from Port Stanley, to avoid contact with the enemy, then march for two or three days to the chosen site of the OP, there was still a real danger of being seen. The pilot therefore hardly touched the ground, but mostly hovered a couple of feet above it as the SAS team jumped down and offloaded their kit. While they were doing this, Danny moved away from the LZ to act as sentry, his M16A2 assault rifle held at the ready. When the kit had been offloaded, the men hurried out of the whirlwind created by the spinning rotors and Ricketts waved the helo away. It ascended vertically, all its lights dimmed, and soon disappeared in the cloudy night sky.

For the rest of this first night no words would be spoken. Instead, Ricketts ordered his men forward with the use of hand signals. Similar signals became the sole means of communication throughout the long, dangerous march, which took them along the valley, then over the hills, skirting around the frost gleaming in the moonlight, always on the lookout for mines. The wind moaned eerily around them, shaking the sparse vegetation, making it difficult to hear the sounds that would have warned them of Argentinian patrols. Everything that moved or made a sound was a potential enemy.

Using an illuminated compass, and aligning landmarks and roads with the map to follow their pre-set route, they moved along in file formation with young Danny well in front, taking the 'point' as lead scout and constantly checking what lay ahead through the night-sight of his rifle. The other three were strung out behind him, a good distance apart, maintaining irregular space between them to avoid unnecessary, or too many, casualties if attacked.

Marching behind Danny, Ricketts as PC was second in line, with Paddy Clarke third as signaller and big Andrew bringing up the rear as 'Tail-end Charlie'. As lead scout, Danny's job was to cover an arc-shaped area in front of the patrol. Ricketts and Paddy covered arcs to the left and right respectively, while Andrew had to regularly swing around to face the direction from which they had come, not only covering their rear but also ensuring that the patrol had no blind spots. Each man had to constantly look left and right for signs of enemy movement, as well as check repeatedly that the men in front and behind him were still in place. It was a rigorous, demanding routine that could not be ignored.

Added to the mental strain of being constantly alert while not allowed to speak, was the sheer physical burden imposed by the extra weight the men had to carry on this particular patrol. Each of their bergens now contained extra link belts, magazines, explosives and other ammunition; spare radios or replacement parts and batteries; rations and water; a sleeping bag and spare clothing. Even more demanding were personal kit belts laden with additional survival gear, medical equipment, water bottles, emergency rations, and smoke and fragmentation grenades. Together, the bergens, kit belts and extra weapons made up a load that would have broken most men's backs on a hike such as this.

Nevertheless, tough as it was, to Ricketts there was a sublime logic and beauty in the very concept of the four-man patrol. Conceived by David Stirling, the creator of the SAS, the four-man patrol was the basic building block of the Regiment, a self-contained unit within a Sabre squadron, and one dependent on the absolute, unwavering trust between each of its members. This was one of its salient features. Another was the fact that though each member of the patrol had been given Cross-Training, to enable him to be proficient in all SAS skills, for the purposes of the four-man patrol each had his specialist role: in this instance, Danny as scout and tracker, big Andrew as linguist and medic, Paddy as signaller and demolitions expert, and Ricketts as PC, which required the ability to take over any of the other specialist roles should one of the men be wounded or killed. The four-man patrol was, then, a microcosm of the whole SAS – and an almost perfect, self-sustaining unit into the bargain.

Now, marching across the hills of central East Falkland, Ricketts felt a great pride that overruled his simmering frustration at the patrol's lack of progress. Because of the constant threat of contact with enemy foot patrols or of being seen by helicopters with electronic aids or solar imagers, as well as the need to always be on the alert for mines, progress was agonizingly slow.

By dawn the next day, though they had neither seen nor been in contact with the enemy in any form, they had covered only ten miles.

'We'll have to hide during the day,' Ricketts said, finally able to speak because dawn was breaking through the mist wreathing the distant, brooding hills and the grey sea beyond. 'So make yourselves a scrape and climb into it. Danny and Andrew will sleep first. You and me, Paddy, we'll rest next. Two hours on and two off for each man. OK, lads, get at it.'

'Right, boss,' Paddy said, clearly relieved he could talk at last and continuing to do so as he unstrapped his short-handled spade. 'I don't mind waiting my turn. Very sensible to let the babies rest first. You can tell the poor shites are already worn out and in need of their sleep.'

'Beauty sleep,' Andrew replied, digging his spade into the hard, frozen soil. 'When you're born black and beautiful, like me, you've a moral responsibility to remain that way. So it's beauty sleep, you ugly little bastard. That's all I need it for.'

'If you're beautiful, I'm a fucking orang-utan.'

'Who's arguing?' Andrew asked.

'Just shut up and dig,' Ricketts said. 'We haven't got all day, lads.'

'Hard at it, boss,' Danny said, digging the soil out with his spade and throwing it over his frail shoulder. 'It'll be done in no time.'

The 'scrape' is a small hollow scraped or dug out of the ground and covered with wire, which is then strewn with local vegetation. It is a temporary measure used for short-term rest by day or night, in the lying-up position, or LUP, which is actually *any* position chosen by the patrol.

In this case the men only dug, or scraped, hollows deep enough to stretch out in – two to sleep under the camouflaged roof of wire and turf, the other two to keep watch, with these functions being swapped every two hours.

It made for a long, wet, cold and miserable day in which psychological as well as physical strength was vital. Nor could they eat properly, since they dare not light a fire or use their hexamine stove; instead, they could only sustain themselves with snacks of cheese, biscuits and chocolate.

Having been particularly well trained in combating the torments of the mind, as well as those of the body, Ricketts and his men, while not especially liking the scrapes, took them in their stride and managed to survive an interminable day, during which they saw only the occasional Argentinian helicopter or aircraft, but no foot patrols.

By nightfall, they were on their way again, on another long march through dark countryside.

Inevitably, as they neared Port Stanley, they began to see, if not Argentinian troops, at least their positions, from the camp-fires glowing eerily in the darkness. When this happened, they recced that area and kept a record of the information, but did not radio it back to the fleet, for fear that the signal might be picked up by the enemy, leading to their location.

Occasionally they saw enemy foot patrols moving, like them, through the moonlit, misty darkness. When this happened they always dropped to the ground and kept the enemy under cover. But they didn't open fire, since their first objective was reconnaissance, not combat, and an engagement, even if won, would have blown their cover to enemy intelligence, thus jeopardizing the forthcoming assault. Though the temptation to open fire was very strong, they never gave in to it.

If the first day had been bad, the second was even worse. They could do little but hide in their scrapes until darkness fell again, either sleeping or keeping their eyes peeled for signs of enemy activity. Their psychological training was such that they were able to do this, though all of them did it in different ways.

Phil Ricketts was married and the father of two children, Julia, 10, and Anna, 11. His wife, Maggie, came from Wood Green, North London, was working-class and proud of it. She was a secretary in a mortgage company in the high street, and was independent, sensual and good-humoured. While the marriage was secure and Ricketts truly loved his wife, he was sometimes disturbed by the fact that he preferred a man's life, away from home and hearth, doing what only men could do. This wasn't gambling or getting drunk or screwing around; it was simply the need for adventure and the sharpened sense of life offered by constant danger.

Before joining the Army, Ricketts had worked as a toolpusher on the North Sea oil rigs. Though it was hard, dangerous work, he had always enjoyed being out there more than being at home. Some men are like that – they can't lead a normal life – and when Ricketts finally accepted that he was one of that breed, he sensibly enlisted in the Army.

At first Maggie had resented it, wondering what she had done wrong, but when she realized that he simply loved doing a man's job – that no other woman was involved – she let him get on with it.

Soon, not satisfied with routine work for the Army, Ricketts had applied to join the SAS. Once accepted, he knew he had found his real home. Nevertheless, when he was in an OP or, as now, in a scrape, trying to combat the silence and interminable hours of inactivity, he did it by dwelling on his marriage and why it wasn't enough for him. He had yet to find an answer to all his questions, but thinking about them helped pass the time.

Like Ricketts, young Danny also thought about his home life, though his thoughts ran along simpler lines. Danny had never harboured a doubt about what he wanted to do in life: from childhood, he had wanted to be a soldier – something both of his parents fully understood. He had collected toy soldiers, read war books, watched war movies, played soldiers instead of cowboys and Indians, then started collecting guns. In this sense, he had been a soldier since he was a boy; it just took time to get there.

Danny had always been small and slim, rather quiet and good-natured, but his temper was legendary during his school years and led him into a lot of fights. By the time he left school, at 15, he had decided that he wanted to join the Army and would let nothing stop him. Before he joined, when he was 18, he already knew that eventually he would transfer to the legendary SAS – which he did, passing every test. When at last he was awarded the winged dagger, he was not in the least surprised.

Nevertheless, Danny's confidence in his ability as an SAS trooper was not matched by the same in his personal life. Born and bred in the Midlands, he was the only child of decent, working-class parents who showered a great deal of affection on him and would have been surprised, even shocked, to learn of his violent temper and frequent fist-fights.

Though the fights were real enough, Danny, on leaving school, was too obsessed with getting into the Army to learn about life's other realities, notably sex. Inexperienced with girls, he viewed them too romantically; so, when he first met Darlene in the company of some mates and their girlfriends in a local pub, he could not resist the knowledge that she fancied him and was not shy of showing it.

He loved Darlene desperately, though with certain residual doubts, most based on idle gossip from those very same mates who had intimated that her father was a boozing prat, her mother a tart, and that she, Darlene, was inclined the same way. Though Danny had tried to ignore such comments, which wounded him deeply, they kept coming back to stain his pure love with the shadow of doubt.

So, when in an OP, or LUP in his scrape, Danny wrestled with the gulf between his total confidence as a member of the Regiment and his doubts when it came to personal matters.

Nevertheless, he only did so with one half of his brain, while the other half – always alert and with natural killer's instincts – never failed to concentrate on the job in hand.

Andrew and Paddy had very different kinds of

thoughts, which were, in both cases, much less personal. Though not quite a born killer like Baby Face, big Andrew had remarkable physical strength and, like Ricketts, an unappeasable hunger for excitement. All brute energy on the one hand, he was highly imaginative on the other, and needed to express both aspects of himself to prevent his boiler from bursting. His poetry expressed the inner self – that gentle soul in the enormous body – and the SAS, with its discipline and challenges, took care of the physical side.

Also, as the SAS took no account of his black skin, but judged him purely on his merits, Andrew felt as natural in the Regiment as he did when expressing himself through his poetry.

Not married and not planning to be – at least not yet – he passed the interminable time in OPs or, as now, in his cramped, damp scrape, by dreaming up more lines of poetry about his life with the Regiment.

Though he never forgot – not for one minute, second even – exactly why he was lying in silence in a hole in the ground. It was see or be seen, kill or be killed. He couldn't afford to forget that.

And Paddy? He had no problems. He didn't care if he lived or died. He'd lost both his parents in childhood, in a routine car accident in Merseyside, and been brought up by distant relatives, decent but dull. Fleeing at an early age, he had hitchhiked to London, became a labourer on a building site, drank too much, screwed around too much and routinely squandered his money. Drifting into petty crime, he had kicked a few heads and been kicked in turn, but eventually, after a spell in the nick, he had decided to call it a day. Seeing a TV ad that sold the Army as an adventure, he enlisted and ended up in Belfast, being assaulted with bricks, screamed at by housewives and occasionally fired upon by teenage snipers.

To his surprise, he loved it. The excitement made him whole. Born in Liverpool, he had never felt Irish, so had no problems in Belfast, Londonderry, or even in so-called 'bandit country', where he ambushed terrorists and was in turn ambushed, surviving it all. The 'enemy' was the one he was told to fight, and that's all there was to it.

Posted back to England, he found Army life dull, so decided to try for the SAS. Being a natural survivor and blessed with strong nerves, he effortlessly passed Basic, Continuation and Cross-Training and was soon wearing the beret with winged dagger.

After another spell in Northern Ireland, practising counter-espionage in bandit country, he was posted to Oman, where he proved himself during the bloody, victorious advance on Shershitti. After that, he knew he'd remain an SAS trooper for as long as they let him.

Paddy didn't feel sentimental about being in the SAS – it was just a job he loved doing – and since he didn't have a family, let alone familial feelings, he withstood the mental stress of lengthy, silent vigils in OPs or scrapes by dwelling, as he was doing right here in East Falkland, on the excitements of his past and the ones he might have in the future.

Though in a cold, damp, coffin-shaped scrape, hidden under a false roof camouflaged with turf, hardly able to breathe, Paddy passed the day more easily than the others, feeling no more than boredom. He took his pride from his suffering.

By the third night they were passing through areas patrolled constantly by Argentinian troops, which meant that they had to be particularly careful and, even under cover of darkness, could advance only with great care. The urge to open fire was now stronger than ever – the humiliation of the Royal

Marines at Port Stanley still rankled – but their training stood them in good stead and, instead of firing, they simply laid low again and took note of the troop movements, their numbers and weapons. Similar notes were taken on the movements, now more frequent, of Argentinian helicopters and aircraft.

Eventually, after three days and nights, just before dawn on the third night, they reached the high ground overlooking Port Stanley and located the ridge chosen for the OP.

'This is it,' Ricketts said with confidence, checking his map against the actual location. 'Let's dig in, lads.'

Still protected by moonlit darkness, using spades and pickaxes while Danny stood guard, they quickly, expertly, constructed a rectangular OP, employing the standard techniques that had recently been used by Grenville in South Georgia. So high and exposed was the ridge that there was little natural cover from the elements, enemy patrols or aircraft. For this reason they camouflaged the OP with a roof of turf over the usual supporting material.

If nothing else, this would hide them from the thermal imagers of Argentinian helicopters. Whether or not it would hide them from enemy foot patrols was, as Ricketts knew from past experience, questionable.

Under normal circumstances, from the OP position, their signaller, Paddy, would have established communications with the SAS base, entertainingly located in the ladies' toilet aboard the *Resource*. However, because it was feared that they might be located by the Argentinians through the pick-up of their radio signals, Major Parkinson had ordered them to maintain radio silence until just before returning to the fleet. Therefore, for the next three days, the information already gathered, as well as the fresh intelligence picked up from the OP and by dangerous foot recces down the hill, to near the Argentinian positions in Port Stanley, was not transmitted, but kept in a file that would be destroyed should the enemy close in on them.

The OP had only one narrow aperture, but it offered a good view of Stanley airport and the Argentinian positions in the surrounding hills. Valuable intelligence was gathered daily with the use of black-painted, camouflaged binoculars, telescopes and night-vision aids. Visual information was usually photographed and the details overdrawn on maps and aerial photos taken by previous aircraft recces. Other information was entered in the logbook as it came up.

Throughout the three days, Argentinian helicopters made reconnaissance sweeps over the hillside. Occasionally foot patrols could be seen on the lower slopes leading down to Port Stanley and the airport. This made foot recces more dangerous for Ricketts and his men, but they made them nevertheless, usually under cover of darkness, when they were guided to the enemy positions by the glow of their fires or the lights shining inside occupied buildings.

Sometimes Argentinian soldiers marched past, only a few feet away from where the SAS recce team was lying, pressed tight to the earth.

To just lie there, doing nothing, was not only frustrating, but required unusually cool nerves. Yet all of them preferred the danger to the boredom of spending all day and night in the OP, where the light was too dim even for reading (notes were entered in the logbook by torchlight) and the only distraction was listening to the BBC World Service through muffled headphones. This at least kept them abreast of political and military developments regarding the Falklands.

The situation, they learned, was reaching crisis point. This was proven by the fact that Port Stanley's airport was now being bombed from the air and bombarded from sea every night, offering the men in the OP a tremendous, fiery spectacle that illuminated the dark port while blotting out the stars with billowing black smoke.

Always, when this happened, the Argentinian helicopters took off from the erupting airport, crossing directly over the OP as they fled inland. Just as often, when they returned, some of them would be missing, having been shot down by the fleet's Harrier jets after being located by other SAS OPs, located much further away from the Argentinian positions and so not under radio restrictions.

The nightly bombings and bombardments became an enjoyable form of distraction for the men in the OP.

After gathering all the information he could reasonably expect to find, Ricketts took a chance and radioed it back to base, with a request that the team be picked up as soon as possible. Confirmation came that the helicopter was on its way and would be there in approximately forty minutes.

'Right, men,' Ricketts said, 'let's pack up and leave. Danny, you take point as sentry while we dismantle and fill in the OP.'

'OK, boss,' the baby-faced trooper said, immediately picking up his M16, clambering out of the

OP, and slithering down the slope for about fifteen yards, to take up his position behind an outcrop of rock, overlooking the lights of the otherwise darkened port. Ricketts, Paddy and Andrew then packed up their kit, dismantled the OP and buried as much as possible beneath the earth, which they then flattened and covered with loose soil.

Fifteen minutes before the helo was due to descend for the pick-up, an Argentinian foot patrol made its way up the hill, the three men in triangular formation, weapons at the ready. It was obvious they had located the approximate area of the OP from the radio call made by Ricketts to the fleet.

The Argentinians investigated the dark, slightly moonlit ridge in a criss-crossing pattern, then spread out even farther as they advanced towards the summit – one, the scout, being too far ahead of the others for his own good.

Ricketts cursed softly and was about to tell his men to open fire – which might have exposed them to other enemy troops hidden lower down the slope – when Danny waved his right hand behind him in an up-and-down motion, signalling that Ricketts and the others should stay flat and remain out of sight. They obeyed his instruction just as the Argentinian scout stepped past Danny's position, missing him by inches, to advance straight up the hill towards Ricketts.

The other Argentinians were not even looking when Danny rose silently, a mere shadow against the skyline, and applied the silent killing technique by coming up behind his victim, covering his mouth with one hand and swiftly slashing his jugular vein with his Fairburn-Sykes commando knife. He held the body tightly while lowering it to the ground before it could go into spasm and start thrashing noisily.

Danny killed the man skilfully, with great stealth and speed, and was moving, crouched over, towards his next victim even before the first soldier was dead.

The second death occurred in darkness, completely hidden from view. There was just a brief thrashing sound – a falling body crushing bracken – then the last Argentinian, hearing the noise, looked around him in panic. His face was visible in the moonlight, eyes wide, searching frantically, but even as he started turning his rifle to fire, a white hand covered his mouth and jerked his head back, enabling a gleaming, moonlit blade to slit his throat.

The soldier's body shuddered convulsively as Danny's other hand slipped around it. His rifle fell from twitching fingers as he spasmed, staying upright, held tightly by his killer, then was lowered gently, almost tenderly, to the ground, to be rolled over and pressed face down into soft soil, which silenced his final, dying gurgle.

Eventually, after checking that the man was dead, Danny stood up and extended his right hand, waving it in towards his body, signalling: 'As you were.'

Ricketts and the others heaved a sigh of relief, then stood up to gather their kit together and await the helo's arrival.

Danny walked back up the slope, his rifle slung across his shoulders, wiping his bloody blade on a cloth and smiling dreamily at them.

'No problem,' he conveyed without speaking, simply raising his thumb in the air. Ricketts replied in kind.

The helo arrived on time, hardly visible in the dark sky, its presence only evident from the sound of its engine and spinning rotors, first a distant throbbing sound, then a drumming and whipping, and finally a roaring that decimated the silence. It descended quickly, hovering just above the ground, whipping up a minor hurricane of flying debris. Then it was ascending again even before the last of the men, Ricketts, had heaved his heavy kit aboard and clambered in after it.

'Piece of piss,' Andrew said.

9

'I've called this briefing,' Captain Grenville said in the ladies' toilet of the *Resource*, 'because we're going in on another urgent recce.'

Corporal Jock McGregor and troopers Taff Burgess and Gumboot Gillis glanced at one another with the air of men being offered a release from prison. They were also pleased to be given the chance to do something, now that the war with Argentina had truly begun.

The day after Ricketts and his patrol had been inserted on East Falkland, the British submarine HMS *Conqueror* had sunk the Argentinian heavy cruiser the *General Belgrano*. This had led to jubilation among the members of the fleet, but this was brutally extinguished when, two days later, an Exocet missile fired from an Argentinian Super Etendard warplane sank HMS *Sheffield*, resulting in many British dead and wounded.

During that time three British Harriers were also lost, one shot down, two colliding over the sea. The war with Argentina was well and truly engaged, making the frustrated members of the SAS itch to take part and make amends for their own recent disasters.

'The various recce patrols of East Falkland,' Captain Grenville continued, 'produced enough intelligence to enable us to launch a major offensive against the island as the first step on the road to Port Stanley. The intended landing beaches are at San Carlos Water, on the west coast of East Falkland, but before the landings can take place we have to destroy any Argentinian aircraft that are within range of the beaches. At the moment, all we know is that those aircraft are based on a grass strip near the only settlement on Pebble Island.'

'Our destination,' Jock said.

'Exactly.'

'Do we know anything else about the aircraft?' Gumboot asked, scratching the broken nose that lent a distorted appearance to his ferret-like face.

'Only that they include 1A-58 Pucara ground-attack planes built in Argentina for use against lightly armed forces. Each carries 20mm cannons, four 7.62mm machine-guns and bombs or rockets, all of which can be used when flying slowly, to strafe our ground troops.'

'How many?' Taff Burgess asked, rubbing his big belly and offering the other two his familiar, distant smile.

'That's what we have to find out.'

'Then we destroy them.'

'No. Then we report back here. Once we've brought the intelligence back, the green slime will decide the next course of action.'

'Shit,' Jock said, then coughed into his fist and glanced around him. It was difficult to breathe in the toilet because of the dense cigarette smoke, most of which came from the constantly burning fags of the radio operatives set up near the toilet booths. 'Hell of a place for our base,' Jock observed. 'Makes me feel right queer, boss.'

'Maybe that's because you *are* queer,' Gumboot responded.

'Yes, dear,' Taff said.

'Come on, men, cut the bullshit,' Captain Grenville said. 'We've no time to spare.'

'So what do we know about Pebble Island?' Jock asked sensibly.

'We believe there's a radar station on the island, although electronic checks have shown that if there is one, it's not being operated. However, they may just be maintaining radio silence until the right moment and we can't risk having our amphibious ships detected as they near Pebble Island, en route to San Carlos Water – so eyeball recces, rather than airborne or electronic surveillance, are required.'

'The good old-fashioned way,' Jock observed.

'Right, Corporal,' Captain Grenville said. 'Which is why we're going in by boat again, instead of by helo.'

'Suits me,' Taff Burgess said. 'When do we leave?'

'When you're kitted out, Trooper.'

'So let's go and do it.'

Leaving the cramped, smoky toilet, they made their way down through the creaking, throbbing bowels of the ship to the SAS requisition area. When they entered the hold filled with makeshift tables laden with all kinds of military clothing, including tropical and Arctic wear, and stacked with crates of weapons, radios and food supplies, they found Ricketts and his team handing back the equipment they had used for their recent OP overlooking Port Stanley. Ricketts was signing his name on a form while the others, some smoking, were waiting for him.

'Well, well,' Jock said with a wicked grin directed at Ricketts, Paddy, Danny and big Andrew, 'the Boy Scouts managed to find their way back after their day out.'

'So where are you lot off to?' Ricketts replied, handing the requisitions clerk the pen and paper, then turning to face the Boat Troop. 'Another Girl Guides' outing, is it, lads?'

'You'd know more about the Girl Guides than we would,' Gumboot said, 'since they're in the only age range you could manage – *if* you could manage it.'

'Another recce?' young Danny asked, baby-faced yet more serious than the others.

'Right,' Taff said with a distant smile.

'Come down to us for some advice, have you?' big Andrew asked, brown eyes bright in that handsome ebony face. 'You know we're dependable.'

'I'd be safer depending on a fucking Argie,' Paddy said. 'Advice from *you* lot? Don't come it, mate!'

'OK,' Captain Grenville said, 'that's enough of the bullshit. This is a confidential mission, Sergeant Ricketts, so get your men out of here.'

'Yes, boss,' Ricketts replied. He turned to the rest of Grenville's team. 'Don't take any notice of these lads. They're just trying to be helpful. Given the reputation of the Boat Troop, they figure you need it.' He turned away while the mocking comments flew thick and fast. 'Come on, lads, let's go. Let the girls do their business.'

Hoots of derision followed the laughing exit of the Mountain Troop, then, after quietening down his men, Captain Grenville requisitioned the weapons and equipment needed for the recce. These included waterproof clothing, special survival suits, life-jackets, a waterproof PRC 319 radio system, and SARBE rescue beacons.

While the men were putting on their waterproof clothing, Grenville phoned through to the docking bay, asking them to prepare two Klepper canoes for his four-man patrol. By the time he had put on his own waterproof gear, the men had received their packed, heavy bergens and were checking their weapons. When they were satisfied, Grenville led them out of the hold and even deeper into the bowels of the ship, until they arrived at the docking bay, which was open and flooded, with the canoes already placed in the water by the Naval ratings who worked here.

As it was nearly midnight, the interior of the docking bay, which resembled a vast hangar, was eerily lit by dimmed spotlights that could not be seen by enemy aircraft, but made the open stern, as well as the sea beyond it, seem even darker and more mysterious than it was. Large Landing Craft, Vehicle Personnel, or LCVPs, were anchored in the water between the three great steel walls, with the smaller Rigid Raiders, five metres long and with fibre-glass hulls, suspended from cranes directly above them. Inflatable Geminis, now all deflated, hung from the walls.

'They look like giant johnnies', Jock observed, 'but they'd be too small for me.'

Taff chuckled.

'Quiet, troopers,' Grenville said, picking up his bergen onto his shoulders, raising his waterproof cape over his head and gazing down at the Klepper canoe just below him. 'Gumboot, you come with me. You two,' he said to Jock and Taff, 'can share the other canoe. OK, let's move it.'

Luckily, the sea was calm, enabling them to load their bergens and weapons into the prow and rear areas of the canoes, cover the hull with a waterproof covering and insert themselves into the two holes in the covering. Once seated, one man behind the other, they tightened the waterproof covering around their waists, picked up their oars and told the Naval ratings to untie the ropes and push them away from the dock. When the ratings had done so, setting them free in the water, they rowed the canoes out of the docking bay and into the dark, open sea.

Normally, the patrol would have cross-decked to a submarine and let it take them close to the shore, but in the absence of a suitable submarine, the *Resource* had sailed under radio silence close enough to the shore for Pebble Island to be visible to the naked eye. What the men in the canoes now saw was a strip of featureless, dark land with few visible hills.

Taking his bearings from the moon and stars, which that night were clearly visible, Grenville led the second canoe towards the approximate area of the chosen LZ, confident that when he drew closer to the shore, he would be able to arrive at the exact location by using the landmarks he had memorized from intelligence briefings. As the ship had managed to get to within a couple of miles of the shore, the canoes were soon in shallow water, with the beach clearly visible, striped by shadow and moonlight, and leading gently up to low hills on which patches of ice gleamed blue and white.

Still paddling with the others, Grenville scanned

the length of the shore for camp-fires or other signs of the enemy presence. So far there was nothing. After bending his right arm, hand raised to indicate 'halt', he again took his bearings, this time with a combination of compass reading and a visual check of the fall of land. Now knowing exactly where the LZ was located, he took the time to jot down useful notes of the tides (which he had observed during the journey), beach gradients that would be suitable for amphibious landings and general topographical details that would help in selecting the best areas for the advance by foot soldiers. This done, he pocketed his pen and notebook, then gently waved his outstretched hand up and down, practically touching the water's surface, to indicate that the other canoe should follow him.

Starting to row again, with Gumboot expertly doing the same behind him, he was soon gliding through shallow water and coming up on the beach. At his signal, Gumboot and the others stopped rowing, anchored the canoes, removed the protective waterproofing from the top of the hull, then carefully clambered out and splashed down into the water. After offloading their kit and weapons, which they carried bit by bit to the shore, they pulled the canoes in, carried them carefully across the beach to ensure that they would not be damaged, stored them under sparse, overhanging foliage, then constructed chicken-wire covers for them. These were then camouflaged with turf and more local foliage.

Finally, with the canoes safely hidden, they strapped the overloaded bergens onto their backs and, at another silent signal from Captain Grenville, hurried off the exposed beach and began the march up the gentle, moonlit slopes of wind-blown grass towards where the Argentinian airstrip was located. They had not spoken a word since leaving the ship forty minutes ago.

The march took them over the low hills and back down again, then along a narrow waist of land with the sea on each side, open and exposed, without natural cover anywhere. This eventually led them to the estimated mile-and-a-quarter field where the aircraft, visible in moonlight, were dispersed.

Viewing them through binoculars, from behind a hedgerow on a slight rise about two miles from the grass airfield, Grenville was able to see the heavily armed Argentinian troops guarding them. Swinging the binoculars in both directions, to view the sea on both sides of the long, narrow strip, he saw the camp-fires of many other enemy positions, placed there as protection against attacks from the sea. According to the green slime, an estimated one hundred Argentinian troops were surrounding the airfield.

'Let's dig in here,' Grenville said, speaking for the first time since leaving the ship. 'We'll recce the whole area as quickly as we can, then get the hell out. They want us back with the fleet as soon as possible, so let's waste no time. Jock, you stick with the radio and be guard.'

'Aye, aye,' Jock said, then moved forward to a more advantageous viewpoint, offering the protection of bushes from where he could see the still darkened airstrip, as well as all around him.

'We'll only be here a short time,' Grenville said. 'So make the OP a star shape.'

'Right, boss,' Taff said, unstrapping his bergen, lowering it to the ground, then opening it, as Gumboot was also doing, to withdraw his pick-axe and spade for the digging.

The star-shaped OP serves the same function as the rectangular, but is smaller and easier to construct. It is shaped like a cross with four arms of equal length: one for the sentry, one for the observer, one as a personal admin, or short-term rest bay, the last as a proper rest bay for a longer, more comfortable sleep in a sleeping bag. Covered, like the rectangular OP, in ponchos, turf and other available materials, such as local brush or shrubbery, it has an open drainage well in the middle, into which excess water, such as rain, will run, and it also contains a kit-well. Giving good all-round visibility, it is excellent as a short-term OP that can be quickly constructed and just as quickly filled in and disguised, as if it had never been.

With the OP constructed, Grenville took the sentry arm, which overlooked the grassy strip and airfield. Studying it through his binoculars as the sun came up, he was able to count eleven Pucaras. As the sun rose higher in the sky, he saw that the Argentinian troops were indeed spread right around the airfield and along the narrow strip of land with the sea on both sides. He also noticed, with a slight shock, that the ground on which the planes were parked was on the top of another rise that put it on the same level as the OP.

'Damn!' Grenville whispered.

'What's that, boss?' Jock asked from the personal admin rest bay.

'I thought we were on a rise, but the slope rises again to put the airstrip on the same level as the OP. That's going to make it damned difficult to get away from here without our movements being noticed by the Argies, even in darkness. We're going to be silhouetted by the sky.'

Jock sat up and expertly scanned the area. 'Aye, you're right there. On the other hand . . .' His eyes moved left and right, then settled on the right. He jabbed his index finger in that direction. 'There's a slight depression over there, running back towards the sea in the general direction of the LZ. We'll have to take our chances and crawl along that.'

Grenville studied the depression with some care. 'Right,' he said eventually. 'Let's do that. We don't have much choice. We'll take off when darkness falls. In the meantime, let's take note of as much as possible without leaving the OP.'

Jock studied the airstrip and both sides of the strip through his own binoculars. 'Those sentries don't look particularly alert to me,' he said with a slight trace of contempt. 'I reckon you could go for a Sunday walk and they wouldn't even notice.'

'I reckon you'd get your balls shot off, so don't try it, Corporal.'

'Aye, aye, boss, I hear you.'

As the day progressed it became increasingly evident that the Argentinian sentries were indeed not very alert and certainly not expecting to find British soldiers spying from the edge of their well-guarded, wind-blown airstrip. And yet it was also clear that any attempt to move out of the OP would result in being spotted immediately. Grenville and his men therefore settled in for a long, cramped, tedious watch, taking turns in the sentry arm and passing on to the others anything they had seen that might be of the slightest interest.

Of most interest was the fact that the enemy sentries were obviously not expecting a British assault in the immediate future – a mistaken notion that had made them lax – and that their aircraft, the eleven Pucaras, were not being used and probably would not be until the actual assault began. It would certainly therefore be wise to put them out of action before D-Day.

While the Argentinian troops moved constantly up and down both sides of the strip throughout the day, sometimes on foot, more often in jeeps and trucks, they never ventured away from the airstrip, nor came in the direction of the OP. By the time the sun had started sinking, Grenville knew all there was to know about the airstrip and its defences.

'Time to move out,' he said.

The star-shaped OP was demolished and filled in under the cover of darkness, though that in itself was dangerous enough. Mission completed, they packed everything back into their bergens, checked their weapons, took one last look at the airstrip, where lights were winking on here and there, then ran, crouched low, to the slight depression that snaked around the top of the hill and led back towards the sea. Unfortunately, it did so in a way that took them dangerously close to the Argentinian sentries, which is why, even before they reached the depression, they had to drop onto their bellies and virtually crawl to it.

'Shit!' Taff exclaimed in a whisper.

'What?' Grenville enquired.

'My bergen's jutting over the top of the depression.'

'So's mine,' Gumboot whispered.

They stared at one another, eyes gleaming in descending darkness, then Grenville said, 'We don't have a choice. We'll have to take the bergens off and leave them here.'

'If they're found,' Jock pointed out, 'the Argies will know we've been here and guess that the British assault is imminent.'

'I know,' Grenville replied, 'but we still don't have a choice. It's either that or be seen for sure.

We've been here all day and the Argies haven't come near this area, so let's just pray that they won't for the next few days. Come on, chaps, let's dump them.'

The four of them struggled out of their bergens, which wasn't easy to do without sitting up, but eventually, when they had been discarded, they moved off again, holding their M16s out ahead of them as they wriggled on their bellies along the depression, practically chewing the soil.

This agonizingly slow, physically draining form of movement had to be continued for approximately half a mile, which took them a torturous three hours to cover. By the time they were out of sight of the Argentinians, they were sweating even in the freezing cold; they were also covered in dirt and breathing harshly. Nevertheless, now out of sight of the enemy, they climbed to their feet and began the rest of their six-mile march back to the beach.

Still blessed by darkness, they uncovered the Klepper canoes, carried them back to the water, anchored and loaded them, clambered in, pulled the anchors in and rowed themselves back out to sea. When they were out a reasonable distance, seeing nothing but the stars sharply cut off by the sea's black horizon, Jock used the radio for the first time, informing the *Resource* that they were on their way back and giving their location. In return, he was informed that the ship was coming in as close to the shore as possible to pick them up. He was to signal the ship with his Morse-code lamp as soon as he saw it.

About forty minutes later, when they were rowing in a black sea reflecting the star-bright sky, they glided into a patch of dense fog. A few minutes later the *Resource* came into view, materializing eerily out of the fog-filled darkness, towering over them as an immense rectangle on which lights glowed dimly.

Jock picked up his signalling lamp and sent a message in Morse code, identifying the two Kleppers, giving the name of their occupants and asking for permission to row around the ship and enter the docking bay. Permission was received by another light flashing in Morse code. It flashed on and off high above them, then signalled 'Over and out' and blinked off, leaving only the darkness.

With his right hand Jock signalled 'Follow me', then he and Grenville started rowing, leading Taff and Gumboot around the ghostly ship, illuminated dimly by the lights that shone high above them.

In the darkness, beyond the fog, the great

ship creaked and groaned as if alive. The sea, though relatively calm, beat and splashed relentless against its hull, making a dull drumming sound.

Eventually the stern of the ship came into view, first as a mere sliver of light on the black water, then as a vertical rectangle of light in which tiny, silhouetted figures moved back and forth, finally as a towering square of light that appeared to be burning out of three immense walls of steel – actually the inside of the ship's hull – from which hung deflated Geminis. Below the inflatables were suspended Rigid Raiders and, in the water between the steel catwalks, anchored LCVPs.

As the two canoes drifted into the docking bay someone cried out, 'Welcome home!'

The four men in the canoes gave the thumbs-up, grinning like Cheshire cats.

10

'The date for the assault on Pebble Beach,' Major Parkinson informed captains Hailsham and Grenville on the deck of the Fleet flagship HMS *Hermes* shortly after the Squadron had been cross-decked by helicopter from the *Resource*, 'has been brought forward from 21 to 15 May.

'Why?' Hailsham asked, since this would drastically reduce the time his Mountain Troop had for briefing and preparation. 'That only leaves us two days.'

Major Parkinson sighed. 'I know. The problem is that the three Sea King helos required for the insertion are only available for ten hours each day. As they have to be serviced, and since the nights of the sixteenth and nineteenth are scheduled for the re-supply and debriefing of recce patrols, any landing on Pebble Island will have to be made before the sixteenth. The raid has therefore been rescheduled to the early hours of the fifteenth. We'll just have to make do.'

Shading his eyes with one hand to protect them from the wind and spray, Parkinson was forced to squint as he studied the many activities taking place on the enormous deck of the ship. Despite the aircraft-carrier's size, the *Hermes* was presently steaming into strong headwinds that made her roll heavily in the surging waves. Because her secondary role of anti-submarine helicopter carrier had added many helos to her complement of Harrier jets, she had a flight deck angled at 6.5 degrees with a 7-degree, gleaming white ski-jump ramp that appeared, from where Parkinson was standing, to soar all the way up to the stormy sky. The immense deck, which was rising and falling hypnotically against a backdrop of stormy sea, was littered with Sea Harrier jets. Sea King helicopters, with folded blades, were parked forward, near piles of strapped-down 1000lb cluster bombs. Four LCVP landing-craft were slung in davits. The jackstay rigs and derricks were a brilliant, blinding yellow against the off-white ship and surrounding grey sea.

With 1027 ratings and 143 officers, the *Hermes* was like a floating Air Force base, always busy, noisy, and wind-blown, with huge waves – though the sea seemed impossibly far below – often smashing noisily against the hull, hurling spray over the deck and soaking the busy ratings. Major Parkinson, not easily impressed, was very impressed.

'There's another small problem,' he said quietly.

'Please *do* tell me, boss,' Captain Hailsham enthused sarcastically.

'These headwinds have prevented the helos being prepared in advance, which is going to cause another slight delay. The storm is expected to abate by this afternoon, but because we'll be late in loading the helos, our time to complete the mission will be reduced from 90 minutes to 30.'

'With all due respect, boss, that's asking an awful lot from our lads.'

Parkinson sighed again. 'I know, but I'm sure they can manage. Get in, do the job, and get out. It's a hit-and-run mission. At least we're no longer expected to eliminate the Argentinian ground crews and the rest of the island's garrison, as well as destroying the planes. As our time has been reduced from 90 minutes to 30, the attack has been limited to destroying the aircraft and ensuring that our helos are back aboard the *Hermes* before daylight. This in turn will ensure that she and her escorts will be well to the east of the islands before the Argentinian Air Force can attack them, if they decide to do so.'

'Let's make sure we hit every plane on the ground,' Captain Hailsham said. 'Every damned one of them.'

'I still say we insert by boat,' Captain Grenville offered, sounding aggrieved.

'No,' Parkinson replied. 'We don't have the time. This is a surprise attack, so we have to insert by helo. Sorry, Larry, but you're out of this one. You'll be back here acting as base, in constant radio contact. You'll get us in and out.'

Hailsham raised his eyebrows at Grenville and gave a broad, mocking grin. 'Ah, well,' he said. 'A man's got to do what a man's got to do. Shall we adjourn to the briefing room?'

'Yes,' Parkinson said. 'The Squadron's already been gathered together there. They're all primed and waiting.'

'Then let's talk to them, boss.'

After another glance at the immense, swaying deck and the stormy sea beyond, Parkinson turned away and slipped through the nearest hatchway, leading the other two into the depths of the ship, down steel ladders, through more hatchways, along creaking corridors, past cabins and lockers and the operational area, to the hold containing the ship's large briefing room. The members of the Mountain Troop, together with the SBS members who had just made the recce, were sitting in chairs in front of the big black-board, now covered in maps of Pebble Island.

The babble of conversation died away when Parkinson entered the room with his two officers and took his place on the small, raised platform in front of the maps. He picked up a pointer and tapped the map behind him, letting the pointer rest on Pebble Beach.

'There it is, gentlemen – our LZ. The beach on Pebble Island. That island is the stepping-stone to San Carlos Water, which is, of course, the back door to Port Stanley. Our job is to ensure the safety of the forthcoming landings by putting all the Argentinian aircraft on Pebble Island out of business. How does that grab you?'

A cheer went up from the assembled men, only dying away when Parkinson waved them into silence.

'What about the Argies?' Ricketts asked.

'Right,' Danny said, looking and sounding, as always, like a choirboy. 'Do we mop 'em up?'

'No,' Parkinson said. 'We no longer have time for that. We've had an hour lopped off our schedule, which only leaves 30 minutes for the actual raid on the airstrip. Our job, therefore, is to ensure that all their aircraft are immobilized in that time – then we get the hell out. We're not interested in taking prisoners or a high body-count. Our sole interest has to be the aircraft.'

'How many?' Ricketts asked.

'Eleven Pucaras.'

Big Andrew gave a low whistle. 'That's some job to do in thirty minutes, boss.'

'You don't think you can manage it?'

'Didn't say that, boss. Merely observing that the time is pretty limited for that number of targets.'

'No argument, Trooper.'

'Who does what?' Jock McGregor asked.

'The Mountain Troop, led by myself and Captain Hailsham, will attack the planes, using LAW 66mm one-shot anti-tank rockets and small-arms fire. This will be done under cover of the Squadron mortars, to be handled by the Boat Troop, as well as a barrage from the fleet's big guns. We'll be guided from the LZ to the target by the members of the Boat Troop who performed the original recce . . .'

'The Girl Guides!' Paddy Clarke cried out, prompting an outburst of laughter and applause.

'At least we know our way around,' Gumboot retaliated with a grin. 'We don't get lost and return like a bunch of snowmen. We don't melt in the heat.'

This time it was the members of the Boat Troop who laughed and cheered while the Mountain Troop hurled good-natured insults.

'OK! OK!' Captain Hailsham said, raising his hand. 'That's enough of the bullshit. Quieten down now.'

Major Parkinson waited until the noise had abated, then continued: 'Let me repeat: the Boat Troop will lead us to the target, then man the mortars. A second troop will seal off the approaches to the airstrip, with a third troop held in reserve. When the planes are all hit, we retreat, still being covered by the mortars and the guns of the fleet. We don't detour en route back to the beach – no unnecessary engagements with the Argies, no laying of booby traps. We just retreat to the beach and get lifted off. Is that understood?'

There followed much nodding and shrugging, disgusted looks and the odd, disappointed, 'Yeah, yeah'.

'So,' Parkinson said, 'any questions?'

'When's the insertion?' big Andrew asked.

'The day after tomorrow. Midnight.'

'And the full briefing?'

'Tomorrow. You'll be at it all day. Intelligence from the green slime, kitted out by the REMFs, weapons-checking and practice all afternoon, a full inspection that evening. This procedure will be repeated the following day, with a final briefing just before insertion. You'll be kept busy, chaps.'

This produced groans, the shaking of heads and much rolling of eyeballs.

'Right, lads, class dismissed.'

The men pushed their chairs back and filed out of the briefing room, leaving Parkinson, Hailsham and Grenville alone by the blackboard.

A lot of bullshit was flying in the hold of the ship, where the SAS troopers were preparing for the raid by urinating, defecating, having a shower, shaving, resting on their cramped steel bunks, one practically on top of the other, writing last-minute letters – or, in Andrew's case, some fine lines of poetry – smoking, drinking – though only non-alcoholic beverages were permitted

179

before a raid – arranging their equipment in their bergens and checking their weapons. The hold was gloomy and sweltering, filled with sweat and the stench of farts, but this was the time they most enjoyed, so nobody cared – even though they certainly noticed the farting and used it for bullshit.

'Christ, that stench is goin' to kill me!' Paddy said. 'Who the hell farted?'

'I's innocent, Massa Abe,' Andrew cried out melodramatically, doing his plantation-nigger act, rolling his brown eyes and flashing his teeth. 'Lord have mercy upon me!'

'I'd recognize that stench anywhere,' Gumboot said, 'and it doesn't come out of a white man's arse. Own up, poet – you did it.'

'Leave him alone,' Taff said, smiling dreamily into his bergen, trying to work out what to put where. 'Being a poor black, he gets enough flak in Civvy Street. We don't want him breaking down in tears here because we've been cruel to him.'

'That's what I like to hear,' Andrew said. 'A little bit of compassion. Especially when it comes from the bastard who started this whole filthy conversation. Own up, Taff! Only a Welshman smells like that, so no point in denying it.'

'My arse isn't black, Trooper.'

'I've never seen mine,' countered Andrew. 'If you've managed to get a look at your own, I'd like to know when and how come. In your salty youth, was it?'

'Now that's wicked,' Jock said. 'That's stickin' it to him where it hurts. I'd be buggered before I'd wear that suggestion. So how *did* you see it, Taff?'

'Why are you all picking on me?'

'Because you fart like a camel.'

'You do that every time you open your mouth, Jock, so don't land on me. In fact, it was probably little baby-faced Danny Boy, now pretending he's deaf.'

Danny didn't respond. He just blushed and checked his weapons, concentrating fiercely on the job and looking at no one.

'Don't pick on that boy,' Jock said, trying to untangle his webbing, ammunition belts resting on his crossed legs, his kit littering his bunk. 'Innocence is bliss. Baby Face is as clean as his dagger when it slits a man's throat. His fart must smell like perfume.'

'I agree,' Gumboot said. 'Let's not upset Danny Boy. When it comes to the crunch tomorrow, when the heat's on, he's the one we'll depend on. He has nerves of steel, that kid.'

181

'And a rod of iron,' Taff said.

'Ah, jealousy!' Andrew said. 'I only know that when push comes to shove, it's the kid who's right in there.'

'Thanks, Andrew,' Danny said, checking his weapons, keeping his eyes down, speaking as softly as a girl. 'I don't want any bullshit from these bastards. I just want to take out some Argies and show them who's boss.'

'Quite right, too,' Andrew agreed. 'I like a man who knows his own mind. It's nice to know you'll be the boss in your own home when you and Darlene get married.'

'When's that, then?' Paddy enquired.

'Haven't decided yet,' Danny said. 'We were just about to work something out when the Argies gave aggro.'

'Most inconvenient,' Andrew said.

'Oh, I dunno,' Gumboot put in. 'I think Danny might be happier fighting Argies than banging his missus.'

'She's not his missus yet, Gumboot. They're only engaged at this point. And naturally you'd be cynical about that, given the state of *your* marriage.'

'His missus left him for a farmer,' Paddy explained helpfully to Danny. 'Gumboot won't tell us why and we're not about to pry, but we figure it's that problem between his legs. It's not a problem you'll have, kid.'

'Go fuck yourself,' Gumboot said.

'I hear poetry!' Andrew cried. 'Paddy Clarke has just spoken. Won't tell us why and we're not about to pry. I have serious competition in the ranks. Irish genius is rampant!'

'We're a talented race.'

'He's a Scouse, not an Irishman.'

'I'm whatever you farts want me to be, because I'll need you tomorrow.'

'What you need you may not get.'

'I stick my neck out for no one.'

'At least it's a proper assault at last and not another OP.' Taff finished packing his bergen and hung it from his bunk, then picked up his short M203 grenade-launcher to check that it fitted into the clip beneath his M16 rifle. It seemed to work all right. 'I'm fed up sitting in mud, rain and piss in a hole in the ground. I want out and about again.'

'So do I,' Danny said, checking his weapons, thinking of Darlene, secretly shocked that it was hard to visualize her when he had work to do. 'I want to shoot me some Argies.'

'You're like my own son,' Gumboot said. 'I

mean the son I might have had. Judging by my missus he'd have been a lot like you – an innocent, sweet-faced little psychopath with a cutting edge to him. My fucking missus is barmy.'

'I'm just a soldier,' Danny said. 'I take pride in my work. I mean, there's nothin' personal in it at all – it's just a job to be done.'

'Then do it tomorrow, Danny. Get in there and shoot some Argies. This time we're going in for the jackpot and a nice bit of aggro. I'm sure you'll be pleased, kid.'

Danny was holding an L1A1 self-loading rifle, inspecting the magazine release catch, slamming the magazine in, ensuring that the Trilux sight clipped on properly, then checking the foresight. Satisfied, he put the rifle down and pulled out his commando knife, turning it slowly before his eyes to let the dim light flash off it. 'Yeah,' he said, drawling like an American or a rock star, blissed out, distracted, 'I guess you're right there.'

'That's no bullshit,' Andrew said.

Parkinson studied the empty chairs in the briefing room, trying to recall all the faces of his troopers, filled with pride at their courage, proud to be their commander, but also concerned at how much they were being asked to do in such a short time.

'Thirty minutes,' he said eventually, almost whispering, really talking to himself. 'It's not too long at all.'

'No,' Hailsham agreed, 'it's not . . . But perhaps it'll work to our advantage. In and out while the Argies are still blinking, wondering what the hell's happening.'

'Let's hope so,' Grenville said.

The three officers smiled at one another, then left the briefing room, going their separate ways at the next hatchway, each with his own job to do.

11

At 30 minutes before midnight on the night of 15 May, HMS *Hermes* was sailing under radio silence through calm, moonlit waters.

Not so calm was the immense flight deck, where, under brilliant spotlights, three Sea King helicopters were being prepared by Naval ratings to carry the many SAS troops milling about them. After two days of briefing by the green slime, weapons training on the open deck and repeated inspections of their weapons and equipment, the men were raring to go.

Grouped around the helos, they were surrounded by a vast array of weapons, including L1A1 self-loading rifles, or SLRs; L7A2 7.62mm general-purpose machine-guns, or GPMGs; M72 light anti-tank weapons, or LAWs; M16 and M203 grenade-launchers with cartridge-launched grenades; L16 ML 81mm mortars with calibrated dial sights; white-phosphorus, smoke and frag-mentation hand-grenades; and even the beloved Browning 9mm high-power handguns.

As the plan was to get in and out quickly, the bergens did not have to carry rucksacks and sleeping bags, but some still weighed up to 140lb because of the additional burdens of heavy weaponry, including the mortars, extra 200-round belts for the GPMGs, radio systems, batteries, binoculars, emergency rations and per-sonal first-aid kits.

The heaviest equipment was being packed in net-covered pallets by the Navy's flight-deck par-ties for transportation as underslung loads on the helos. But the rest of it had to be carried by the Troop in their bergens, which is why, com-bined with their bulky Gore-tex weatherproof battle jackets, the men looked bowed down and unwieldy.

Wearing ear protectors to combat the incessant noise, or headsets for communications, the Royal Naval Squadron ground crew and flight-deck parties – all with their ranks and names on a patch on their back for easy recognition – worked ceaselessly at checking and loading the helicopters. The Sea Harrier pilots – relatively slim and dashing in their G-suits and thermal liners, but with 9mm Browning automatic pistols on their hips – looked on, grinning widely, mixing encouragement with friendly banter.

The noise was atrocious. Even as the helicopters roared into life, with their rotor blades spinning and whipping up the air, some of the Sea Harriers lined along the edge of the deck were also revving up to make their way cautiously to the angled flight deck on the bow of the ship. Ignoring the planes, some of the SAS troops were running last-minute checks on their weapons by firing them off the edge of the flight deck at the stately white-capped waves. At the same time the bright-yellow jackstay rigs were moving equipment across the forward deck, before it was cross-decked to another ship later that day. Last but not least was the bawling of many men, trying to communicate with one another above the combined roaring, whining, screeching and clanging – not forgetting the moaning wind and the ceaseless bass rumbling of the sea as it hammered the ship's hull.

'Move it!' Major Parkinson yelled, scanning the sky beyond his helo and seeing a pale moon and myriad stars in the vast night sky. 'Let's do it! Go!'

As Ricketts was urging his men into the Sea Kings, one of the Sea Harriers roared into life, belching flames and smoke, then moved along the deck, raced up the angled flight deck and soared into the sky. Ricketts felt the blast from the take-off, as well as a wave of heat, even as his helo roared even louder and its spinning rotors, increasing their speed, created a minor hurricane that threatened to sweep him off his feet.

After glancing at the sea far below the helipad, Ricketts followed Paddy Clarke into the helo, moved along the cramped, vibrating interior, and strapped himself in between big Andrew and Danny. He was adjusting his belt when another Sea Harrier took off with a mighty roar that seemed to fill the already noisy interior of the helo, before fading away far out to sea.

As Ricketts was last in, the RAF Sergeant Air Loadmaster in charge of the hold, wearing an olive-green flying suit, zip-up boots and a headset for communication with the crew and ground crew, slammed and locked the door. After saying something into the mouthpiece of his headset, he disappeared behind the pallets stacked up along the front of the SAS Troop. A minute later, with much shaking and roaring, the helo lifted off the helipad, swayed from side to side, ascended vertically, hovered for a moment, then headed for the shore.

Glancing over his shoulder, through the window behind him, Ricketts saw the aircraft-carrier far below, cutting through the grey sea, its immense deck decorated with white-painted guide lines for the aircraft, the ski-jump ramp curving gracefully over the bow, the yellow jackstays a startling contrast in colour even from this great height. The second Sea King was ascending just below, coming closer, and the third was rising off the helipad on the carrier's deck to follow the second. It was a sight worth seeing.

'How's it going, troopers?' he asked. 'No pissing in the pants? No diarrhoea?'

'Lots of uncomfortable smells down here, boss, but all of them are coming from the Boat Troop.'

When the laughter died away, Gumboot replied: 'The only diarrhoea down here, Trooper Winston, is the bullshit coming out of your mouth. It flows fast and free.'

Andrew yelped with pleasure, his teeth gleaming white. 'Oh, man, we got a gilded tongue there. These Girl Guides are so fast.'

'Fast and efficient. Competent and cool. You want poetry, Mr Poet, there it is. You can always call on the Boat Troop.'

'They always come when we call,' Paddy said deadpan.

'They come at the very sight of us,' Andrew added. 'They're so desperate, the poor dears.'

'Glad you're all still awake,' Ricketts said. 'I like my Girl Guides and Boy Scouts to be alert, even if just with bullshit. It keeps my pulse beating at a normal rate – but that's enough for now, children. Keep the lid on it.'

'Yes, boss, we hear you.'

The banter, which was competitive, was also good-humoured, relied on not only to pass the time during the flight, but to ease the tension felt by even the most courageous, experienced troopers before going into battle.

Ricketts had known a similar kind of banter when on the North Sea oil rigs, where the constant danger and daily isolation had created the same kind of camaraderie. It was exactly what held the SAS together and made it such an effective fighting unit. Ricketts liked being part of it. Married though he was, good father that he was, he now knew he could never live a normal life outside the Regiment. For him, it all began and ended here, no matter what the danger.

'Keep your arses on your seats,' Gumboot said thirty minutes later. 'Here comes the Navy!'

'Actually, I'm RAF,' the Sergeant Air Load-master replied with an easy grin, returning to take his place by the exit door, 'and we're the guys that always get the ladies – we don't need you toy soldiers. Now unhitch yourselves and stand up, boyos. We're coming in for the landing.'

The repartee stopped immediately as the men concentrated on the job in hand, first unclipping their safety belts, then standing upright with a noisy jangling of weapons and turning into line, ready to leap out one by one when ordered to do so. The Loadmaster opened the door when the helo was still descending, letting the air rush in and howl through the hold, beating and tugging furiously at the men and their colliding weapons. Ricketts saw the sky outside, a stretch of darkness filled with stars, then a darker, tilting length of coastline as the helo changed its direction, heading for the LZ.

'Ten, nine, eight, seven,' the Loadmaster called, counting down. 'Three, two, one, zero . . . *Go!*'

The troopers jumped out one by one as the helo hovered in the air, swaying dangerously from side to side, mere feet off the ground. The first men down formed a protective ring around the helo, their weapons at the ready, while others released the underslung loads containing the heavy equipment. The helos remained in the air, creating a storm directly below, with sand and shrubbery spinning wildly, but the troopers fought against the swirling wind to spread out even farther.

When the men were all on the ground, either spreading out in a defensive circle or opening the underslung loads, the helos rose vertically, hovered briefly, in salute, then flew back towards the Fleet, leaving the LZ in a calmer state and letting the men get to work.

The helos had touched down on an LZ marked by the Boat Troop and located approximately six miles from the airstrip. Once the pallets had been broken open and the equipment dispersed, Major Parkinson quietly briefed the other officers, then divided the Squadron into three separate groups.

'Group One will seal off all approaches to the airstrip,' Parkinson explained, 'to ensure that the Argies can't get in *or* out. Group Two, led by myself, will blow up the Argentinian aircraft. The third group – and I know you won't like this – will be held in reserve.'

When the men in Group Three started beefing, Parkinson silenced them with a wave of his hand.

'Sorry, men, but that's the way it has to be.

I just can't commit all of you. Now where are the men who went on the original recce?' Jock, Gumboot and Taff raised their hands. 'Right,' Parkinson said. 'It's up to you three to lead us off the beach and guide us to the airstrip, stopping at the previously laid base-plate to set up the mortar. You do *remember* the route?'

'Yes, boss,' Jock said.

'And you *did* lay down a base-plate for the mortar en route back to the LZ?'

'That's A1 as well, boss.'

'OK, then, let's move out.'

This time, when they embarked on their long march, there were no jokes about Girl Guides.

In fact, the bright moonlight made most of them feel vulnerable as they hiked across four miles of desolate, exposed moorland to the site chosen by the Boat Patrol for the mortar base-plate, approximately two and half miles from the airstrip. Each member of the squadron was carrying two bombs for the mortar, which they left with the selected mortar crew – Gumboot and Taff – by the steel base-plate earlier laid down by them in this clearing, within a handily protective circle of piled rocks.

'Now I believe in miracles,' Paddy said. 'They actually remembered to lay it down.'

'Fucking right, we did,' Jock said. 'When we do a job, we do it properly. You need lessons? Just ask.'

'OK, troopers,' Ricketts said. 'That's enough of the mutual admiration. Now go about your business.'

'Good as done,' Gumboot said, then he and Taff, observed thoughtfully by Major Parkinson and Ricketts, set up the L16 ML 81mm mortar, which would be fired indirectly at a target identified by a forward observer placed with the assault group at the airstrip and using a PRC 319 radio system for communication with the mortar crew.

As the mortar had a range of three miles, it was well within range of the target airstrip, approximately two and a half miles distant. The forward observer would be Corporal Clarke.

'Right, boss,' Gumboot said, sitting back on his haunches and admiring the mortar now fixed to its base-plate. 'We're all set to go.'

'Good,' Parkinson replied. 'We'll be in contact as soon as we reach the airstrip. Tune that radio, Trooper.'

'Will do, boss. No sweat.'

'And keep your eyes and ears open for any Argentinian patrols.'

'It doesn't have to be said, boss. Good luck.'

'Same to you.'

After a brief exchange of banter from their closest friends, notably Andrew and Jock, Gumboot and Taff were left behind while the other members of the Squadron continued their march through the dark, wind-blown, freezing night.

Two and a half miles on, having met no opposition from the enemy, Jock led them to positions that gave a clear, moonlit view of the aircraft on that narrow strip of land thrusting into the sea. The lights of camp-fires burned all around the airstrip and along the front of the ammunition and supply dumps, carelessly giving away the Argentinian positions where the uniformed sentries, though armed, did not appear to be too attentive. It was almost like being offered a gift.

'Beautiful!' Parkinson whispered, back in action at last. 'Those Argie sentries look comatose. We're going to take them out, gentlemen.'

Signalling silently with his free hand, he motioned the third, reserve group to take cover as best they could, then sent the first group off in various directions, as previously instructed, to seal off the approaches to the airstrip. When they had gone, he nodded at Jock, who signalled 'Follow me' by swinging his right hand into his hip, then led the assault group closer to the airstrip – not quite as far as his OP, but near to where he and the others had been forced to crawl belly-down on the ground.

Moving in for the attack, with speed more important than safety, the assault group advanced at the crouch, weapons at the ready. When they were less than 300 yards from the airstrip, which was within the firing range of their LAWS, M203 grenade-launchers, and other small arms, Parkinson signalled them to prepare for the engagement, then he contacted the fleet on the radio system. Using the designated code, he told them to commence the covering barrage without delay. Receiving confirmation, he handed the phone back to Paddy Clarke.

'Get in contact with the mortar crew,' he said, 'and give them compass bearings. I want them to start firing immediately.'

'Yes, boss,' Paddy said.

Resting on one knee, Parkinson raised his right hand, preparing to give the signal to open fire. Behind him, the assault squadron were also kneeling and taking aim with their wide range of small arms. At the same time, the troopers with the 66mm LAWS extended the 90cm tube, removed the protective cap from each end of the launcher, thus making the folding sights pop up, held the launcher against the shoulder and prepared to press the trigger switch.

For a full minute, each second an eternity, the assault group knelt there in the darkness, wrapped in silence. The first sound was a high, keening wail that came from the direction of the sea, reached a climax right over the airstrip, and was cut off abruptly when the para-flares fired from the *Glamorgan*'s guns exploded noisily, spectacularly, to illuminate the airstrip below.

Major Parkinson instantly dropped his hand – and the assault group opened up on the Pucaras with their small arms.

Almost simultaneously, the first of the bombs from the L16 ML 81mm mortar fired by Gumboot and Taff, two and a half miles away, from compass bearings given over the radio by Paddy, exploded between the Pucaras in a fountain of fire, smoke and bellowing, erupting soil.

Paddy was bawling a revised calibration into the phone as the troopers pressed the triggers of their LAWs, sending rockets racing like tracers into the same area. Other troopers opened fire with their GPMGs, peppering the area with 200 rounds per minute.

Explosions from all these sources erupted

between the aircraft as the Argentinian sentries, taken by surprise, either ran for cover or instinctively fired back with rifles and other automatic weapons.

Hit by a LAW shell fired by Andrew, one of the Pucaras exploded, with pieces of metal and perspex flying in all directions and the cockpit engulfed in crackling, vivid-yellow flames.

Even as this spectacular strike illuminated the area, more air-burst shells were exploding overhead. Also, mortar explosions from the rounds being fired two and a half miles away were erupting between the aircraft to crater the runway.

In the silvery, flickering, artificial light, and with air-burst shells from the fleet, as well as the mortar bombs, causing further havoc, the Argentinians were forced to take cover, running back to their slit trenches at the edge of the airstrip, and aiming only occasional bursts of inaccurate machine-gun fire at the SAS.

'Let's go!' Major Parkinson bawled, boldly leading his men on to the dispersal areas. There, even as they were being fired on, with bullets tearing up concrete in jagged lines all around them, they ran from one plane to the other, coolly rigged explosives to those not already being destroyed with LAW rounds and vicious bursts from the GPMGs, placing the charges to destroy front undercarriages and nose-cones housing avionic equipment.

When the charges exploded, the nose-cones were blown off and the undercarriages demolished, causing the planes to tilt forward with their smashed noses deep in the ground and smoke belching from them.

As the troopers were thus engaged, more shells from the fleet's barrage were falling farther away, making the ground erupt in a series of explosions directly in front of the enemy's defensive positions, eventually striking the base's petrol store and ammunition dump.

Both buildings exploded spectacularly, with searing yellow, red and blue flames stabbing vividly through black, oily smoke. This billowed skyward, then was carried back on the wind to blanket and choke the Argentinian troops. While the Argentinians were temporarily blinded, the last of the charges rigged to the Pucaras by Parkinson's men exploded one by one, causing more flames, smoke and flying debris as the men backed away.

Making his escape beside Major Parkinson, under cover of an arc of continuous fire from Ricketts's SLR, young Danny glanced back over his shoulder, practically skidded to a stop – thus halting Parkinson – and turned back to the airstrip.

'One of the Pucaras is still untouched!' he shouted.

'Damn!' Parkinson exclaimed.

'Bugger that for a joke!' Danny said, then ran back to the planes, ignoring the Argentinian troops, who, in their smoke-wreathed slit trenches, were recovering from their shock and clambering out to spread across the airstrip, firing directly at him. The ground was erupting around him in jagged lines of spitting earth as he raced back to the untouched aircraft, Parkinson and Ricketts right behind him, both firing their SLRs on the move.

Some of the Argentinians went down, spinning like skittles, collapsing, even as Paddy Clarke, still on the PRC 319 radio system, corrected the mortar being fired two and a half miles away and the next rounds, looping in with more accuracy, landed spot on, the explosions throwing the broken bodies of the enemy soldiers high in the air. They fell back like rag dolls, hitting the ground with dreadful force, sometimes practically bouncing off it and appearing to shrivel up where they lay, some visibly scorched and still smouldering, all with broken or crushed bones.

Reaching the untouched Pucara, Danny expertly rigged the explosive charge, under the protective fire of Parkinson and Ricketts. He then waved them away and dropped back to the ground just as some Argentinians rushed at him. Resting on one knee, ignoring the bullets whistling around him and thudding into the Pucara, he fired his SLR with cool, murderous accuracy, downing the four men advancing on him. He then jumped up and fled from the aircraft.

It exploded behind him with a deafening roar. The shock from the blast punched him forward, throwing him face down on the strip. A wave of intense heat swept over him, momentarily suffocating him, then mercifully faded away. He jumped back to his feet and continued racing back to his own men, who were keeping up a relentless barrage of fire as they backed away from the airstrip.

When Danny reached them, stopping between Parkinson and Ricketts, he studied the airstrip and counted eleven blazing, smouldering aircraft.

'Terrific,' he said.

Parkinson checked his wristwatch. The attack had lasted fifteen minutes. He raised his right hand above his head and bawled, 'That's it, men! *Move out*!'

Still keeping up a protective wall of fire, the men backed away from the Argentinians advancing across the airstrip, weaving left and right between the blazing aircraft and the many explosions from the mortars. In the brilliant, silvery light from the air-burst shells they looked faceless, insubstantial, almost ghostlike.

Suddenly, from the direction of the blazing petrol and ammunition dump, a truck filled with Argentinian troops raced at the retreating men.

Jock appeared from nowhere, running back to the strip. He dropped to one knee, raising a 66mm LAW to his shoulder. The ground nearby erupted, hit by a mortar shell, and he was thrown down, rolling over a couple of times, as the smoke swirled about him.

When he sat upright, shaking his head, slapping his own face to help himself recover, his clothes were torn by shrapnel, with blood leaking from wounds to his face and body.

The truck was still racing at him. His fellow troopers poured fire at it. Grimly determined, Jock wiped blood from his face, adopted the kneeling position, removed the protective cap from each end of the launcher, held the weapon against his shoulder, then aimed along the pop-up sights. When he pressed the trigger switch, the backblast made him jerk violently, but the rocket shot straight to its target, creating a stream of flame, and the truck, which was almost on top of him, was hit and blew up. Careening sideways with a squealing of brakes, it crashed into a blazing Pucara, which also exploded.

Though covered in blood, Jock climbed to his feet and made his way unsteadily back to his mates.

Argentinian soldiers jumped out of the truck, some on fire, screaming hideously, flapping at their own burning bodies with smouldering hands. Some of the SAS troopers were undecided what to do about these unfortunates, but young Danny stepped forward, his angelic features highlighted ethereally by the flames, and cut them down in a hail of withering fire from his SLR.

'Put 'em out of their misery,' he explained, turning back to his mates. 'Only thing to do.'

'Yeah,' Andrew said. 'Right.'

'Pull back!' Parkinson shouted, waving his right hand. 'Let's move it! *Go!*'

As the assault group withdrew from the blazing, smoking airstrip, still under cover of mortar fire and naval support from the *Glamorgan*, some brave Argentinians attempted another counterattack, emerging from the smoke swirling across the strip and firing their weapons. Still kneeling on the ground behind his powerful GPMG, big Andrew let rip with a 200-round burst that cut some of the men down and forced the others to beat a hasty retreat. Then Andrew jumped up, slung his heavy weapon over his shoulder and followed the rest of the Troop back towards the sea.

A sudden explosion made the ground erupt violently in their midst, hurling one trooper high in the air. Crashing back down in a shower of debris, he hit the ground with a bone-breaking thud. His body actually bounced off the earth before rolling over, the bloody bone of a smashed kneecap thrusting out through torn pants, a white rib exposed through shrapnel-slashed flesh. Mercifully concussed, he made no sound.

'Damn!' Ricketts exclaimed. 'The bastards set off a remote controlled land-mine.'

'Medics!' Parkinson yelled.

As the troopers near the concussed man shook their heads to clear their ears, the medics, who had just been waved away by the bloody Jock, rolled their patient onto a stretcher and then hurried off. The troopers closed in behind them to form a protective wall.

Reaching the summit of the low hill that over-looked the airstrip, Parkinson glanced back to take stock of the situation.

In the still flickering, eerie light of the air-burst shells from the Fleet, all of the eleven Pucaras were either burning or smouldering. Craters littered the runway and the ground between the burning planes, ensuring that the airstrip could not be used in the immediate future. There were many dead bodies.

Satisfied, Parkinson was about to turn away when he heard the steady roar of other GPMGs and small arms from the sea road on one side of the airstrip.

Obviously the SAS troopers in the second group, sent there to seal off the approaches to the runway, were stopping the advance, or flight, of Argentinian troops trying to get along the sea road.

Even as Parkinson was gazing in that direction, a series of explosions sent smoke pouring into the sky in the vicinity of the GPMG and small-arms fire, indicating that someone in the group had called in for support from the *Glamorgan*'s big guns. A few minutes later the sound of battle died away – an indication that the second group had stopped the Argentinians and was now also heading back to the LZ.

'Good men,' Parkinson whispered.

The two-and-a-half mile march back to the location of the mortar base-plate was uneventful. There, they picked up Gumboot and Taff, then proceeded back to the LZ. The Sea Kings returned in time and the Squadron was lifted back to the *Hermes*, where the men had a warm welcome from Captain Grenville. Though disappointed that he had not been on the raid, he was delighted that the invasion could now commence.

12

Jock was the first to be shipped back, but not the last. When the shrapnel had been removed, he was a quiltwork of scars, some left to heal on their own, others stitched up, and no matter which way he turned, he lay on a bed of pain. This did not stop the mocking comments from flying thick and fast when he was visited in the ship's sick bay by other members of the Regiment, shortly before being shipped back to Ascension Island and from there on to England.

'I hear your arse is a hot-spot,' big Andrew said, flashing his teeth.

'Don't worry about the shrapnel in your prick,' Paddy said. 'I'm told that if you can manage a hard-on, the wounds open and the pieces just fall out.'

'That's *if* you can get one,' Gumboot clarified,

'which in Jock's case is an issue of doubt. Can I lend you a hand, Jock?'

'Ha, ha,' Jock responded stiffly, lying there like an Egyptian mummy, wrapped from head to toe in bloody bandages, but refusing to show his pain.

'You look pretty good, all told,' Taff informed him, studying the head-to-toe bandages with an experienced eye. 'Like a babe in swaddling clothes. Red and white becomes you.'

'It's just a pity,' Andrew said, 'that the shrapnel missed your mug. You could do with some rearranging there, so a good chance was missed.'

'Still, you'll get a rest,' young Danny said, being more concerned than the others. 'A nice little trip back to Blighty.'

'Right,' Gumboot said. 'Where they should have pretty nurses instead of these blokes. That should perk you up, mate.'

'Then you might get it up,' Andrew added, 'and the stitches will fall out.'

'Fuck you, Andrew,' Jock said. 'Fuck you all, come to that. I don't have stitches in my arse or dick, so go screw yourselves.'

'Even I can't get *mine* around that far,' Paddy said. 'Though if I could, I'm sure I'd have a good time.'

'Christ,' Jock said, rolling his eyes, 'do I have to endure this?'

'You need visits from friends to cheer you up,' young Danny said solemnly. 'That's why we're here.'

'I'm cheered up,' Jock said. 'Thanks a lot. You can all piss off now.'

'He's so ungrateful,' big Andrew said, glancing around as Sergeant Ricketts entered the sick bay and approached the bed. Ricketts glanced dispassionately at Jock, noting the bloodstains on the bandages, then studied each of the other troopers in turn.

'So what are you pisspots doing here?' he asked.

'Cheering him up,' Andrew said.

'Offering sympathy,' added Gumboot.

'Letting him know we all care,' Taff explained.

'I'll bet,' Ricketts grinned, then turned back to Jock. 'Giving you a hard time, are they?'

'Don't worry, boss, I can take it. You can smell the bullshit before they speak it, so I'm well prepared for it.'

'Good,' Ricketts said. 'It shows you've been well trained. A man who can take any kind of flak. A real SAS trooper.'

'That's me,' Jock said, grinning defiantly from his bed of pain. 'So what's happening, boss?'

'You're being medevacked this morning,' Ricketts told him. 'Cross-decked to another ship that'll take you to Ascension Island, then flown from there back to Blighty, where some sympathetic nurse might give you a hand-job under the sheets. What more could you want?'

'To take part in the invasion,' Jock said.

'Not in your state, Trooper. As for you bullshit artists,' Ricketts said, turning to the men gathered about Jock's bed, 'the British landing at San Carlos Water has been scheduled for the twenty-first. As a diversion, we've been tasked with mounting a raid against the Argies at Darwin, East Falkland. This is scheduled for tomorrow, so we're being cross-decked to the *Intrepid* this evening. I therefore suggest that you go and get your kit in order. Say goodbye to this useless case on the bed, then get the hell out of here. We've no time to waste.'

'Gee, thanks,' Jock said. 'It's nice to know I'm valued.'

'I'll see you back in Hereford,' Ricketts said, 'when you're out of those bandages. You'll be more valued then. Keep your pecker up, Jock.'

'Aye, boss, I'll do that. Best of luck for tomorrow.'

Ricketts nodded, glanced briefly at the other

men, then raised his hand and spread his fingers. 'Five minutes,' he said, then left Jock to the mercy of his comrades.

'You hear that, Jock?' Andrew said. 'You've got to keep your pecker up.'

'I'll go fetch some splints,' Paddy said. 'I think Jock's going to need them.'

'OK, you bunch of shites,' Jock said, 'you've all had your fun. Now piss off and leave me alone. I've got things to think about – like a hand-job from a saucy wee nurse in Hereford while you're getting your balls shot off.'

'There's still life in this corpse,' Andrew said. 'I take that as a hopeful sign.'

'Amen,' Taff added.

Before any more could be said, the medics came in to prepare Jock for his cross-decking. Ordered out of the sick bay, the troopers shook Jock's hand, offered a few more parting shots, then went up to the flight deck to see him off.

Jock was brought up on a stretcher and mocked relentlessly while being carried across the deck to the Sea King. He waved once, weakly but defiantly, before being hoisted up into the helicopter. Then the door was slammed shut and the helo roared into life, creating a wind that whiplashed the watching troopers before lifting off. It hovered above the helipad like an indecisive bird, then ascended and headed south, joining the many other helos already in the air, noisily cross-decking men and supplies from one ship to the other in the build-up for the forthcoming assault on San Carlos Water.

Ricketts, who was leaning against the railing near the helipad, glanced across at the many other ships of the fleet – aircraft-carriers, destroyers, frigates, hospital ships and landing vessels – now gathering together for the definitive assault on the Falkland Islands. Seeing him there, Danny joined him.

'The first of us to be shipped back,' he said, his gaze focused on the helo that was taking Jock back to Ascension Island.

'Yes,' Ricketts replied distractedly. Then he added ominously: 'Let's hope he's the last.'

Two hours after sunset, nearly thirty members of the Squadron, wearing full belt kit and life-jackets, as well as carrying the usual complement of weapons, boarded a Sea King for the five-minute cross-decking from the *Hermes* to the *Intrepid*, now cruising a mere half-mile away. From there, the Troop would be inserted by sea onto Darwin, East Falkland.

Within minutes the helicopter was in the air and heading across the relatively short stretch of dark sea. In the equally dark, cramped passenger compartment of the helo, the noise was deafening and the atmosphere claustrophobic.

'Thing I most dislike about this whole business,' Andrew said, distractedly checking the ammunition belts criss-crossing his chest, 'are these damned chopper flights. Like being in a coffin. Even worse than a chartered flight to Spain. It don't do me no good, man.'

'It's not a chopper,' the Loadmaster said. As it was only a five-minute flight, he was still standing by the door, getting ready to open it. 'It's a *helicopter* – or a *helo*. Get your terminology right, soldier. We don't like the word "chopper".'

'Strike me dead, man, for using the wrong word, but whether it's a helicopter or a helo, I still don't like it, period.'

'You're just scared of heights is all.'

'I can't see no heights, man. I can't see a damned thing. All I can see is your white face in that overhead light there.'

The Loadmaster grinned. 'More than I can see, friend. In the darkness, you're practically invisible. Must be useful in your line of business. Is that why they took you on?'

'Ha, ha, very funny.' Big Andrew was not amused. He ran his fingers up and down his M203 grenade-launcher, then checked that its incendiary bombs were still in the pockets of the belt criss-crossing his chest. 'You want a tan like this, man, you've got to go and cook in the sun. With me it comes natural.'

'So how come you take charter flights to Spain?'

'I like the rain on the plain.'

The Loadmaster laughed and looked out of the window. 'We're about 300 feet up,' he said. 'We'll be coming in to land any minute, so you've no need to fear.'

'That guy's talking to himself,' Andrew said. 'He can't be talking to me. I don't know what fear means. Hey, Danny, have you ever been scared? Do you know what fear is?'

'I think it's RAF slang,' Danny replied. 'They know lots of words we don't.'

Andrew chuckled at that. 'Right on, my little brother. They've got a language all their own. Phrases like "scared shitless" and "crapping your pants" and "turning white around the gills" and so forth – all the things they know from personal experience, right?'

'Right,' Danny said.

Andrew let the Loadmaster hear his healthy

bellow of laughter. He stopped laughing when the Loadmaster listened intently to his earphones, glanced out of the window again, then said with an evil grin: 'Sorry, guys, but we've got a bit of a delay. Another helo's still sitting on the *Intrepid*'s flight deck, so we're going to have to complete a second circuit.'

'What?' Andrew asked. 'Are you putting me on, man?'

'No, Trooper, I'm not putting you on. We're going to have to stay aloft for a while. But don't worry, it's free. Hey, I notice you haven't gone white around the gills yet. Is that a good sign or simply a physical impossibility?'

Andrew rolled his big brown eyes. 'Oh, we've got a clown on board. Someone should give him a clip-on nose and a striped, cone-shaped hat. Another circuit, for Christ's sake!'

Some of the men were still laughing, but they stopped when they heard a very loud, unusual bang.

The noise was still reverberating through the passenger compartment when the helo tilted sharply, throwing the Loadmaster to the floor, scattering the other men and their equipment, then plunged screaming and shuddering towards the ocean.

'We're going down!' someone bawled.

Stars exploded in Ricketts's head when a boot kicked his temple. He opened his eyes to find himself pinned to the floor – or perhaps the ceiling – in a tangle of writhing bodies – men bawling, weapons clanging – as the helo continued its clamorous dive towards the ocean, shuddering wildly, going into a spin, its engines roaring unnaturally, as if about to explode. Ricketts took a deep breath and reached out for his SLR – too late.

The helo plunged into the sea with a dreadful roaring, tearing noise, metal buckling and shrieking before the water poured in, drenching him, completely submerging him, cutting off all sound. Ricketts was picked up, turned over, battered, sent spinning like a top, then smashed against something hard in that terrible silence. He may have blacked out briefly – he couldn't be sure – but consciousness returned with a sudden inrush of noise – splashing water, bawling men, clattering weapons, twanging metal – and he surfaced beneath the tilting ceiling of the helo, coughing water, surrounded by other bobbing heads, drifting webbing and clothing.

'We're turning over!' someone cried out. 'It's starting to sink!'

That much was true. As Ricketts trod water, unable to find the floor beneath him, he saw that the helo was tilting to the side, sinking, with the water pouring in through the smashed perspex of the cockpit, where the pilot, waist-deep in water, the navigator dead beside him, was clambering out, holding a distress flare in his hand.

With only inches between himself and the ceiling – now actually the overturning side – of the helo, Ricketts had to frantically tread water while being dragged under by his ammunition belts and webbing. Out of the corner of his eye, he saw Andrew's wide eyes and flashing teeth; clinging to a door handle, he was tugging young Danny up out of the water to enable him to shuck off the heavy bergen that was dragging him under. Beyond Andrew, in a jagged frame of shattered perspex, silhouetted by the night sky, now outside the helo and balanced precariously on the smashed nose, the pilot was firing his distress flare.

It shot up out of sight with a whoosh, making the pilot's arm jerk and almost throwing him off the nose, then exploded directly above to illuminate the crashed, sinking helo.

Even as Ricketts felt a brief exhilaration, a dead body surfaced near him, then another, and a third, as the helo turned turtle and sank completely. Ricketts saw the pilot waving his arms wildly and toppling off the turning nose. He caught a glimpse of Andrew and Danny falling into one another and plunging into the rising water. Then he too was submerged as the water reached the turning wall, forcing him down into total darkness, silence, and a numbing cold.

He lost all sense of direction, not knowing up from down, but managed to wriggle out of his webbing and get rid of his heavy boots before he ran completely out of breath and again started blacking out. He forced himself to stay calm and resisted unconsciousness.

It was darkness and silence. A bottomless well. Ricketts was only made aware of himself by the objects, or bodies, bumping into him. *Open your eyes*! he thought. It was hard, but he managed it. Objects darker than the darkness of the water were swirling and turning around him. *Dead bodies*, he thought. The sea's darkness was streaked with light ... *Light*? *What light*? he wondered. *Where's the light coming from*? His lungs were about to burst. He could hardly think straight. His thoughts went in and out like faulty gears as he slipped towards unconsciousness. *Light*! he said in his shrinking mind. *The light's streaking that water filled with dark shapes*. It was dimly illuminating the bodies bobbing and sinking around him. A light coming from somewhere.

He forced his eyes to stay open, though they stung from the salt water. Numbed by cold, bereft of air, Ricketts was sinking and drifting out of himself when he saw where the light was. It looked like a star, now expanding, now contracting, its striations spreading out all around him like a pale, shivering web in which the dark, drifting objects, the drowned bodies, appeared to be trapped.

Ricketts turned towards the light, fighting oblivion, kicking his legs, and reached out to take hold of the star and let its light warm him. He surfaced to a burst of sound – splashing water, bawling men – and saw that the light was the moon beaming down on the sea.

He had made his escape from the sinking helo by swimming up through the hole in the smashed nose, now sinking below him.

Getting his senses back, he realized that the SARBE surface-to-air rescue beacon – essentially a small radio used for communication between the helo and the ship – had probably kept sending out its distress signal until the helo sank beneath the waves. With luck, an SAR, search and rescue, helicopter would soon be on its way. Meanwhile, like the other survivors bobbing around him, he had to stay afloat and hope to be rescued before suffering from hypothermia or even freezing to death.

As the helo sank, bubbles rose to the surface and the high waves turned into a minor whirlpool that picked Ricketts up and swept him in a circle with the other survivors and debris – mostly webbing and clothing. Wiping the water from his eyes as best he could with numbed fingers, he saw Andrew clinging to a rescue dinghy, its automatic search-and-rescue beacon transmitting while the pilot let off more flares. Beyond them, surprisingly far out to sea, Danny Porter drifted all alone. Between them, and between Andrew and Ricketts, were other survivors. Some of them, badly battered in the crash, were already dying and sinking.

The whirlpool created by the sinking helo subsided, leaving the waves to rise and fall as usual. Picked up on the waves, then swept along in the rushing troughs, Ricketts knew he was safe in his life-jacket. He also knew that he was starting to freeze and could do nothing about it.

The dead and their debris were floating all around him when he saw an SAR helicopter emerging from the darkness, its searchlights beaming down on the sea, to illuminate Danny, floating alone, drifting south towards Antarctica.

Even as the helo descended to just above the surface, its spinning rotors sucking the sea up in angry waves that threatened to submerge Danny before he could grab the unfurling lifeline, the lights of a cutter materialized in the distance, obviously coming from the direction of the fleet and heading steadily for the scene of the crash.

Picked up on a high wave, then sucked down through a trough, Ricketts briefly lost sight of Danny. When he was swept back up on the crest of the same wave, he saw Danny in mid-air, swinging from side to side, being winched up to the SAR helo, unreal in the silvery beam of the searchlights, obscured by spray from the surging sea.

The helo flew back towards the fleet, with Danny being winched up as it went, then disappeared into the darkness, taking Danny with it.

Clinging to the rescue dinghy, but seeing the approaching cutter, the resolute pilot of the crashed helo set off another flare. It exploded high above in a brilliant fireworks display, bathing the black sea in its silvery light. In that eerie glow Ricketts saw the other survivors; he also saw the dreadful debris of the crash, including dead bodies kept adrift by their lifebelts, some staring skyward.

Aware that he was freezing, hardly able to feel his limbs, Ricketts kept moving as best he could. It was, he assumed, like having amputated limbs: he could sense them there and will them to move, but he couldn't really feel them. Nevertheless, he was moving – the splashing water told him that – and he kept doing so until the cutter arrived and started picking the men up.

Ricketts was lucky, being one of the first. Rolling onto the deck and being immediately wrapped in blankets, he couldn't feel a thing – not the deck, not his own body – but experienced an enormous exhilaration. Big Andrew followed shortly after, his face wet and gleaming, groaning, 'Christ, man, I'm cold, so damned cold. What the fuck happened, man?' He was rolled onto a stretcher, covered in blankets, given a brandy, then picked up and carried away with Ricketts, who realized, when he floated up beside Andrew, that he, too, was being carried on a stretcher. He was too numb to feel it.

Ricketts, Andrew and Danny spent the rest of the night in bed in the sick bay, recovering from mild hypothermia and unable to sleep properly because the pain, which was caused by the return of feeling to their limbs, made them too uncomfortable.

Early next morning, when Major Parkinson came to see them, he told them that the cause of the crash was unknown, but that it may have been caused by a large seabird being sucked into an engine intake.

'Whatever the reason,' Parkinson said, 'it's been an absolute disaster. Few of the men made it to the surface. Eighteen are dead. You three were lucky.'

'Is the assault on the Falklands still scheduled?' Ricketts asked.

'Yes, Sergeant, it is.'

'What about the diversionary assault on East Falkland? The one we should have made?'

'That's still scheduled as well. We simply can't let this dreadful incident stop us. The diversion is vital.'

'And us?' Ricketts asked, indicating Andrew and Danny in the adjoining beds.

'Just get some rest, Sergeant.'

Parkinson left the sick bay without saying another word. When he had gone, Andrew turned to Ricketts and said, 'He didn't actually answer the question. What does *that* mean?'

'If it means what I think we won't be happy, but let's wait and see.'

Thirty minutes later, the ship's doctor arrived. After examining his three patients in turn, he said: 'Well, lads, aren't *you* the lucky ones? I'm going to have to ship you back to Hereford for recuperation.'

'What recuperation?' Ricketts asked. 'There's nothing wrong with us, doctor.'

'You're suffering from hypothermia.'

'We *were* suffering from that. It was mild and we're not suffering any more. We don't need to recuperate.'

'Yes, you do, Sergeant. This condition is unpredictable. You could even be suffering from shock without knowing it, so you have to go back.'

'Bullshit,' Ricketts said. 'Feed that birdseed to the others. We were first out of the water and we weren't in it long. Trooper Porter – five minutes. Me – about ten minutes. Trooper Winston – a couple of minutes longer than me, but he's as strong as an ox. We're not suffering from hypothermia, Doc, and we're not going back.'

'You'll all do what you're told, Sergeant Ricketts, and that's all there is to it. Now lie down and shut up.'

'Yes, Doc,' Ricketts said. He waited until the

doctor had left the sick bay, then turned to Andrew and Danny. 'So now you know what Parkinson meant. We're not going to take part in the final assault on the Falkand Islands. We're being dropped from the Task Force and sent home to be mended.'

'Mended?' Andrew responded, outraged. 'Who the fuck needs mending? I'm as fit as a fiddle and raring to go, so I don't need no spell in a hospital in Hereford, tucked up nice and cosy with a bunch of whining wimps and premature geriatrics. Fuck it, man, we've come all this way, doing a good job, and now they're planning to send us back. It's a bag of unwholesome shit.'

'I agree,' Ricketts replied.

'So do I,' Danny said. 'I don't think it's fair at all. I'm already bored lying in this bed and we've only been here one night. I want to be part of the assault and take out some more Argies. We've earned that right, Sarge.'

'How do you feel?' Ricketts asked him.

'The same as always. I'm not suffering from hypothermia, I don't have a temperature, and I've got a lot of energy to burn. I don't want to go back, boss.'

'What's that fucking doctor know?' Big Andrew was working himself into a lather. 'He sits on his arse all day, treating a lot of poncy sailors, sticking thermometers up their arses, probably his swollen dong as well, and expressing sympathy when they say they have a cold or got ill drinking mother's milk. He's a fucking Navy doctor – a soft twat treating wimps. He'd send a sailor back for recuperation if he just stubbed his toe. So who's he to say we're not fit enough to fight? Tell him to go bang a few more sailors and let us get on with it.'

His increasingly venomous monologue was only interrupted when Paddy, Gumboot and Taff – who had not been assigned to the diversionary mission to East Falkland and were therefore hale and hearty – arrived at the sick bay for some mischief. When they saw the grim expression on Ricketts's face, the jibes died on their lips.

'Where are our uniforms?' Ricketts asked.

'In the laundry,' Gumboot informed him. 'Being cleaned and pressed.'

'Since last night?'

'Yes, boss.'

'Then they're ready.'

'I guess so.'

'Go and get those three uniforms, Gumboot, and bring them back here.'

'You want your underclothes as well, do you, boss?'

'Don't piss around with me, Gumboot. I want everything – uniforms, underclothes, socks and boots – and I want them right now.'

'I'm on my way, boss.'

Gumboot departed and returned soon enough with the clothing. Ricketts slid out of bed, carelessly washed and dressed himself, combed his dishevelled hair, then marched grimly to the ladies' toilet, still housing the SAS HQ. Major Parkinson was there, leaning over a cluttered table, thoughtfully studying a map of East Falkland with captains Hailsham and Grenville. They all looked up in surprise when Ricketts entered.

'What are you doing here, Sergeant Ricketts?' Parkinson asked. 'I thought you were confined to the sick bay, prior to being flown back to Hereford.'

'I don't want to go back to Hereford, boss. Neither do troopers Winston and Porter. We all want to stay here.'

'What you want is irrelevant, Sergeant. The doc says you must . . .'

'Fuck the doc, boss. He doesn't know shite from shinola. He says we have to go back to recuperate, which is pure bloody nonsense. We were only in that water five minutes and we know how we feel – and we're all feeling fine.'

'I don't give a damn how you feel – you're all going back.'

'No, we're not, boss.'

Parkinson straightened up, glanced at Hailsham and Grenville, then stared unflinchingly at Ricketts. 'You're being insubordinate, Sergeant.'

'What's that mean, boss? That sounds like an RAF or Navy word. It's not a word that I know.'

'A smart ass,' Hailsham said.

'A hard head,' Grenville added.

'A smart-assed hard head,' Parkinson said, 'who's asking for trouble.'

'Him and his troopers,' Hailsham said. 'They're all begging for aggro.'

'Then let's give them a bit of aggro,' Grenville added with a sly grin. 'As much as the bullshit artists can take. It's the least we can do.'

'OK, Sergeant,' Parkinson said, his gaze steady and bright, 'you have heard judgement passed by your superior officers. If it's trouble you want, you can have it.'

'Yes, boss,' Ricketts said.

'We insert tomorrow,' Parkinson told him.

'We're 18 men down, but their replacements are parachuting in tonight. Take care of them, Sergeant.'

'Yes, boss. Thank you, gentlemen.'

A jubilant Ricketts returned to the sick bay, where he eagerly informed Andrew and Danny about the boss's decision. They both raised their clenched fists in the air and let out a loud cheer.

That evening Ricketts, Andrew, Danny, Gumboot and Taff were leaning on the railing of the flight deck, looking out over the calm, moonlit sea as the replacements for the 18 dead jumped out of the tailgate of a Hercules C-130 flying over the fleet. Picked up by the slipstream and spread across the sky, they descended silently on billowing white parachutes, falling silently, gracefully, like pollen in a field at night, to splash one after the other into the sea, rising and falling on foam-capped, murmuring waves.

The replacements popped their life-jackets and floated freely with the tide, waiting patiently for the crew of the Rigid Raiders from the *Hermes* to reach them and pull them to safety.

For a while 18 parachutes drifted like flowers in the black sea.

Eighteen flowers for the 18 dead.

13

The following evening, 60 men of D Squadron landed near Goose Green with GPMGs, a MILAN anti-tank weapon, an American Stinger surface-to-air (SAM) missile system, 81mm mortars, and the usual collection of automatic and semi-automatic rifles, favouring the L1A1 SLR, the Heckler & Koch G3, and the ever-reliable M16. This time their intention was not to hide from the Argentinians, but to let them know they were there and create the impression that a battalion ten times their number had landed.

This would merely be one of several diversions being created that night to distract the enemy's attention from the main landings on the opposite coast, far to the north of Goose Green.

Inserted on East Falkland by Sea King helicopters, the Squadron, led by Major Parkinson and including captains Hailsham and Grenville, embarked on a twenty-four-hour forced march south, across rolling fields of marshy peat and tussock grass whipped constantly by sleet and freezing wind. It was an arduous march offering little respite, but endured with a combination of physical strength and the traditional, though now mostly whispered, bullshit.

'To think you could have escaped this,' Gumboot said to Andrew, 'by letting yourself be shipped back to England and a Hereford rest home. You three must be mad.'

'Dedication, Gumboot. It's a word you won't know. One used by the kind of individual who stands too tall for you to see.'

'Wanking again, are you, Andrew? Tugging that big, purple dong. In real terms I stand taller than you by a mile and a half, so your size doesn't bother me.'

'You mean the size of his purple dong?'

'No, Paddy, I don't. I'm talking about real stature, my friend, though that's a word *you* won't understand.'

'I befriend him and he turns on me. Insults my intelligence. In fact, I once saw a statue in a museum – a naked man with a white dong. I was only a teenager, on an outing with my school class, and the size of the dong on that stature gave me problems for years.'

'It's not the size – it's the quality,' Taff advised with a solemn nod.

'I learnt that too late in life,' Paddy explained, 'which is why I lack stature like my friend here – the Jock with the fantastic vocabulary of words he can't actually spell.'

'You must be talking about Andrew,' Jock said. 'He's the one with the banana-republic education and the need to assert himself. Now me, I'm white as snow with no hang-ups . . .'

'Which is why he stands tall,' Andrew interjected, 'though only five foot five inches in stature. Who the fuck's kidding whom?'

'Quiet back there,' Ricketts said, trying to glance over his shoulder, one eye visible around the edge of his packed bergen and gleaming in the darkness. 'Keep your voices down. You're not supposed to be a bunch of car salesmen, advertising your presence. Zip your lips and pick those feet up. We've a long way to go yet.'

'Yes, boss!' they chorused in a whisper, then did as they were told, leaning into the wind, forcing themselves to go faster, marching throughout the night, resting up before dawn, having a breakfast of cold snacks and water, helping the grass grow with their urine and excrement, then moving on again, into the day's sleet-filled grey light, marching, ever marching, towards the horizon and what lay beyond. Twenty-four hours later, back in early morning's darkness, exhausted but not defeated and still raring to go, they arrived at the Argentinian garrison.

Remarkably, it was brightly illuminated, its defensive slit trenches clearly visible in the lights beaming out of the many huts raised behind them. The sentries, placed well ahead of the trenches, were completely exposed.

'Looks like they're not expecting us,' Parkinson whispered.

'So let's give them a little surprise,' Grenville replied.

'Why not?' Hailsham asked.

After dividing the Squadron into three groups – one led by Hailsham, another by Grenville and the third by himself – Parkinson spread them out over a wide arc as part of his strategy for making the Argentinians believe that they were being attacked by a vastly greater number of men. When the 80 troopers were all in place, Parkinson contacted the *Ardent*, out at sea, requesting that the previously agreed support barrage from its single 4.5in gun be implemented immediately. After the ship had confirmed, Parkinson knelt beside Ricketts and waited.

'Here goes,' Parkinson whispered.

Ricketts merely showed his crossed fingers and gave a broad grin.

The sound of the *Ardent*'s big gun was heard by the Squadron as a distant, muffled boom. Hardly more than a second later the first shell exploded with a mighty roar and the ground erupted in front of the Argentinian slit trenches.

Immediately Parkinson dropped his arm, letting his group open fire with everything they had, including mortars and small arms, causing another shocking, deafening din. Simultaneously Paddy Clarke, as signaller, relayed the firing command to the other two groups, thus releasing a barrage of fire along an arc at least half a mile wide and angled towards the Argentinian positions, as if about to surround them.

Between the *Ardent*'s single gun and the mortars, explosions were now taking place all over the field in front of the enemy positions. Meanwhile the troopers were firing their small arms without letting up. Even before the Argentinians could gather their senses enough to return fire,

Paddy had given new calibrations to the mortars placed farther back. Soon shells were falling between and behind the slit trenches.

Eventually, with mortar and big-gun shells exploding along the length of the Argentinian positions, filling the air with flying soil and wreathing the area in smoke, the enemy returned fire with their small arms.

Noting this, Parkinson had Paddy contact the other two groups by radio and order them to start changing positions, moving even farther apart, to convince the enemy that the line of attack was much wider and involved at least a full battalion.

Even as Paddy did so, and while Sergeant Ricketts was fitting the MILAN anti-tank weapon to its tripod, big Andrew was expertly raking the slit trenches with automatic fire from his roaring GPMG.

Having set up the MILAN, Ricketts lay behind it, beside Taff Burgess, who already was squinting down into its optical sight. Getting the target centred in his thermal-imaging sight, which would bring the SACLOS semi-automatic guidance system into play, Taff placed one hand firmly over the carry handle, to hold the MILAN steady, then carefully pressed the trigger grip.

The backblast rocked his body, as if tugging him off the ground, and the anti-tank missile shot out of the exit point and raced on a plume of fire-streaked smoke towards the enemy position. The ground erupted just in front of the prefabricated buildings lined up behind the slit trenches, filling the air with billowing smoke and showering the men in the trenches with raining soil.

'Too short,' Ricketts said.

'Give me a chance,' Taff replied. 'The next one won't be too short, boss. Just hold on to your hat.'

Glancing across the field, Ricketts saw that the Argentinians, though returning the SAS fire, had still not left their trenches.

'It's working,' he said to Major Parkinson. 'They obviously think we're a whole battalion and they're scared to come out.'

'Let's hope it stays that way,' Parkinson said.

More shells from the mortars and another from the *Ardent* caused havoc to the Argentinian defensive trenches, the air above and in front of them filled with smoke, raining soil and debris.

Smiling dreamily, Taff inserted another missile with folded wings into the launcher tube of the MILAN, squinted down into the optical sight, centred his target and pressed the trigger grip.

The backblast was deafening and rocked him again, but this time he was on target and one of the buildings behind the slit trenches was hit, exploding in flames, its roof being blown off, the walls collapsing in on the flames and causing a great shower of sparks.

'Good one, Taff,' Ricketts said.

'Damn right, it's a good one,' Taff replied. 'Right on the nose, boss!'

Hot debris from the explosion rained down on the slit trenches as some Argentinian troops, screaming in agony, tried to climb out. Big Andrew, monolithic behind his GPMG, cut them down with a short, precise burst. The Argentinians threw up their arms as soil and dust spat about them. They jerked and shook epileptically, toppled over in all directions, hit the ground beneath the still showering debris or rolled back down into the trenches.

'Take that, you cunts,' Andrew hissed, continuing to rake the area with murderous fire as young Danny, right beside him, methodically picked off single targets with his SLR, whispering, 'One, two, three', as he did so, like a kid playing marbles in the schoolyard, counting them off as he hit them, the number growing each time. The Argentinians were falling like flies, but they didn't seem real from where he was.

'The rest are still keeping their heads down,' Ricketts observed. 'They think we're here in our hundreds.'

Parkinson checked his wristwatch. 'Good,' he said. 'Paddy, get me HQ on that radio.' Handed the phone, he plugged his free ear with his finger, to cut out the ferocious noise of the battle taking place on both sides and to the front, then listened intently to what he was being told by HQ on the *Hermes*.

Passing the phone back, he said: 'The invasion of the Falklands has commenced. *Fearless* and *Intrepid* are anchored off Jersey Point, West Falkland, with the troops already disembarked from the LCUs and advancing inland. *Brilliant*, *Canberra*, *Norland*, *Fort Austin* and *Plymouth* are anchored in the Falkland Straits. The *Antrim*'s guns are shelling Fanning Head in support of the landings there. More ships are presently steaming into San Carlos Water and Port Stanley is under constant air attack. This is it, gentlemen.'

Again taking the phone, Parkinson contacted the other two groups, led by Hailsham and Grenville, told them the news, then ordered them to spread out even more and continue the mock assault on the Darwin defences. That they did so was soon indicated by the increased size of the arc of fire, which now seemed at least a mile long.

Parkinson moved his own men, then moved them again, and kept doing this as the others were doing the same. They kept this up throughout the morning, never letting up on their fire, and the Argentinians, obviously thinking that they were being attacked by a full battalion, returned the fire in a confused, desultory manner, but never left their slit trenches.

By the hour before dusk the three groups had advanced and spread out until they were practically forming an immense semicircle around the burning, smoking enemy defences. Keeping contact by radio, Parkinson told them to keep firing until dawn, then advance under cover of the morning's remaining darkness and meet up at their chosen grid location well north of the confused Argentinian troops.

By this time, too, he had learned from constant radio communication with the fleet that 12 British ships were now in the Falkland Straits, another five warships were patrolling just outside, and the landing troops, including

40 Commando and 2 Para, were occupying Port San Carlos and Ajax Bay.

By the early hours of the following morning, when the three SAS groups had stopped firing, circled around the blazing, smoking Argentinian positions, and met up north of Darwin, to embrace each other, shake hands and settle down to a good breakfast, the landings on the opposite coast had been a complete success and the battle for the Falkland Islands was well under way.

14

'I'm proud to say,' Major Parkinson informed his troops when they had gathered north of Darwin, though still in sight of the smoke rising from the burning buildings of the Argentinian garrison, 'that the British landing troops were guided in by the torches of the SBS already ashore and hiding out in OPs. Congratulations, Captain Grenville.'

'Thanks, boss. They knew what they were doing. Now what about the 80 men we have here? What do we do with them?'

'Create havoc,' Parkinson said. 'We break up into 16 groups of five, all heading north, but each covering different areas, and we gradually make our way to Port Stanley, harassing the enemy in whatever way we can – wherever we can.'

'Sounds good to me,' Captain Hailsham said.

'Keep the Argies dancing on tiptoe, turning left and right.'

'Hit and run,' Parkinson said. 'Disorientation and confusion. Outside the normal chain of command. All the way to Port Stanley.'

'Naughty, but nice,' Grenville said.

'Better than sitting here waiting to be lifted out,' Captain Hailsham added. 'A positive contribution.'

'Might cause a little annoyance at HQ,' Grenville reminded them.

'Who dares wins,' Parkinson said with a grin.

Pleased with themselves, they divided the men into 16 groups of five, with Parkinson getting Sergeant Ricketts and troopers Winston, Porter and Gillis, the latter acting as signaller.

With one man placed in charge of each group, the teams were given individual grid references before moving off in open formation, all heading north, but in slightly different directions, thus gradually losing sight of one another in the broad, mist-wreathed fields.

Soon Parkinson and his team were all alone in the visible landscape, marching in file formation, with Danny well in front, taking the 'point' as lead scout, Parkinson second in line as PC, Gumboot third as signaller, Ricketts protecting

Gumboot, and Andrew, heavily burdened with an American Stinger SAM system, as well as his GPMG and packed bergen, bringing up the rear as Tail-end Charlie.

By nine that morning they learnt from Gumboot's radio that the only casualty during the landing at San Carlos Water was the loss of three Royal Marines air-crew, forced down when fired on by enemy ground forces. However, over the next hour they saw many Argentinian aircraft, including Pucaras, Skyhawks and Daggers, flying from the mainland and Port Stanley, towards the sea and back, obviously attacking the fleet and the landing force.

The sound of bombing was clear even from where they were marching, now farther north of Darwin, though they were encouraged to learn, both visually and from Gumboot's radio, that Port Stanley and the enemy positions around it were being attacked relentlessly by Sea Harriers dropping air-burst shells and 1000lb bombs, as well as by Vulcans firing American Shrike radiation-homing missiles. The smoke darkening the sky on the horizon was boiling up from Port Stanley.

After a four-hour march, the men had encountered no enemy forces, though they had seen an enormous build-up in the number of British aircraft heading to and from Port Stanley. Stopping for a light lunch of biscuits, chocolate and water, Parkinson checked the southern landscape through binoculars and saw troops advancing across the high ground south of San Carlos Water. Giving Gumboot the grid location and asking him to check on the radio, he was informing that the advancing troops belonged to 2 Para.

'They'll capture what's left of Darwin,' he told Ricketts. 'This advance won't be stopped now. Come on, let's get moving.'

The farther north they advanced, the closer they came to the many inland Argentinian positions, including airstrips. For this reason, flights of enemy aircraft to and from the sea increased, and grew ever closer, the harsh, relentless chatter of their automatic weapons soon adding to the distant noise of exploding bombs.

Late that afternoon they heard over the radio that in San Carlos Water, now dubbed 'Bomb Alley', their support ship, the *Ardent*, had been sunk, the *Argonaut* crippled, and the *Antrim*, *Brilliant* and *Broadsword* all hit by enemy bombs, each suffering different degrees of damage, most of it serious. Also, one Sea Harrier and two

245

helicopters had been lost. In return, 12 Argentinian aircraft had been destroyed and the British force, having gained a foothold on the Falklands, was poised to break out and advance on Port Stanley.

Parkinson and his four men spent that first night in a star-shaped OP, taking turns to sleep, listening to the distant sounds of relentless bombing and assiduously keeping notes on the movements and frequency of Argentinian aircraft. No enemy troops were seen, so at first light they filled in the OP and moved out again, continuing their long march to Port Stanley, following the bleak, windswept coast-line.

By dusk they had still seen no enemy troops, so they built an OP and spent another night listening to the radio, sleeping in turn and observing the movements of enemy aircraft.

By dawn they were on the move again, all alone in the vast landscape, but still hearing the sounds of battle in the distance and seeing enemy aircraft flying to and from Port Stanley. During a break for lunch, again cold snacks and water, they learnt from the radio that three more British ships had been hit by Argentinian bombs and Exocet AM.39 missiles, two already sunk, the third sinking.

'The Argentinians are being foolish,' Major Parkinson said. 'They're concentrating all their attacks on the warships in Falkland Sound while ignoring the landing and supply ships. No wonder our troops are advancing with relative ease.'

'I'm glad to hear it,' Ricketts replied.

'I just wish we'd run into some Argies,' young Danny said. 'I'm bored just wandering about here.'

'Right, man,' Andrew said. 'I agree with that sentiment.'

'A right pair of bloody warmongers, you two,' Gumboot informed them. 'Always after the action.'

'It's in the blood,' Andrew retorted. 'We're the sons of the Regiment. Come on, Argies, where the hell are you? I want to cop me an Argie!'

He got his wish soon enough.

Just before dusk they arrived at a lonely farmhouse in a wind-blown valley between Fitzroy and Bluff Cove, with the sea of Port Pleasant Bay visible beyond the edge of the distant cliff. Signalling for the others to drop to the ground, Parkinson, also belly-down, examined the farmhouse through his binoculars.

A single track snaked from the horizon, across that desolate valley of gorse, to the lonely farmhouse. An enemy troop truck was parked in front of it. Smoke was rising from its chimney, indicating that the fire inside was being used. Armed soldiers were wandering casually in and out by the front door, some drinking from mugs. Between Parkinson's group and the house, but well away from it, an Argentinian private was standing guard – though he was in fact sitting on an upturned bucket, smoking a cigarette, distractedly studying his own feet instead of the landscape, his rifle resting carelessly on his crossed legs.

'A sitting duck,' Danny whispered.

'That's a mobile radio patrol,' Parkinson said, noting the makeshift antenna on the roof of the house. 'They're probably using that place as an OP – making daily trips around the area, reporting back what they learn about our troop movements. I don't think we should let them.'

'Absolutely not,' Ricketts replied.

'Let's take it.' Parkinson lowered his binoculars and rubbed his tired eyes. 'Trooper Porter?'

'Yes, boss,' Danny replied, not even having to ask, knowing exactly what was expected and already unstrapping his bergen, to lower it to the ground and leave himself free to move easily. This done, he removed his Fairburn-Sykes commando knife from its sheath, held it firmly in his right hand, then advanced crouched low, with the stealth of a cat, dropping down and rising up and running crouched low again, until he was coming around, then behind, the unsuspecting guard.

Meanwhile, as big Andrew was unslinging his GPMG and holding it across his upturned left arm in the Belfast cradle, Ricketts and Gumboot were covering the distant house with their M16s.

The unwary guard was still studying his booted feet, his clothes flapping in the moaning wind, when Danny rose up behind him, as silent and insubstantial as a wisp of smoke, to slide one hand over his mouth, blocking off all sound, and slash his jugular with the commando knife.

The guard quivered like a bowstring and kicked out with one leg, but Danny dragged him off the bucket and pulled him down to the ground before he could make any sound or further movement. They both vanished in the gorse, Danny on top of his victim, waiting for his final, despairing breath and the stillness of death.

Eventually Danny reappeared, resting on his

knees, waving inward with his raised right hand, signalling the rest of them forward.

'Fucking great!' Andrew whispered.

Still cradling the GPMG, he advanced to where Danny was waiting for him. There, ignoring the dead man, he fixed the machine-gun to its tripod, checked the alignment and prepared to fire on the farmhouse. Changing his mind, he signalled to the others, now coming up behind him, to take cover again, which they did by lying belly-down on the ground. Andrew then clipped his M203 grenade-launcher to the underside of the barrel of his M16, slid the barrel forward and loaded the grenade, then stood up in full view of the enemy troops milling about in front of the farmhouse.

One of the Argentinians looked across the field, directly at Andrew, just as he took the firing position, squinted along the pop-up sight of the M203, braced himself by spreading his thick legs, and fired the grenade.

The Argentinian shouted a warning and threw himself to the ground as the backblast rocked even Andrew's huge bulk and the grenade smashed through a window of the house, sending glass everywhere. The grenade exploded a second later, blowing the other windows out, as Ricketts, Danny and Gumboot opened fire with their M16s, raking the front of the farmhouse, cutting down the few Argentinians who had been too shocked to throw themselves to the ground. The other soldiers started crawling back to the house, where the walls were spitting concrete, but Andrew fired his M203 again, and this time, when the grenade exploded inside the house, it ignited some form of gas – either a cooker or a container – and yellow flames curled out through the windows, clawing at the darkening sky.

The front door burst open and some men rushed out, screaming and slapping at their burning uniforms. They either collapsed of their own accord, rendered unconscious by pain, or were cut down by the semi-automatic fire of the M16s. Then big Andrew placed his M203 on the ground, knelt behind the machine-gun, and proceeded to rake the front of the house, left to right, up and down, until the wall was a living thing, spitting concrete and dust, and the men on the ground in front, trying to crawl back indoors, became whirling dervishes in clouds of exploding soil, their screams lost in the clamour.

Parkinson raised his right hand and waved it in a forward direction, indicating 'Advance'. As Andrew changed the belt in the GPMG, Ricketts, Danny and Gumboot followed Parkinson across the field to the farmhouse, all still firing their weapons as they advanced. Reaching the troop truck, which remained untouched, they saw that the Argentinians in front of the house were either dead or close to it. Some were badly scorched, others soaked in their own blood. The few still alive would not live long and were scratching instinctively at the earth, needing something to cling to.

Knowing that Andrew was keeping them covered, Parkinson led the others into the house. It was a mess. The fragmentation grenades had caused utter havoc, with dead Argentinians peppered with shrapnel, the walls scorched, floorboards torn up and splintered, and the flames, still flickering out through the windows, coming from a punctured portable gas container used for the stove. The Argentinian radio equipment, also badly damaged in the explosions, was sparking and smoking.

'No more messages through that,' Parkinson said with satisfaction. 'No tales about the British advance. A job well done, men.' He went to the table in the middle of the room, which was covered in papers, some of them starting to curl at the edge from the heat of the flames. Flipping through them, at first carelessly, then more intently, he said: 'Well, well, what have we here?' He picked the papers up and waved them in front of Ricketts. 'Precise details of the Argentinian defences. These could be useful. I don't think we can hang around here, Sergeant. We have to get to Port Stanley. That truck outside was untouched, I believe?'

'Yes, boss.'

'Then let's take it. We can get to Port Stanley earlier than planned and set up an OP. However, first I've got to talk to HQ and give them this info.'

After leading them back outside, Parkinson told Ricketts to give Andrew the all-clear, which the latter did with a hand signal. As Andrew was packing up his GPMG and walking up to join them, Parkinson wandered around the front of the house, checking the Argentinian dead and wounded, all of whom were covered in dust and mud. The wounded, however, continued to moan and claw at the earth.

'Let's put them out of their misery,' Baby Face said, stroking the knife sheathed on his hip.

'No, Trooper,' Parkinson said. 'Let's attend to them.'

'There's only the five of us here, boss. We don't have any medics.'

'We have our personal first-aid kits.'

'For personal use, boss. Besides, these men are pretty badly wounded; we can't do much for them.'

'We can stop their bleeding and give them morphine,' Parkinson said. 'Don't shit me, Trooper.'

'Sorry, boss,' Danny said. He glanced at Gumboot, who just shrugged, then withdrew his first-aid kit from his bergen. The others did the same and they all pooled their first-aid kits. Gumboot, who was well trained in medical emergencies, began patching up the Argentinian wounded as best he could as Andrew joined them, setting his GPMG on the ground and flexing his fingers.

'That's some heavy fucker,' he said, 'though she's well worth the effort. What are *you* doing, Gumboot?'

'Patching up these wounded Argies.'

'What the hell for? Those are *our* first-aid kits, man!'

'You don't like it, Trooper?' Major Parkinson asked.

'Just passin' a comment, boss.'

'Weren't you trained in first-aid, Trooper?'

'Sure enough, boss.'

'Then take over from Trooper Gillis. I need

him to stay with me on that radio. Gumboot, get in touch with HQ. Trooper Winston is going to play doctor. He's a man in a million.'

'Sure am, boss,' big Andrew said, looking disgusted. 'Right on, boss, I'm in there.'

Danny stood guard by the truck while Andrew reluctantly patched up the Argentinian wounded, Ricketts gave them cigarettes and water, and Parkinson, with the help of Gumboot, contacted HQ on the *Hermes* and relayed the information he had found in the papers of the enemy patrol. HQ expressed their thanks. They did no more than that. Though the information would hasten the reconquest of Port Stanley, its source would never be revealed. Parkinson and his men were not supposed to be here, so officially they weren't here.

'Thank you, boss,' Parkinson said over the radio to his superior aboard the *Hermes*. 'Over and out.' Handing the phone back to Gumboot, he glanced back over his shoulder at Andrew, still patching up the Argentinian casualties, and asked. 'How are they?'

'Not good, boss. Fucked, actually. No minor wounds here. I've patched them up and filled them with morphine, but they need more attention.'

'We can't take them with us,' Parkinson said, 'so let's leave them some food and water and send someone back later.'

'You're too kind, boss.'

'These poor sods didn't ask for this war. They're just like you and I, Trooper.'

'We're a bit short on food and water ourselves, boss.'

'You're a member of the Regiment, Trooper, and should rise to a challenge.'

'Yes, boss, I hear you.'

In fact the few surviving Argentinians were so badly wounded, so deeply in shock, that they could hardly mutter their thanks when the SAS troopers each contributed half of their rations to a small food-well for them. Ricketts threw in a couple of extra packets of cigarettes as Major Parkinson was climbing up into the front of the Argentinian troop truck and the rest of the men were getting into the back. Ricketts waved goodbye to the dust-covered, moaning Argentinians, then he climbed up into the driver's seat of the truck, beside Major Parkinson, and drove off, the truck bouncing and rattling along the muddy, wind-whipped road, heading for the stormy horizon way past Bluff Cove.

'This will save us boot leather as well as

time,' Major Parkinson said. 'It's so nice to go travelling.'

'I'll second that,' Ricketts said.

They drove through the night and stopped just before dawn, well on the road to Port Stanley. Breakfasting on the last of their meagre dry rations – the rest had been given to the wounded Argentinians – they learned over the radio that the enemy garrisons at Darwin and Goose Green, psychologically destroyed by the SAS diversionary raid, had fallen to the 2nd Parachute Regiment, with 1300 Argentinians taken prisoner. Since then, the 550 Marines of 42 Commando had yomped eastward, all the way from Ajax Bay on San Carlos Water, to Teal Inlet, about ten miles north-west of Port Stanley, which they had secured with the aid of SBS teams already placed there.

'Another medal for Captain Grenville,' Parkinson said with a smile of pleasure and pride. 'OK, men, let's go.'

They had only been driving for thirty minutes, into increasingly hilly terrain, when they were attacked by a British Sea Harrier. Flying in from the west, obviously engaged in an inland recce, the pilot could not resist a lone Argentinian troop truck and swept in low to rake it with his guns.

Momentarily forgetting that he was driving an enemy truck, Ricketts was shocked by the attack, accelerated automatically, then realized what was happening and slammed on the brakes, thus throwing the vehicle into a skid, with the men in the rear tumbling about and bawling. Careering across the road, the truck ploughed into soft earth, bounced up and down, shuddered violently and came to rest, as the Harrier roared directly overhead and away again, its bullets still stitching lines of spitting soil across the field by the road.

'Shit!' Ricketts exclaimed, opening his door and dropping down to the ground as Major Parkinson did the same and the other men jumped out of the rear, not forgetting to throw their kit and weapons out first.

'Take cover!' Major Parkinson shouted. 'Get as far away from the truck as possible. He's coming back! *Go now!*'

True enough, the Sea Harrier was completing a great circle in the sky above the Atlantic, beyond the edge of the field.

The men scattered as it returned, first seeming to glide, then rushing and roaring at them, its guns roaring also, the bullets preceding the aircraft by creating lines of spitting soil that raced across the field and peppered the truck, including the petrol tank, making it explode with a godalmighty clamour.

Ricketts and the others were just throwing themselves to the ground when the truck's doors were blown off, its tyres burst into flames and melted instantaneously, and its canvas top became a great bonfire under a mushroom of oily smoke. The Harrier had already ascended and disappeared in the distance when the truck, already a blackened shell wreathed in flame and smoke, hiccuped from internal convulsions and collapsed onto wheels devoid of tyres, the melted rubber still smouldering.

'Shit!' Ricketts exclaimed again.

'There goes our transport,' Gumboot said.

'A British Harrier!' Andrew burst out. 'I don't fuckin' believe it!'

'OK, men,' Major Parkinson said, climbing back to his feet and wiping the earth from his Gore-tex jacket, 'if we must yomp, we must. Pick up your kit and let's go. No point staying here.'

'Yes, boss,' Danny said.

Falling automatically into single file, in the usual order, they continued their march to Port

Stanley. Now crossing the empty fields between Bluff Cove and Sapper Hill, they were seeing more aircraft, both British and Argentinian, as well as hearing the sounds of battle more clearly. There was smoke in the distant sky, boiling up from the horizon, and they knew that it was coming from Port Stanley, now being bombed daily.

Later that afternoon, they were attacked by another aircraft, this time an Argentinian Pucara that roared out of nowhere, all guns firing, stitching the earth all around them, then flew off again and circled to come back. Now mad as hell, big Andrew removed his American Stinger SAM system from where it was strapped to his bergen, inserted a missile canister armed with a 3kg high-explosive fragmentation warhead, and stood up in full view of the approaching aircraft.

As the Pucara flew low, already firing its guns and creating lines of spitting soil that raced dangerously towards Andrew, he coolly fitted the Stinger's shoulder-rest into his shoulder, held the foregrip, squinted into the aiming sight and pressed the trigger located in the grip.

Armed with an infrared seeker and sensors that could track its target by the heat of its exhausts, the Stinger's surface-to-air missile streaked upwards and hit the Pucara as it was levelling out to ascend. The plane exploded with a mighty roar, turning into a spectacular ball of searing white flame and boiling black smoke, with its debris thrown far and wide, to rain down on the field. Andrew lowered the Stinger to his side and raised his free hand in the air, clenching his fist.

'How's that, fucker?' he bawled.

'I don't think he's going to answer,' Ricketts said. 'I think the cat's got his tongue.'

Andrew laughed and shook his head, as if bemused by Ricketts's statement, then hugged the Stinger to his chest. 'Sheer poetry,' he said.

Parkinson watched the ball of fire shrinking away in the sky, disappearing in the smoke being dispersed by the wind. 'I think the closer we get to Port Stanley, the more exposed we'll become. We're going to have to restrict ourselves to night marches and hide out in the daylight. I think a long-term OP should be made right here. Get to it, gentlemen.'

A rectangular OP was constructed in no time and the men, hidden under its camouflaged roof, became one with the barren earth.

15

During the next ten days Parkinson and his men holed up in their OP and only ventured out on deep-penetration patrols or to ambush Argentinians on the snow-covered hills. Their unfortunate victims, mostly inexperienced conscripts, usually on foot patrol, invariably in small groups, were cut down with relative ease by a combination of Andrew's GPMG, the M16s of the other men and the occasional fragmentation grenade.

More than once, usually at night, Danny was called upon to despatch a guard, which he always did with his customary deadly skill. This was often the prelude to an attack on an enemy OP or radio station; once the attack was completed, the radio would be destroyed and the printed data removed by Major Parkinson, to be relayed from the SAS OP to HQ on the *Hermes*, still out at sea with the fleet.

In their own small, anonymous way, Parkinson's group – and the many other SAS groups spread out across East Falkland – caused confusion and fear among the enemy, while also disrupting their communications and practising psychological warfare, or 'psyops' against them, so making the advance on Port Stanley easier for the other British troops.

When not thus engaged, the men hid out in their damp, claustrophobic, camouflaged OP, either observing and detailing enemy troop and aircraft movements or listening to the progress of the war on the BBC World Service. Through the latter they learnt that although the British now had air superiority, a briefly revitalized Argentinian Air Force was relentlessly bombing British forces on Fitzroy, Bluff Cove and Mount Kent.

'That won't last too long,' Gumboot said with an air of satisfaction. 'If they're the same as the Argies we encountered at Darwin and Goose Green – the ones who didn't have the nerve to climb out of their bleedin' trenches – I'd say those pilots will soon be finding excuses to have themselves grounded.'

'The Argentinians on Pebble Island were courageous,' Ricketts said, 'and if their pilots are of the same calibre, they could fight on for ever.'

'No way,' Gumboot replied. 'We've demolished half of their fucking planes. They're now flying on a wing and a prayer, just waiting to come down.'

'Meanwhile they're doing a lot of damage,' Andrew said, carefully oiling his weapons, 'so it's not over yet.'

More encouraging was the news that the British were patrolling the mountains around Port Stanley. When, on 11 June, Parkinson learnt from HQ that the battle for Port Stanley was about to begin, with night attacks against the major mountains of East Falkland – Longdon, Two Sisters and Harriet – he decided it was time to move on.

'We've done all we can do here,' he informed the men lying, half frozen, on both sides of him in their dug-outs in the OP. 'There's no more need for reconnaissance or harassment in this area. It's time to be heading for Port Stanley, where we'll be of more use.'

'When do we go?' Ricketts asked him.

'Why not right now?' Parkinson replied rhetorically, having already made up his mind. 'Let's pack up our kit, fill in the OP and get moving. We can march throughout the night while the main attacks are being launched, arriving at Port Stanley some time tomorrow. That's when we'll be useful.'

The men did as they were told, dismantling the OP, filling in the dug-out and carefully hiding anything that would reveal they had been there. Then they set off on the road to Port Stanley.

Marching throughout the night, sticking close to the coastline, intending to come in south of Port Stanley, they were whipped constantly by heavy wind, sleet and snow. They were, however, encouraged by the sounds and sights of battle, most a couple of miles to the north where the attacks on Mount Harriet, Tumbledown and Mount William were being undertaken by Nos 4 and 7 Infantry Regiments, as well as the crack 5 Marine Battalion.

The battle being engaged, the night sky was criss-crossed with dazzling white phosphorus tracers, coloured crimson, yellow and blue by fire, stained black by smoke. For most of the march they could hear 155mm and 105mm Argentinian artillery, the return fire of the 4.5in guns of the fleet, 105mm howitzers, 66mm anti-tank rockets, exploding 81mm mortar shells, chattering machine-guns and whining, growling aircraft, most of them British. Other explosions, Parkinson assumed, were being caused by enemy minefields, which reminded him to warn the patrol to watch the ground in front of them, as best they could, in the stormy, snow-whitened darkness.

When dawn broke they found themselves in a rugged, hilly, mist-wreathed landscape devastated by war. The battle for the three mountains around Port Stanley had been fought with bullets, grenades and bayonets under cover of mortar, artillery and machine-gun fire. Now, in an area pock-marked with shell holes, some caused by mines, the enemy trenches and sangars camouflaged in rocky outcrops were scorched black and filled with corpses buried in debris.

Luckier, but not looking appreciative, were the hundreds of weary, shocked Argentinian prisoners who were being marched at gunpoint to makeshift camps of barbed wire and canvas, where they would be held until the reconquest of Port Stanley, then almost certainly shipped back to Argentina.

Making their way across the rocky ridges and rugged spines of the hills around Port Stanley, Parkinson and his group came into contact with battle-weary Scots Guardsmen, Welsh Guards, Marines, Commandos, Paratroopers, Gurkhas, REMFs, and even Forward Observers from 148 Commando Battery Royal Artillery.

Port Stanley was now visible from the heights, though covered in smoke from the exploding shells of the Naval gunline bombarding the airport, the racecourse and Sapper Hill. As the port had not yet been taken, British and Argentinian aircraft were still flying to and fro, the former bombing Port Stanley and inland, the latter attacking the Fleet. Helicopters, all British, were landing and taking off in a race to transport the growing numbers of wounded to the Forward Dressing Stations of Teal and Fitzroy, or the Main Dressing Station at Ajax, further away on San Carlos Water.

All of this could be seen from the desolate, mountainous region, south of Port Stanley, through which Parkinson and his men were reso-lutely marching. They were therefore surprised when they saw another farmhouse, isolated at the end of a track that snaked between windswept fields, being used by Argentinian troops. As the house offered a clear view of Port Stanley, it was clearly an observation post.

Parkinson signalled his men to go belly-down,

then he studied the house through binoculars.

'No doubt about it,' he told Ricketts. 'It's being used as an OP. There's a temporary aerial on the roof and a telescope thrusting out of one window. They're observing the movements of our troops around Port Stanley. Passing the info to their aircraft and big guns. We must have wandered into one of the few areas still not held by our own men. This is an Argie stronghold.'

Ricketts glanced about him, at the bleak, rolling hills, seeing nothing but swirling snow, wind-blown gorse, and the boats of the British Fleet, some bombed, still smouldering and sinking, in the grey sea beyond. 'The only Argies I see are outside that house,' he told Major Parkinson.

'Which means there are more *inside* the house.'

'So I suggest we take out the house and then be on our way – in fact all the way down to Port Stanley, to meet the rest of the Regiment. What say you, boss?'

'I say we don't have a choice, Sergeant. We go around it or through it.'

'Let's go through it, boss.'

Doubtless because this OP was close to Port

Stanley and surrounded by an advancing British army, instead of a single sentry distractedly studying his own feet, it was guarded by a pair of three-man trenches, one on each side of the dirt track leading up to its gardens. Both slit trenches had machine-gun emplacements, which made them formidable.

'A short, sharp shock,' Parkinson whispered.

'Fragmentation grenades to clear the trenches,' Ricketts suggested, 'then smoke grenades to cover our run up to the house. That should just about do it.'

'Let's hope so,' Parkinson said.

Signalling with his hands, he sent Danny and Andrew in opposite directions, both crouched low and advancing on either side of the dirt track, offered slight protection by the fall of the land in the frost-covered fields. As they were doing this, Parkinson, Ricketts and Gumboot, still flat on their bellies, covered the house with their M16s and SLRs. Danny and Andrew then also dropped down, both in protective furrows, and crawled forward, each on opposite sides of the dirt track, until they were in line with the slit trenches, just behind the line of vision of the sentries. They were out of sight for a moment, as if they had never existed, though some snow was then seen to move where they were obviously contorting to get at their webbing. Then two hands appeared, one on each side of the trenches, swinging in deceptive slow motion, releasing the smoke grenades.

One of the sentries glanced sideways, hearing the noise of Danny's throw, and shouted a warning – too late – as the smoke grenade fell into the trench. Danny's grenade exploded noisily, followed immediately by Andrew's, then the fragmentation grenades also looped into the trenches, even as smoke was billowing up to choke the panicking sentries. The second explosions were catastrophic, devastating the trenches, with soil and debris spewed at the sky on billowing mushrooms of black smoke.

The screaming of the sentries caught in the explosions was drowned out by the sudden, savage roar of the SAS small arms.

'Go!' Parkinson bellowed, jumping up and running forward, followed closely by Ricketts and Gumboot as Danny and Andrew, also jumping to their feet, ran in towards one another to check the trenches. Ignoring the trenches, Parkinson, Ricketts and Gumboot raced straight for the house, firing from the hip, hidden by the smoke from the grenades and further protected by the element of surprise. As they plunged into the smokescreen created by the grenades, Danny and Andrew were closing in on both sides of them, converging on the trenches, and putting paid to the survivors, if such there were, by automatically peppering them with deadly bursts from their SLRs.

Oblivious, Parkinson, Ricketts and Gumboot were bursting out of the clouds of smoke, still firing from the hip, to race over the gardens in front of the house where the enemy troops were bellowing, screaming, quivering like bowstrings, and collapsing in the hail of bullets from the three semi-automatic weapons.

Reaching the front of the house, where trucks and a jeep where parked, Parkinson quickly scanned the area, noted the dead and dying – no threat posed here any more – then pressed his spine to the wall beside the front door, which was open. A savage burst of gunfire suddenly came from the windows as Ricketts and Gumboot, ducking low and diving forward, reached the other side of the door, from where the latter hurled a grenade into the house.

The subsequent explosion filled the house with flame and smoke, letting Parkinson slip in through the front door, already firing his weapon in a wide arc taking in the whole room. He saw vague figures in smoke and dust, rising up, falling down, then Ricketts and Gumboot were right there behind him, also firing their weapons. The room reverberated with screaming, but no shots were fired back. Parkinson went in further, shooting anything that moved, and only stopped when the smoke escaped through the open door and smashed windows, letting him see that the house was devastated – and that all the Argentinians on the floor were either dead or dying.

'There's their damned radio,' Ricketts said. 'Fuck that for a joke.' He let rip with a burst of fire from his M16. The radio, which had been receiving British broadcasts, exploded and burst into flames. '*Adiós*,' Ricketts said.

Parkinson was already rifling through the Army documents littering the kitchen table, which had been used for a desk, when a mortar shell exploded in the front garden, shaking the whole house, spewing dust and soil through the smashed windows.

'Christ!' Parkinson exclaimed softly, not even ducking, but looking out through the front door, 'was that us or them?'

Before Ricketts could answer, Danny raced

through the open front door, practically pirouetting to a halt, to gasp: 'We're surrounded by Argies! They were dug in all around the house, as far as four or five hundred yards out. They're moving in on us, Major.'

'*All* around us?' Parkinson asked as Andrew followed Danny into the house.

'Yes, boss!' Andrew said, his eyes as bright as diamonds. 'We're completely surrounded, boss.'

'Damn!' Parkinson hammered his fist on the table, glanced at the door and windows, then focused his gaze on the charred, bloody, dead men in the room. 'They're not about to take prisoners after this. They won't have time for small talk.'

'We have to leave,' Ricketts said. 'It's get out or be done in.'

'Two-man teams,' Parkinson said. 'One man looking after the other. Out the back door and run like the clappers, trusting in God or luck. You and Danny go first, Ricketts, then Andrew and Gumboot.'

'What about you, boss?'

'Two-man teams,' Parkinson said. 'Each man depending on the other. It's the best – the only – way in these circumstances. Get going, Ricketts.'

273

'That leaves you alone, boss.'

'Two and two, Ricketts. *Go!*'

'You're the CO of the Squadron,' Ricketts said, 'so I can't leave you here.'

'I'm responsible for my men,' Parkinson said, 'and they have to take orders.' Another mortar shell exploded out in the front garden, shaking the house, showering more soil and dust through the open door and smashed windows. When the explosion had done its worst and subsided, the hoarse shouts and firing weapons of the Argentinians could more clearly be heard. 'Time's up,' Parkinson continued. 'And an order is an order, Sergeant Ricketts, so get the hell out of here.' He turned to Andrew. 'Leave the GPMG, Trooper Winston. Goodbye and good luck.'

Andrew unshouldered the heavy GPMG, laid it carefully on the floor, then stood up and took a deep breath. 'OK,' he said, 'who goes first?'

'You and Gumboot,' Ricketts said. 'And don't waste any time.'

'Yeah, boss,' Andrew said.

'I'm staying behind,' Gumboot said to Parkinson, 'and that's all there is to it. This Squadron needs its damned CO. With your permission, boss, I'm saying get the hell out the door with that handsome black bastard.'

Parkinson glanced at Ricketts, who nodded his approval. 'As you wish, Gumboot,' Parkinson said, sounding a little choked up. 'Good luck to you.'

'Good luck, boss.'

Holding his M16 in the Belfast cradle, Andrew marched through the shattered front room, kicking furniture aside, letting it fall over the dead men, and didn't stop until he reached the back door. Leaning sideways, he glanced out of the window, saw nothing immediately threatening, so checked that Parkinson was behind him, then took a deep breath. He grabbed the door handle, jerked the door open, screamed 'Go!' and hurled himself out.

Parkinson followed – and was followed almost immediately by Ricketts and Danny – just as a mortar shell exploded in the back yard, spewing fire and smoke, tearing up more soil and debris. The four men, breaking into two groups, raced hell for leather across the broad field, aware only of the roaring, erupting earth and the need to be free of it.

Back in the house, Gumboot mounted the machine-gun on its tripod, loaded a 200-round magazine, and sat patiently in that room filled with dead, waiting for the enemy. Their gun barrels appeared first, poking in through both smashed windows, and Gumboot pressed the trigger of the machine-gun even as the Argentinians' gun barrels spat flame in his general direction, then blindly raked the room.

The machine-gun shook his body, pierced his flesh with countless spikes, then he realized that the shaking and the burning were part of his dying.

The hail of bullets threw him backwards, made him gasp, killed all feeling, but he had a sudden glimpse of his wife at home in Devon, tending the garden, not particularly attractive and inclined to wander at times, but the only woman he'd ever cared about or felt the pain of love for.

She wasn't bad at all, he thought as he died, *and life could have been* . . .

He was dead before the men who had shot him burst into the room.

16

Ricketts and Danny zigzagged through the erup-
tions of mortar shells, glimpsing shadowy figures
aiming at them through swirling smoke. Hearing
gunshots, seeing the soil spitting around them,
firing back as they ran, crouched low, they
somehow managed to get away.

Escaping from the chaos, stumbling down a
rocky, frost-covered gradient, Ricketts, followed
by Danny, came to a halt in a gully filled with
snow, offering a panoramic view of Port Stanley
and the war being waged there.

Parkinson and Andrew were there, also, the
trooper already on the radio, calling in grid
references to the fleet and asking for aircraft
support. The Sea Harriers were there in minutes,
bombing the hell out of the hilltop, turning it into
an inferno of flame and smoke before giving the
all-clear.

'Damn it,' Parkinson said. 'We can't leave him there. He's got to be taken all the way. Who's going back with me?'

'We're *all* going,' Ricketts said.

They clambered back up the hill and returned to a field of dead, the ground surrounding the house pock-marked by shell holes and littered with scorched, tattered bodies. The farmhouse, as Andrew had instructed, had been left intact.

'I hate giving credit to the RAF,' Andrew said; looking in admiration at the dreadful carnage around the untouched farmhouse, 'but in this case I have to. The proof's in the pudding, right?'

Hardened though they were, they had a problem with Gumboot. He had been shot so many times, by so many, he looked no more than a heap of tattered, dust-covered rags, buried in over-turned, splintered furniture. Choking back their rage and grief, they dragged him out from where he lay, rolled him onto a makeshift stretcher of wood and Argentinian webbing, then proceeded to carry him down to Port Stanley.

Ricketts was silent, but his cheeks were stained with tears.

'Oh, Lord, my man,' Andrew said, 'but this is one death we don't need.'

Baby-faced Danny revealed little: out ahead, on point, leading them downhill, he never relaxed his guard for a moment, keeping his thoughts to himself.

Major Parkinson was more emotional, having to fight to control himself; he managed to do so by taking the radio from Andrew, getting in touch with HQ, and filling them in on events.

'Just part of the damned job,' Andrew was heard to mutter as they entered liberated Port Stanley. 'We all pay our dues and take our chances, so no point thinking about it.'

'One more fucking word,' Ricketts said, 'and I'll tear your head off. Do you understand, Andrew?'

'Yes, boss,' Andrew said.

Ricketts smiled and placed his hand on Andrew's shoulder, squeezing gently, affectionately. 'Sorry, Trooper.'

'No sweat, boss.'

Still carrying Gumboot on his improvised stretcher, they marched through the recaptured streets of Port Stanley, past wooden-framed houses miraculously untouched, damaged British ships still smouldering in the docks, 42 Commando Marines, the Red Berets of 2 Para, and dejected Argentinian prisoners huddled around open fires beside piles of discarded weapons and helmets. They also marched past traffic jams of Land Rovers, troop trucks, Panhard armoured cars and Mercedes jeeps; under a sky filled with Sea King, Lynx, Scout, Chinook and Wessex helicopters, as well as Sea Harriers and Vulcan bombers – marched resolutely to the one place where they knew that Gumboot, even dead, would wish to be on this great day of liberation.

Resting the stretcher that bore the body of their beloved friend on a couple of tables in the Upland Goose bar, Ricketts and his troopers, trying desperately not to cry, ordered drinks for everyone in the house.

They were not refused service.

17

In Port Stanley, at 9.00pm local time on 14 June, 1982, Major General Mario Menéndez formally surrendered all the Argentinian Armed Forces in East and West Falkland to Major-General J.J. Moore. The British flag was raised again over Government House.

Throughout the next couple of days, while thousands of dejected Argentinian soldiers were rounded up by British forces and imprisoned near Stanley airport, before being shipped back to Argentina, the members of the various five-man SAS teams came marching into Port Stanley to be reunited with their friends, swap stories, and express their grief over the death of Gumboot, whose body had already been shipped back to Hereford.

During lively drinking sessions in the Upland Goose, when Ricketts, Danny, Andrew and

Major Parkinson were trading experiences with their friends, it emerged that Captain Grenville had linked up with other SBS men, returned to the fleet, then taken part in the daring SBS raid designed to set fire to oil storage tanks in Stanley's harbour installations, coming ashore from high-speed raiding craft and withdrawing without serious casualties. Also in the harbour at that time were Captain Hailsham, Corporal Paddy Clarke and Trooper Taff Burgess, who had actually managed to infiltrate enemy defences to hide in the hulk of a wrecked boat, keep a watch on the harbour, and report back to the fleet with daily details of Argentinian movements. Other groups had, like Parkinson and his men, simply foraged across the land, disrupting enemy communications, harassing their patrols and committing many invaluable acts of sabotage. SAS casualties, with the tragic exception of Trooper Gillis, had been minimal.

'So here's to Gumboot,' Ricketts said.

They all touched glasses, saluting their dead friend, then drank to his memory.

A few days after the surrender of the Argentinian forces, when the harbour was secured and the cleaning-up process had begun, the media descended like wolves on Port Stanley, anxious to tell the 'true' story of the Battle for the Falklands.

Though the fighting had stopped, explosions were still taking place in the hills around Port Stanley as anti-personnel mines were located and set off by British sappers. Piles of abandoned weapons, equipment and other stores were being removed. On the runway of Stanley airport, damaged Pucaras were surrounded by strewn debris, stores, ammunition, flapping tents and the burnt-out skeletons of other vehicles. The walls of the terminal were scarred with bullet holes, when not completely destroyed by the explosions of shells from the fleet's big guns. The wind that howled and blew sleet through the broken windows of the same building, also froze the thousands of dejected, mud-covered Argentinian prisoners who were huddled near the airstrip, wrapped in blankets and ponchos, waiting to be embarked on the *Canberra* and shipped home. In Port Stanley itself there was an acute water shortage because, though the wooden buildings remained untouched, the town's sole filtration plant had been destroyed in the bombings.

As they investigated the area, interviewing victorious British troops and defeated Argentinians, the reporters gradually picked up a lot of seemingly fantastic stories about the SAS. Intrigued, they tried to track down some members of the legendary Regiment and ended up, perhaps inevitably, in the Upland Goose.

They could find no members of the SAS. The Squadron had packed up and gone, leaving no trace behind.

'The SAS?' a local said to one of the journalists. 'That regiment's just a myth, mate. You guys must have invented it.'

That remark would have been hugely appreciated in the pubs of Hereford.

SOLDIER C: SAS

SECRET WAR IN ARABIA

PRELUDE

Framed by the veils of his Arab *shemagh*, the guerrilla's face was good-humoured, even kindly. This made it all the more shocking when he expertly jabbed his thin-bladed knife through Sa'id's eyelid and over the top of his eyeball, twisting it downward to slice through the optic nerve at the back of the retina and gouge the eye from its socket.

The old man's pain was indescribable, exploding throughout his whole being, drawing from him a scream not recognizably human and making him shudder and strain frantically against his tight bonds. Glancing down through the film of tears in his remaining eye, he saw his own eyeball staring up at him from the small pool of blood in the guerrilla's hand.

'Will you now renounce your faith?' the guerrilla asked. 'What say you, old man?'

Racked with pain and disbelief, his heart racing too quickly, Sa'id glanced automatically across the clearing. He saw the troops of the Sultan's Armed Forces lying on the ground, shot dead with pistols, soaked in blood. Directly above them, the bodies of other village elders were dangling lifeless from ropes.

Beyond the hanged men, clouds of smoke were still rising from the smouldering ashes of homes put to the torch. The sounds of wailing women, screaming girls and pleading men rose above sporadic outbursts of gunfire and hoarse, self-satisfied male laughter.

Life in this and the other villages of the country had become nightmarish in recent months, but today, in this particular village, all hell had broken loose.

First, at dawn, the Sultan's troops had encircled the village to accuse the people of aiding the guerrillas and to prevent them doing so in the future. This they did by torching the whole settlement, cementing over the well without which the villagers could not survive, and hanging a few suspected communist sympathizers from ropes tied to poles hammered hastily into the ground. Then, in the late afternoon, the communist guerrillas had arrived to terrorize the already suffering Muslim villagers and, in particular, to pursue their merciless campaign of making the repected elders of each community renounce their faith.

'So, old man,' the guerrilla taunted Sa'id, still holding the bloody eyeball in his hand for him to see, 'will you renounce your vile Muslim faith or do I gouge out the other one?'

Still in a state of shock, barely aware of his own actions, Sa'id nevertheless managed to croak, 'No, I cannot do that. No matter what you do to me, I cannot renounce my faith.'

'You're a stubborn old goat,' the guerrilla said. 'Perhaps, if you don't care for yourself, you'll be more concerned for your daughters.' Casually throwing Sa'id's eyeball into the dirt, he turned to the armed guerrillas behind him. 'Take the Muslim bitches,' he said, 'and make proper whores of them.'

'No!' Sa'id cried out in despair, as the men raced into the ruins of his half-burnt home and the screams of his virgin daughters rent the air. It went on a long time: the girls screaming, the guerrillas laughing, while Sa'id sobbed, strained against his bonds, tasted the blood still pouring from his eye socket, and mercifully slipped in and out of consciousness.

But he was still coherent when his three adolescent daughters, their clothes bloody and hanging in shreds from their bruised, deflowered bodies, were thrown out of the ruins of his mud-and-thatch hut to huddle together, sobbing shamefully, in the dust.

Even as the horrified Sa'id stared at them with his one remaining eye, the guerrilla with the good-humoured face turned to him and asked, '*Now* will you renounce your faith, old man?'

When Sa'id, too shocked to respond, simply stared blankly out of his good eye, the guerrilla snorted with disgust, gouged out his other eye, slashed through his bonds even as the old man was screaming, and stepped aside to let him fall to the ground.

Sa'id could hear his daughters wailing, even though he could not see them. Nor could he see the other raped and beaten women, the men dangling from ropes, the shot SAF troops, the burned ruins of the village huts and the life-giving well sealed with cement. All he saw was the darkness in which he would spend the rest of his days.

Sa'id wept tears of blood.

1

'Badged!' Trooper Phil Ricketts said, proudly holding up his beige beret to re-examine the SAS winged-dagger badge stitched to it the previous day by his wife, Maggie. 'I can hardly believe it.'

'Believe it, you bleedin' probationer,' said Trooper 'Gumboot' Gillis, who was wearing his own brand-new badged beret. 'You earned it, mate. We *all* did!'

'I'm surprised I actually made it,' said Andrew Winston, a huge black Barbadian, glancing around the crowded Paludrine Club and clearly proud to be allowed into it at last, 'particularly as I almost gave up once or twice.'

'We probably all thought about it,' said Tom Purvis, 'but that's all we did. Otherwise we wouldn't be drinking in here.' He glanced around the noisy, smoky recreation room of 22 SAS Regiment. 'We're here because, although we may have thought about it, we didn't actually give up.'

'I thought about it once,' Ricketts said. 'I'll have to admit that. Once – only once.'

He had done so during that final, awful night on the summit of Pen-y-fan. At other times during the 26 weeks of relentless physical and mental testing, he had wondered what he was doing there and if it was all worth it. But only that once had the thought of actually giving up crossed his mind – in the middle of that dark, stormy night in the Brecon Beacons, where, for one brief, despairing moment, he thought he had reached the end of his tether.

Even now, he could only look back on the rigours of Initial Selection, 'Sickeners One and Two', Continuation Training, Combat Training and, finally, the parachute course, with a feeling of disbelief that he had actually undergone it and lived to tell the tale. He had arrived at the SAS camp of Bradbury Lines, in the Hereford suburb of Redhill, in the full expectation that he was in for a rough time, but nothing had quite prepared him for just how rough it actually turned out to be.

'What you are about to undergo,' the Squadron Commander, Major Greenaway, had informed over a hundred recruits that first morning as they sat before him on rows of hard seats in the training wing theatre, or Blue Room, of Bradbury Lines, 'is the most rigorous form of testing ever devised for healthy men. No matter how good you believe yourselves to be as soldiers – and if you didn't think you were good, you wouldn't be here now – you will find yourselves tested to the very limits of your endurance. Our selection process offers no mercy. You can fail at any point over the 26 weeks. Some will fail on the first day, some on the very last. If you are failed, you will find yourselves standing on Platform Four of Redhill Station, being RTU'd.' A few of the listening men glanced at each other, but no one dared say a word. 'There is no appeal,' Greenaway continued. 'Only a small number of you will manage to complete the course successfully – a *very* small number. Let that simple, brutal truth be your bible from this moment on.'

It was indeed a brutal truth, as Ricketts was to discover from the moment the briefing ended and the men were rushed from the Blue Room – passing under a sign reading 'For many are called but few are chosen' – to the Quartermaster's stores to be kitted out with a bergen backpack, sleeping bag, webbed belts, a wet-weather poncho, water bottles, a heavy prismatic compass, a brew kit, three 24-hour ration packs and Ordnance Survey maps of the Brecon Beacons and Elan Valley, where the first three-day trial, known as Sickener One, would take place.

Once kitted out, they hurried from the QM's stores to the armoury, where they were supplied with primitive Lee Enfield 303 rifles. Allocated their beds, or 'bashas', in the barracks of the training wing, they were allowed to drop their kit off in the 'spider' – an eight-legged dormitory area – and have a good lunch in the cookhouse. Immediately after that, the harsh selection process began.

'Christ,' Gumboot said, placing his pint glass on the table and licking his wet lips, 'it seems a lot longer than it was. Only six months! It seems like six years.'

Ricketts remembered it only too well. The few days leading up to Sickener One were filled with rigorous weapons training and arduous runs, fully kitted, across the deceptively gentle hills of the Herefordshire countryside, each one longer and tougher than the one before, and all of them leading to a final slog up an ever-steeper gradient that tortured lungs and muscles.

The first of the crap-hats, or failures, were weeded out during those runs and humiliatingly RTU'd, or returned to their original unit. Those remaining, now fully aware of just how many failures there would be, instinctively drew into themselves, not wanting to become too friendly with those likely to soon suffer the same fate.

'And to think,' Tom Purvis said, shaking his

head from side to side in wonder, 'that at the time we thought nothing could be worse than Sickener One!'

'It's helpful not to know too much,' Jock McGregor said.

'It sure is, man,' big Andrew added, flashing his perfect teeth. 'If we'd known that Sickener One was just kids' stuff compared to what was coming, we'd never have stuck it out for the rest.'

It was a greatly reduced number of SAS aspirants from various British Army regiments who had awakened in the early hours of a Saturday morning, showered, shaved, pulled on their olive-green uniforms, or OGs, picked up their rifles and dauntingly heavy bergens, then hurried out to the waiting four-ton Bedford trucks. After being driven north along the A470, they were eventually dropped off in the Elan Valley, in the Cambrian Mountains of mid-Wales. An area of murderously steep hills and towering ridges, it had been chosen for its difficult, dangerous terrain and harsh weather as the perfect testing ground for Sickener One. This gruelling three-day endurance test is based on hiking and climbing while humping a heavily packed bergen and weapons, then repeatedly 'cross-graining the bukits'.

Derived from the Malay – Malaysia was

where the exercise was first practised – this last expression means going from one summit or trig point to another by hiking up and down the steep, sometimes sheer hills rather than taking the easy route around them. It takes place in the most rugged terrain and the foulest weather imaginable, including fierce wind, rain or blinding fog. Each conquered summit is followed by another, and the slightest sign of reluctance on the part of the climber is met by a shower of abuse from a member of the directing staff (DS), or – a psychological killer – by the softly spoken suggestion that the candidate might find it more sensible to give up and return to the waiting Bedfords.

Those taking this advice seriously were instantly failed and placed on RTU, never to be given the chance to try again. This happened to many during the three days of Sickener One.

Those who survived the first day, even though exhausted and disorientated, then had to basha down at the most recent RV, or rendezvous, no matter how hostile the terrain. Invariably, when they did so, they were frozen and wet, often with swollen feet and shoulders blistered by the bergen. They were then forced to spend the night in the same appalling weather, eating 24-hour rations heated on portable hexamine stoves, drinking tea boiled on the same, before bedding down in sleeping bags protected from the elements only by waterproof ponchos.

Given the filthy, windy weather – for which that time of the year had been deliberately chosen – few of the men got much sleep and the next day, even wearier than before, they not only cross-grained more bukits, but were faced with the dreaded entrail ditch, filled with stagnant water and rotting sheep's innards, standing in for the blood and bone of butchered humans. The candidates had to crawl through this vile mess on their bellies, face down, holding their rifles horizontally – it was known as the 'leopard crawl' – ignoring the stench, trying not to swallow any of the mess, though certainly swallowing their own bile when they brought it up. Failure to get through the entrail ditch was an RTU offence which further reduced the number of aspirants.

'I fucking dreaded that,' Tom said, lighting a cigarette and puffing smoke. 'It was only the thought of Platform Four that kept me going when things got rough.'

'Right,' said Bill Raglan, who was born and bred in Pensett, in the West Midlands, and had little education but a lot of intelligence. Bill's face was badly scarred from the many fights he had been in before the regular Army channelled his excess energy in a more positive direction. 'Can you imagine the humiliation, standing there with

11

the other rejects? Then having to go back to your old regiment with your tail between your legs. That kept *me* going all right!'

At dawn, after a second night of sleeping out in frozen, rainswept open country, numb from the cold and with their outfits still stinking from their encounter with the entrail ditch, they had been ordered to wade across a swollen, dangerously fast river, holding their rifles above their heads as the water reached their chests. One man refused to cross and was instantly failed; another was swept away, rescued and then likewise failed. While both men were escorted to the waiting Bedfords, the others, though still wet and exhausted from contending with the river, were forced to carry one of their DS supervisors, complete with his bergen and weapons, between them on a stretcher for what should have been the last mile of the hike. However, when told at the end of that most killing of final legs that the Bedfords had gone and they would have to hike the last ten miles – in short, that they had been conned – some of them lost their temper with their supervisors, while others simply sat down wearily and called it a day.

The latter were failed and placed on RTU. A few more were lost on that draining ten miles, leaving a greatly reduced, less optimistic group to go on to the torments of Sickener Two.

'I mean, you can't believe what those fuckers will dream up for you, can you?' Jock asked rhetorically, really speaking to himself in a daze of disbelief as he thought back on all he had been through. 'You get through Sickener One, thinking you're Superman, then they promptly make you feel like a dog turd with Sickener Two. Those bastards sure have their talents!'

In fact, between the two exercises there had been more days of relentless grind in the shape of long runs, map-reading, survival and weapons training, and psychological testing. Then the dreaded first day of Sickener Two finally arrived, beginning with the horror of the Skirrid mountain, which rises 1640 feet above the gently rolling fields of Llanfihangel and is surmounted by a trig point ideal for map-reading. Naturally, for the SAS, the only way to the top was by foot, with the usual full complement of packed bergen, heavy webbing and weapons.

In addition, the route specially chosen by the DS for the exercise carefully avoided the gentler slopes and forced the candidates up the nearly vertical side. As part of the tests, each man had to take his turn at leading the others up the sheer face to the summit, using his Silvas compass, then guiding them back down without mistakes. This procedure was repeated many times throughout the long day, until each man had taken his turn as leader and all of them were suffering agonies of body and mind.

Some collapsed, some got lost through being dazed, and others simply dropped out in despair, while those remaining went on to week three. For this the teams were split up and each man was tested alone, with the runs becoming longer, the mountain routes steeper and the bergens packed more heavily every day until they became back-breaking loads. Added to this was an ever more relentless psychological onslaught, designed to test mental stamina, and including cruel psychological ploys such as last-minute changes of plan and awakenings at unexpected times of the day or night. On top of all this, even more brutal, unexpected physical endurance tests were introduced just as the men reached maximum exhaustion or disorientation.

The climax of this week of hell on earth was a repeated cross-graining of the peaks of the Pen-y-fan, at 2906 feet the highest mountain in the Brecon Beacons, one day after the other, each hike longer than the previous one, with extra weight being added to the bergens each time. On even the highest peak, the DS was liable to leap out of nowhere, and hurl a volley of questions at the exhausted, often dazed applicant, who, if he failed to supply an answer, would be sent back down in disgrace, bound for Platform Four.

By the fifth day of the third week, after a final, relentlessly punishing, 40 miles solo cross-graining of the bukits, known as the 'Fan Dance' – across icy rivers, peat bogs, pools of stagnant water and fields of fern; up sandstone paths and sheer ridges, in driving rain and blinding fog, carrying a 45lb bergen, as well as water bottles and heavy webbing – most of the candidates had been weeded out. In the end, under two dozen of the original hundred-odd men were deemed to have passed Initial Selection and allowed to go on to Continuation Training.

Phil Ricketts was one of them. He had had his moment of doubt on the summit of Pen-y-fan, when in a state of complete exhaustion, cold and hungry, whipped by the wind, feeling more alone than he had ever done before, he wanted to scream his protest and give up and go back down. But instead he endured and went on to do the rest of the nightmarish exercise and return to the RV by the selected route. He felt good when he finished and was applauded by his stern instructors.

Given a weekend break, Ricketts spent it with his wife in Wood Green, North London, where Maggie lived with her parents during his many absences from home. Even in the regular Army, he had never felt as fit as he was after Initial Selection, and he made love to Maggie, to whom he had only been married a year, with a passion that took her breath away. As they were to find out later, their first child, Anna, was conceived during that happy two days.

'You remember that first weekend break we got?' Ricketts asked his mates. 'Immediately after passing Initial Selection? What did you guys do that weekend?'

'I went back to Brixton,' Andrew said, 'to see my white Daddy and black Mammy, then screw my Scandinavian girlfriend. It was well worth the journey, believe me.'

'I banged a whore in King's Cross,' Jock said without emotion.

'Bill and I shared a hired car and drove back to the Midlands,' said Tom. 'Though my folks come from Wolverhampton they're now living in Smethwick, which isn't too far from where Bill lives, in Pensett. So since neither of us were keen to spend too much time with our families, we drove between the two towns, having a pint here, another pint there, and gradually getting pissed as newts.'

'I can hardly remember the drive back,' Bill said with a broad grin, 'so I like to think we only made it because of our SAS training. Who dares wins, and so on.'

'And you, Gumboot?' Ricketts asked. 'Did you go and see your wife?'

'No,' Gumboot answered, puffing smoke and sipping his beer at the same time.

'But you'd only been married six months,' Ricketts said.

'Six months too fucking long,' Gumboot said. 'Got her pregnant, didn't I? Besides, we only had one weekend, which leaves no time to go all the way to Devon and back.'

'You could have travelled on Friday night and come back on Sunday,' Andrew pointed out.

'OK, I'll admit it,' Gumboot said pugnaciously. 'I didn't want to spend my free weekend with a bloody bean bag, so I slipped into London. I'm amazed I didn't run into Jock, since I had a few pints in King's Cross on Saturday evening.'

'I probably saw you and avoided you,' Jock replied. 'I can be fussy at times.'

'Up yours, mate.' Gumboot swallowed some more beer, wiped his lips, and grinned mischievously. 'Ah, well, it was only a weekend – and over all too soon.'

On that, at least, they all agreed.

When they had returned to Hereford that Monday morning, some with blinding hangovers, others simply sleepless, they had been flung with merciless efficiency into their fourteen weeks of

Continuation Training, learning all the skills required to be a member of the basic SAS operational unit: the four-man patrol. These skills included weapons handling, combat and survival, reconnaissance, signals, demolitions, camouflage and concealment, resistance to interrogation, and first aid. Continuation Training was followed by jungle training and a static-line parachute course, bringing the complete programme up to six months.

Though Ricketts and the others had all come from regular Army, Royal Navy, RAF or Territorial Army regiments, and were therefore already fully trained soldiers, none of them was prepared for the amount of extra training they had to undergo with the SAS, even after the rigours of Initial Selection.

Weapons training covered everything in the SAS arsenal, including use of the standard-issue British semi-automatic Browning FN 9mm high-power handgun, the 9mm Walther PPK handgun, the M16 assault rifle, the self-loading semi-automatic rifle, or SLR, the Heckler & Koch MP5 sub-machine-gun, the MILAN anti-tank weapon, various mortars and a wide range of 'enemy' weapons, such as the Kalashnikov AK-47 assault rifle.

In combat and survival training they were taught the standard operating procedures, or

SOPs, for how to move tactically across country by day or night, how to set up and maintain observation posts, or OPs, and how to operate deep behind enemy lines. This led naturally to signals training, covering Morse code, special codes and call-sign systems, the operation of thirty kinds of SAS radio, recognition of radio 'black spots', the setting-up of standard and makeshift antennas, and the procedure for calling in artillery fire and air strikes.

As one of the main reasons for being behind enemy lines is the disruption of enemy communications and transportation, as well as general sabotage, particularly against Military Supply Routes, or MSRs, this phase of their training also included lessons in demolition skills and techniques, particularly the use of explosives such as TNT, dynamite, Semtex, Composition C3 and C4 plastic explosive, or PE, Amatol, Pentolite and Ednatol. Special emphasis was laid on the proper placement of charges to destroy various kinds of bridge: cantilever, spandrel arch, continuous-span truss and suspension.

Many jokes were made about the fact that those lessons led directly to instruction in first aid, including relatively advanced medical skills such as setting up an intravenous drip, how to administer drugs, both orally and with injections, and the basics of casualty handling and care.

This phase of Continuation Training culminated in escape and evasion (E&E) and Resistance to Interrogation (RTI) exercises. E&E began with a week of theory on how to live off the land by constructing makeshift shelters from branches, leaves and other local vegetation, and sangars, or semicircular shelters built from stones, and by catching and cooking wild animals. (Repeated jokes about rat stew, Ricketts recalled, had raised a few queasy laughs.) Those theories were then put into practice when the men were dropped off, alone, in some remote region, usually with no more than their clothing and a wristwatch, knife and box of matches, with orders to make their way back to a specified RV without either becoming lost or getting caught by the enthusiastic Parachute Regiment troopers sent out to find them.

Those caught were hooded, bound, thrown into the Paras' trucks and delivered to the interrogation centre run by the Joint Services Interrogation Unit and members of 22 SAS Training Wing, where various physical and mental torments were used to make them break down and reveal more than their rank, name, serial number and date of birth. Those who did so were failed even at that late stage in the course. Those who managed to remain sane and silent went on to undertake jungle-warfare training and the parachute course.

'For me,' Bill said, 'that was the best bit of all. I loved it in the jungle. I mean, even though it was tough all I could think of was how I'd come all the way from the Stevens and Williams Glassworks to the jungles of fucking Malaysia. I was in heaven, I tell you.'

'It wasn't Malaysia,' Andrew corrected him. 'It was just *close* to there. It's the only British dependency inhabited by Malays that didn't join the Federation of Malaysia.'

'He's so fucking educated,' Gumboot said, 'you'd never think he'd been up a tree. What the fuck's the difference? It was *jungle*, wasn't it? That's why you couldn't possibly fail there, mate. You must have felt right at home.'

'My family, comes from Barbados,' Andrew said, flashing Gumboot a big smile, 'where they have rum and molasses and white beaches. No jungle there, Gumboot.'

'Anyway,' Tom said, looking as solemn as always, 'I agree with Bill. I was a lot more relaxed when we went there. It was too late to fail, I thought.'

'So did some others,' Jock reminded them, 'and the poor bastards failed. One even failed during the parachute course. Can you fucking believe it?'

'That would have killed me,' Ricketts said. 'I mean, to be RTU'd at that stage. I would have opened a vein.'

'Hear, hear,' Andrew said.

Jungle-warfare training was a six-week course in Brunei, the British-protected sultanate of North-West Borneo, forming an enclave with Sarawak, Malaysia, where the SAS was reborn after World War Two and where it learnt so many of its skills and tactics. There the candidates were sent on four-man patrols through the jungle, some lasting almost a fortnight. During that time they had to carry out a number of operational tasks, including constructing a jungle basha, killing and eating wildlife, including snakes, without being bitten or poisoned, and living on local flora and fauna. Most importantly, they had to show that they could navigate and move accurately in the restricted visibility of the jungle. Failure in any of these tasks resulted in an even more cruel, last-minute, RTU.

Those who returned successfully from Brunei did so knowing that they had only one hurdle left: a four-week course at the No 1 Parachute Training School at RAF Brize Norton, Oxfordshire, where Parachute Jump Instructors, or PJIs, taught them the characteristics of PX1 Mk 4, PX1 Mk 5 and PR7 (reserve) parachutes, then supervised them on eight parachute jumps. The first of these was from a static balloon, but the others were from RAF C-130 Hercules aircraft, some from a high altitude, some from a low altitude, most by day, a few by night, and at least one while the aircraft was being put through a series of manoeuvres designed to shake up and disorientate the parachutists just before they jumped out. Those who made this final leap successfully had passed the whole course.

The men drinking around this table in the Paludrine Club had all just done that.

'I still don't believe it,' Andrew mused, 'but here we all are: in a Sabre Squadron at last. I think that's reason enough for another drink.'

'I think you're right,' Jock said, going off to the bar for another round.

Once badged, the successful candidates were divided between the four Sabre Squadrons, with those around this table going to Squadron B, where they would spend their probationary first year. They were also allowed into the Paludrine Club to celebrate their success and get to know each other as they had not been able to, or feared to, during the past six months of relentless training and testing.

'So,' Gumboot said, raising his glass when Jock

had set down the fresh round of drinks. 'Here's to all of us, lads.'

They touched their glasses together and drank deeply, trying not to look too proud.

2

The day after their celebratory booze-up with the other successful troopers, which was followed by a farewell fling with wives and girlfriends in the camp's Sports and Social Club, the six men allocated to B Squadron were called to the interest room to be given a briefing on their first legitimate SAS mission. As the group was so small, the briefing was not taking place in that room, but in the adjoining office of the Squadron Commander, Major Greenaway. To get to his office, however, the men had to pass through the interest room, which was indeed of interest, being dominated by a horned buffalo head set high on one wall and by the many photographs and memorabilia of previous B Squadron campaigns that covered the other walls, making the room look rather like a military museum.

Andrew was studying photographs of the Malaysia campaign, as well as items of jungle equipment, when a fair-haired SAS sergeant-major, built like a barrel but with no excess fat, appeared in the doorway of Major Greenaway's office.

'I'm your RSM,' he said. 'The name is Worthington, as befits a worthy man and don't ever forget it. Now step inside, lads.'

Following the Regimental Sergeant-Major into the office, they were surprised to find one wall completely covered by a blue curtain. Major Greenaway had silvery-grey hair and gazed up from behind his desk with keen, sky-blue eyes and a good-natured smile.

'You all know who I am,' he said, standing up by way of greeting, 'so I won't introduce myself. I would, however, like to offer you my congratulations on winning the badge and warmly welcome you to B Squadron.' When the men had murmured their appreciation, Greenaway nodded, turned to the wall behind him and pulled aside the blue curtain, revealing a large, four-colour map of the Strait of Hormuz, showing Muscat and Oman, with the latter boldly circled with red ink and the word 'SECRET' stencilled in bold black capital letters across the top.

Greenaway picked up a pointer and tapped the area marked 'Southern Dhofar'. 'Oman,' he said. 'An independent sultanate in eastern Arabia, located on the Gulf of Oman and the Arabian sea.

Approximately 82,000 square miles. Population 750,000 – mainly Arabs, but with substantial Negro blood. A medieval region, isolated from the more prosperous and advanced northern states by a 400-mile desert which rises up at its southern tip into an immense plateau, the Jebel Massif, a natural fortress some 3000 feet high, nine miles wide, and stretching 150 miles from the east down to, and across, the border with Aden, now the People's Democratic Republic of Yemen. The Gulf of Oman, about 300 miles long, lies between Oman and Iran, leading through the Strait of Hormuz to the Persian Gulf and the oil wealth of Saudia Arabia. So that's the place.'

The major lowered the pointer and turned back to face his new men. 'What's the situation?'

It was a rhetorical question requiring no answer other than that he was about to give. 'Oman has long-standing treaties of cooperation with Britain and is strategically important because Middle East oil flows to the West through the Strait of Hormuz. If the communists capture that oil, by capturing Oman, they'll end up controlling the economy of the Free World. The stakes, therefore, are high.'

Resting the pointer across his knees, Greenaway sat on the edge of his desk. Ricketts, who had worked on the North Sea oil rigs as a toolpusher before joining the regular Army, had been impressed by many of the men he met there: strong-willed, independent, decisive – basically decent. The 'boss', who struck him as being just such a man, went on: 'The situation in Oman has been degenerating since the 1950s with Sultan Said bin Taimur's repressive regime forcing more and more of the Dhofaris in the south – culturally and ethnically different from the people in the north – into rebellion. After turning against the Sultan, the rebels formed a political party, the Dhofar Liberation Front, or DLF, which the Sultan tried to quell with his Sultan's Armed Forces, or SAF. The rebels were then wooed and exploited by the pro-Soviet Yemenis, who formed them into the People's Front for the Liberation of the Occupied Arabian Gulf – the PFLOAG. This greatly improved the situation of the rebels, or *adoo*, and the Sultan's regime, falling apart, failed to mount an effective counter-insurgency war. Which is where we come in.'

He studied each of the men in turn, checking that he had their full attention and that they all understood him.

'What's "*adoo*" mean, boss?' Tom asked.

'It's the Arabic word for "enemy",' Greenaway informed him. 'Can I continue?'

'Yes, boss!'

'The SAF has long had a number of British ex-officers and NCOs as contract advisers, but they were facing a losing battle in the countryside. Exceptionally cruel, punitive actions, such as the public hanging of suspected rebels and the sealing of their life-giving wells, were only turning more of the people against him. As it wasn't in British interests to let the communists take over Oman, in July last year the Sultan was overthrown by his son, Qaboos, in an almost bloodless coup secretly implemented and backed by us – by which I mean the British government, not the SAS.'

A few of the men laughed drily, causing the major to smile before continuing. 'However, while Qaboos, with our aid, gradually started winning the hearts of those ostracized by his father's reactionary regime, the PFLOAG – backed by the Russians, whose eyes are focused firmly on the oil-rich countries of Arabia – continued to make inroads into Oman. Now the *adoo* virtually control the Jebel Dhofar, which makes them a permanent threat to the whole country.'

Ricketts glanced at the other troopers and saw that they were as keen as he felt. What luck! Instead of Belfast, which was like Britain, only grimmer, they were going to fight their first war in an exotic, foreign country. Childish though it was, Ricketts could not help being excited about that. He had always needed changes of scenery, fresh challenges, new faces – which is why he had first gone to the North Sea, then joined the regular Army. While Belfast might have similar excitements, it was not the same thing. Ricketts was thrilled by the very idea of Oman, which remained a mysterious, perplexing country to all but a few insiders. Also, he was drawn to hot countries and desert terrain. Of course, Maggie would not be pleased and that made him feel slightly guilty. But he could not deny his true nature, which was to get up and go, no matter how much he loved his wife. He felt like a lucky man.

'What we're engaged in in Oman,' the boss continued, 'is the building of a bulwark against communist expansionism.' Standing again, he picked up the pointer and turned to the map. 'That bulwark will be Dhofar,' he continued, tapping the name with the pointer, 'in the south of Oman, immediately adjacent to communist-held Aden, now the People's Democratic Republic of Yemen. Our job is to back Sultan Qaboos with military aid and advice and to win the hearts of his people by setting up hospitals and schools, by teaching them the skills they need, and by crushing the *adoo* at the same time. The so-called hearts-and-minds campaign is already in progress, with British Army Training Teams, or BATT, based at Taqa and Mirbat. Our job is to tackle the *adoo*. Any questions so far?'

'Yes, boss,' Ricketts said, already familiar with SAS informality and determined to put it to good use. 'It's clearly a laudable aim, but how do we win the military side of it?'

Greenaway smiled. 'Not everyone considers our aims to be laudable, Trooper. Indeed, Britain has been accused of supporting a cruel, reactionary regime merely to protect its oil interests. While I happen to think that's the truth, I also believe it's justified. We must be pragmatic about certain matters, even when our motives aren't quite laudable.'

'Yes, boss,' Ricketts said, returning the major's wicked grin. 'So how do we fight the war, apart from winning hearts and minds?'

Greenaway put down the pointer, sat on the edge of the desk, and folded his arms. 'Since early last year, with the aid of the *firqats* – bands of Dhofari tribesmen loyal to the Sultan – we've managed to gain a few precarious toe-holds on the coastal plain immediately facing the Jebel Dhofar. Now, however, we're about to launch an operation designed to establish a firm base on the Jebel, from where we can stem the *adoo* advance. That operation is codenamed Jaguar.'

'Is this purely an SAS operation?' Andrew asked, realizing that this was a typical SAS 'Chinese parliament', or open discussion.

'No. In all matters relating to Oman, the SAF

and *firqats* must be seen to be their own men. For this reason, B Squadron and G Squadron will be supporting two companies of the SAF, Dhofari *firqats* and a platoon of Baluch Askars – tough little buggers from Baluchistan. Nearly 800 fighting men in all.'

'Are the SAF and the *firqats* dependable?' Gumboot asked, gaining the confidence to speak out like the others.

'Not always. The main problem lies with the *firqats*, who are volatile by nature and also bound by Islamic restrictions, such as the holy week of Ramadan, when they require a special dispensation to fight. But they have, on occasion, been known to ignore even that. When they fight, they can be ferocious, but they'll stop at any time for the most trivial reasons – usually arguments over who does what or gets what, or perhaps some imagined insult. So, no, they're not always dependable.'

'What about the *adoo*?' Ricketts asked.

'Fierce, committed fighters and legendary marksmen. They can pick a target off at 400 yards and virtually melt back into the mountainside or desert. A formidable enemy.'

'When does the assault on this Jebel what's-its-name begin?' Bill asked, nervously clearing his throat, but determined to be part of this Chinese parliament.

'About a month from now,' Greenaway

informed him. 'After you've all had a few weeks of training in local customs, language and general diplomacy, including seeing what previous SAS teams have been up to with schools, hospitals and so forth. It's anticipated that the assault on the . . .' – the major looked directly at Trooper Raglan with a tight little smile before pronouncing the name with theatrical precision – 'Jebel Dhofar will begin on 1 October. The Khareef monsoon, which covers the plateau with cloud and mist from June to September, will be finished by then, which will make the climb easier. Also, according to our intelligence, there'll be no moon that night, which should help to keep your presence unknown to the *adoo*.'

'Who, of course, have the eyes of night owls,' said Worthington, who had been standing silently behind them throughout the whole briefing. Only when Major Greenaway burst out laughing did the men realize that the RSM was joking. Still not quite used to SAS informality, some of them grinned sheepishly. Worthington managed to wipe the smiles from their faces by adding sadistically: 'Rumour has it that there are over 2000 *adoo* on the Jebel. That means the combined SAF and SAS forces will be outnumbered approximately three to one. Should any of you lads think those odds too high, I suggest you hand in your badges right now. Any takers?'

No one said a word, though some shook their heads. 'Good,' said the RSM, before turning his attention to Major Greenaway. 'Anything else, boss?'

'I think not, Sergeant-Major. This seems to be a healthy bunch of lads and I'm sure they'll stand firm.'

'I'm sure they will, boss.' The RSM looked grimly at the probationers. 'Go back to the spider and prepare your kit. We fly out tomorrow.'

'Yes, boss!' they all sang, practically in unison, then filed out of the office like excited schoolboys.

3

The four-engined Hercules C-130 took off the following afternoon from RAF Lyneham, refuelled at RAF Akroterion in Cyprus, then flew on to RAF Salalah in Dhofar, where the men disembarked by marching down the tailgate, from the gloom of the aircraft into the blinding, burning furnace of the Arabian sun.

On the runway of RAF Salalah stood Skymaster jets, each in its own sandbagged emplacement and covered by camouflage nets. Three large defensive trenches – encircled by 40-gallon drums and bristling with 25lb guns and 5.5 Howitzers, and therefore known as 'hedgehogs' – were laid out to the front and side of the airstrip. Overlooking all was an immense, sun-bleached mountain, its sheer sides rising dramatically to a plateau from the flat desert plain.

'That must be the Jebel Dhofar,' Ricketts said to Andrew.

'It is,' a blond-haired young man confirmed as

he clambered down from the Land Rover that had just driven up to the tailgate. 'And it's crawling with heavily-armed *adoo*. I'm Sergeant Frank Lampton, from one of the BATT teams. I'm here to guide you probationers through your first few days.' He grinned and glanced back over his shoulder at the towering slopes of the Jebel Dhofar, the summit of which was hazy with the heat. 'How'd you like to cross-grain the bukits of that?' he asked, turning back and grinning. 'Some challenge, eh?'

'It'd dwarf even the Pen-y-fan,' Andrew admitted. 'That's some mother, man.'

'Right,' Lampton said. Slim and of medium height, the sergeant was dressed in shorts, boots with rolled-down socks and a loose, flapping shirt, all of which were covered in the dust that was already starting to cover the new arrivals. A Browning 9mm high-power handgun was holstered on his hip. Squinting against the brilliant sunlight, he pointed to the convoy of armour-plated Bedfords lined up on the edge of the runway. 'Stretch your legs,' he told the men, 'and get used to the heat. When the QM has completed the unloading, pile into those trucks and you'll be driven to the base at Um al Gwarif. It's not very far.'

While the men gratefully did stretching exercises, walked about a bit or just sat on their bergens smoking, the Quartermaster Sergeant, a flamboyant Irishman with the lungs of a drill instructor, organized the unloading and sorting of all the squadron's kit by bawling good-natured abuse at his Omani helpers, all of whom wore *shemaghs* and the loose robes known as jellabas. The new arrivals watched them with interest.

'Fucked if I'd like to hump that stuff in *this* heat,' Gumboot finally said, breaking the silence.

'You soon will be,' Lampton replied with a grin, puffing smoke as he lit a cigarette. 'You'll be humping it up that bloody mountain, all the way to the top. That's why you'd better get used to the heat.' He inhaled and blew another cloud of smoke, then smiled wryly at Ricketts. 'Now these Omanis,' he said, indicating the men unloading the kit and humping it across to the Bedfords, 'they'd probably down tools if you asked them to do that. That's why they call the SAS "donkey soldiers" or *majnoons* – Arabic for "mad ones". Are they right or wrong, lads?'

'Anything you say, boss,' Bill said, 'is OK by me.'

'An obedient trooper,' Lampton replied, flicking ash to the ground. 'That's what I like to hear. Which one of you is Trooper Ricketts?' Ricketts put his hand in the air. 'I was informed by the

RSM that you're the oldest of the probationers,' Lampton said.

'I didn't know that, boss.'

'You're the oldest by one day, I was told, with Trooper McGregor coming right up your backside. That being the case, you'll be my second-in-command for the next few days. I trust you'll be able to shoulder this great responsibility.'

Lampton, though a sergeant, was hardly much older than Ricketts, who, feeling confident with him, returned his cocky grin. 'I'll do my best, boss.'

'I'm sure you will, Trooper. The RSM also said you put up a good show at the briefing. Fearless in the presence of your Squadron Commander. Right out front with the questions and so forth. That, also, is why you'll be in nominal charge of your fellow probationers while you're under my wing.'

'This sounds suspiciously like punishment, boss.'

'It isn't punishment and it isn't promotion – it's a mere convenience. Do you want to beg off?'

'No, boss.'

'You gave the correct answer, Trooper Ricketts. You're a man who'll go far.' Glancing towards the Bedfords, Lampton saw that Major Greenaway and RSM Worthington were already allocating the other members of B Squadron to their respective Bedfords. 'The unloading must be nearly completed,' Lampton said, dropping his cigarette butt to the tarmac and grinding it out with his heel. 'OK, Ricketts, collect the other probationers together and follow me to that truck.'

Ricketts did as he had been told, calling in his small group and then following Lampton across to one of the Bedfords parked on the edge of the airstrip. When they were in the rear, cramped together on the hard benches, already covered in a film of dust and being tormented by mosquitoes and fat flies, Lampton joined them, telling another soldier to drive his Land Rover back to base. The Bedford coughed into life, lurched forward, then headed away from the airstrip to a wired-off area containing a single-storey building guarded by local soldiers wearing red berets. The Bedford stopped there.

'SOAF HQ,' Lampton explained, meaning the Sultan of Oman's Air Force. Removing a fistful of documents from the belt of his shorts, he climbed down from the Bedford and went inside.

Forced to wait in the open rear of the crowded Bedford, Ricketts passed the time by examining the area beyond the SOAF HQ. He saw a lot of Strikemaster jet fighters and Skyvan cargo planes in dispersal bays made from empty oil drums.

The Strikemasters, he knew from his reading, were armed with Sura rockets, 500lb bombs and machine-guns. The Skyvan cargo planes would be used to resupply, or resup, the SAF and SAS forces when they were up on the plateau, which Ricketts could see in all its forbidding majesty, rising high above the plain of Salalah, spreading out from the camp's barbed-wire perimeter. The flat, sandy plain was constantly covered in gently drifting clouds of wind-blown dust.

Returning five minutes later with clearance to leave the air base, Lampton climbed back into the Bedford and told the driver to take off. After passing through gates guarded by RAF policemen armed with sub-machine-guns, the truck turned into the road, crossed and bounced off it, then headed along the adjoining rough terrain.

'What the matter with this clown of a driver?' Jock McGregor asked. 'The blind bastard's right off the road.'

'It's deliberate,' Lampton explained. 'Most of the roads in Dhofar have been mined by the *adoo*, so this is the safest way to drive, preferably following previous tyre tracks in case mines have been planted off the road as well. Of course, even that's no guarantee of safety. Knowing we do this, the *adoo* often disguise a mine by rolling an old tyre over it to make it look like the tracks of a previous truck. Smart cookies, the *adoo*.'

All eyes turned automatically towards the road, where the Bedford's wheels were churning up clouds of dust and leaving clear tracks.

'Great,' Gumboot said. 'You take one step outside your tent and get your fucking legs blown off.'

'As long as it leaves your balls,' Andrew said, 'you shouldn't complain, man.'

'Leave my balls out of this,' Gumboot said. 'You'll just put a curse on them.'

'Any other advice for us?' Ricketts asked.

'Yes,' Lampton replied. 'Never forget for a minute that the *adoo* are crack shots. They're also adept at keeping out of sight. The fact that you can't see them doesn't mean they're not there, and you won't find better snipers anywhere. You look across a flat piece of desert and think it's completely empty, then – pop! – suddenly a shot will ring out, compliments of an *adoo* sniper who's blended in with the scenery. They can make themselves invisible in this terrain – and they're bold as brass when it comes to infiltrating us. So never think you're safe because you're in your own territory. The truth is that you're never safe here. You've got to assume that *adoo* snipers are in the vicinity and keep your eyes peeled all the time.'

Again, they glanced automatically at the land they were passing through, seeing only the clouds of dust billowing up behind them, obscuring the sun-scorched flat plain and the immense, soaring sides of the Jebel Dhofar. The sky was a white sheet.

'Welcome to Oman,' Tom said sardonically. 'Land of sunshine and happy, smiling people. Paradise on earth.'

After turning off the road to Salalah, the truck bounced and rattled along the ground beside a dirt track skirting the airfield. About three miles farther on, it came to a large camp surrounded by a barbed-wire fence, with watch-towers placed at regular intervals around its perimeter. Each tower held a couple of armed SAF soldiers, a machine-gun and a searchlight. There were stone-built protective walls, or sangars, manned by RAF guards, on both sides of the main gate.

'This is Um al Gwarif, the HQ of the SAF,' Sergeant Lampton explained as the truck halted at the main gate. A local soldier wearing a green *shemagh* and armed with a 7.62mm FN rifle checked the driver's papers and then waved the Bedford through. The truck passed another watch-tower as it entered the camp. 'Home, sweet home, lads.'

Had it not been for the exotic old whitewashed fort, complete with ramparts and slitted windows, located near the centre of the enclosure and flying the triangular red-and-green Omani flag from its highest turret, the place might have been a concentration camp.

'That's the Wali's fort,' Lampton explained like a tour guide. 'That's W-A-L-I. Not wally as you know it. Here, a Wali isn't an idiot. He's the Governor of the province. So that's the Governor's fort, the camp's command post. And that,' he continued, pointing to an old pump house and well just inside the main gate, beyond one of the sangars, 'is where our running water comes from. Don't drink it unless you've taken your Paludrine. There, behind the well, to the right of those palm trees, is the officers' mess and accommodations.' He pointed to the lines of prefabricated huts located near the Wali's fort. 'Those are the barracks for the SAF forces. However, you lads, being of greater substance, are relegated to tents.'

He grinned broadly when the men let out loud moans.

As the Bedford headed for the eastern corner of the camp, Ricketts saw that many of the SAF men were gathering outside their barracks, most wearing the same uniform, but with a mixture of red, green, sand and grey berets.

'The SAF consists of four regiments,' Lampton explained. 'The Muscat Regiment, the Northern Frontier Regiment, the Desert Regiment and the Jebel Regiment. That, incidentally, is their order of superiority. While in the barracks, they can be distinguished from each other by their regimental beret. However, in the field they all wear a green, black and maroon patterned head-dress, known as a *shemagh*. As it's made of loose cloth and wraps around the face to protect the nose and mouth from dust, you'll all be given one to wear when you tackle the plateau.'

'We'll look like bloody Arabs,' Bill complained.

'No bad thing,' Lampton said. 'Incidentally, though there *are* a few Arab SAF officers, most of them are British – either seconded officers on loan from the British Army or contract officers.'

'You mean mercenaries,' Andrew objected.

'They prefer the term "contract officers" and don't you forget it.'

The Bedford came to a halt in a dusty clearing the size of a football pitch, containing two buildings: an armoury and a radio operations room. Everything else was in tents, shaded by palm trees and separated by defensive slit trenches. One of them was a large British Army marquee, used as the SAS basha, and off to the side were a number of bivouac tents.

The rest of the Bedfords had already arrived and were being unloaded as Ricketts and the others climbed out into fierce heat, drifting dust and buzzing clouds of flies and mosquitoes.

Once the all-important radio equipment had been stored in the radio ops room, they picked up their bergens and kit belts and selected one of the large bivouac tents, which contained, as they saw when they entered, only rows of camp-beds covered in mosquito netting and resting on the hard desert floor. After picking a spot, each man unrolled his sleeping bag, using his kit belt as a makeshift pillow. Already bitten repeatedly by mosquitoes, all the men were now also covered in what seemed to be a permanent film of dust.

Even as Ricketts was settling down between Andrew and Gumboot, Lampton came in to tell them that they only had thirty minutes for a rest. 'Then,' he said as they groaned melodramatically, 'you're to report to the British Army marquee, known here as the "hotel", for a briefing from the "green slime".' This mention of the Intelligence Corps provoked another bout of groans. When it had died down, Lampton added, grinning: 'And don't forget to take your Paludrine.'

'I hear those anti-malaria tablets actually *give* you malaria,' Bill said.

'Take them anyway,' Lampton said, then left them to their brief rest.

'What a fucking dump,' Gumboot said, lying back on his camp bed and waving the flies away from his face. 'Dust, flies and mosquitoes.'

'It's all experience,' Andrew said, tugging his

boots off and massaging his toes. 'Think of it as an exotic adventure. When you're old and grey, you'll be telling your kids about it, saying how great it was.'

'Exaggerating wildly,' Jock said from the other side of the tent. 'A big fish getting bigger.'

Ricketts popped a Paludrine tablet into his mouth and washed it down with a drink from his water bottle. Then, feeling restless, he stood up. 'No point in lying down for a miserable thirty minutes,' he said. 'It'll just make us more tired than we are now. Half an hour is long enough to get a beer. Who's coming with me?'

'Good idea,' Andrew said, heaving his massive bulk off his camp-bed.

'Me, too,' Gumboot said.

The rest followed suit and they all left the tent, walking the short distance to the large NAAFI tent and surprised to see a lot of frogs jumping about the dry, dusty ground. The NAAFI tent had a front wall of polyurethane cartons, originally the packing for weapons. Inside, there were a lot of six-foot tables and benches, at which some men were drinking beer, either from pint mugs or straight from the bottle. A shirtless young man smoking a pipe and sitting near the refrigerator introduced himself as Pete and said he was in charge of the canteen. He told them to help themselves, write their names and what they had had on the piece of paper on top of the fridge, and expect to be billed at the end of each month. All of them had a Tiger beer and sat at one of the tables.

'So what do you think of the place?' Pete asked them.

'Real exotic,' Gumboot said.

'It's not all that bad when you get used to it. I've been in worse holes.'

'Who else is here?' Ricketts asked.

'Spooks, Signals, BATT, Ordnance, REME, Catering Corps, Royal Corps of Transport, Engineers.'

'Spooks, meaning green slime,' Ricketts said.

'Yes. You're SAS, right?'

'Right.'

'They'll keep you busy here.'

'I hope so,' Andrew said. 'I wouldn't want to be bored in this hole. Time would stretch on for ever.'

'At least we've got outdoor movies,' Pete said, puffing clouds of smoke from his pipe. 'They're shown in the SAF camp. English movies one night, Indian ones the next. Just take a chair along with a bottle of beer and have yourself a good time. Me, I'm a movie buff.'

'I like books,' Andrew said. 'I write poetry, see? I always carry a little notebook with me and jot down my thoughts as they come to mind.'

'What thoughts?' Gumboot asked.

Andrew shrugged. 'Thoughts inspired by what I see and hear around me. I rewrite them in my head and jot them down.'

'You've got me in your notebook, have you?' Jock asked. 'All my brilliant remarks.'

'Ask no questions and I'll tell you no lies,' Andrew replied with a big grin. 'It's just poetry, man.'

'I didn't think you could spell,' Gumboot said, 'but maybe that doesn't matter.'

'Say, man,' Andrew said, taking a swipe at a dive-bombing hornet trying to get at his beer, 'how come there's so many frogs in this desert?'

'Don't know,' Pete said. 'But there's certainly a lot of 'em. Frogs, giant crickets, flying beetles, hornets, red and black ants, centipedes, camel spiders and scorpions – you name it, we've got it.'

'Jesus,' Tom said. 'Are any of those bastards poisonous?'

'The centipedes and scorpions can give you a pretty serious sting, so I'd recommend you shake out anything loose before picking it up. Those things like sheltering beneath clothes. They like to hide in boots and shoes. So never pick *anything* up without shaking it out first.'

'What about the spiders?' Bill asked, looking uneasy.

'They look pretty horrible, but they don't bite.

One has a small body and long legs, the other short legs and a big, fat body. You'll find them all over the bloody place, including under your bedclothes – another reason for shaking everything out.'

Bill shivered at the very thought of the monsters. 'I *hate* spiders!' he said.

The thunder of 25-pounder guns suddenly shook the tent, taking everyone by surprise.

'Christ!' Jock exclaimed. 'Are we being attacked?'

'No,' Pete said. 'It's just the SAF firing on the Jebel from the gun emplacements just outside the wire. You'll get that at regular intervals during the day and even throughout the night, disturbing your sleep. It's our way of deterring the *adoo* hiding in the wadis from coming down off the Jebel. It takes some getting used to, but eventually you *will* get used to it – that and the croaking of the bloody frogs, which also goes on all night.'

'Time for our briefing,' Ricketts said. 'Drink up and let's go, lads.' They all downed their beer, thanked Pete, and left the tent. Once outside, Ricketts looked beyond the wire and saw one of the big guns firing from inside its protective ring of 40-gallon drums, located about a hundred yards outside the fence. The noise was tremendous, with smoke and flame belching out of the long barrel. The backblast made dust billow up around the Omani gunners, who had covered their ears with their hands to keep out the noise.

'That's one hell of a racket to get used to,' Jock said.

'Plug your ears,' Gumboot told him.

The briefing took place in the corner of the marquee known as the 'hotel', where Sergeant Lampton was waiting for them, standing beside another man who, like Lampton, was wearing only a plain shirt, shorts and slippers.

'Welcome to Um al Gwarif,' he said. 'I'm Captain Ralph Banks of SAS Intelligence and I don't like to hear the term "green slime".' When the laughter had died down, he continued: 'You may have noticed that I'm not wearing my green beret or insignia. You may also have noticed that everyone else around here is like me – no beret, no insignia. There's a good reason for it. While we're all here at the Sultan's invitation, there are those, both here and in Great Britain, who would disapprove of our presence here, so to avoid identification we don't wear cap badges, identification discs, badges of rank or formation signs. This also means that the *adoo* won't know who we are if they capture us, dead or alive. Of course, if they capture you alive, they may try some friendly persuasion, in which case we trust that your interrogation training will stand you in good stead.'

The men glanced at one another, some grinning sheepishly, then returned their attention to the 'Head Shed', as senior officers were known.

'I believe you were briefed in Hereford,' he said, 'about the general situation here in Oman.'

'Yes, boss,' some of the men replied.

'Good. What I would like to fill you in on is what you'll be doing for the next few days, before we make the assault on the Jebel Dhofar and start ousting the *adoo*.' Banks turned to the map behind him. 'As you've already been informed, everything that happens here must be seen to be the doing of the Omanis. With our help, the Sultan's Armed Forces have established bases all around this area. At Taqa,' he said, pointing the names out on the map, 'Mirbat and Sudh, all on the coast, and also here in the western area at Akoot, Rayzut, where a new harbour is being built, at Thamrait, or Midway, on the edge of the Empty Quarter, and even on the Jebel itself, at the Mahazair Pools, which will be your first RV when the assault begins.' He turned back to face them. 'While the next military objective is the assault on the Jebel, it's imperative that you men first learn about the workings of the BATT, who assist the SAF with training, advice and community welfare. Also, before you make the assault on the Jebel you'll have to learn how to deal with the *firqats*, who can be a prickly, unpredictable bunch.'

He nodded at Sergeant Lampton, who took over the briefing. 'The *firqats* are irregular troops formed into small bands led by us. Many of them are former *adoo* who sided with Sultan Qaboos when he deposed his father and started his reforms. As they know the *adoo* camps and bases, those particular *firqats* are very useful, but they aren't overly fond of the Sultan's regular army and, as Captain Banks said, they can be very difficult to deal with. For this reason, part of the work of the BATT teams is to be seen doing good deeds, as it were, in the countryside, thus impressing the *firqats* with our general worthiness and strengthening their support for the Sultan. So it's imperative that you learn exactly what the BATT teams are doing and how they go about doing it. Therefore, for your first week here, you'll be split up into small teams, each led by a BATT man, including myself, and given a guided tour of the area, plus special training relating to warfare in this particular environment. At the end of that week, the assault on the Jebel will commence. Any questions?'

There was a brief silence, broken only when Ricketts asked: 'When do we start?'

'Tomorrow morning. You have the rest of the day off. As the sun is due to sink shortly, it won't be a long day. Any more questions?'

As there were no further questions, the group was disbanded and went off to the open mess tent to have dinner at the trestle tables. Afterwards they returned to the NAAFI tent to put in a solid evening's drinking, returning at midnight, drunk and exhausted, to their bivouac tent. After nervously shaking out their kit to check for scorpions and centipedes, they wriggled into their sleeping bags for what was to prove a restless night punctuated by croaking frogs, irregular blasts from the 25-pounders and attacks by thirsty mosquitoes and dive-bombing hornets. Few of the men felt up to much the next day, but they still had their work to do.

4

For the next five days, Ricketts, Andrew and Gumboot were driven around the area in Lampton's Land Rover, with Ricketts driving, the sergeant beside him and the other two in the back with strict instructions to keep their eyes peeled at all times. To ensure that they did not dehydrate, they had brought along a plentiful supply of water bottles and *chajugles*, small canvas sacks, rather like goatskins, that could be filled with water and hung outside the vehicle to stay cool. Just as the Bedfords had done the first day, Ricketts always drove alongside the roads, rather than on them, to minimize the risk from land-mines laid by the *adoo*.

The heat was usually fierce, from a sky that often seemed white, but they gradually got used to it, or at least learned to accept it, and they frequently found relief when they drove along the beaches, by the rushing surf and white waves of the turquoise sea. The beaches, they soon discovered, were covered with crabs and lined with wind-blown palm trees. Beyond the trees, soaring up to the white-blue sky, was the towering gravel plateau of the Jebel Dhofar, a constant reminder that soon they would have to climb it – a daunting thought for even the hardiest.

As they drove through the main gates that first morning, the big guns in the hedgehogs just outside the perimeter fired on the Jebel, creating an almighty row, streams of grey smoke and billowing clouds of dust. Just ahead of their Land Rover, a Saladin armoured car was setting out across the dusty plain, right into the clouds of dust.

'The *adoo* often mount small raids against us,' Lampton explained. 'They also come down from the Jebel during the night to plant mines around the base or dig themselves in for a bit of sniping. That *Saladin* goes out every morning at this time to sweep the surrounding tracks, clear any mines left and keep an eye out for newly arrived *adoo* snipers. The same procedure takes place at RAF Salalah, which is where we're going right now.'

Reversing the same three-mile journey they had made the day before, when they first arrived, with the Land Rover bouncing constantly over the rough gravel-and-sand terrain beside the dirt track, they soon passed the guarded perimeter of RAF Salalah, then came to the main gate by the single-storey SOAF HQ. Their papers were checked by an Omani soldier wearing the red beret of the Muscat Regiment and armed with a 7.62mm FN rifle. Satisfied, he let them drive through the gates and on to where the Strikemaster jets and Skyvan cargo planes were being serviced in the dispersal bays encircled by empty oil drums.

'Stop right by that open Skyvan,' Lampton said. When Ricketts had done so, they all climbed down. Lampton introduced them to a dark-haired man wearing only shorts and slippers, whose broad chest and muscular arms were covered in sweat. Though he was wearing no shirt, he carried a Browning 9mm high-power handgun in a holster at his hip. He was supervising the loading of heavy resup bundles into the cargo bay in the rear of the Skyvan. The heavy work was being done by other RAF loadmasters, all of whom were also stripped to the waist and gleaming with sweat.

'Hi, Whistler,' Lampton said. 'How are things?'

'No sweat,' Whistler replied.

'You're *covered* in bloody sweat!'

Whistler grinned. 'No sweat otherwise.' He glanced at the men standing around Lampton. 'These bullshit artists have just been badged,' Lampton said, by way of introduction, 'and are starting their year's probationary with us. Men, this is Corporal Harry Whistler of 55 Air Despatch Squadron, Royal Corps of Transport. Though he's normally based on Thorney Island and was recently on a three-month tour of detachment to the army camp in Muharraq, he's here to give us resup support. As his surname's "Whistler" and he actually whistles a lot, we just call him . . .'

'Whistler,' Andrew said.

'What a bright boy you are.'

Everyone said hello to Whistler. 'Welcome to the dustbowl,' he replied 'I'm sure you'll have a great time here.'

'A real holiday,' Gumboot said.

'You won't be seeing too much of Whistler,' Lampton told them, 'because he'll usually be in the sky directly above you, dropping supplies from his trusty Skyvan.'

Grinning, Whistler glanced up at the semi-naked loadmasters, who were now inside the cargo hold, lashing the bundles to the floor with webbing freight straps and 1200lb-breaking-strain cords.

'What's in the bundles?' Rickets asked.

'Eighty-one-millimetre mortar bombs, HE phosphorus and smoke grenades, 7.62mm ball and belt ammo, compo rations, water in jerrycans – four to a bundle. Those are for the drops to our troopers at places like Simba, Akoot and Jibjat, but we also have food resup for the *firqats* out in the field, since those bastards are quick to go on strike if they think we're ignoring them.' Whistler pointed to some bundles wrapped in plastic parachute bags for extra protection. 'Tins of curried mutton or fish, rice, flour, spices, dates, and the bloody oil used for the cooking, carried in tins that always burst – hence the parachute bags. As well as all that, we drop the propaganda leaflets that are part of the hearts-and-minds campaign. It's like being a flying library for the illiterate.'

'Whistler will also be helping out now and then with a few bombing raids,' Lampton informed them, 'though not with your regular weapons, since those are left to the Strikemaster jets.'

'Right,' Whistler said. 'We're already preparing for the assault on the Jebel.' He pointed to the six 40-gallon drums lined up on the perimeter track by the runway. 'We're going to drop those on the Jebel this afternoon, hopefully on some dumbstruck *adoo*, as a trial run.'

'What are they?' Ricketts asked.

'Our home-made incendiary bombs. We call them Burmail bombs.'

'They look like ordinary drums of aviation oil.'

'That's just what they are – drums of Avtur. But we dissolve polyurethane in the Avtur to thicken it up a bit; then we seal the drums, fix Schermuly flares to each side of them, fit them with cruciform harnesses and roll them out the back of the Skyvan. They cause a hell of an explosion, lads. Lots of fire and smoke. We use them mainly for burning fields that look like they've been cultivated by the *adoo*. However, if help is required by you lads on the ground, but not available from the Strikemasters, we use the Burmail bombs against the *adoo* themselves.'

'Why are they called Burmails?' asked Andrew, a man with a genuine fondness for words.

'"Burmail" is an Arabic word for oil drums,' Whistler told him. 'Thought by some to be a derivation from Burmah Oil, or the Burmah Oil Company.'

'What's it like flying in on an attack in one of those bathtubs?' Gumboot asked with his customary lack of subtlety.

'Piece of piss,' Whistler replied, unperturbed. 'We cruise in at the minimum safe altitude of 7000 feet, then lose altitude until we're as low as 500 feet, which we are when we fly right through the wadis on the run in to the DZ. When those fucking Burmail bombs go off, it's like the whole world exploding. So anytime you need help, just call. That's what we're here for, lads.'

* * *

On the second day Lampton made Ricketts drive them out to the Salalah plain, where they saw Jebalis taking care of small herds of cattle or carrying their wares, mostly firewood, on camels, en route to Salalah. This reminded the troopers that life here continued as normal; that not only the *adoo* populated the slopes of the Jebel Dhofar and the arid sand plain in front of it.

That afternoon the group arrived at the old walled town of Salalah. At the main gate they had to wait for ages while the Sultan's armed guards, the Askouris, searched through the bundles of firewood on the Jebalis' camels to make sure that their owners were not smuggling arms for the *adoo* supporters inside the town, of which there were known to be a few. Eventually, when the camels had passed through, the soldiers' papers were checked, and they were allowed to drive into the town, along a straight track that led through a cluster of mud huts to an oasis of palm trees, lush green grass and running water. They passed the large jail to arrive at the Sultan's white, fortified palace, where Lampton made Ricketts stop.

'When Sultan Sa'id Tamur lived there,' Lampton recounted, 'he was like a recluse, shunning all Western influence, living strictly by the Koran and ruling the country like a medieval despot. Though his son, Qaboos, was trained at Sandhurst, when he returned here he was virtually kept a prisoner – until he deposed his old man at gunpoint, then sent him into exile in London. He died in the Dorchester Hotel in 1972. A nice way to go.'

'And by reversing his father's despotism,' Andrew said from the back of the Land Rover, 'Qaboos has gradually been finding favour with the locals.'

'With our help, yes. He's been particularly good at increasing recruitment to the army and air force. He's also built schools and hospitals, plus a radio station whose specific purpose is to combat communist propaganda from Radio Aden. He's trying to bring Oman into the twentienth century, but I doubt that he'll get that far. However, if he wins the support of his people and keeps the communists out of Oman, we'll be content.'

'Our oil being protected,' put in Ricketts.

'That's right,' Lampton said. 'Wait here. I'm going in to give Qaboos a written report on recent events. He likes to be kept informed. When I come out, I'll give you a quick tour of the town.'

'It's more like a bleedin' village,' Gumboot complained.

'It might be a village in Devon,' Lampton said as he got out of the vehicle, 'but here it's a town. Relax, lads. Put your feet up. This could take some time.'

In fact, it took nearly two hours. While Lampton was away, Ricketts and the other two had a smoke, repeatedly quenched their thirst with water from the water bottles and *chajugles*, and gradually became covered in a slimy film composed of sweat and dust. Already warned to neither stare at, nor talk to, the veiled women who passed by with lowered heads, they amused themselves instead by making faces at some giggling local kids, giving others chewing gum, and practising their basic Arabic with the gendarmes who were indifferently guarding the Sultan's palace, armed with .303 Short-Magazine Lee Enfield, or SMLE, rifles. When Lampton emerged and again offered them a quick tour of the town, they politely refused.

'We've seen all there is to see,' Gumboot said, 'and we're frying out here, boss. Can we go somewhere cooler?'

Lampton grinned as he took his seat in the Land Rover. 'OK, lads. Let's go and see some of the BATT handiwork. That'll take us along the seashore and help cool you down.'

He guided Ricketts back out through the walled town's main gates and down to the shore, then made him head for Taqa, halfway between Salalah and Mirbat. The drive did indeed take them along the shore, with the ravishing turquoise sea on one side and rows of palm and date trees on the other. A cool breeze made the journey pleasant, though Ricketts had to be careful not to get stuck in the sand. Also, as he had noticed before, there were a great many crabs, in places in their hundreds, scuttling in both directions across the beach like monstrous ants and being crushed under the wheels of the Land Rover.

'I get the shivers just looking at 'em,' Gumboot told them while visibly shivering in the rear of the Land Rover. 'I'd rather fight the *adoo*.'

'There's a BATT station at Taqa,' Lampton said, oblivious to the masses of crabs, 'so you can see the kind of work we do there. You know, of course, that the SAS has been in Oman before.'

'I didn't know that,' Gumboot said to distract himself from the crabs. 'But then I'm pig-ignorant, boss.'

'I know they were here before,' Andrew said, 'but I don't know why.'

'He's pig-ignorant as well,' Gumboot said. 'Now I don't feel so lonely.'

'It was because of Britain's treaty obligations to Muscat and Oman,' Lampton informed them. 'In the late 1950s we were drawn into a counter-insurgency campaign when the Sultan's regime was threatened by a rebellious army of expatriate Omanis from Saudi Arabia. As their first major move against the Sultan, they took over the Jebel Akhdar, or Green Mountain, in the north of Oman, and declared the region independent from him.'

'Which did not amuse him greatly,' Andrew said.

'Definitely not,' Lampton replied. 'We Brits were called in to help. When British infantry, brought in from Kenya in 1957, failed to dislodge the rebels from the mountain, D Squadron and A Squadron of 22 SAS were flown in to solve the problem. In January 1959 they made their legendary assault on the Jebel Akhdar, winning it back from the rebels. Once they had done that, they implemented the first hearts-and-minds campaign to turn the rest of the locals into firm supporters of the Sultan. Unfortunately, with his medieval ways, Sultan Qaboos's old man undid all the good done by the SAS. Now Qaboos has another rebellion on his hands.'

'Which is why we're here,' Andrew said.

'Yes. What we did in 1959, we're going to have to do again twelve years later: engage in another hearts-and-minds campaign, while also defeating the *adoo* on the Jebel Dhofar.'

'What exactly does a hearts-and-minds campaign involve?' Ricketts asked him.

'The concept was first devised in Malaya in the early 1950s and used successfully in Borneo from 1963 to 1966. It's now an integral part of our counter-insurgency warfare methods. Its basic thrust is to gain the trust of the locals of any given area by sharing their lifestyle, language and customs. That's why, for instance, in Borneo, SAS troopers actually lived with the natives in the jungle, assisting them with their everyday needs and providing medical care. In fact, medical care is one of the prime tools in the hearts-and-minds campaign. We even train some of the BATT men in midwifery and dentistry. Those skills, along with basic education, building small schools and hospitals, and teaching crafts that create work, have won us lots of friends in many regions.'

'Fucked if I'd deliver a baby,' Gumboot said. 'There's a limit to duty.'

'You'd be surprised at the number of SAS men who've delivered babies and pulled teeth in emergencies.' Lampton turned to Ricketts. 'Watch out for the water here. This bay leads to Taqa.'

Even as Lampton was speaking, the Land Rover was driving into the shallow water of a bay surrounded by small cliffs. By using four-wheel drive, Ricketts got them across to dry land, where they passed more cliffs and sand dunes, before arriving at another beach. There, flocks of seagulls were winging repeatedly over piles of rotten, stinking fish that were scattered between the beached fishing boats. After passing the boats and the Arab fishermen sitting in them repairing the nets, they arrived at a small village of mud huts. At the end of its single, dusty street were two buildings taller than the others, being three storeys high, with the Omani flag flying from one of them.

'Taqa,' Lampton said. 'Stop here.' Ricketts pulled up, then followed the others out of the vehicle. 'The building with the flag,' Lampton told them, 'is the Wali's house. The other tall building is the BATT house. Now let's meet the BATT men.'

Three of the latter were on the first floor of the BATT house, brewing tea on a No 1 burner and placing tin mugs on the trestle table that took up most of the tiny room. The shelves were stacked with tins of compo rations and cooking utensils, indicating that the room was used as a combined kitchen and mess room. SLR and M16 rifles were piled up in a corner, along with boxes of grenades, webbing, phosphorus flares and other ammunition.

When introductions had been made, the tea was poured and the BATT men, constantly interrupting one another, explained that they were still working to win the hearts and minds of the villagers. They were having problems, however, because some of the men of the village were suspected of belonging to the *adoo* – for they often disappeared for weeks at a time – and the villagers, including the Wali, were worried about possible reprisals against them once the BATT teams moved out.

'So one of our jobs,' Corporal Roy Coleman said, 'is to persuade the villagers that we won't be leaving until the *adoo* have been defeated militarily and forced off the Jebel once and for all. Another problem is that these villagers are still pretty primitive, and although we give them medical treatment we're up against a lot of their old beliefs and superstitions.'

'Is this the whole BATT team?' Ricketts asked, indicating the three troopers with a nod of his head.

'No. There's eight of us. Some are sleeping, a couple are in the Wali's fort, keeping their ear to the radio, and the rest are performing their duties in the village. Let's go outside and see what's happening. If you hear gunshots, don't worry. We're giving firing lessons to some of the gendarmes on a makeshift firing range on the beach. It's not the *adoo*.'

Leaving the house, Coleman led them to the back of the building, where a tent had been set up as a basic, open-air surgery. Gunshots did indeed ring out from the direction of the beach as they approached the Omanis queuing for medical treatment at the tent. The SAS medic was standing behind a trestle table, sweating in the afternoon heat as he went about his work. Introduced to the probationers, he talked to them as he continued cleaning and bandaging cuts, lancing boils, treating bad burns and dispensing a wide variety of tablets.

'Some of the tablets are genuine and some are piss-takes,' he said. 'You get hypochondriacs even in this place, believe me. I was trained at the US Army's special forces medical school at Fort Sam, in Houston, and Fort Bragg, North Carolina – the best of its kind – which means that although I'm not a doctor I can deal with just about anything short of major surgery. Here, the most common problems are boils, burns, ruptures, messed-up circumcisions, conjunctivitis, dysentery, malaria, yellow fever, sand-fly fever and dengue from mosquitoes . . .'

'Don't tell me!' Gumboot interrupted sardonically.

'. . . trench fever from lice, spotted fever from ticks, every kind of typhus, even leprosy and the dire results of floggings ordered by the Wali. Like the other medics, if I come across something I can't handle I simply call the BATT doctor at Um al Gwarif. Nevertheless, I have two major problems. One is being up against the primitive practices of the local witch doctors, who tend to cure all ills by branding the pained area with a red-hot iron. The other is trying to work out which of the villagers are really sick and which are just becoming pill heads. Gradually, however, more and more of them are coming to depend increasingly on us while rejecting the advances of the *adoo*. That's the whole point.'

'It's also the point of the school we've recently built for them,' Coleman said as he led them away from the medical tent, 'and for the firing practice we give to the gendarmes. The more we give them, the less they appreciate the *adoo*. And that, in a nutshell, is what's known as the hearts-and-minds campaign.'

The following day they were at Mirbat, on the south coast of Dhofar. It was little more than a collection of dusty mud huts and clay buildings, with the sea on one side and a protective barbed-wire fence running north and east. The settlement included a cluster of houses to the south; a market by the sea; some thirty armed Omanis, housed in an ancient Wali's fort to the west; another small fort about 500 yards to the west, holding 25 men of the Dhofar Gendarmerie, or DG; and, near the market in the middle of the compound, a mud-built BATT house holding nine BATT men under the command of the 23-year-old Captain Mike Kealy. Eight hundred yards north of the northern perimeter, on the slopes of Jebel Ali, was another Dhofar Gendarmerie outpost.

'We've won the hearts and minds of this town,' Captain Kealy informed them, 'but the *adoo* harass us all the time and, so it's rumoured, are determined to capture the town and wipe out the defenders as an inspiration to their own wavering troops and a warning to all those who oppose them.'

'What kind of defences do you have?' Ricketts asked him.

'You mean, apart from the men?'

'Yes.'

Kealy shrugged. 'Not much. The only heavy weapons are an old 25-pounder in a gun-pit next to the DG fort, a single 7.62mm GPMG on the BATT house roof, an 81mm mortar emplaced beside the building and a 0.5in-calibre heavy machine gun.' Kealy shrugged again. 'That's it.'

'That's not much.'

'If they come,' Kealy said, 'we'll be waiting for them. Don't doubt that, Trooper.'

'I won't,' Ricketts replied.

Leaving the BATT house, they were introduced to other members of B Squadron, including three Fijians – the enormous Corporal Labalaba, known as Laba, Valdez, and Sekonia, known as Sek. They were told that all three had joined up during the British Army's major recruitment drive in Fiji and were veterans of the Keeni Meeni operations in Aden, as well as later missions in Borneo.

'What's "Keeni Meeni" mean?' Gumboot asked, almost tripping over his own tongue.

The enormous Labalaba, who was even taller than Andrew, looked down at Gumboot and grinned. 'Keeni Meeni? It's a Swahili phrase used to describe the movement of a snake in the grass. In Aden we'd disguise ourselves as Arabs, infiltrate our chosen district and seek out the enemy, quickly pull our Browning handguns from our *futahs*, the traditional Arab robes, neutralize the enemy with a "double-tap", then melt back into the scenery – just like snakes in the grass!'

'You mean, you'd blow the poor fucker away.'

'You've got it, Trooper.'

Leaving the sandbagged gun-pit, where the three Fijians had been cleaning the big gun, they saw their first *firqats*, just down from the hills and returning their FN rifles and other weapons to the armoury in the Wali's fort. Though they all had similar *shemaghs*, the rest of their clothing was widely varied, ranging from the loose robes worn by most locals to Khaki Drill (KD), or Light Tropical, uniforms. Festooned with webbing, ponchos and bandoliers of ammunition, and with the large Omani knives called *kunjias* tied around their waists, they looked like a particularly fierce band of brigands.

'I wouldn't like to fucking tangle with them,' Gumboot said admiringly.

'Don't,' warned Lampton. 'They're extremely efficient with those knives and quick to use them. Only last year, they murdered a British officer in his tent when he refused to give them what they wanted. And those men, believe it or not, are the ones you depend on. Now let's get back to the basha and have a couple of cooling beers.'

'The word's *soothing*,' Andrew corrected him, glancing back over his shoulder at the fierce-looking *firqats*. 'Let's all go for a *soothing* beer.'

They drove gratefully back to base.

5

The indoctrination tour continued. Lampton had Ricketts drive them to Rayzut, where British Army engineers were constructing a new harbour from large blocks raised around the bay and an SAS BATT team was inoculating the local labour force. Many of the latter, Ricketts noticed, were so intrigued by modern medicine that they queued up eagerly to have their jabs.

At Arzat, which was little more than a random collection of mud huts with a small garrison of Dhofar Gendarmerie, they found an SAS BATT team showing the locals how to purify the water tanks with fluoride and transform their rubbish into fuel. SAS veterinary surgeons were also present, showing the locals how to improve the breeding of their cattle and training them in basic veterinary medicine.

At Janook, the probationers were given an enthusiastic lecture by a four-man BATT 'Psyops' team, formerly of the Northern Ireland regiments and now responsible for Psychological Operations in Oman. These activities included, apart from the writing of the propaganda leaflets dropped from the Skyvans, the showing of British and Hollywood movies to the locals.

'The theory,' they were informed by Corporal Hamlyn of the BATT team, 'is that with little or no command of English, the locals can receive the benefits of Western civilization more easily from moving images than they can from the printed page.'

'Never attack the written word,' Andrew said, jotting some in his notebook, presumably for future poems. 'There are aspects of humanity that the moving image can never describe.'

The corporal looked up in surprise at the immense black newcomer. 'What's that, Trooper? I'm not sure I heard that right.'

'The moving image is severely limited in its payload. It's the printed word that will always knock 'em out.'

'Not in this case, Trooper. These folk in their jellabas and *shemaghs* don't speak any English, so it's easier to show them some movies, preferably action-packed.'

'Charles Bronson,' Gumboot said.

'Clint Eastwood,' Ricketts added.

'I'm with you,' Andrew said. 'Movies that

demonstrate Democracy in action – lots of guns and dead bodies.'

'Are you taking the piss, Trooper?'

'Just bouncing a few ideas, Corporal.'

'He's just stopped living off bananas,' Gumboot explained, 'and has withdrawal symptoms.'

'Piss off, you lot,' Hamlyn said.

Andrew was more impressed when, at Suda, another windswept, dusty village scattered around a lovely bay on the Arabian Sea, they spent some time with a BATT team who were teaching the local children English with the aid of carefully selected illustrated books that showed them the wealth and wonders of the West – none of which, the BATT team repeatedly emphasized to their impressionable pupils, would be supplied by the communists.

'See what I mean?' Andrew said triumphantly. 'When it really gets down to the nitty-gritty, the printed word is what matters.'

'Not forgetting the pretty pictures,' Gumboot reminded him.

'They're only there to support the words.'

'Every kid I saw was looking at the pictures,' Ricketts chipped in. 'Not reading the words.'

'A mere diversion,' Andrew insisted. 'They were merely stopping to think a bit. The pictures visually confirmed what the words had conveyed to them, but it's the words, not the pictures, that they'll be able to use in the future. We're talking language here, man!'

'That's quite a mouthful, Andrew.'

'It's verbal diarrhoea,' Gumboot insisted, 'caused by all those bananas.'

'Better than mental constipation,' Andrew retorted, 'of the kind you know so well.'

'Cut out the bullshit,' Lampton said. 'These matters are serious. The point is that whether with pictures or prose, movies or chewing gum, we're showing these people what they can have if they side with us instead of the communists. Call it brainwashing if you like, but that's what we're about here.'

Finally, during the late afternoon of their fourth day, Lampton guided Ricketts – still driving while Andrew and Gumboot kept a constant watch for *adoo* snipers – to a desolate village located in rough, gravel flatland west of the Jebel Dhofar, in a region once patrolled by the rebels but now back in the hands of the SAF.

'Never forget,' Lampton told them as they approached the village in four-wheel drive, bouncing over the rough, rocky ground, 'that the *adoo* are fanatical communists, backed by the Soviet Union and the Chinese. Often removed from their parents to be schooled in the PDRY – the People's Democratic Republic of Yemen, formerly Aden – or sent to guerrilla-warfare schools in Russia and China, they're returned to their mountain villages as fanatics. There they establish communist cells, breaking down former loyalties, organizing their converts first into village militias, then into seasoned battle groups who show absolutely no mercy to the Muslims. They ban all religious practices, torture village elders into denying their faith and routinely rape their women. In other words, they're engaged in a campaign of terror designed to wipe out Islam altogether and establish communism in Oman – and they're ruthless in doing it.'

The Land Rover bounced down off the rough ground on the lower slopes of the Jebel, then travelled along the flat gravel plain until it arrived at a dusty village of clay huts, Arabs in traditional dress and a surprising variety of animals, including cattle, mountain goats, mangy dogs and chickens.

The sun was just beginning to sink, casting great shadows over the village, when Lampton told Ricketts to stop the Land Rover near the two wells, where a group of SAS men had gathered. Explosive charges, detonating cords, primers and other demolition equipment could be seen in opened boxes on the ground by their feet.

'Are those sappers?' Andrew asked.

'Yes,' Lampton replied. 'Under the command of one of our demolition specialists.'

As Lampton climbed out of the Land Rover and approached the men around one of the wells, followed by the others, the men, in two groups, both being watched attentively by many villagers, including children, were leaning over the walls of the two wells and shouting down into them. The voices of men down inside the wells came back up with a hollow, reverberating quality, though what they said could not be made out.

'You look like you're ready to take a dive,' Lampton said, stopping just behind one of the men leaning over the bricked parapet of the well. 'What's going on?'

The man straightened up and turned around to gaze at Lampton. He had unkempt red hair, a beakish, broken nose, and a face flushed from sunshine or booze – possibly both. He was still in his twenties, but his dour expression and a couple of scars made him seem older.

'Hi, Sarge,' he said. 'We're trying to open these wells.'

'What do you mean by *trying*?'

'The problem is that in blowing the concrete apart, we might also destroy the walls, covering the concrete with more debris and fucking the wells up for good.'

'Which means we fuck up the village for good.'

'Yes, boss, that's it.'

Lampton glanced at the well behind the man, his attention drawn by what sounded like the tapping of a hammer coming up from its depths. 'What are the chances of success?'

'Pretty good,' the man said, 'but not guaranteed. It's a calculated gamble, I guess, but I've orders to try it.'

'Why not?' Lampton said, glancing at the villagers gathered together across the clearing, though being kept a safe distance away by some troopers. 'If it fails, those poor sods won't have lost any more than they've lost already. This village is dead as we stand here. We can't kill it off more.'

When the red-haired man's sharp blue gaze focused on Ricketts and the other two, Lampton introduced them, then said: 'This is Corporal Alfie Lloyd, formerly a Royal Engineer sapper, then ammunition technician with the Royal Army Ordnance Corps, now an SAS demolition specialist.' He turned back to Lloyd. 'So how's it going, Alfie?'

'Fine, boss. We're all set to go. The wet concrete was originally poured in from mechanical mixers and hardened at the bottom of the walls. We think it's about six foot deep. We've drilled about halfway through it and filled the hole with C3 plastic explosive. There's a man down each well right now, fixing the time fuse, blasting cap and det cord.' He indicated the coils of detonating cord resting on the ground by each well, with one end looped over the wall and snaking down to the bottom, where the sapper below would now be fixing it to the blasting cap. 'We're hoping that with just the right amount of explosive we can shatter the slab concrete without doing damage to the walls around it. If we're successful, the pieces of broken concrete can be hauled up from the bottom of the well in buckets, giving access to the water still below.'

Lloyd turned away from Lampton as the men who had been at the bottom of the wells clambered back over the sides, their bodies criss-crossed with webbing that held explosives, blasting caps and various tools, including wire-clippers and a small, light hammer. When they were completely over the walls, their companions pulled up the rope ladders.

'OK?' Lloyd asked. Both men put their thumbs up. 'Right. Run the other ends of those det cords across to the detonators and let's get this show on the road.' He turned back to Lampton. 'I'd stand over there, if I was you, a safe distance away. About the same distance as those gawking Arabs, in case we've miscalculated.'

'Now you wouldn't do that, would you, Corporal Lloyd?'

'It's best not to take chances.'

'*I'm* not taking any chances,' Gumboot said. 'When I was in Northern Ireland, doing a tour in bandit country, we were called to the scene where some IRA wally had blown himself up by accident when planting a bomb. They gave us plastic rubbish bags and told us to pick up the pieces, which were scattered all over the fucking place. You couldn't tell his dick from his fingers. That put me off explosives for life, so just tell me where to stand.'

'Over there by those houses. Beside the Arabs. Where you belong, mate.'

Clearly knowing that Lloyd had no sense of humour whatsoever, Lampton led the others back across the clearing, until they were level with the detonators on either side of them. As they waited for the sappers to move their demolition gear away from the wells and fix the detonating cords to the detonators, Ricketts asked: 'Were those wells sealed by the SAF?'

'Correct,' Lampton replied. 'As I said, the *adoo* are fanatical communists. About sixteen months ago, just before the old Sultan was deposed by his son, Qaboos, he was informed that this village was sympathetic to the *adoo*, who were then in control of much of the region.

Reacting as he always did, the Sultan sent his SAF troops in to hang the suspected *adoo* and seal the wells, the lifeblood of the village, by pouring in gallons of wet cement direct from mixers. But this didn't stop the *adoo* from carrying out their customary brutalities against the same unfortunate Muslims. They came into the village that very afternoon, while some of the Sultan's victims were still dangling from ropes – deliberately kept up there as a grim reminder to the villagers, and guarded by SAF troops. The *adoo* shot the troops, then engaged in their usual practice of trying to persuade the village elders to publicly renounce Islam. As is one of the *adoo* customs, when the elders refused, their eyes were gouged out and their daughters repeatedly raped. When the *adoo* then melted back into the wadis of the Jebel, the villagers were left without their life-giving water and, even worse, with many of their menfolk dead or blinded. In short, the village was doomed.'

Lampton stopped for a moment to watch the sappers fix the detonating cords to the detonators under the eagle eye of the dour corporal.

'What a fucking awful story!' Gumboot said to Ricketts and Andrew. 'First you get it from one side, then from the other – just like the protection gangs in Northern Ireland.'

'Oh, yeah?' said Andrew. 'What did they do?'

'A bunch of fucking gangsters masquerading as freedom fighters,' Gumboot said. 'First, a Protestant gang would visit a shop and demand payment for so-called protection against the Catholics. If the shopkeeper refused, they either wrecked his shop or burned it down completely. If he accepted, he'd then receive a visit from a Catholic gang demanding payment for so-called protection against the Prods. If he refused, they did the same as the Prods – turned his shop over. If he agreed, the Prods came back and burned the shop down to keep the money from going to the Catholics. The poor fuckers didn't know which way to turn. Often it was just a matter of who got to them first. Just like this place!'

'Religion and politics,' Andrew intoned in a mock-solemn voice, 'are excuses for many evil deeds. Personally, I wash my hands of both and stick to my poetry.'

'Look at those mad fuckers,' Gumboot said, indicating with a nod the sappers, who were kneeling on the ground by the detonators, a hundred yards from the wells, fixing the end of the detonating cords to the charge terminals. 'Did you see that Corporal Lloyd? He had a broken nose and scars on his face and we all know what from – his own fucking explosives. Some job to have, eh?'

'Rather him than me,' Ricketts said.

Satisfied that the sappers were getting on with their business, Lampton turned back to his probationers and continued: 'What was I saying? Ah, yes, the village was doomed . . . Well, that's why we're here. Now that this area is back in Sultan Qaboos's hands, it's our job to rescue formerly doomed villages like this, righting the wrongs of the previous Sultan in the name of his son and reminding the Muslims what will happen to them should they let the *adoo* return. In this case, our first task is to open up those wells and give water, therefore life, back to the villagers. Once that's done, we'll bring in some BATT teams, including medics and veterinarians, to restore the sick to health and help the rest get the most out of the water, the crops it'll bring back, and the livestock it'll help to increase. After that, we'll bring in English teachers, radio sets tuned to Radio Salalah, comics, books and other seductive Western luxuries.'

'Propaganda,' Andrew murmured.

'No, Trooper. Hearts and minds.'

'Ain't no one gettin' *my* mind,' Andrew insisted. 'That's all my own, man.'

'With a mind like yours,' Gumboot said, 'no one would want it. You've no cause for concern there.'

'We've already got it,' Lampton said. 'The trooper just doesn't know it yet.'

After grinning at the doubtful Andrew, Lampton returned his gaze to the sappers who were still kneeling on the ground, one at each detonating plunger. The grim-faced Corporal Lloyd checked that the gawking villagers, particularly the children, were being held back by the troopers, then, without ceremony, he told his men to set off the explosive charges. They pressed down simultaneously on the plungers.

At first, the explosions at the bottom of the two wells were muffled by the solid concrete and sheer depth, but as the concrete exploded, the noise became louder, like the roaring of a buried beast. Suddenly, with an even louder roar, the mouths of the two wells spewed clouds of dust, smoke, pulverized concrete – and finally, water.

The villagers erupted into cheers and cries of joy as the water showered up in the air, then rained back down on them, mixed with dust and powdered concrete. When it had settled down and the smoke and dust had cleared away, both villagers and BATT men rushed to the wells to fight for a position around the walls to look down into the depths.

In both wells the slab concrete had been shattered by the explosions and was piled up as rubble at the bottom. But the rubble was loose and easy to haul up, and soon water was clearly visible below. The village was saved.

6

Any doubts that Ricketts and his two friends might have been harbouring about the reality of *adoo* raids were brutally laid to rest on the final day of their five-day tour. Awakened, as usual, at the crack of dawn, which was just after five o'clock; they rolled off their camp-beds, shocked themselves awake with a quick shower and then returned to the bivouac tent to get dressed.

'What the fuck do we have to get up so early for, anyway?' Bill asked, 'when we're not even on patrol, but just farting about the area, getting lessons in diplomacy and other shit from BATT teams?'

'We have to get up at five in the morning,' Andrew told him, 'because whether or not we appreciate the lessons, our wonderful tour guides, such as Sergeant Lampton, like to fill in every minute of the day, from dawn to dusk.'

'He's a damned good guide, though,' Ricketts

said, slipping into his shorts. 'And a nice bloke as well.'

'You only think that,' Gumboot teased, 'because he put you in charge of us.'

'Go fuck yourself, Gumboot.'

'I agree with Ricketts,' Andrew said. 'Lampton's A1. What's your sergeant like, lads?

'OK,' Jock said. 'Like yours, he never gives us a free minute, but otherwise he's not bad. Good-humoured. Pretty relaxed. No problems there.'

'Fuck the sergeants,' Tom said. 'What's weird to me is the fact that having gone through the hell of Initial Selection and Continuation Training, we're not even allowed to wear our berets, let alone any other insignia. I sometimes think I never really did all that – never really got badged.'

'If you hadn't been badged, you wouldn't be here,' Andrew said, 'so get a grip on yourself. Think positive, man!'

While the men got dressed, the radio beside Tom's camp-bed informed them that the official IRA had condemned a recent pub bombing by the Provisionals in which two people had been killed; that 32 inmates and ten wardens had died in a prison riot at the Attica State Correction Facility in New York state; and that Chelsea had beaten Jeunesse Hautcharage 13–0 in the second round of the European Cup Winners

Cup. The news was followed by the ravings of a demented DJ introducing Rod Stewart's hit, *Maggie May*.

Tom switched the radio off when they all left the bivouac tent, but Gumboot and Bill were singing *Maggie May* as they crossed the dusty clearing to the open mess tent. Inside, they joined the queue to the servery, where they engaged in a little waken-up bullshit with the cook. He had weary eyes and sweat on his vest.

'What's that?' Andrew asked, pointing to the heaped, steaming baked beans. 'Have you been robbing the bog again?'

'You don't like it, Trooper, go climb a tree and pick the kind of grub you're used to.'

'That still leaves us,' Gumboot said, 'and we're in need of some decent grub, though that isn't exactly what I see here. Is that compo sausage or stewed cock?'

'If it's the latter, I'm sure you've tasted it before, so why not try it again?'

'He's just insulted your manhood, Gumboot.'

'He's not a man if he stoops to that. Hey, chef, is that bacon you're putting on my plate or just one of your old shoes?'

'It's tongue,' the cook replied wearily as he slapped the bacon down on Gumboot's plate between the sausage and baked beans. 'It was torn from the throat of the fucker

89

who insulted me yesterday. Now move along, Trooper.'

'A nice man,' Gumboot said, moving along to the tea urn. 'I'm told he washes his hands once a week – when he has his day off.'

Andrew studied his mug of tea. 'A strange colour, folks. It also has an odd smell. Has anyone ever seen that cook in the ablutions or does he piss somewhere else?'

'Smells familiar,' Ricketts said.

'Pungent,' Andrew clarified.

'Close your eyes and think of England,' Gumboot said, 'when you have to swallow the stuff.'

'Hey, you bunch,' the cook bawled, glaring at them, 'you're holding up the whole queue. Clear off to the tables.'

'Yes, mother!' Andrew piped.

They sat around one of the trestle tables near the open end of the tent, from where they could see the rest of Um al Gwarif, including the other SAS tents, the whitewashed Wali's fort, the SAF barracks, and the officers' mess and accommodations partially hidden behind a row of palm trees. When a 25-pounder roared from beyond the perimeter, they all looked automatically in that direction, actually seeing the shell leave the smoking barrel. A few seconds later, a column of smoke and dust billowed up where the shell exploded on the lower slopes of the Jebel.

'I'm amazed there's any *adoo* left up there at all,' Tom said, holding a fork heaped with baked beans to his mouth. 'Those 25-pounders fire on the Jebel every couple of hours, day in and day out. It must be sheer hell up there.'

'They rarely hit anything,' Ricketts said as Tom swallowed his baked beans. 'Or if they do, it's just by accident. They're just firing at random to keep the *adoo* on their toes and preferably sleepless.'

'That's why we're all so exhausted,' Bill put in. '*We're* the ones kept awake!'

As the sand and dust thrown up by the big gun drifted back down over the hedgehog, slightly obscuring the view of the plateau, an unshaven white man wearing a filthy striped jellaba and loose *shemagh* stopped at the adjoining, empty table. He had an L42A1 7.62mm bolt-action Lee Enfield sniper rifle slung across his back and his webbing bristled with ten-round box magazines and L2A2 steel-cased fragmentation grenades. There was a Browning high-power handgun in a holster on his hip and two different knives – the fearsome Omani *kunjias* and a Fairburn-Sykes commando knife – were sheathed on the belt around his waist. Sitting down at the table next to them, neither smiling

SOLDIER C: SAS

nor talking to anyone, he placed his plate of
compo on the table, then unslung his rifle
and aimed it at the smoke still boiling up
from the lower slopes of the Jebel. He pretended to fire, making a clicking sound with
his tongue. Then, still not smiling, he placed
his rifle on the table beside his plate and
began to eat.

Tom leaned sideways and whispered to his
best friend, Bill: 'That's Sergeant Parker! They
all talk about him. They say he's the best sniper
and tracker in the whole SAS.'

'Looks pretty fierce,' Bill said.

'Apparently he is. Dresses up in those old
Arab clothes and goes out there on a camel,
criss-crossing the whole plateau, sniping on
the *adoo* and often bringing prisoners back
for questioning. He's waging a private war
out there and causing a lot of confusion.'

'Glad he's on our side,' Bill said. 'Wouldn't
want him against me.'

'Apparently he's going to be with us when
we make the assault on the Jebel. They say he
now knows as much about the Jebel as any
tribesman.'

'He *looks* like one,' Bill said. 'As mad and as
bad. Well . . .' he sighed melodramatically, 'nice
to know we're protected.'

Hearing what they had just said, Andrew

turned towards the man dressed like an Arab and said with a big smile, 'Hi, there, Sarge!'

Parker stopped eating just long enough to turn his head and stare at Andrew with the steady, fathomless gaze of a cat. He did not say a word.

Glancing briefly at the others, Andrew cleared his throat, kept his smile firmly in place and turned back to Parker.

'How are things up on the Jebel, then?' he asked. 'Pretty hot up there – right, boss?'

Parker just stared at him as if at a blank wall, his fork still raised in the air, with an untouched piece of sausage on it.

Andrew cleared his throat again. 'Still picking off the *adoo*, are you? Still bringing them back down the hill for a talk with the green slime? Good work, Sarge. Keep it up!'

Parker just stared at him, his gaze as firm as it was unreadable, then opened his mouth and popped the sausage in, turning back to his plate. Andrew, clearing his throat for the third time, pushed his chair back and stood up. 'Well,' he said, louder than strictly necessary, 'I think it's time we all left, lads. Lots to do out on the Salalah plain. A long day ahead of us.' He was out of the tent before Ricketts and Gumboot had kicked their own chairs back, but they soon caught up with him. 'Did you see the way he looked at me?' he said. 'With those mad-dog eyes! A born killer if ever I saw one. I'm still shaking, man!'

'You imagined it,' Ricketts said consolingly. 'You're a poet – imaginative. It was all in your head. He's just the quiet type, that's all.'

Andrew shook his head from side to side, clearly not convinced. 'No, man, I didn't imagine a thing – that was one real mean mother. He's the kind to use barbed wire as dental floss, and wipe his arse with sandpaper. You say the wrong thing to him, man, and you'll end up as mince-meat on his plate. Hey, I'm still sweatin' and shakin'. Let's go find Sergeant Lampton and get out of here. I need the wide, open spaces.'

'Yes, let's do that,' Ricketts said, glancing sideways and grinning at Gumboot. 'It's time to start anyway.'

Walking the short distance to the motor pool, they found Sergeant Lampton waiting in the Land Rover, pressed back in the front passenger seat with his knees bent and his desert boots on the dash board, smoking. He made a show of looking at his wristwatch when they approached him.

'You were nearly late,' he said.

'Sorry, boss,' Ricketts replied. 'Trooper Winston became involved in conversation with a sergeant named Parker.'

'Dead-eye Dick,' Lampton replied.

'Pardon?'

Lampton slid his feet off the dashboard and sat up straight. 'Dead-eye Dick. That's what they call him. He's probably the best sniper in Oman – and he's quick with those knives, as well. You mean, he actually *spoke* to you?'

'Well, not exactly . . .' Andrew began.

'It was kind of one-sided,' Ricketts explained, 'but Andrew was certainly trying.'

Ricketts, Gumboot and Lampton all burst out laughing.

'Very funny,' Andrew said, heaving his great bulk into the back of the Land Rover.

'*Very* funny!' Gumboot said. 'Fucking had me in stitches!'

'I'll have you in stitches in a minute if you don't shut your mouth.'

'OK, lads, cool it.' Lampton flicked his cigarette butt out of the vehicle. 'We'll start the day with a morning visit to the BATT house at Rakyut, which is somewhere you haven't been before. OK, Ricketts, let's go.'

'Yes, boss.' Ricketts released the handbrake, slipped into gear, pressed his foot on the accelerator and drove towards the main gate. Just before he reached it, there was an explosion from beyond the perimeter, followed by a billowing cloud of smoke.

The sirens on the watch-towers started wailing. Ricketts braked to a halt as two RAF guards sprinted out of the sangars on either side of the main gate, intending to close it.

'Leave it open!' Lampton bawled. 'We're going out!'

As the guards stopped to stare in surprise at Lampton, he turned to Ricketts, slapped his shoulder and shouted, 'Go, damn it!' Ricketts put his foot right down and raced out through the gate, turning in the direction of the boiling cloud of smoke, even as the RAF guards closed the gate and sprinted back to their sangars.

By now the machine-guns in the watch-towers to the front of the camp had started roaring, sending steams of purplish tracers looping over the billowing cloud of black smoke and exploding in the ground further on.

'Bloody *adoo*!' Lampton exclaimed, glancing to where earth and sand was spewing up from the impact of the 7.62mm GPMG shells.

Straight ahead, just beside the dirt track, the Saladin armoured car used for the daily sweep of the terrain was lying on its side, pouring black smoke. A scorched, horribly blistered figure was crawling from the wreckage. Just as Ricketts was accelerating towards him, however, another figure, wearing loose pants, sandals and a *shemagh*, emerged from behind some rocks, darted up to the crawling figure, and drove a *kunjias* through the back of his neck. After grabbing the dead man's wristwatch, pistol and spare ammunition, the Arab hurried back behind the nearby rocks.

'Bastard!' While Ricketts was still driving, Lampton pulled out his Browning handgun and fired a short burst at the fleeing man. Pieces of stone flew off the rocks in clouds of spewing dust, but the Arab disappeared, untouched. Then a fusillade of fire from behind the rocks made Ricketts swerve off the track and brake to a halt beside the smouldering armoured car, which offered protection.

It also offered a grisly view of the RAF guards inside, all dead, either slashed to pieces by flying, red-hot metal or burned alive in the flaming vehicle.

'Shit!' Lampton jumped out of the Land Rover. He was followed by Ricketts, Andrew and Gumboot, who took up positions on either side of the smoking vehicle. Stifling their urge to throw up at the smell of burning flesh, they poured a hail of SLR fire at the mound of rocks, where they assumed the *adoo* assassin was still hiding.

No more gunfire came from behind the rocks, but Lampton still made no move. Only when the tracers from the watch-tower started falling farther away, indicating that the *adoo* were beating a retreat, did he take a chance by racing around the overturned armoured car and heading straight for the mound of rocks.

Ricketts and the other two gave him covering fire until he reached where he was going. He fired a burst behind the rocks, stepped forward, glanced down, then raised his right hand, waving it to and fro, indicating 'Cease fire'. The guns on the watch-towers then fell silent.

Lampton walked back to the blazing armoured car. He glanced with distaste at the dead men inside. The other victim was lying face-down on the ground with the back of his neck pumping blood. Turning the latter on his back, Lampton checked that he was dead, then shook his head.

'Didn't have a prayer,' he said. He glanced back at the mound of rocks from which the *adoo* had been firing. 'And those bastards,' he said. 'The invisible men. They've gone already – all of them – clean away.'

Returning to the Land Rover, he called base on the PRC 319, explaining what had happened and asking them to send out an ambulance and tow truck with crew. Both arrived within minutes, the former to remove the dead bodies, the latter to put out the fire on the overturned armoured car, hoist it the right way up, then transport it back to the wrecker's yard.

Lampton and the others followed in the Land Rover, now destined to spend the rest of the morning in camp, submitting a report of the grim event.

7

Every evening, being covered in a slimy film of dust and sweat, the newcomers trooped off for a cleansing, cooling shower. This was followed by 'prayers', a meeting of personnel where the ops captain would read out the day's news about Dhofar and then a summary of world news. Failure to attend the meeting without good cause led to the standard SAS punishment of a fine. 'Prayers' was followed by dinner in the open-sided mess tent. Then the evening was free. It was spent either in the NAAFI tent, running up a tab with Pete, or at the outdoor cinema, where, on alternate nights, they could watch the latest English or American movies, supplied by the Service Kinema Corporation. The men invariably went straight back to the NAAFI tent after the movie, where they would help themselves to more Tiger beer from the fridge and discuss the film with Pete, the movie buff.

'Close to the fucking bone,' Gumboot said.

'Humping there in the grass in the winter with overcoats on. No wonder Mary Whitehouse and Lord Longford are all up in arms.'

'Well, it *was* called *Carnal Knowledge*,' Andrew reminded him, 'so what *else* could they show?'

'I think the idea was to satirize it,' Pete explained, 'which Mike Nichols did well.'

'It wasn't Mike Nichols,' Bill said, looking a little confused. 'It was that other guy – what's-his-name? Jack *Nicholson*. The one with the leer.'

'Mike Nichols is the director, you stupid prat.'

'Sorry, Pete.'

'That Ann-Margret was gorgeous,' Ricketts said.

'A good actress, too,' Pete pointed out.

'Yeah,' Jock chimed in. 'You could tell that by the size of her knockers. She should get an award.'

'She did,' Pete the Buff said. 'Academy nomination.'

'I saw her in that *Viva Las Vegas*,' Gumboot said, 'with good old hound dog, Elvis Presley. Boy, can that guy sing!'

'I saw that film as well,' Andrew said. 'Ann-Margret walked away with the picture. Christ, she was sexy!'

'She displayed more of her talents in *Carnal*

Knowledge,' Tom said, trying to be as witty as Jock. 'Those enormous, bare boobs!'

'What a bunch of bloody philistines,' Pete said, puffing his pipe and opening another bottle of Tiger. 'It's like talking to Neanderthal men. Where do you guys get off?'

'On Ann-Margret,' Andrew said.

Invariably, during the movies, the nearby 'hedgehogs', picking up a reading of ground movement on their Battlefield Surveillance (ZB) radar, would let rip with 81mm mortars and 7.62mm GPMGs, webbing the starry night beyond the big outdoor screen with tracer fire. This encouraged incoming green tracer from the defiant adoo. Though the noise and spectacular *son et lumière* shows were something of a distraction, they did not actually interrupt the films.

'Shut that racket!' some men bawled.

'Fucking gunners!' cried out others.

'Those guns went off just as Ann-Margret came,' Andrew observed. 'I think that's symbolic.'

As they had only been on the base five days and nights, and as Indian-language films were shown on alternate nights, the new arrivals only managed to see two English-language movies. The second was *Kelly's Heroes*, starring Clint Eastwood.

'Now there's *my* man,' Gumboot said. 'A real actor, old Clint. He's supposed to be as good a shot in real life as he is in the movies. Bloody marvellous, he is!'

'Disappointing in that one, though.' Pete was drunk and thoughtful as he stoked his smouldering pipe. 'I prefer him in those great spaghetti westerns as the Man from Nowhere.'

'Load of shite, that film was.' Jock was on his fourth bottle. 'I mean *Kelly's Heroes*. A straight steal from *The Dirty Dozen*. Did you ever see soldiers behaving that way? Not on your nelly!'

'Yeah, right,' Bill said, smoking a cigarette and sipping his Tiger. 'We're supposed to believe that a bunch of World War Two GIs could march into a German-occupied town and rob the bloody bank. What a load of dog's balls!'

'Not to mention Donald Sutherland,' Tom added. 'They're always casting him as a soldier, yet he walks and talks like the living dead. He didn't convince me a bit.'

'Right,' Gumboot said 'I can't imagine *him* doing Sickener One, let alone Sickener Two.'

'I can't imagine *you* doing them,' Andrew said, 'but you somehow got through.'

'Oh, very funny, Trooper Winston. I can't imagine how they let *you* through the course and gave you a badge.'

103

'It's 'cause they thought I was pretty. Also, I'm as tough as nails, as brave as a lion, and one of the best soldiers in the Regiment. What more can I say?'

'Don't say anything, Andrew. Just let us see what you're like when we tackle the Jebel. You'll be pissing in your pants, shitting bricks, so don't come it with me, mate!'

Big Andrew grinned at him. 'Oh, I'm not worried. I know you'll be right there by my side, my protector and hero. I feel so lucky, Gumboot.'

Noting that Andrew had mockingly lisped the final sentence, Gumboot shook his head in disgust. 'What a ponce!' he said.

But, for all their joking, few of them had forgotten the one subject they rarely discussed – the forthcoming assault on the Jebel Dhofar. Few of them could forget it because it was always there before them, soaring up to the sky and dominating the landscape no matter in which direction they drove across the Salalah plain. From there, at ground level, the plateau looked enormous, too high to be climbed; it was also strewn with wadis which were, as they knew, filled with hundreds of *adoo*, most of them crack marksmen and fanatics only too willing to die for their cause. As Major Greenaway had pointed out, the *adoo* would be a formidable enemy. Also formidable would be the Jebel itself, though they rarely discussed this fact.

On the sixth morning, the day after the armoured car had been ambushed, they were driven out of the base for a few more days of weapons training in the boiling heat and dust of the Arzat ranges. Regardless of the heat, they were kept at it all day every day, practising on the firing range and learning to clean and reassemble their weapons in the harsh, unwelcoming desert.

It was hell on the firing range, the heat relentless, the light too bright, and the dust got up their nostrils and filled their mouths, clogging chambers and barrels and jamming the works. The ground did not really belong to human beings, but to poisonous scorpions and centipedes, as well as hideous camel spiders, while the very air they breathed was filled with fat, buzzing flies, whining mosquitoes and stinging hornets, all of which had to be constantly swatted away while the men were trying to take aim and fire.

'This is useless,' Jock groaned. 'I can't even take aim. Every time I try to squint through the sight, I get sand or dust or some other shit in my eye. As for breathing – forget it. You'll only swallow a fucking hornet. And each time I squeeze the trigger, I get bit by a mosquito, so I jerk and go a mile off the target. I say call it a day.'

'I say keep your trap shut, Trooper,' their instructor, Sergeant Bannerman, said, 'and try to put a bullet in that target instead of moaning and groaning. Annoy me and you'll cop an RTU and find yourself on a plane back to England before you can blink . . . Hey, you! That's right, the big black one! What the hell are you doing?'

'Pardon, boss?' Andrew asked. Having just yelped and rolled frantically to the side, he was looking up at Bannerman with wide, shocked eyes.

'What the hell do you think you're doing, Trooper, wriggling and yelping there like a woman getting a good piece?'

'Bloody spider, boss. A great big hairy thing! It had a body the size of my hand and 'orrible little legs.'

'So?'

'*What*, boss?'

'It's a spider — so what? It wasn't a fucking scorpion or centipede, so what the hell are you worried about? Get back on your belly!'

'But it's still there, boss! Right in front of where I'm lying. It's looking me right in the eye and it gives me the shivers.'

Gumboot sniggered. Bannerman glared at him. 'You think this is funny, Trooper? A big joke to you, is it? If it's so bloody funny, why not go over there and pick up that perfectly harmless camel spider and bring it to me?'

'Er . . .' Gumboot stuttered.

'Go on,' Andrew said, suddenly feeling a lot better at getting his own back, 'let's see you do it.'

'Who gives the orders around here, Trooper?'

'Pardon, boss?' Andrew asked.

'I give the orders around here, Trooper, and don't you forget it. Now roll back on your belly and ignore that bloody spider and put a bullet into the target before I put one in you.'

'Yes, sir!'

Luckily, when Andrew did as he was told, the spider was gone. But the incident, as well as providing some mirth, was a reminder of just how antagonistic the desert was, even here on the firing range, and of what they could expect to find when they started climbing the Jebel. It merely made the firing range more hateful and increased their other concerns about what was to come.

As the *adoo* were renowned marksmen who could chalk up kills from a great distance while remaining well hidden, the troopers were issued, apart from their customary 30-round M16s, with a range of sniper rifles, including the L42A1 7.62mm Lee Enfield bolt-action and the L1A1 SLR semi-automatic. These, in the furnace of the firing range, they were required to repeatedly disassemble, clean of dust and sand, oil, and reassemble – sometimes blindfolded.

However, as the likelihood of close contact with the *adoo* was likely, they were also issued with Heckler & Koch MP5 9mm sub-machine-guns, or SMGs, and practised firing them from the sitting, kneeling and standing positions in single shots, three-round bursts, and on fully automatic, using 30-round magazines at a rate of 800rpm. They were also trained in the MP5K, a shorter version of the MP5, with a 15-round magazine, and used as a semi-automatic replacement for the pistol; and in the MP5SD, also a short-barrelled model, but including a visual sight with a tell-tale red dot indicating the mean point of impact, or MPI.

More ominous was the instructors' insistence that they endlessly practice the various methods of firing their standard-issue Browning 9mm high-power handguns. The fact that this insistence was combined with the sudden appearance of the Heckler & Koch MP5 range of SMGs – which were, in effect, automatic pistols – only made the men realize that the Head Sheds, their senior officers, were anticipating more than ordinarily close contact with the enemy – possibly even hand-to-hand fighting.

Be that as it may, they were retrained in the

Hereford lessons for the Browning: the one-handed, two-handed and alert positions; standing, kneeling and prone; breathing, squeeze, and release-trigger hand pressure; adjusting the aim in the midst of firing. These lessons, too, were carried out in the blazing sun, amid the dust and the flies and other insects.

The fact that a couple of the men collapsed in the heat during this retraining did nothing to deter their instructors, who pointed out that they would have to endure similar, and possibly worse, conditions during the assault on the Jebel. Indeed, for this very reason, even while the remaining men were boiling in the heat and choking in the dust, they were severely restricted in their use of water, this being their instructors' way of teaching them to discipline themselves against chronic thirst for long periods of time.

As they sat 'resting' between firing lessons or drills – which in fact meant being tortured further by the heat and dust – they were forced to listen to lectures on ways of combating dehydration, sunstroke, sunburn and, of course, lack of water. Naturally, while listening to such lectures, some of the men started suffering from dehydration, others came close to sunstroke and sunburn, and all of them nearly went mad with the need for a drink.

'It'll be easier up on the plateau,' Andrew gasped, when finally they were allowed to sip some water. 'Nothing on earth could be worse than this.'

'I wouldn't bet on it,' Lampton said.

While in Arzat, they slept at night on the ground, shocked by how cold it was after the day's scorching heat. Yet even in the cold they had to shake out their kit, invariably finding scorpions, centipedes or camel spiders in at least one or two of the canvas sheets. And, though it was cold, the night was still filled with whining mosquitoes, dive-bombing hornets, flying beetles, and bloated flies, none of which ever seemed to sleep, all ravenous for human sweat and blood. The nights were therefore filled with the sounds of muttered curses and hands slapping bare skin.

'I'm amazed I've any blood left at all,' Gumboot said, examining the ugly mosquito bites all over his arms and legs.

'I sympathize,' Andrew said. He had decided to be nice to Gumboot. 'You look like a bloody pincushion and you never stop scratching. Maybe it's syphilis.'

'Ha, ha, very funny,' Gumboot said, still scratching compulsively.

Though an experienced regular soldier, Ricketts also found himself unable to sleep, not only because of the constantly diving, whining hornets and mosquitoes, but also because of persistent thoughts of the attack on the armoured car and the savagery with which the RAF guards had been killed. He was particularly haunted by the recollection of the *adoo* soldier driving the long blade of his *kunjias* through the back of the neck of the burnt man crawling face-down on the ground. The man had made no sound, which suggested that the long blade had gone right through his neck to his throat and vocal cords, but his body had jumped and quivered hideously as the blood gushed out of his neck and splashed over the Arab. That recollection, more than anything else, seemed nightmarish to Ricketts.

Then there was the mountain, the Jebel Dhofar, looming over him even now, where he lay on the hard ground, using his bergen as a pillow, hoping that the cream smeared on his skin would keep the insects and creepy-crawlies away, particularly those with venomous stings, such as the scorpion and centipede. The Jebel was dark now, even darker than the night, and given shape only by the stars that appeared to fall all around it. It was dark, immense, very high, and unknown, probably mined and filled with the *adoo*, who were practically part of it.

Ricketts, though exhausted and full of aches

and pains, wanting to sleep and unable to do so, looked to the mountain with an odd, unfamiliar mixture of fear and excitement. He wanted to brave the very thing that frightened him and thus blow it away. That's what made him a trooper.

Returning to the base at Um al Gwarif, sun-tanned, covered in filth, badly bitten, sleepless, with eyes sore from constantly squinting into the sun, the men were only given time for a quick shower and meal, then ordered to the 'hotel' for a briefing about the assault on the Jebel, due to take place the next day.

Once in the big marquee, they were split into teams and sat around a couple of standard British Army six-foot tables with their individual maps of Dhofar spread out in front of them. The Intelligence Corps officer arrived shortly after, shook the hand of B Squadron's commander, Major Greenaway, and was then introduced as Captain Butler. A larger map of Dhofar was pinned to a board behind the table with the words 'OPERATION JAGUAR – SECRET' stencilled across the top of it.

'Tomorrow's operation,' Butler began, 'code-named Jaguar, has been designed to secure us our first firm base on the enemy-held Jebel around the village of Jibjat. The starting point is a former

Sultan's Air Force base on the plain known as Lympne. The mixed assault force, consisting of SAS, SAF and *firqats*, will total 800 men. It will be split into two. The majority of B Squadron and G Squadron 22 SAS, the Firqat Al Asifat, the Firqat Salahadeen, and the Baluch Askars are tasked to assault the airfield at Lympne on foot. The remainder of the force will be choppered in after a firm base has been established.'

Using a pointer to show the various locations, Butler continued: 'At first light we'll leave the SAF staging post of Midway, located north of the Negd plain. From there, we'll drive south-east until we reach the foothills of the Jebel and the entrance to this major wadi.' He pointed to the beginning of the Jebel. 'We'll follow the wadi bottom until we run out of motorable track. We'll then debus and move on foot to an area known as the Mahazair Pools, where already we have a small base camp. As the monsoon's just finished, there should be plenty of water there, which is why we're making it our rest area.'

As if to remind them all that the *adoo* were still up there on the Jebel, waiting for them, the 25-pounders boomed from just outside the perimeter. A lot of the men glanced at one another, some grinning nervously.

'The actual operation against the airfield will be mounted the following night,' Butler continued. 'The climb into the hills will be exhausting. Almost certainly it will also involve a running battle with the *adoo*. We will, however, have resups from the Skyvans and air support from the Strikemasters. No matter how difficult, we must keep advancing until we reach the rough airstrips and the few watering-holes on the high plain. That's where most of the *adoo* are entrenched. Our task is to get them out for good and take command of the area. If we succeed, we'll deal a serious blow to their morale and gain the support of most of the local populace.'

Captain Butler put the pointer down and faced the men again. 'Any questions?'

'What kind of resistance is expected, boss?' Tom Purvis asked.

'Regarding the makeshift airfield at Lympne, we're anticipating that a diversionary attack to the south will draw the *adoo* away long enough for our main assault force to encircle the area without resistance. Once the *adoo* return, a battle lasting weeks, or even months, is the least we expect. It won't be an easy battle, as the *adoo* are heavily armed with state-of-the-art Soviet and Chinese automatic weapons, including Kalashnikov AK-47s, Simonev semi-automatics, RPG 7s, RPD light machine-guns, GPMGs and 82mm mortars. The battle, however, no matter how brutal and lengthy, will be followed by the surrender of the *adoo* before the next monsoon season, beginning in June. Nobody has ever stayed on the Jebel through the monsoon, so it should be over by then. Any *more* questions?'

'Did you say *months*, boss?' Bill Raglan asked.

'You heard me, Trooper.'

'No more questions, boss.'

The men left the 'hotel' to prepare their kit, a task which took up most of the remainder of the evening. This done, they shook out the sheets on their camp-beds, checking for scorpions and centipedes, then tried to catch the last remotely decent sleep they would have for a long time.

They were up again at the crack of dawn.

8

The men did not set out at the crack of dawn. Instead, after they had dressed in their OGs and jungle hats, they had a long morning of personal kit and weapons inspection, conducted by Sergeant Lampton and RSM Worthington, both of whom displayed a ruthless talent for spotting even the slightest speck of dirt or sand in the weapons, a loose strap or damaged webbing. More than one man was sent on the double to the armoury or the Quartermaster's stores to replace faulty parts or damaged items, returning shamefaced to his bivouac for another bollocking from the redoubtable RSM.

Nor did it end there. Once the kit inspections were over, the men were marched to the firing range, where every personal weapon was checked by actually being fired. Nevertheless, by lunchtime, the troop was ready to move and the men were allowed a last visit to the NAAFI tent for a decent lunch.

'Mutton curry!' Bill groaned. 'I don't bloody believe it! We're going to be on the march for days and they serve up compo *curry*!'

'We'll be shitting our pants as we climb the Jebel,' Gumboot said. 'I call that good planning.'

'The planning's in the rice pudding,' Andrew informed them. 'That stuff will stick like glue to your guts and keep the diarrhoea in. It's kind of an antidote.'

'Five minutes!' the RSM bawled from the open end of the tent. 'Bolt it down and get out of there!'

'Bolting your food down causes indigestion,' Tom complained. 'My dear mother swore to that.'

'Diarrhoea, constipation and indigestion,' Jock said dourly. 'We're in for a right mix.'

They nevertheless obeyed the RSM, bolting down their food and hurrying out of the mess tent to gather together by the Bedfords parked outside the armoury. There, though already heavily burdened with their standard-issue US 5.56mm M16 rifle, 9mm Browning high-power handgun, packed bergen, ammunition pouch, smoke and fragmentation grenades, escape/evasion survival kit and water bottles, they were burdened even more with the selective distribution of L42A1 7.62mm Lee Enfield sniper rifles; two different versions of the Heckler & Koch MP5 9mm sub-machine-gun; the L7A2 general-purpose machine-gun, or GPMG, also known as the 'gimpy'; M-72 LAWs, or Light Anti-Tank Weapons; 51mm mortars with smoke bombs and L16 ML 81mm mortars with base plate, tripod and shells; plus Clansman high-frequency and PRC 319 portable radio systems, with generators and rechargeable batteries.

It took a good half hour to hump the kit into the trucks, but eventually the job was done and the men, having already put in a full day's work, were driven out of Um al Gwarif, across the road, then onto the rough ground beside it, where they shook, rattled and rolled the three miles to RAF Salalah.

After being waved through the main gates by an armed SAF soldier, under the watchful eyes of two RAF guards, the Bedfords parked by the dispersal bays for the Skyvan cargo planes. Corporal Harry Whistler of 55 Air Despatch Squadron, RCT, was there with other pilots and RAF loadmasters, most of them stripped to the waist, gleaming with sweat, and covered in the dust that billowed up from the ground every time they moved a crate of supplies to slide it into the cargo bay in the rear of a Skyvan.

'Are these heaps ready to fly?' Major Greenaway asked Whistler as the rest of the men piled off their individual Bedfords and started sorting out their gear.

'No problem, boss,' Whistler said. 'These supplies will soon be back. The men can start boarding immediately. By the time they're all on board, we'll be ready for take-off.'

'Very good, Corporal.' Greenaway turned to RSM Worthington and told him to divvy the hundred SAS men up and get them on board the half-dozen Skyvans. Even with that number, the pilots would have to make quite a few trips to get the whole complement of men and equipment to the SAF staging post of Midway. Worthington therefore divided them into groups, allocated certain of the groups to individual Skyvans, and told the rest to wait in the minimal shade offered by the walls of oil drums. The latter men let out melodramatic groans of misery.

'Stop whining,' Worthington said. 'To save the Skyvan pilots from having to make too many return trips, the CO's roped in the RAF's three Hueys and the Sikorski light chopper. You men will be going in those.' The four helicopters in the dispersal bays 200 yards away roared into life even as he spoke. Glancing at them, then turning back to Greenaway, Worthington said: 'They're leaving sooner than I thought. What about you, boss?'

'You and I are going in the Sikorski,' Greenaway

said. 'So let's get these men in the Hueys first.'

'Right, boss.' Worthington turned to the troopers who had been moaning and groaning. 'OK, you men, come with us.' The men fell in behind Greenaway and Worthington, following them towards the helicopters as overdone groans came from the men waiting to board the Skyvans.

'OK, lads,' Sergeant Lampton said to Ricketts and the other newcomers, 'we've been lucky. Good old Whistler's going to put us onto his personal Skyvan, so we'll be one of the first groups to take off. Come on, let's go.'

Having assumed that Lampton would be remaining with the BATT teams, Ricketts had been surprised, though pleased, to learn that he was in fact taking part in Operation Jaguar as their platoon leader. Now he was glad to follow him across to Whistler's Skyvan. The RAF corporal was standing by the cargo hold, stripped to the waist as usual, his dark hair falling over his bloodshot eyes, shoulders and arms glistening with sweat, his face red from the sun.

'Hello again!' he said to Ricketts and the others. 'How did your week go?'

'Pretty good,' Ricketts said.

'I hear you had a little trouble at Um al Gwarif.'

'First blood,' Lampton said. 'But they did okay.'

Whistler's grin broadened. 'A taste of what's to come, lads. The *adoo* aren't scared of man or beast – as you'll find out soon enough.' He jerked his thumb back over his shoulder. 'OK, we'll soon be finished here, so get in the plane and take a seat. We'll be taking off in no time.'

'Just don't leave us to fry in there,' Gumboot said, 'with a long wait in this heat.'

'I won't,' Whistler said.

Some of the Skyvans had already roared into life and even as Whistler spoke were taxiing out of the dispersal bays, heading for the runway. At the same time, first one, then two of the American-built Hueys also roared into life, adding their din to that of the aircraft. Suddenly, the whole area had become a hive of activity, with restraining blocks being pulled away from wheels, Skyvan cargo-hold doors being closed, spinning helicopter rotors creating clouds of swirling dust, the Bedfords whining noisily as they reversed and turned away, empty, and line men, or marshallers, with ear defenders driving out in jeeps to the runway to guide the aircraft with hand signals to the holding point on the runway.

Meanwhile, Lampton led his team of probationers into the passenger cabin of the Skyvan, where they strapped themselves into the cramped seats, three to a row, with no aisle down the middle. Ricketts was sitting between Lampton and Andrew.

'Christ,' Andrew complained, 'it's like a furnace in here.'

'Not much space, it's true,' Lampton said, 'but at least the flight will be brief.'

'*How* far is the LZ?' Ricketts asked.

'About fifty-fives miles north of the Jebel.'

'Get me out of this plane and I'll *run* the fifty-five miles,' Andrew said.

Lampton grinned. 'Don't you like planes, Trooper?'

'I hate the bloody things – particularly bathtubs like this. The old Hercules transport isn't so bad, but this . . .' Andrew shrugged. 'Do we flap our arms or what?'

'You just twist the rubber bands and let them go,' Ricketts replied. 'The propellers should spin then.'

'If this thing takes off and lands in one piece, I'll start believing in God.'

'Don't let Whistler hear you saying things like that,' Lampton warned him. 'He's in love with this plane and he'd throw you out without thinking twice.'

'My lips are sealed from this moment on.'

The Skyvan did at least have windows, through

which Ricketts could see the first of the Hueys taking off, rising vertically, heavily, like the bloated flies he had seen so often since coming to Oman. A metallic grinding noise, followed by loud banging, came from behind him as the rear cargo-hold door was wound down and locked. Less than a minute later, Whistler entered the aircraft by the front door and disappeared behind the wall dividing the pilot's cabin from the rest of the plane. The loadmasters, Ricketts knew, would be sitting in the rear loading bay, communicating with Whistler through their headphones and mikes. Glancing out the window, he saw the Sikorski taking off, whipping up immense clouds of dust, rising towards the last of the three Hueys, all heading for Midway. At that moment, the Skyvan's STOL twin engines roared into life, making the rotors spin, and the aircraft shuddered violently, then moved forward, taxiing out of its dispersal bay and heading for the runway. Within minutes it was racing along the runway and lifting off, following the other aircraft and choppers into the brilliant, blue-white sky above the Salalah plain.

The journey took no time at all, which was a small mercy, as the interior of the Skyvan was suffocatingly hot, and they landed at the SAF staging post of Midway. The disused oil exploration camp consisted of no more than a number of Twynam huts scattered around an old airstrip in the desolate wasteland of the Negd plain and guarded by SAF troops wearing *shemaghs* and carrying 7.62mm FN rifles. A lot of Bedfords had been already brought in and were lined up along the runway near the huts, where the troops just lifted in by the helicopters were milling about, stretching their legs, smoking, drinking water and making wry jokes.

'Heaven on earth,' Gumboot said sourly, glancing around him, then spitting on the dusty ground at his feet. 'A real home from home.'

'It could be worse,' Andrew replied, mopping the sweat from his face with a handkerchief as the helicopters took off again. 'Just think – you could be back home in Devon, ankle-deep in cow crap and being nagged by your missus. Thank God for small mercies.'

'Well,' Whistler said when his men had unloaded everything from the rear cargo hold and were drawing the door down, 'I'm on my way again, though I guess I'll be coming back with the *firqats*. Best of luck up there, lads.'

'We'll call you if we need you,' Ricketts said, 'so have some Burmail bombs ready.'

Whistler grinned and stuck his thumb up. 'Will do,' he said, then turned away and got back in the Skyvan. As the aircraft was taking off, creating a hell of swirling dust and sand, the men picked up what kit they did not have on them and hurried away from the slipstream. They stopped by the Bedfords at the edge of the runway. The CO and Worthington were near the old huts, shaking hands with the SAF commander, who, like the rest of his men, was wearing a dark-green *shemagh*. Looking in the other direction, Ricketts watched one Skyvan after another take off and disappear into the darkening late-afternoon sky.

'All right, you men, gather round!' Worthington suddenly bawled. 'The CO wants to speak to you.'

When the men had assembled in front of Greenaway, the major said, 'It's going to take all day for the Skyvans and choppers to bring in the remainder of the assault force. We'll therefore be spending the rest of the afternoon and all night here, then move out at first light. In the meantime, you can basha down on that strip of waste ground near the SAF barracks' – he pointed to the dusty old huts – 'and boil up a brew. Don't plan on a rest, as you'll be needed to help with the unloading, which should take half the night. All right, men, that's it.'

When Greenaway and Worthington walked off with the SAF commander, the troopers scattered to find a place on the waste ground to the right of the SAF barracks.

'Fucking typical,' Tom said. 'The A-rabs get the barracks and we get the bloody desert floor.'

'It should be the other way around,' Bill complained. 'I mean, those bastards *come* from the bloody desert.'

'And we don't even get a rest,' Jock added. 'We've been up since dawn and now he says we're gonna work half the night. Bloody cheek, if you ask me.'

'Who's asking?' Andrew asked.

'I mean, unloading!' Jock burst out. 'Why the fuck can't the loadmasters do that and let us get a sleep?'

'It would take too long,' Ricketts said. 'We'd never get it done by dawn. We have to be on our way by first light, so we have to help them unload.'

'Then let the SAF do it instead of hanging around like ponces. I'm amazed they didn't ask us to guard duty as well, to give those SAF sods a rest.'

'On the ground again,' Gumboot said. 'We'll get bitten to death. Every creepy-crawlie known to man and beast is gonna be creeping and crawling over us, after our sweat and blood. Filthy fucking bastards.'

'Poetry and alliteration!' Andrew exclaimed with a wide, mocking smile. 'Hey, Gumboot, you're a real original – pure genius. I'm burning up here with envy.'

'The day you can speak better than me I'll put on a monkey suit. Who fancies a cuppa?'

'Me!' they all cried at once.

Having checked the area for scorpions, centipedes and the like, they put their sleeping bags down and brewed up by boiling water in their mess tins heated on lightweight hexamine stoves.

'Bloody beautiful!' Gumboot said, swiping flies, mosquitoes and hornets from his face and sipping his steaming tea.

The first of the Skyvans arrived back within the hour, when the grey evening light was turning to darkness and the boiling heat was starting to chill. That Skyvan was soon followed by another, then another, all disgorging more supplies and SAF soldiers and *firqats*, the latter looking as fierce as they had done when Ricketts and the other new arrivals had first seen them. Luckily, they were marched off to bed down for the night in another strip of waste ground at the far side of the runway, while the SAF soldiers, of whom the *firqats* did not approve, were given beds or floor space in the SAF barracks.

The extra supplies, of which there were many, kept coming in on plane after plane to be unloaded by the already weary SAS troopers and transported directly to the Bedfords lined up by the runway and guarded by other SAS troops.

'Can't trust those fucking SAF bastards to do it,' Gumboot observed, 'so they lumber us with it. Some fucking deal!'

'*What's* that, Trooper?' The RSM had appeared from nowhere. He was standing there, large as life, in front of Gumboot and glaring at him. 'Did I hear a complaint?'

'Complaint, boss? No! No complaints. I think you must have misheard me.'

'If that word's in the English language,' Andrew said, 'I'll give up writing for good.'

'You couldn't write your name on a cheque, so get back to work,' the RSM said, marching away again.

'Yes, boss!' Andrew bawled.

And work he did. As did most of the others. Not through the whole night, but certainly until well after midnight, by when the last of the Skyvans had been and gone, letting silence descend at last with the settling dust.

Reprieved at last, the more fortunate men left the airstrip, leaving the unlucky few to stand guard on the loaded-up Bedfords. The former made their way back to the waste ground, where they shook everything out, then, still wearing their OGs, wriggled gratefully into their sleeping bags.

Ricketts closed his eyes, but could not sleep. There were too many whining mosquitoes, too many itchy places on his skin. Also, every time he drifted off, the image of his wife floated before him, jerking him awake. He tried to shut her out, to make his mind a blank, but the silence, which in fact was filled with rustling and shifting sounds, only drew him back to tormenting visions of her body and face.

Then Ricketts heard a ghostly moaning. At first he thought he was imagining it. Startled, then a little frightened, he opened his eyes. The moaning was growing louder; it gradually turned into a groaning. When Ricketts turned his head to the side, the sound had become almost anguished. It was coming from Andrew.

'What the fuck's the matter with you?' Ricketts heard Gumboot ask.

'Oh, man,' Andrew groaned, 'this is the worst time of all. I've got a hard-on that's as big as the Jebel and I can't stop thinking of tits and ass. It's a monster and it just won't go down and I'm trapped in this sleeping bag. Oh, man, this is awful.'

'Jesus Christ!' Gumboot said.

When Andrew moaned yet again, Ricketts smiled and at last dropped off to sleep.

9

At first light the following morning, the 250 men, including SAS, SAF and *firqats*, were driven out of the staging post in Bedfords, following a Saladin armoured car which had taken the lead position to give them some protection from mines. For added insurance against mines, the lengthy convoy drove cross-country, though parallel to the road.

The journey was hell, taking them across the Negd plain, a sun-scorched moonscape inter-laced with dried-up stream beds, each of which caused the trucks to lurch wildly, as if about to topple over. In the rear of their Bedford, Ricketts and the other probationers, all in Sergeant Lampton's charge, were repeatedly thrown into each other, their weapons and water bottles colliding noisily. The Bedfords were open-topped, which at least meant they had air, but as the sun rose in the sky, casting a silvery light on the desert, they began to feel the heat and knew, with a feeling of unease, that it was going to get much worse. Surprisingly, even in the wind created by the truck's movement, the flies and mosquitoes were still present in abundance, buzzing and diving, growing more frantic the more the men sweated and attracted them.

'As long as I live I'm going to remember these little bastards,' Ricketts said, swiping another mosquito from his face. 'I've never seen so many of them in my life. They bloody torment me.'

'And me!' Andrew said.

'I thought you'd be used to them,' Gumboot said, ducking and weaving. 'What with where you come from and all.'

'Brixton,' Andrew said.

'I thought you said Barbados.'

'My *mother* comes from Barbados,' Andrew explained, slapping his own cheek, 'but I was born in Brixton.'

'You're going down in my estimation every minute. You're not even exotic!'

'Sorry, Gumboot.'

'I come from Smethwick,' Tom Purvis said helpfully, 'but the family then moved to Wolverhampton. I hope you think *that's* exotic.'

'Not as exotic as Pensett,' Bill Raglan said, 'which has a grammar school, a glassworks, a Miners' Welfare Club, and, of course, Wolverhampton Wanderers. How does that grab you?'

'I pity you,' Gumboot told him. 'But now at last I know why you're both halfwits – no stimulation.'

'There's lots of that in Devon, then? Lots of moo-moos and dung. Incest in the barns every Friday, followed by home-brewed cider. I feel deprived just thinking of it.'

'Christ,' Gumboot said, ignoring the dumb twat and slapping frantically at the mosquitoes and flies swarming around his face, 'these things are driving me crazy.'

'Your natural state,' Andrew said.

As usual, they relied on banter of this kind to keep the blues at bay, but as the morning wore on and the heat increased dramatically, making them sweat even more, thus attracting more flies and mosquitoes, they felt less inclined to crack jokes. Also, as the journey progressed, the gravel plain became rougher, filling up with patches of sand, and the bucking of the trucks became much worse.

By noon, the convoy was still on the move, with the Arabian sun blazing relentlessly on the desert and turning it into a featureless white haze. Heat waves rose from the desert floor, making the land beyond shimmer, and the trucks front and rear, when visible through the swirling sand, appeared to contract and expand, as if made from black jelly.

The men seemed just as unreal – or at least, they felt so – assailed by flies and mosquitoes, sometimes by stinging hornets, while being forced repeatedly to wipe grimy sweat from their faces or sand from their parched lips, bloodshot eyes, sweat-soaked clothing and hot-barrelled weapons. With the sand came the dust – floating everywhere, rising up through the floorboards, and blown in from the billowing clouds being churned up by the wheels of the Bedfords.

Even worse was the heat, now a veritable furnace, making even the slipstream of the trucks suffocatingly warm.

'I can hardly breathe,' Gumboot rasped. 'This air's thick with dust and sand. It's so warm, it makes me almost choke. I feel bloody nauseous.'

'So do I,' Tom said.

'My stomach's churning,' Bill added.

'They've got to stop and let us out for a bit,' Andrew insisted, looking out across the vast, sun-scorched plain and its drifting dust clouds. 'They've got to give us a break from this.'

'They won't,' Lampton said. 'We don't have the time. We've got to reach the RV by last light, so they won't have a break.'

'Oh, fuck!' Bill groaned, then closed his mouth and choked, his cheeks suddenly bulging, and clawed his way past Gumboot and

Tom to hang over the truck's tailboard and throw up.

'That was decent of him,' Lampton said as Bill continued vomiting, his body heaving convulsively. 'If he'd done it where he was sitting, it would have gone all over you lot. Now, at least, he's put it all behind us.'

Gumboot laughed uneasily at that, but a few minutes later, when Bill was back in his seat, gasping for breath and cleaning his messy lips with a handkerchief, Gumboot – either smelling Raglan or imagining he could smell him – was likewise suddenly obliged to claw his way to the rear and throw up over the tailboard. He was soon followed by Tom, then, as Ricketts noticed, by some of the men in the other Bedfords, front and rear, now distorted beyond the shimmering heat waves and obscured by the boiling sand.

'If anyone comes after us,' Lampton said, 'they won't have a problem. They've only to follow the trail of . . .'

'Do you mind?' Andrew interrupted.

'What's that?' Lampton asked.

'No offence, boss, but the mere mention of that word will just set them all off again.'

'Got you, Trooper,' Lampton said with a broad grin, clearly as fit as a fiddle and enjoying himself.

Though men continued being ill along the

whole length of the column, the drivers did, as Lampton had warned, keep going without a break. They reached the wadi by late afternoon, when the fierce white sun had cooled to a more mellow golden light that brought detail back to the landscape.

Glancing along the wadi, with its sheer granite slopes casting stark black shadows on the sun-bleached gravel of the valley floor – a barren, silent, almost eerie terrain – Ricketts was reminded of the boulders and craters of the moon, which he had seen on TV coverage of the Apollo 15 landing in July, three months earlier. This in turn reminded him that he was a long way from home and in a new, totally alien environment. It made him feel slightly disorientated and remote from himself.

Entering the wadi, heading straight for the towering Jebel, the lengthy column of trucks soon left the sand-filled Negd behind and drove over a smoother surface of tightly packed gravel and small stones. Mercifully, the shadows cast over the convoy by the high rock faces on either side brought the men further protection from the sun and wind. Eventually the sun went down, cooling the men even more.

'Thank God for the evening,' Ricketts said. 'A little relief at last.'

'It'll soon be so fucking cold you'll have frost

on your nuts,' Gumboot replied. 'If it isn't one thing, it's another. This place is a pisser.'

Now out of the wind and dust, the men were removing the magazines from their SLRs and other weapons to clean them again, working the cocking handles to ensure that they were back in good order. Some were hurrying to finish this task when the convoy ground to a halt because the wadi had narrowed so much that they would have to go the rest of the way by foot.

Ricketts placed a 7.62mm round back in the magazine of his SLR, fixed the magazine to the weapon and cocked the action. He had time to quickly squeeze oil onto the side of the breech before following the other troopers out of the Bedford.

Standing on the gravel floor of the wadi as the other SAS, SAF and *firqats* also jumped down, rapidly filling up the formerly empty, silent area, he was surprised to see Sergeant 'Dead-eye Dick' Parker with a nearby group, still wearing his jellaba and *shemagh*, which, with his bandoliers and two knives, made him look as fearsome as the tribesmen. In fact, even as Ricketts saw him, he moved away from the SAS group and went to join the Arabs, talking to them in a low murmur and receiving solemn nods from them by way of reply.

'Fucking Lawrence of Arabia,' Gumboot said.

'And probably just as mad,' Andrew added.

'A damned good soldier,' Lampton informed them. 'At least the *firqats* respect him.'

'They respect men as mad as they are.' Gumboot was checking his M16. 'They know he'd slit your throat as quick as look at you. That's what they respect.'

'OK, you men!' RSM Worthington bawled, standing mere feet away, his barrel chest heaving. 'Don't stand there like limp dicks at a wedding. Clean out those Bedfords!'

The equipment was unloaded and divided among the men. As number two of the GPMG sustained-fire team, Ricketts would be carrying a steel tripod weighing over 30lb, plus a thousand rounds of 7.62mm ammunition belts – half wrapped around his body, the other half in his bergen – and four 20-round SLR magazines on his belt. He also had his Browning handgun, belt kit with smoke and fragmentation grenades, rations, first-aid kit, and three full water bottles. Also in his team were Jock as gun controller, Gumboot as observer and Andrew as number one, or trigger man. Between them, apart from personal gear, they had to hump the tripod, two spare barrels weighing 6lb each, spare return spring, dial sight, marker pegs, two aiming posts, aiming lamp, recoil buffer, tripod sighting bracket, spare-parts wallet, and the gun itself, weighing 24lb. Burdened with all this, they would have to climb out of the wadi, up onto the flat, open area of the Mahazair Pools, which was their night basha spot.

'This is gonna fucking kill us,' Jock McGregor said.

Gumboot studied the Arab fighters conversing solemnly with Dead-eye Parker. 'Those bastards aren't carrying much,' he said. 'Only personal weapons.'

'They don't need as much as us,' Lampton explained. 'They'll be out front, facing the *adoo*, while we give them covering fire. Let that console you.'

'Donkey soldiers,' Andrew said. 'Isn't that what they call us? Because we hump all this heavy gear. *Donkey soldiers*! The bastards must be having a good laugh at us.'

'If I hear any of them calling me that, I'll give them what for.'

'Since you don't speak their language, Gumboot, you won't hear a damned thing,' Andrew corrected him.

'Prepare to saddle up!' the RSM bellowed. 'We haven't got all night!'

In preparation for the climb, Ricketts unlocked the front leg-clamp levers of the GPMG tripod, swung them forward into the high-mount position and relocked them. Then, with Andrew's help, he humped the tripod up onto his shoulders with the front legs resting on his chest and the rear one trailing backwards over his bergen. His total burden now weighed a crippling 130lb, and he was carrying his SLR with his free hand.

All along the wadi, in the dimming afternoon light, the other men were doing the same, making a hell of a racket. There were 250 of them in all, spread out over approximately a quarter of a mile, between and around the parked Bedfords.

'OK, men,' Worthington bellowed, his voice reverberating eerily around the wadi, as if amplified. 'Saddle up!'

The men moved out, falling instinctively into a lengthy, irregular file formation, spreading more and more apart, until the line was a good half mile long, snaking back from the slopes of the wadi to the trucks below.

Within minutes, the metal of the tripod cradle was digging viciously into the back of Ricketts's neck, letting him know that it was going to hurt. He turned his head left and right, but this only rubbed the skin of his neck against the steel leg, making it hurt even more. In less than an hour the pain was worse, shooting down through his shoulder blades, and the sweat was starting from his forehead and dripping into his eyes.

He glanced at his nearest friends and saw

that they were suffering the same – if not with a tripod, certainly with other gear – and sweating every bit as much as he was. No one spoke. They were trying to save their breath. To make the hike more tortuous, they were assailed, as usual, by flies, mosquitoes and the occasional hornet, but this time they could not slap them away as they were either carrying weapons or holding onto heavy equipment, just as Ricketts had to do with his tripod. Now it was hurting more than ever, sending darting pains through his shoulders, and those pains, combined with his increasing exhaustion, made him start wondering if he could actually stand the strain.

Ricketts's fears were in no way eased when, one after the other, a number of troopers vomited from the strain and were pulled out of the column and ordered by the RSM to 'rest up, then catch up'. This brought no respite to the others, since the column continued moving. However, it stopped shortly after, the men banging into one another, as voices called down the line for the medics. When those voices faded away, a series of hand signals came down the line, indicating that the men were to rest up until further notice. Gratefully, the men around Ricketts all sank to the ground.

'What's up?' Ricketts asked.

'I don't know,' Lampton replied, 'but I'm going to find out.'

As the sergeant hurried away towards the front end of the column, Gumboot wriggled out of his bergen and lay on his back.

'Ah, God,' he said breathlessly, 'that's wonderful. That's just bloody beautiful.'

Andrew wiped sweat from his gleaming black forehead as he lay back with his head on his bergen. 'I don't give a shit what's happened, so long as it buys a rest.'

'Which it has,' Ricketts said.

'I've thrown up twice already,' Tom told them, 'and I still don't feel too good.'

'Who does?' Bill asked rhetorically. 'Not me, mate.'

They fell silent after that, trying to get their breath back, not wanting Lampton to return and make them get up again. Unfortunately, he did so five minutes later.

'Heart attack,' he said. 'A radio corporal. He collapsed with his radio, got stuck between some rocks, and had a heart attack trying to free himself. He's conscious again, but he's going to have to be carried on a stretcher to the RV, from where he can be casevacked back to base.'

'Lucky bastard,' Tom said.

'The poor bastards who have to carry him

aren't so lucky,' Lampton replied. 'OK, men, on your feet.'

'What?' Andrew's head jerked around. 'You mean we're moving already?' Lampton nodded towards the front of the line. When they all turned in that direction, they saw a series of hand signals coming towards them, indicating that the march was recommencing. 'Shit!' Andrew exclaimed.

Luckily, they were near the end of their journey. They had been marching for two hours and the sun was going down. After another three-quarters of an hour the slopes became less steep, indicating that they were nearly out of the wadi. Eventually, as the sun sank, a breeze, blowing down from the level ground, cooled the sweat on their foreheads.

Ricketts was beginning to believe that he was on his last legs – stabbing pains in his shoulder blades, his neck aching, his lungs on fire – when, just before darkness fell, they emerged from the wadi and headed across an open area, where pale moonlight was reflected off the water in the Mahazair Pools, in the shadow of the mighty Jebel Dhofar.

They could rest up at last.

10

The rest only lasted a few minutes. At last light, with the eerie wailing of the mullah rending the silence, the *firqats*, their faces half hidden by *shemaghs*, knelt in circles and bowed their heads to pray while holding their rifles between their knees.

'I don't think we can depend on these geezers,' Gumboot whispered out of the corner of his mouth to Ricketts and Andrew. 'They're not allowed to fight during the holy month of Ramadan – and that's due to begin later this month.'

'Right,' Andrew said, nodding. 'But these guys have been let off on the grounds that they're Islamic warriors fighting a Holy War.'

'That's convenient,' Ricketts said.

'And the fact that they're praying right now,' Sergeant Lampton informed them, 'is a sign that Operation Jaguar's about to begin.'

'What, already?' Bill asked, glancing automatically up at the mighty Jebel, then across at the *firqats* kneeling in prayer, their rounded shoulders bathed in the moonlight when they bowed their covered heads.

'Yes,' Lampton said. 'Already. We have to make the climb tonight, under cover of darkness.'

'There's no way we can do that,' Tom said. 'Not after a day like the one we've put in. It's asking too much.'

'Do you want to keep that badge or don't you?' Lampton asked him.

'You know the answer to that, boss.'

'Then it's not asking too much. Zero hour is thirty minutes from now and you'd best be prepared.'

Realizing that they were actually going to have to get up and go, the men drank more mugs of tea, cleaned and oiled their weapons, filled magazines and water bottles, and stared curiously at the still kneeling, praying tribesmen, now bathed in the moonlight. Beyond them, near one of the pools, was the collection of tents and lean-tos of the SAS base camp that had been established here a few weeks before. Some of the troopers were outside their tents, brewing up in the open.

'I don't envy them their job,' Andrew said,

glancing at the men in the base camp. 'Stuck up here for weeks on end with sweet fuck all to do.'

'It's good training for OP work,' Lampton told him, 'and you'll get plenty of that in the future. That's why you had all that psychological flak during Sickener Two – to prepare you for days, sometimes weeks on end, in an observation post with only yourselves for company and not much to do, other than keep tabs on enemy movements. It's the worst, the most difficult, job of all.'

'It couldn't be worse than climbing the Jebel,' Jock insisted.

'Don't even think about that,' Lampton warned him. 'It won't help you a bit. You'll just give up before you start.'

Glancing up at the vast, imposing plateau, now almost jet-black and ringed by stars in the gathering darkness, Ricketts was reminded of his last night on the Pen-y-fan, during Sickener Two, and had a good idea of the tortures awaiting him.

The thought was disturbing, but also undeniably exciting, a contradiction of emotions that he had learned to live with ever since he had worked on the North Sea oil rigs. He was not a hard man, nor did he think himself cruel, but he definitely had a low boredom threshold and the need for adventure.

Thank God Maggie understood that. His wife was a treasure. Like Ricketts in that she was sentimental and romantic, she missed him not being at home a lot, but was satisfied that he was not fooling around when out of her sight. She knew him enough to know that he was not that kind of man, but merely needed the kind of excitement that normal life did not offer. The line between that need and the love of violence was thin, but, as Maggie well understood, her husband was on the right side of it. Though understanding the moral ambiguity of what he was doing, Ricketts could not still his urge for adventure, no matter how dangerous. So, he accepted it, while remaining wary of it, careful not to let it run amok.

Nevertheless, only when he experienced that odd combination of fear and excitement – as he was doing right now, in the shadow of the mighty Jebel – did Ricketts feel truly, electrically alive. This was a truth he could not deny.

'Any minute now,' Lampton said, checking his wristwatch. 'In fact, any *second* now.'

He was right. It was now completely dark, with no sign of the moon, and the sudden sound of equipment being moved in the *firqats*' area indicated that the operation was under way.

Clambering to his feet with the others, Ricketts checked his kit and weapons, then again let

Andrew help him hump the heavy GPMG tripod onto his shoulders. The rear leg bit immediately into his neck, reminding him of what he was in for, but also making him resolve to endure it, no matter what the cost.

The *firqat* guides led off in the darkness, heading south-east, and the rest of the assault force, including the SAF, now all wearing *shemaghs* instead of berets, followed in a single file that gradually stretched out to form an immense human chain, snaking up the lower slopes of the Jebel. At first the slopes were gentle, presenting no real challenge, but soon they rose more steeply, sometimes almost vertically, turning the hike into a mountain climb that tortured body and mind. The steeper gradients were often smooth, making the men slip and slide, and often, where the gradients were less steep, loose gravel led to the same problems. A lot of cursing passed down the line. Men fell and rolled downhill. The climb was made no easier by the moonless darkness, which hid dangerous outcrops and crevices. The column nevertheless continued to snake upwards, making slow, painful progress.

'Take five,' were the words passed down the line an hour later, by which time most of the men were sweating, out of breath and aching all over.

Removing the tripod, Ricketts slumped to the ground with the others and, like them, gratefully gulped water from one of his three, rapidly emptying bottles.

'God,' he said, 'this is murderous.'

'It's what we joined for,' Andrew reminded him.

'I can't remember why I wanted the badge,' Gumboot said. 'I must have been mad.'

Still gasping for breath and soaked in his own sweat, Ricketts glanced along the line and saw Sergeant Parker squatting on the ground near the *firqats*, dressed just like them, as impassive as them, and not displaying one drop of sweat.

'Right,' Andrew whispered. 'Don't say it. I know just what you're thinking. That bastard, Dead-eye Dick, is sitting there as cool as a cucumber, not fazed at all.'

'He's not normal, that bastard,' Gumboot said. 'I'd lay odds he's a fucking psychopath. He gets his kicks out of suffering.'

'How good do you think he really is?' Ricketts asked no one in particular.

'He's exceptional,' Lampton told him. 'He's as good a marksman as any *adoo* – and that's saying a lot.'

'Thanks, Sarge,' Andrew said, 'for those encouraging words. It's nice to know that we're going up against an enemy that shoots better than we do.'

'No point in telling lies.'

'Little white lies have their moments.'

'In this kind of war,' Lampton insisted, 'it's best to know what you're up against. And the *adoo*, believe me, are good. They have the eyes of eagles.'

'Fucking wonderful,' Gumboot said. 'That's all I need to know. After killing ourselves climbing this bloody mountain, we'll get picked off like flies. Let's all kneel in prayer.'

Five minutes later, they were on the move again, killing themselves as they slogged up the ever-steeper mountainside, slipping and sliding in loose gravel or on smooth stone, catching their feet in fissures, banging their heads or elbows against outcrops hidden in darkness.

For the next five hours, they halted every hour and wetted their parched throats with more water. They soon began to run short.

'According to the *firqats*,' Lampton said, 'there was a well four hours march from the Mahazair Pools. We've now been on the march for five hours and there's still no sign of it.'

'Apart from knowing how to slit enemy throats,' Bill said, 'those A-rabs don't know a damned thing.'

'They better,' Lampton said, 'because they're the ones guiding us up this mountain.'

'I'll believe it when we see it,' Tom said, 'and I don't think we'll see it.'

'Let's hope that at least they find the well,' Andrew said, 'before our water runs out.'

'I'm low,' Ricketts said.

'So am I,' Gumboot told him.

'Stop talking about it,' Lampton advised them, 'and you won't feel so thirsty. Also, you won't feel so breathless. You've still got a long climb ahead of you, so try conserving your breath.'

An hour later, after six hours of climbing, they halted again – unfortunately not for the well, but because another of the men, laden with three radios and marching right in front of Ricketts, suddenly choked, vomited and collapsed.

Andrew, who had had special medical training, dropped immediately to his knees beside the unconscious man, loosened his webbing, removed the radios and other heavy kit, then hammered on his chest in an attempt to revive him. When this failed, he applied mouth-to-mouth resuscitation, but this was also to no avail. Without thinking about his own diminishing supply, Andrew opened the only one of his three bottles still containing water and poured some down the unconscious trooper's throat. The man coughed and spluttered back to dazed consciousness just as Major Greenaway and RSM Worthington appeared on the scene, having walked back from the front of the column.

'Christ!' Greenaway exclaimed in frustration. 'Not another heart attack!'

'Don't know, boss,' Andrew said, 'but whatever it is, it's not fatal. He's not in the best condition, but he's conscious and I think he'll be OK.'

'Can he walk?'

'I wouldn't ask him to try just yet.'

Greenaway turned to Worthington. 'If we call in a casevac chopper, we could compromise the whole operation. We'll have to send him back to the base camp. From there, he can be casevacked back to RAF Salalah.'

'That means a stretcher, boss, and two men carrying it. No easy job on this mountain.'

'We're not here for easy jobs, Bob, so get this man on a stretcher.'

'Yes, boss, will do.' As Greenaway marched back to the head of the column, a lot higher up the mountain, the RSM looked around him, then jabbed his forefinger at two troopers. 'You and you,' he said.

'Aw, shit, no!' one of the men protested.

'Right, boss,' the other said. 'We've been through hell to get this far and now you're sending us back. It isn't fair, boss.'

'It isn't a question of fairness,' Worthington replied. 'It's a matter of necessity. We can't afford to lose any medics before the battle commences, so he has to be taken down by two troopers and I've chosen you.'

'Why us?'

'You happen to be nearest. Now shut up and wait until I send down a stretcher. Then take this man back to base.'

A few minutes after the RSM had hiked back up the mountain, towards the front of the column, two medics came down with a rolled-up stretcher. After unrolling it, they hoisted the groaning trooper onto it, then turned to the men chosen by the RSM to carry him back to base.

'OK,' a medic said, 'he's all yours.'

'He *should* be all yours,' one of the troopers replied.

The medic shrugged and grinned. 'It's all in the lap of the gods, meaning the lap of the RSM. Have a good trip, lads.'

Before the troopers could reply, the medics hurried back uphill. The troopers, looking disgusted, hoisted the stretcher up between them. 'Fucking diabolical,' one of them said, as they started downhill with the groaning man.

'OK,' Lampton said, 'let's move out again.'

Knowing that first light would be at 0530

hours, Greenaway marched his men mercilessly, following the hardy *firqats* uphill through the darkness, still with no sign of the promised well and its life-giving water. Even at this time of the morning, in that total, moonless darkness, the heat was considerable, clammy, suffocating and rendered worse by the dust kicked up by hundreds of marching feet. More men choked and were sick.

Ricketts began to suffer from heat exhaustion and dehydration: dry mouth and throat, swollen tongue, cracked lips. He also began to hear lurking *adoo* with every sound and to see them in the dark outlines of rocks and outcrops. Aware that the *adoo* were superb marksmen, able to pick off enemy troops at distances so great they had been called the 'phantom enemy', his imaginings along these lines became increasingly vivid.

As they pressed on, the *firqats* up front decided to lighten their heavy loads by discarding valuable items of kit, such as ration cans, portable hexamine cookers and blocks of hexamine fuel. These littered the upward trail and made the going even more difficult for the SAS troops behind them. When reprimanded by RSM Worthington, the Arabs started screaming angrily, threw their weapons and kit to the ground, and threatened to return to the base camp. Appeased by their diplomatic friend,

Dead-eye Dick Parker, they picked up what they had just thrown down and continued the march.

'Selfish fucking bastards!' Gumboot managed to groan between anguished breaths.

Nevertheless, the climb continued, with more men collapsing and either being revived and made to keep going or, if they were in serious condition, sent back to the base camp.

About half an hour before first light, the men ahead began disappearing one by one over the skyline, filling Ricketts with the hope that this must be the top of the plateau.

In fact, it was a false crest, only leading down into another wadi. The men gathered together at the bottom of that wadi just as dawn's light appeared in the east. At the head of his hundred men, but behind the SAF and *firqats*, Major Greenaway consulted with RSM Worthington, both of them studying their maps by torchlight, neither looking pleased.

'We should have been on Lympne by now,' Greenaway said loudly, in exasperation. 'Those *firqat* guides have led us in the wrong direction. We should be on high ground.' He glanced angrily at the masked guides. 'Those stupid bloody . . .' Not wanting to cause trouble with the notoriously proud and temperamental Arab fighters, he let his voice trail off, scratched his chin in deep thought, then turned to the RSM. 'Go and talk to the scouts,' he said. 'Find out just where we are.'

The RSM went off, embroiled himself in a heated discussion with the *firqat* guides, then had a talk with the fearsome-looking Sergeant Parker. The latter nodded, then hurried away, clambering up the steep face of the wadi with the agility of a mountain goat, eventually disappearing in the darkness. When he had gone, the RSM, looking frustrated, returned to Greenaway.

'Those bloody *firqats* aren't sure where the track leading to Lympne is, so I've sent Sergeant Parker on ahead to do a recce. He's the best tracker we've got and if anyone can find the trail, he can.'

'Right,' Greenaway replied. 'We might as well make the most of the opportunity. Tell the men to take five.'

In a state of exhaustion made worse by lack of sleep, the men squatted on the ground as best they could while still wearing their bergens. As even glowing cigarettes could betray their position to the enemy, they were not allowed to smoke, but they compensated for this lack with chocolate and chewing gum, and by releasing their frustration over the *firqats*.

'Fucking typical!' Gumboot exploded. 'We've

been trained for this kind of work, but they leave it to the A-rabs and before you can say boo we're lost. I could piss on their heads!'

'I wouldn't try it,' Andrew said. 'They might chop your dick off. Not that you'd even realize it was missing, given what you've not done with it – but still, it might hurt.'

'It's no joke,' said Bill. 'I side with Gumboot here. I've heard a lot about these *firqats* and none of it was good, so I don't see why we're supposed to depend on them.'

'It's because *they* know the mountains,' Tom said sarcastically. 'That's why we're all sitting here on our arses, with not a clue where we are – the dependable *firqats*.'

'So one of our own men goes on ahead to find out where the trail is,' Gumboot said, spitting to emphasise his contempt.

'Fucking choice, ain't it? It all gets back to us. And I suppose if Dead-eye *does* find the track, those *firqat* bastards will go on strike.'

'They're not that bad,' Lampton said.

'I've heard they go on strike, boss.'

'There are times when they down arms and turn to prayer instead, but given that we're in a Muslim country, you have to accept that. It's not like going on strike.'

'Same difference to me.'

'You lack a world view, Gumboot.'

'I lack patience with any fucking scout who gets me lost in the mountains. What a malarkey!'

A lot of the men's aggravation was due to exhaustion, but that didn't make it any less real. Luckily, they were only there fifteen minutes before Parker returned to say he had found what he thought was the track leading up to Lympne.

An hour later, ninety minutes after they should have been there, and just after the sun had risen, they arrived, with churning stomachs and aching muscles, on the plateau of the mighty Jebel Dhofar.

11

As expected, the scrub ground being used as a makeshift *adoo* airstrip was deserted. This was confirmation that the other SAS troop's diversionary attack to the south had been successful in drawing the *adoo* away – hopefully long enough for the assault force to get entrenched above and around the airstrip, where they would wait for the enemy to return.

Nevertheless, receiving instructions from a combination of radio messages and hand signals, the 250 men sank to the ground in a line that snaked in an enormous arc around the airstrip. Major Greenaway then moved the assault group, team by team, across the open ground, meeting no resistance whatsoever.

Lying belly-down on the ground, watching the mass of men advance towards the airstrip in small groups, jumping up and darting forward under cover of the others, then dropping down and jumping up again, Ricketts had the chance to study the terrain in the dawn light. Around the makeshift airstrip there were rocky, parched hills, but on the flatlands, on high elevations, he could see other improvised runways and water gleaming in the area's few watering-holes. It was the latter, he knew, that made this area so valuable to the *adoo*, and they would certainly fight fiercely to defend it. The airfields were little more than strips of level ground, levelled more carefully by hand, and surrounded by defensive trenches and the occasional hut of wood or corrugated iron. There were no control towers or even watch-towers. As for this particular airfield, known as Lympne, the *adoo*, in their zeal to defeat the SAS's diversionary attack to the south, had failed to leave even one man on guard. It was completely deserted.

'They may be crack marksmen,' Andrew said, 'but they can't be that bright.'

'They don't have to be too bright,' Gumboot said. 'They're fucking ferocious. That's what makes them hard to beat.'

'Still, it's kind of them,' Ricketts said, 'to leave us this whole airstrip for our own use. Presumably that's where the rest of the assault force is going to land.'

'That's right,' Bill said. 'That's the LZ – presuming the rest of the assault force manages to get here before the *adoo* return.'

Lampton, who had been in consultation with Greenaway, came crawling up to them with his M16 cradled in his arms. 'Right,' he said. 'I want the machine-gun team to take up a position on the eastern flank of the airstrip, halfway up that hill overlooking it. You can build yourselves a sangar up there and turn it into a nice home from home. The rest of you will stay with me, taking up a position lower down the same slope. The SAF and *firqats* will be leading the advance against the *adoo* and we'll give covering fire. OK, lads, get going.'

With practically no rest, the very thought of climbing to his feet so soon filled Ricketts with weariness. But he did so, shouldering the tripod again with Andrew's help, then leading him, Gumboot and Jock towards the hills rising east of the airstrip. The hike was longer than anticipated, taking almost an hour, and when they finally arrived at their position they were sweaty and breathless.

From here they had a panoramic view of the nearby hills and the valleys far below. The SAF and *firqats* had completely surrounded the airstrip. SAS troops were marking the runway with coloured smoke grenades for the reinforcements being flown in. It was now 0815 and the grey light of morning was growing brighter, creating a jigsaw of shadow and light over the parched hills and plains.

'Quite a view,' Andrew said, scribbling in his notebook. 'It was worth that hellish climb just to see this. My soul soars like an eagle.'

'Stash that notebook,' Ricketts said, 'and let's build a sangar. Then we can fix the machine-gun and brew up and have us some breakfast.'

'Sounds good to me,' Gumboot said.

Downing their bergens and kit, Ricketts, Andrew and Gumboot started to build the sangar by wrenching boulders out of the ground with their bare hands and stacking them in a rough circle. Meanwhile, Jock kept watch and also listened for incoming calls on the PRC 319.

The sangar took the shape of a semicircular drystone wall three feet high and eight feet in diameter. When it was completed, the men laid their bergens, kit and personal weapons around the inner wall, then mounted the machine-gun, placing the tripod on its triangular legs and relocking the clamp levers. After levelling the cradle for a good firing angle, Ricketts withdrew the front mounting pin. Jock had already serviced the gun for mounting, with the gas-regulator correctly set and the recoil buffer fitted. He now inserted the rear mounting pin into the body of the GPMG, lifted the gun into position on the cradle slot projection, pushed it fully forward, then locked it with the front mounting pin. With the gun prepared, Andrew, the trigger man, was able to open the top cover, load a belt of 200 rounds, cock the action and apply the safety catch.

'So,' he said, sitting back against the wall of the sangar, 'she's all set to go.'

Glancing over the wall, down the hillside, Ricketts saw that many other SAS teams had constructed similar sangars on the slopes over-looking three sides of the airstrip and were covering it with L7A2 GPMGs, M-72 LAWs and L16 ML 81mm mortars. Below him, some 2000 yards down the hill, Sergeant Lampton was sharing a sangar with troopers Purvis and Raglan, as well as a two-man mortar team. Not far to the right, all on his own, the dangerously eccentric Dead-eye Dick Parker was smoking a cigarette, studying the landscape and resting his free hand on the L42A1 7.62mm Lee Enfield sniper rifle lying on the wall of his small, one-man sangar. At the very bottom of the hill, on the level ground around the airstrip, SAF, *firqat* and Baluchi troops had taken over the unprotected *adoo* defensive trenches and appeared to be eating and drinking contentedly.

'Let's have a brew-up,' Ricketts said.

'No water left,' Gumboot replied, spitting over the wall of the sangar. 'We're all dry as a bone.'

'Shit,' said Jock in disgust.

'The back-up force is arriving,' Andrew told them. 'Let's hope they've brought water.'

Ricketts spotted the first of the Skyvans appearing in the sky to the south. Soon the air was filled with them as lift after lift came in, followed by Huey and Sikorski helicopters. One after the other, they landed on the airstrip improvised by the absent *adoo*, their propellers and rotors whipping up enormous, billowing clouds of dust that obscured the men pouring out of the aircraft and across the runway, carrying artillery pieces, mortars, ammunition, rations and, most important of all, water.

By the time the last of the aircraft had landed, the assault force had reached a total strength of 800 men, including 100 SAS, 250 SAF, 300 *firqat* members and 150 Baluchi tribesmen.

Just as they had arrived, so the aircraft took off one by one, creating more clouds of dust. While Ricketts and the others were watching this spectacle, an SAS trooper with an M16 across his back, obviously one of the new arrivals, laboriously climbed the hill, bringing with him two jerrycans of water. Reaching the sangar, he placed the jerrycans on the ground and puffed, 'What a hike! Who's got a cigarette?'

'It's the least we can offer you,' Gumboot said, giving the man a cigarette from his own packet. 'Sit down. We're just about to brew up.'

'Thanks,' the new man said, taking the cigarette and accepting a light from Gumboot. 'I'm bloody exhausted already.' He sat on the ground beside Gumboot. 'And I haven't even climbed the Jebel,' he said, blowing a cloud of smoke. 'What was it like?'

'It could have been worse,' Gumboot said modestly. 'But it was pretty exhausting.'

'I'll bet,' the new man said. 'I'm Dave Greaves, by the way.'

Gumboot introduced himself and the others as Jock set up his hexamine stove and boiled water in his mess tin. The others took out their tin mugs and put tea bags in them, waiting for the water to boil.

'Any news from down below?' Ricketts asked.

'Not much,' Greaves replied, inhaling and blowing another cloud of smoke. 'Apparently, the diversionary attack to the south was a success, drawing the *adoo* away from here and resulting in no SAS casualties. The attack's over now, though, and the *adoo* are believed to be on their way back. Expect fireworks very soon.'

When the water had boiled, Jock poured it into the five tin mugs set out on the ground. The men then added sugar and powdered milk from packets, and sat back to enjoy their brew-up.

'So what's happening about food?' Gumboot asked, glancing down over the wall to where the SAF, *firqat* and Baluchi troops, spread out around the airfield, were having breakfast. The last of the aircraft and helicopters had taken off, leaving the dust to settle back down over the airstrip and the trenches formerly used by the *adoo*.

'I was told to tell you to use the high-calorie rations in your escape belts. They'll be replaced later in the day with fresh rations brought in on the Skyvans. The field kitchens won't be set up until later in the day, so you won't get a proper meal till tonight.'

'And even that may not happen,' Ricketts said, 'if the *adoo* attack.'

'Fucking wonderful!' Gumboot exclaimed. 'Meanwhile, those A-rabs down there are having a banquet.'

'They brought their own food,' Andrew pointed out, 'and I don't think you'd eat it.'

'Damned right, I wouldn't,' Gumboot replied. 'It's good old British tucker for me. I don't want to poison myself.'

'Then have your dry breakfast and shut up. Thank God for small mercies.'

'Hallelujah!' Jock said.

After finishing his tea, Trooper Greaves waved goodbye and headed back down the hill to his own position. He had not reached Lampton's sangar when the whole hill erupted.

12

The first explosions lacerated the ground near Greaves, showering him in soil and then picking him up and hurling him sideways. He hit the ground like a rag doll, bouncing off it, limbs flapping, before becoming lost in swirling smoke and more raining soil as the ground erupted again.

'Christ!' Ricketts exclaimed, ducking down behind the sangar wall and automatically picking up his SLR. More explosions ripped the hillside, making a catastrophic din, as Ricketts stared at the others, all of whom were staring back, then tentatively raised his head above the wall to look out again. A stream of green tracer, surprisingly luminous in the morning light, snaked out of the boiling smoke, first appearing to almost float, then zipping overhead at fantastic speed to spend itself a good distance away. Another series of explosions erupted across the hillside, spewing earth and more smoke.

'The *adoo*!' Andrew yelled, huddling up beside Ricketts with his M16 propped up between his knees.

'Right,' Ricketts said. Holding his SLR, he hugged the wall as the western perimeter came alive with the stutter of incoming small-arms fire. Raising his head again, he saw that the tracer was coming from the rim of the western hillside. The *adoo* GPMGs, he reckoned, were located just beyond that rim, as were their mortars. Even as he deduced this, a series of explosions erupted in a line that ran from the airstrip to the base of the eastern hill, tearing through the defensive trenches in which the SAF troops were now sheltering. More soil spewed upwards and rained down through the clouds of black smoke.

'Mother of God,' Jock whispered. 'Those bastards aren't fooling!'

Lower down the hill, Greaves, miraculously still alive, was raising himself up on hands and knees, shaking his head to clear it. Soil dropped off his arched back as he vomited convulsively, then another explosion tore up the earth beside him and flipped him over again.

'Shit!' Gumboot hissed, then darted out of the sangar. He was starting down the hill when he was stopped by another burst of green tracer, which, whipping just above his head, made him throw himself to the ground.

'Gumboot!' Ricketts bawled.

'We've got to help him!' Gumboot shouted back while lying belly-down on the ground with tracers ripping through the air above him. 'That poor bastard is . . .'

His last words were drowned by the roar of another explosion that made the sangar shake and rained soil on it. Andrew was up and over the wall, even as the smoke blew in. He careered the few yards to Gumboot, and helped him back to his feet.

'Damn it, Gumboot, he's too far away! Get back in the sangar!'

They raced back to the sangar as more explosions erupted around them, causing soil to rain down and filling the air with dense smoke. They piled back into the sangar, crouching beside Ricketts and Jock as the shelling continued.

Using the PRC 319, Jock contacted base, located by the airstrip, and requested a medic to be sent up. The reply was affirmative. As Jock put the phone down, another series of mortar explosions tore up the hill below.

'Fucking hell!' Gumboot gasped.

'Keep your head down,' Andrew told him.

Gumboot reached for the GPMG, wanting to retaliate, but Ricketts slapped his hand off, saying, 'No! They're too far away. We can't do much from here. It's up to the others.'

'Who?' Andrew asked.

'The ones dug in on the western slope. They'll be the first to be attacked if the *adoo* advance.' Glancing over the wall, he saw the wavering green lines of tracer coming towards him, whipping above him, while more explosions erupted along the airstrip and on the lower slopes of the hill below. 'But they're not advancing at the moment,' he continued. 'In fact, there isn't a sign of them. The foot soldiers are obviously grouped beyond the rim of the western hill, but they're staying put while their mortars and machine-guns soften us up. Right now we can't do a thing. We just have to sit tight.'

'Fuck,' said Jock. Joining Ricketts, he looked over the wall as more explosions obscured Greaves in smoke and showered soil all around. When the smoke had cleared, Greaves was still there, flat on his back, almost certainly unconscious.

Two SAS medics were scrambling up the hill towards the trooper, one with a rolled-up stretcher on one shoulder, the older man shouldering a packed medical bag. Another series of explosions forced the pair to the ground, but when the turbulence died away they jumped up and completed their run. While one examined

Greaves, the other rolled out the stretcher. The
latter fell onto his belly as more green tracer
whipped through the air above him, and then
he jumped up again and helped his friend roll
Greaves onto the stretcher. They hurried back
down the hill, carrying Greaves between them, as
more explosions erupted all around them. They
disappeared in the swirling smoke.

'Good men,' Ricketts whispered.

The attack continued for another twenty
minutes, with the mortars hitting the western hill, the area between the trenches by
the airstrip and the lower slopes of the hill
itself, where SAF troops were also entrenched
and returning the fire with their own GPMGs
and 81mm mortars. Soon, the whole area was
covered in a grey pall of smoke punctuated
by criss-crossing lines of green tracer from the
adoo and the purplish tracer of the SAF, SAS
and other troops.

'Might as well finish our tea,' Andrew said.
'Not much else we can do.'

'True enough,' Ricketts replied.

They sipped hot tea as the green tracers
continued to streak over the sangar and more
explosions occurred lower down the slope. Occasionally, through the drifting smoke on the western perimeter, they saw SAF troops, including
the *firqats* and backed by covering fire from the

SAS, making their way uphill, trying to get closer to the *adoo* hidden beyond the rim. However, long before they reached it the *adoo*'s attack slackened until only sporadic firing could be heard. Gradually even this died away and silence descended.

Glancing down the slope, Ricketts saw a couple of SAS troopers loping across the airstrip, from the western side, then up the hill to the sangar. It took them a long time to complete the journey and when finally they arrived, they were breathless.

'And I thought I was a fit man!' one of the troopers said, gasping. 'I'm Roy Baker and this' – he indicated the other soldier with a jerk of his thumb – 'is Taff Burgess, of A Squadron. Shit, what a hike!'

'Have a cup of tea,' said Ricketts.

'Appreciate it,' Baker replied, still gasping. He and Burgess slumped to the ground inside the sangar, both leaning back against the wall until tin mugs of steaming tea were in their hands. Breathing normally again, they drank gratefully, then lit up cigarettes.

'So what's happening over there?' Ricketts asked.

'Are you guys probationers?'

'Yes.'

'Your sergeant must have a lot of faith in

you, letting you run this machine-gun post unsupervised.'

'He's just down the slope a bit,' Ricketts explained, 'and we're in radio contact.'

'Still, he must trust you,' Baker said, sipping more tea. 'A very nice brew, this.'

'So what's happening?' Andrew asked.

'A force of between twenty and thirty *adoo* hit the positions over on the west with AK-47s and RPD light machine-guns as back-up. The SAF took no casualties, but had two hits, which makes us one up.'

'Why has the attack tapered off?'

'We think the *adoo* were just testing our strength. Some of the SAF got over the rim of the hill and found them already gone. The generally received wisdom is that they've retired to their stronghold at Jibjat, six kilometres west of here. That's where we're going tomorrow.'

'Why?' Ricketts asked.

'Because the Head Shed,' Baker replied, referring to their CO, Major Greenaway, 'thinks that makeshift airstrip down there, on Lympne, is fucking useless. Apparently it's already breaking up from this morning's resup landings. So tomorrow, at first light, we're going to march on Jibjat.'

'That's only 7500 yards away.'

'Right,' Baker said with a grin. 'A short hike to the enemy.'

'Who dares wins,' Ricketts said.

Before first light, after a night in the sangar during which they took one-hour turns on watch, or stag, they packed their bergens and prepared the GPMG and tripod for carriage. They destroyed their sangar, dismantling it brick by brick, then moved down the hill to join Sergeant Lampton and the others. The ground around Lampton's sangar was pock-marked with shell holes and the structure itself had been partially damaged by an explosion. Tom and Bill were still cleaning the weapons that had been clogged up with falling soil and dust. They both looked exhausted.

'Bloody marvellous,' Tom said. 'I cleaned these weapons at Um al Gwarif, I cleaned them again at the Mahazair Pools, I cleaned them when we climbed up to here, and then, after that fucking attack, I had to clean them again. Gravel, sand and dust spewing in every time a shell hit. A right fucking misery!'

'At least it wasn't your guts spewing out,' Bill said philosophically. 'Count your blessings, I say.'

'So what's happening, boss?' Ricketts asked.

'We're marching to Jibjat,' Lampton replied.

'Six kilometres west with all our gear in the heat of the noonday sun. Mad dogs and Englishmen.'

'Terrific,' Tom said. 'More sand, dust and other shit. More cleaning of weapons. Absolutely terrific.'

'This bothers you?' Lampton asked.

'It gets on my fucking wick.'

'You're still on probation,' Lampton said. 'If you don't like it, pack it in.'

'What?'

'I think you heard me, Trooper.'

'Jesus, boss, I didn't mean . . .'

'Don't take anything for granted,' Lampton said, 'just because you've been badged. All you people are on one year's probation, so never forget it.'

'Forget every word I uttered,' Tom said. 'Just wipe it out of your mind. OK, boss, what's the rope?'

'The rope is six kilometres long and it takes us to Jibjat. Do you walk or stay here?'

'I walk, boss. I'm on my feet already. I'm raring to go.'

'Then let's go,' Lampton said.

Impressed by Lampton's deceptively gentle demolition job on Purvis, Ricketts and the others helped to destroy the sangar, taking it apart stone by painful stone, as they had just done with their own; then they picked up their heavy loads and took their position in the spectacular gathering of some 800 men, broken up into dozens of extended, snake-like lines, stretching down the eastern hill, across the airstrip, then up the lower slopes of the western hill. All of them were wearing camouflaged clothing, with the *firqats* half hiding their faces in their wind-blown *shemaghs* and looking all the more fearsome by so doing. When everything was in order, a series of hand signals came down the line and the men moved out.

There was no talking. The various lines stretched out a long way, over the western hill, but the only noise was the jangling of kit and weapons hanging from webbing. At first the air was cool, but the sun was rising fast, and before long, as the last men crossed the hill, the heat made itself felt. Ricketts wiped sweat from his face; he swatted flies and mosquitoes. Though physically uncomfortable, he felt oddly at one with the great column of men snaking down the hillside, towards the flatland where the Jibjat airstrip lay. He knew that the *adoo* would be there, waiting for them, ready to fight, but even that thought filled him with a kind of wonder, rather than fear.

The march did not take long and soon the airstrip came into view in the distance, enclosed in a great horseshoe of high, rocky terrain, where the *adoo* were almost certainly entrenched. Immediately, as if communicating with body language, a subtle change came over the hundreds of marching men as they instinctively became more tense and watchful. They moved slightly away from one another, spreading out across the desert plain, until they were covering the broad area leading up to the rocky bottleneck leading to the airstrip. All of this was accomplished without a word.

Then the first shots rang out. Surprisingly, they were single shots from Kalashnikov rifles, fired by the *adoo* with unerring accuracy to pick off some of the SAF troops up front and perhaps demoralize the others. Some men fell, but the others kept marching, first walking as before, picking up speed, then gradually breaking into a run as they raced for the bottleneck. More shots rang out and more SAF troops fell, then a distant thudding sound indicated that mortars had just been fired.

The first explosions erupted on a wide arc where the troops were advancing, ripping up the ground between them and sending up a screen of boiling sand and smoke. The men at the head of the column disappeared into this as the *adoo* opened up with their machine-guns.

Green tracer illuminated the murk, exploding in silvery flashes, and making jagged, spitting lines in the sand that sent some of the advancing troops into convulsions before jerking violently backwards. The other troops continued to race into the turmoil as the medics ran to and fro, crouched low, bravely tending to the wounded, the dying and the dead.

'What the fuck are those bastards firing?' Gumboot asked, 'that can reach us from the far side of that airstrip?'

'Twelve-point-seven-millimetre Shpagin heavy machine-guns,' Lampton said as they all gradually broke into a trot. 'They can outrange anything we have, so we'll have to get a lot closer before returning their fire. Come on, lads, pick your feet up.'

Ricketts and his team tried to run as best they could while carrying the separate parts of the dismantled GPMG. For Ricketts it was hell, with the legs of the tripod biting into his neck and chest, but eventually he found himself in the thick of the smoke-filled, spewing sand, where the mortar shells and heavy machine-gun fire were causing most havoc. Here the other men advancing through the gloom were no more than shadows.

'Christ!' Andrew said, running beside him, 'I can't see a damned thing.'

Ricketts almost fell, one foot slipping into a shell hole, but Andrew grabbed him by the shoulder and tugged him upright, then pushed him ahead. Gumboot was there beside him, his face streaked with sand and sweat, running beside Tom and Bill – a trio of ghosts. The mortar shells were still exploding, making the sand roar and swirl about them, and green tracer zipped through the air with a vicious, spitting sound.

Suddenly, from the gloom of the swirling sand, they plunged back into daylight. For a moment it was dazzling, seeming brighter than it really was, but then, when Ricketts managed to adjust to it, he saw that the bottleneck leading to the airstrip had been blocked with a barricade of trees and barbed wire. Then he saw the *adoo* retreating across the airstrip, firing on the move, and gradually scattering up the rocky slopes beyond, where they could hide behind boulders.

'We should be in range!' Lampton shouted. 'Set up the machine-gun!'

Relieved to be unburdened, Ricketts dropped to his knees and, with Andrew's assistance, set up the GPMG. Once it was on place on its heavy tripod, he closed the top cover on a belt of 200 rounds and Andrew hammered out a test burst of 50. He then slipped the hinge-clip off the foresight of the barrel, took the foresight blade between his thumb and forefinger and screwed it up into position. After replacing the hinge-clip, he again took up his firing position, index finger on the trigger and thumb behind the pistol grip, so as not to accidentally move the gun with the natural pull of his fingers. Then, with Ricketts feeding in the belts, he started pouring fire into the hills where the *adoo* were sheltering.

It was difficult to tell what effect Andrew was having personally as by now the other SAF machine-gunners were also peppering the hill and the mortar crews were laying down a barrage that soon covered the whole area in smoke. The *adoo*, however, were in retreat, moving back up the hill, allowing the SAS demolitions team, led by the dour, red-headed Corporal Alfie Lloyd, to race across to the bottleneck to begin the task of blowing away the trees and barbed wire blocking the way to the airstrip. They were given covering fire, not only by the many machine-guns, but by a fusillade of fire from the 7.62mm FN rifles of the SAF, *firqat* and Baluchi troops now massed on both sides of the barricade.

With Ricketts feeding in the belts and Gumboot acting as observer, Andrew kept hammering away with his GPMG, helping to force the *adoo* back up the slopes of the western hill and over its rim. Meanwhile, Jock was in constant touch with the Head Sheds, who soon relayed the information that the barricade was about to be blown up.

By this time most of the *adoo* appeared to be well up the western hill, clearly retreating back over the rim, out of range of the SAF guns, so the machine-gun fire gradually tailed off. Andrew also stopped firing. Finally, the SAF rifles fell silent and the troops, realizing that the barricade was going to be destroyed, hastily retreated from both sides of it to crouch on the ground near the SAS.

Ricketts borrowed binoculars from Gumboot and scanned the rim of the western hill. Magnified by the binoculars, he could see the *adoo* clearly. Wearing jellabas, *shemaghs* and sandals, they were heavily burdened with webbing, ponchos, bandoliers of ammunition and long-bladed *kunjias*.

To Ricketts's untrained eye, the *adoo* looked just like the fearsome *firqats*. This could, he thought, cause some confusion in the future. Even as he watched through the binoculars, most of them stopped firing and retreated back up the hill, cradling their Kalashnikovs in their arms. Ricketts handed the binoculars back to Gumboot when the last of them were about to disappear over the rim of the hill.

The demolition men had completed their work and were retreating backwards, crouched low, uncoiling the detonation cord as they went. From where he was kneeling, Ricketts could clearly see the plastic explosives taped to the up-ended trees. The det cord, with one end fixed to blasting caps embedded in the explosive charges, was running out from the explosives to the roll being uncoiled by Alfie Lloyd. When he and his assistant had reached the detonator, Lloyd cut through the cord with scissors, expertly bared the wires with a pocket knife, fixed them to the electrical connectors on the detonator, then kneeled above the latter, resting his hands lightly on the plunger.

He scrutinized the barricade to ensure that no one was near it, then glanced at Major Greenaway, who was kneeling about ten yards to his right, beside RSM Worthington and a radio crew. When Greenaway raised and lowered his right hand, Lloyd pressed down on the plunger.

The noise emerged from what seemed like the bowels of the earth to explode with a deafening roar and spew out a mighty mushroom of soil, sand, dust and loose gravel. The trees were blown apart and burst into flames, raining back down through the boiling, dark smoke as a fountain of fire, falling into the murk some way to each side of the bottleneck and causing more dust to billow upwards.

The fading noise of the explosion was followed by another – the spine-chilling, macabre wailing of the excited *firqats*, rising eerily above the cheering and shouting of the SAF and Baluchi troops. As one man, they jumped to their feet and raced through the billowing smoke in the bottleneck, between the exploded, flaming trees, then spread out across the deserted airstrip, firing their weapons repeatedly in the air to announce their triumph.

Bemused by the furore, the SAS men followed them in.

13

Though the position had been taken, it had to be consolidated, a job beginning with the clearing of the airstrip, which was littered with spent shells and the debris of mortar and other explosions. As the runway had not been tarmacked, but was merely level ground cleared and flattened by human hand, the filling in of the few shell holes was relatively easy and completed by men from the Royal Electrical and Mechanical Engineers (REME), most of whom worked stripped to the waist in the boiling heat. The job was almost completed by noon, when the sun was a white ball in the azure sky.

As Major Greenaway well knew, the *adoo* 'retreat' was in fact merely part of a typical guerrilla strategy involving staying out of sight and harassing the enemy with sniper fire, mortar shells, and small, daring hit-and-run raids of the kind the SAS could only admire. These activities went on throughout the morning while the

REME teams filled in the shellholes and cleaned up the airstrip, to enable the planes to bring in more men, supplies and equipment, including some badly needed ground transport. Luckily, most of the mortar shells had fallen on the lower slopes of the western hill, well short of the runway, and the sniper fire, while causing the REME men to jump, also fell well short.

Nevertheless, knowing that small groups of *adoo* snipers would almost certainly sneak down the western slope to fire from behind rock outcrops, within range of the airstrip, the SAF commander, after consultation with Greenaway, sent some of his own teams to patrol the lower slopes.

By mid-afternoon, Ricketts, Andrew, Gumboot and Jock had built another sangar, on a hill due north of the airstrip. There, sitting on their bergens and drinking a brew-up, they were able to rest while observing the work going on below. When not sipping hot tea or surveying the activities around the airstrip, Andrew scribbled more poetry in his notebook.

'What the fuck are you writing about now?' Gumboot asked him.

'What's going on down there,' Andrew replied, not looking up from his notebook.

'How the hell can you write poetry about *that*?'

Gumboot asked. 'I thought poetry was all blue moons and posies.'

'It can be about anything, Gumboot. War and peace, love and hatred, the sound of church bells ringing out over Hereford, the smell of your old socks.'

'One word about my old socks,' Gumboot said, 'and I'll have you for libel.' He glanced down the hill. 'Nice to see those REMF sods doing some work at last.' 'REMF', not to be confused with 'REME', meant rear echelon motherfuckers, which is why Gumboot used it with such relish. 'They've been sitting on their arses since we got here, so let them sweat for a change.'

'They work for their keep,' Ricketts said, 'making life more pleasant for us. So stop complaining.'

Glancing down the hill, he saw that Sergeant Lampton, whose friendship he had already come to value, was again sharing a sangar with Tom and Bill. Obviously, the sergeant was making sure that all of his probationers were in sight and easy to reach. Below, around the airstrip, the REME were opening a lot of packing crates and removing some of the tools they would need to construct the camp. More tools and the heavier equipment would be brought in on the planes.

'I wonder how Greaves was,' Jock asked,

removing his shirt and wiping the sweat off his white skin. 'He looked a right bloody mess.'

'He was scorched by the blast,' Ricketts said, 'and peppered with shrapnel. He won't walk for a long time.'

'A lot of SAF troops copped it as well,' Jock said, putting his shirt on again to ensure that his white skin did not burn, 'and they won't walk at all.'

'No, I guess they won't, Jock. They were pretty fearless, weren't they?'

'Aye, they were.'

'Not like those fucking *firqats*,' Gumboot said. 'Ready to lay down their arms at the least excuse.'

'That's not cowardice,' Andrew said, slipping his notebook into his breast pocket. 'They never stop fighting because they're scared. They either do it on an impulse because of something else that's come up – say, they feel offended by something – or for religious reasons, such as Ramadan.'

'I don't give a shit about their reasons,' Gumboot said. 'My concern is that the bastards aren't dependable. That's what has *me* worried.'

'You're always worried about something, Gumboot. A regular bundle of anxieties, you are. Go ask the doc for some Valium.'

'A couple of pints would do me better,' Gumboot sighed.

'Sweat and suffer,' Ricketts said, then contented himself with looking down the hill, at all the work going on far below in the increasing light and heat.

As the REME finished clearing the airstrip and organized the building of defensive 'hedgehog' emplacements and sangars, as well as marking out the separate areas of the camp they would create here, Alfie Lloyd's demolitions team blew up the last obstructions placed by the *adoo* between the airstrip and the western hill, leaving the way clear for a full-scale advance at a later date.

Remarkably, the first of the resup aircraft were flying in before last light. The very first Skyvan brought in the keenly awaited marquee tent to be used as a mess, a proper field kitchen, supplies of compo food, water and mobile electrical generators to be used for general lighting around the camp and for recharging radio, vehicle and other batteries. The second Skyvan brought in dismantled 25-pounders, for emplacement in the 'hedgehogs'. The three Hueys and single Sikorski helicopter began the lengthy process of landing more men while the first Skyvans took out the wounded and dead, including Greaves, for casevac from RAF Salalah back to England.

All of this was observed by Ricketts and his mates from their sangar halfway up the northern slopes. During the morning and afternoon, they were baking in the heat and, as usual, driven mad by flies and mosquitoes, but as last light came the air started turning cold, reminding them that they were in for an uncomfortable night. They were, however, heartened to see the mess tent being put up by the REME while the kitchen staff unloaded the equipment brought in on a Skyvan. By last light, the kitchen was in operation and men were queuing up at the mess tent, now brightly illuminated inside with lamps lit by the mobile generators.

Tired of living off brew-up and high-calorie rations from his survival belt, Jock contacted Lampton on his PRC 319 radio. 'We have a bit of a problem up here, boss,' he said while gazing at the sangar further down the hill, where he could actually see Lampton with his own radio.

'Hear you loud and clear, Trooper. What's the problem?'

'An acute shortage of high-calorie rations, boss, hand in hand with the desperate yearning for a decent meal.'

'I still hear you loud and clear, but this sangar has no kitchen, so why are you bothering me, Trooper?'

Jock grinned at Ricketts. 'Seems to us, boss,

190

that there's bright lights and a healthy queue down in that mess tent.'

'I have eyeball contact, Trooper, and *can* confirm. In fact, I'm just on my way down there myself to tag onto that queue. Any more problems, Trooper?'

'A little problem of permission, boss, given that we're on watch. Not complaining, mind you.'

Lampton broke down and laughed, then spoke through a wave of static. 'OK, Trooper, you win. The Regiment respects persistence. Two men have to be on watch at any given time, which means one man at a time down in the mess. My recommendation's for a Chinese parliament to decide. Either that or toss a coin if you've got one. Over and out.'

Not having a coin between them, they scratched a head on a small, flat stone and flipped it three times, with the first loser being condemned to go downhill last, the next loser second to last, the third loser second and the winner first. Ricketts, however, rigged it so that Jock could have first go as a reward for getting on the blower.

While Jock was in the mess tent below, making up for his two days of enforced dieting, Ricketts and the other two carefully shook out their gear, then rolled out two sleeping bags in the sangar. Only two of them would be allowed to sleep at any one time, with the other two keeping watch together, with each one ensuring that the other was still awake.

Waiting for Jock's return, Gumboot huddled up in the sangar, protected by the wall of stones, and had a smoke. Ricketts and Andrew, their weapons resting lightly on the wall on either side of the GPMG, kept watch in all directions. After the heat of the day, the night was bitterly cold.

When Jock returned, Gumboot hurried downhill and Jock took Andrew's place on watch, letting the latter huddle down behind the wall to warm himself and have a cigarette. Andrew went down next, with Gumboot taking Ricketts's place beside Jock, allowing Ricketts to huddle beneath the wall, out of the biting wind. By the time Andrew returned, Ricketts was feeling a lot warmer and hurried down the hill to the mess, in the mood to eat.

After the dark and cold of the hill, the mess tent seemed brilliantly illuminated, warm and inviting. It was, indeed, packed and noisy, with everyone in a good mood, and Ricketts relished his compo sausages, mashed potatoes, green peas and baked beans, followed by apple pie and hot custard. He was there for forty minutes, had a good talk with some other troopers, then reluctantly climbed back up the hill to relieve Jock on watch. The men then took turns at watch, or stag, two on, two off, until first light.

Sleep, when it came, was constantly interrupted as the *adoo*, still pursuing their guerrilla tactics, fired their rifles and mortars at irregular intervals throughout the night.

The resup flights had also continued throughout the night and by first light the following day Skyvans, Caribou transport planes and helicopters had lifted in defence stores and ordnance; full and empty oil drums, the latter to be used to build defensive walls; water and rations; jeeps, trucks, Saladin armoured cars; donkeys for carrying heavy loads on mountain patrols; and even live goats to be killed, cooked and eaten by the *firqats*.

'Talk about special privileges!' Gumboot complained. 'We eat compo rations and those A-rabs get live goats for their fucking couscous. A diabolical liberty!'

'The food's part of their religion as well,' Andrew explained, 'which is why they get those so-called special privileges.'

'How come religious people get everything and we sinners get nothing?'

'It's the same back in England,' Andrew said. 'The same in America. Religion excuses every damn thing.'

'Still, it's a fucking liberty. We get sausage and beans and they get bloody couscous.'

'Would you actually eat couscous, Gumboot?'

'Are you fucking crazy? That shit's for the birds!'

'There you are, then.'

'Never mind what I'll eat or not, Andrew. It's the fucking *principle*, mate!'

'Couscous for breakfast, dinner and tea,' Jock said, 'must be a wonderful, stomach-wrenching experience.'

'You'd be farting like a whale with gastritis,' Gumboot warned him. 'Stay well away from it, mate!'

From their vantage point high on the northern hill, Ricketts and Andrew, in particular, found it fascinating to observe with what speed and efficiency the base camp was built around the original, largely featureless airstrip. Artillery positions consisting of 40-gallon-drum hedgehogs were built on all four sides of the runway and manned with 25-pounders and Browning 0.5in heavy machine-guns, the latter having a range of 1400 metres and a firing rate of up to 500 rounds per minute. Sangars were placed at regular intervals between the hedgehogs and armed with Browning 0.3in medium machine-guns – range 900 metres and 400–500 RPM – and Carl Gustav 84mm rocket launchers. Other sangars were equipped with the same MMGs, but had 81mm mortars instead of the rocket launchers. The combination of heavily armed hedgehogs and sangars formed a natural defensive perimeter around the base camp.

The work was completed by lunchtime the second day. By late afternoon, marquees and bivouacs were sprouting all over the area, with many of the latter in two sets of three lines, making an accommodation area for the SAS, SAF and Baluchi troopers, each with their individual lines. The two sets of tents were divided by an area of flat land to be used as a football pitch and general recreation area. Portable showers and chemical toilets were raised near the tents. An artificial wall was created from piled Burmails to protect the rows of bivouacs from the four LZs specially cleared for the helicopters. South of the airstrip, near the cleared bottleneck, was a fenced-in armoured car parking area. Above it, near the eastern hill, were the officers' tent lines and toilets, the mess tent, and a captured enemy personnel, or CEP, tent. North of the airstrip, obliquely below Ricketts's sangar, were marquees used as the rations, equipment and ammunition stores. Located well away from those and the accommodations areas, in order to avoid the smell, was a donkey handler's tent with fenced-in area for the donkeys, plus a similar area for the goats and goatherds. As they were not bothered by the smell and indeed had sole use of the goats as a source of food, the *firqats* had their own camp, located near the base of the western hill. From there they could constantly patrol the hill with the support of SAF troops.

By last light on the second day, the camp was a thriving community, with goats and donkeys braying; SAF and Baluchi troops being noisily and rigorously drilled by their officers; REMFs hammering, drilling and shouting instructions; SAS troops playing football on the new pitch; *firqat* members slaughtering a squealing goat, draining it of blood, skinning it, and cooking it over an open fire; jeeps and Saladin armoured cars roaring and rattling all over the place; helicopters ascending and descending from their four LZs; and Skyvans and Caribou transports continuing to land and take off on the runway, bringing in more supplies and taking out what was no longer required.

All of this took place while *adoo* mortar shells and FN rifle fire continued to tear up the earth on the slopes above the western perimeter.

Shortly after the last of the four-man team in Ricketts's sangar had returned from the mess tent, Sergeant Lampton came up the hill at the crouch to squat beside them and tell them what was happening.

'The force is being split into two fighting units, or fire groups,' he told them. 'The first, called the Eastern Group, will be tasked with probing deeper into the eastern area. As the *adoo* beyond the western hill are gathered around the Ain watering-hole, the second group, the Western Group, of which you'll be part, are going to start clearing them out tomorrow. This sangar, including the machine-gun, will be taken over by some other troopers while you lot rejoin Purvis and Raglan to gain experience in close-contact mountain fighting, under my guidance. We move out at . . .'

'First light,' Andrew interrupted him.

Lampton grinned. 'You're obviously learning, Trooper. Now have a good night.'

The sergeant slithered his way back down the hill, to the sangar he was sharing with Tom and Bill.

Later, close to midnight, the *adoo* released their most sustained volley of fire since surrendering the airstrip. From Ricketts's position in the sangar, he could see the eerily beautiful, gracefully arching, green tracer gliding out from the pitch-black western hill, picking up speed as it curved down towards the airstrip, then exploding either on the ground or spending itself in silvery bursts in the darkness above the many tents of the new camp. It was a magical sight he would never forget.

Though he did not know it then, it was the beginning of five days of bloody fighting.

14

The intermittent rifle and mortar fire of the night allowed Ricketts and his mates very little sleep. Struggling awake at first light, when Gumboot and Jock were still on watch, he felt sleepless, cold and full of faint aches and pains. Sitting upright and rubbing the sleep from his eyes, he glanced over the sangar wall just as another mortar explosion shook the lower slopes of the western hill, sending a column of sand, soil and smoke into the pearly-grey air.

'Christ,' he said, 'I feel shattered.'

'Aye,' Jock agreed, a cigarette dangling from his lips as he leaned on the wall beside the GPMG with his M16 rifle resting across the stones. 'Me and Gumboot, we've just been saying the same thing. What a fucking night!'

'Right!' said Gumboot. 'Fireworks all night long. Just to keep our eyes open. I can't remember when I last had a good sleep. My eyes feel like lead.'

Andrew, who had been sleeping beside Ricketts, groaned and also sat upright. 'Shit,' he said, 'I feel terrible.'

Jock and Gumboot laughed. 'You better get used to it,' Jock said. 'I don't think we'll get much rest today – nor tonight for that matter. Here come our replacements.'

Ricketts glanced over the wall again and saw the new four-man team making their way laboriously up the steep hill. A similar group was already at Lampton's sangar, replacing the sergeant, Tom and Bill, who were presently making their way downhill. Pale sunlight was falling on the dry earth, streaking the grey light with silvery striations that heralded the heat. On the western hill, there was no sign of the *adoo*, who had been firing on and off all night and were continuing to do so. Most of them were hidden behind the rim of the hill, but others, Ricketts suspected, were sniping from behind the slope overlooking the camp – the slope that he and the others would soon be climbing. The thought filled him with a slight, healthy tension that would stand him in good stead.

The replacement team finally reached the sangar. Exchanging greetings, they sounded breathless.

'That's some climb,' one of them said.

'Sure is,' Andrew replied, rolling up one of the

two sleeping bags and stuffing it back into his bergen. 'It clears out the lungs, right?'

'Right,' the replacement replied.

Jock and Gumboot were enthusiastically humping their bergens onto their shoulders as Ricketts rolled up his own sleeping bag and stuffed it into his bergen. This done, he hoisted the bergen onto his shoulder, picked up his SLR and stepped out of the sangar.

'Good luck,' he said to the four men as they took over the sangar.

'And to you,' one of them said. 'You're the ones who'll need it.'

After waving goodbye, Ricketts scrambled with the others down the hill and into the newly erected camp. The rich aroma of boiled lamb and spices reached them from the *firqats'* camp near the base of the western hill, where the Arabs, all wearing their jellabas and *shemaghs*, were kneeling around an enormous communal pot piled high with couscous, which they were scooping into their mouths with their fingers.

Gumboot screwed his face up in disgust, then held his nose as they passed the goats. But by the time they reached the mess tent, they were well out of range of the smell and were greeted instead with the welcoming aroma of bacon and eggs.

Entering the tent, they found it packed, the men queuing up along the servery and then taking their plates to the trestle tables. After the usual bullshit with the cook, they had a slap-up fried breakfast washed down with hot tea, their weapons stacked up around them, then made their way to the ammunition store, where they had to collect spare ammo and meet Lampton. The sergeant was waiting for them when they arrived.

'Morning, lads. Got a good night's sleep, did you?'

'Wonderful!' Jock said. 'Slept all of ten minutes.'

'Now we're bright-eyed and bushy-tailed,' Gumboot added, 'and rarin' to go.'

They had to join another queue to pick up their spare weapons, which included, as well as their standard-issue Browning high-power handguns and SLR or M16 rifles, Heckler & Koch MP5 9mm sub-machine-guns and, for some of them, 7.62mm Lee Enfield sniper rifles. Tom and Bill were given an M-72 LAW, and others, Ricketts noticed, were collecting 51mm and 81mm mortars with base plate, tripod and shells – heavy loads to be humping up that hill in the increasing heat of the morning. To increase the load even more, each group was carrying at least one PRC 319. It would not be an easy day.

The men then joined the many others grouping together near the hedgehog by the base of the western hill. The group, known as the Western Group, tasked with clearing the eastern slope of the western hill, consisted of the majority of B Squadron and G Squadron 22 SAS, the Firqat Al Asifat, the Firqat Salahadeen and the Baluch Askars. Being organized by British officers, notably Major Greenaway, they were surprisingly indifferent to the mortar explosions erupting at irregular intervals on the hill. In fact, the explosions were all fairly high up, out of range, as were the occasional *adoo* rifle shots.

'OK,' Lampton said to Ricketts and the others, 'you men will be with me, coming up behind that group of *firqats* gathering over there.' He indicated the Arab fighters with a nod of his head. Bristling with bandoliers, webbing and weapons, looking as fierce as usual, they were listening intently to Dead-eye Dick as he gave them instructions. With his L42A1 7.62mm bolt-action Lee Enfield sniper rifle slung across his back, his webbing bristling with ten-round box magazines and L2A2 steel-cased fragmentation grenades, a Browning high-power handgun holstered on his hip, and his two knives – a *kunjias* and a Fairburn-Sykes commando knife – sheathed on the belt around his waist, Parker looked every bit as fearful as his *firqat* comrades.

'Shit,' Gumboot whispered, 'are we going with *him*?'

'Yep,' Lampton said, grinning.

'That bastard terrifies me,' big Andrew said. 'I'm not sure I like this.'

'He's a good man,' Lampton said. 'Good tracker, great sniper. He's a good man to have in your area, so you should be thankful you've got him. Whoops! Here comes the briefing.'

Standing on a wooden crate, so that everyone could see him, Major Greenaway gave a short speech, saying that their ultimate task was to clear the Ain watering-hole and take command of the whole plateau, but that before that they would have to take the western hill and thus ensure the safety of the Jibjat airstrip.

'Therefore,' he said, 'you will climb the hill in your separate groups, flushing out the *adoo* where you find them and hopefully taking some prisoners for interrogation. It's anticipated that you'll be on the rim of the hill by last light. From that vantage point, you'll direct the fire of the 25-pounders onto the *adoo* positions on the other side. We will keep this barrage going all night.'

'There goes our sleep,' Gumboot whispered.

'At first light,' Greenaway continued, 'you will make your way down the other side, pushing the *adoo* back to the watering-hole. Once that's been accomplished, you'll all regroup at the bottom of the hill in preparation for the final assault on the watering-hole and ultimately the Wadi Dharbat, where most of the *adoo* are entrenched. Any questions?' The major looked around him, but saw only heads shaking from side to side. 'No? Good. You may now proceed with all speed.'

The first of the SAF, *firqat* and Baluchi troops were already starting up the hill when Greenaway jumped down off his box and headed back to his HQ tent in the camp, accompanied by RSM Worthington. At the same time Sergeant Parker walked up to Lampton, nodded at him, then turned to Ricketts and the others, to study them with icy grey eyes.

'We go up the hill together,' he said finally, 'but well spread out, with me and the *firqats* out front, you lot behind us. We advance at the crouch, from one outcrop to another, never standing fully upright and making sure that we're never fully exposed for more than a few seconds.' His voice was soft, almost a whisper, with hardly any timbre or intonation; not a comforting sound. 'The *adoo* can see through rocks, use their eyes like periscopes, and have eyes in the back of their heads as well. You stand up and you'll get a bullet through *your* head and fucking deserve it. Don't panic up there. Don't shoot the wrong people. On the other hand, if anything moves, don't take too long to decide. Keep your eyes to the front and to the ground, because there might be land-mines. OK, let's go.'

Ricketts and the others glanced uneasily at one another, then followed Lampton up the lower slopes, behind Parker and the *firqats*. At first the climb was easy, on a gentle incline, but before long the rise was much steeper, the ground underfoot rougher. As Parker had instructed them – and as he and the Arabs were doing now – they spread well apart and made the climb on the crouch, darting from one outcrop to another, trying desperately not to slip on the loose stones and slide back down the hill. A backbreaking activity, sending pains through every muscle, it was made even more difficult by the flies and mosquitoes that buzzed frantically around their lips and eyes. The rising heat only made it worse and they were soon bathed in sweat.

Tying his *shemagh* around his mouth to keep out the flies, Ricketts glanced in both directions and saw the many other SAF, *firqat*, Baluchi and SAS troops, totalling over two hundred, advancing up the lower slopes by the same painfully slow yet effective method. Glancing over his shoulder, he saw the camp spread out below, an apparently chaotic collection of tents, hedgehogs and sangars spread around the airstrip and four helicopter LZs on baking earth covered with wind-blown sand. Reflected heat rose up from the ground, distorting the shape of solid objects, making them appear to bend and wobble. The men down there, whether walking or driving, were indistinguishable from their shadows, which also shifted and changed into bizarre shapes in the shimmering heat.

Ricketts looked to the front again just as rifle shots rang out and an SAF soldier was slammed backwards to the ground, then rolled down the hill in a cloud of dust. Even as those around him were crouching low behind outcrops and raising their weapons to return the fire, more bullets kicked up the sand around them and ricocheted off the rocks. The return fire was quick, exploding from many SAF weapons, turning the hill above into an inferno of angrily spitting, jagged lines of sand.

When it died away, however, there was still no sign of the *adoo* who had killed the SAF soldier.

'The phantom enemy,' Andrew whispered. 'Now we know why they call them that.'

'Move further apart, you two!' Lampton snapped, waving his left hand.

'Yes, boss,' Andrew replied, again putting a good distance between himself and Ricketts, crouched low, then dashing across open space to drop down behind another outcrop.

Parker and the *firqats* were up ahead, moving

in a north-south arc, away from the main assault force. More *adoo* sniper fire rang out from even higher above, causing sand to fly all around the *firqats*. Parker's head popped up and down as he checked the source of the fire, then he leaned out from the sheltering rocks, taking aim with his Lee Enfield, and snapped up three quick shots in a row before pressing himself back into the rock.

A man came rolling down the hill, limbs akimbo, jellaba flapping and dust billowing up around him, only stopping when he crashed into a large rock near the *firqats*. He was still alive, groaning and gargling, his body twitching, but one of the Arabs darted across to where he lay, rolled him over and slit his throat with a *kunjias*.

'Christ!' Gumboot said.

'Keep moving!' Parker shouted, waving them on with one hand and running uphill, crouched low, as the Arab stripped the dead man of his bandolier and weapons, then divided them among the other tribesmen. Ignoring them, Lampton urged Ricketts and the others up the hill, still crouching low and darting from rock to rock as more bullets thudded into the ground around them or ricocheted off the surrounding rocks.

So it went on for a couple of hours – the men jumping up and down, scurrying from rock to rock, dropping low and then jumping up briefly to fire a shot. Another body rolled down the hill. A *firqat* was hit, and threw up his arms, his robes billowing behind him, and jerked back to land on the slope with a sickening thud.

Jock had the PRC 319 and called up the medics. While he was doing so, a mortar shell exploded nearby, creating a spiralling column of smoke and sand. The roar of the explosion was followed by screaming in Arabic and another fusillade of fire from the advancing SAF soldiers, though to what effect no one knew.

The *adoo* were still hard to find. They popped up and down from behind the rocks above, jellabas fluttering, eyes wide above their *shemaghs*, only to disappear and reappear somewhere else, picking off the SAF troops with daunting accuracy. And yet they were in retreat, backing gradually up the hill, and as more of them were hit and tumbled down in clouds of dust, the remainder, of whom there were clearly many, retreated up the hill even faster.

Progress was being made, but it was not easy, and by noon, when the hill was like a furnace, with heat shimmering up off the scorched, dusty rocks and even the insects seemingly dazed, Ricketts, feeling as tired as the others looked, was grateful to take five. In fact, the break lasted for an hour, allowing the men to rest up and eat some high-calorie rations, washing them down with water; but then the PRC 319s started crackling and hissing, relaying the order to move, and the men climbed laboriously to their feet and started the whole thing again.

They had another four hours in hell, burning up in its cruel heat, tormented by flies and mosquitoes, by scorpions and centipedes underfoot, while being picked up by the hawk-eyed *adoo* snipers and, on the odd occasion – when the *adoo* heavy gun teams forgot the danger to their own men – by the erupting soil and flying shrapnel of mortar explosions. More bodies littered the hillside and were carried away by the sweating medics, but gradually, as the afternoon passed into evening, and the heat died down, they began to force the *adoo* back over the hill. By now Parker had led his group well away from the main assault force and was moving towards the summit of the hill in the planned north-south arc.

Ricketts saw the levelling summit and the featureless sky beyond; he was exhilarated enough to forget to stay low when he made his next zigzagging run to another outcrop. An *adoo* sniper fired at him and the bullet, after hitting the stock of his SLR and making the weapon spin out of his hand, ricocheted off the rock he had quickly dropped behind, spraying his face with pulverized stone and temporarily blinding him.

Blinking to clear his eyes, Ricketts saw the *adoo*

sniper running at him, striped jellaba billowing in the breeze, his FN rifle in one hand, a *kunjias* in the other, the latter reflecting the sunlight as the man held it high.

The SLR was out of reach, still lying where it had fallen, so Ricketts quickly tore his Browning handgun from its holster and swung it up into the two-handed firing position: in line with the centre of his body, locking his arms, his free hand holding the firing hand, and with equal pressure between thumb and fingers as he pressed gently, precisely on the trigger.

A double-tap – two shots fired in quick succession – and the Arab was stopped, staggering back, dropping his knife, then turning aside, as if trying to be polite, before falling face-down in the dirt.

Ricketts lowered the handgun and took a deep breath. After checking that the man was dead, he holstered the weapon, picked up his SLR, noted with relief that it was OK, and then followed the other men up to the summit.

It was a rocky plateau, scorched white by the sun, stretching out quite a distance before falling away again. Beyond the slope of the eastern side of the plateau, the desert stretched out for what seemed to be for ever, though it was merely that the horizon was virtually invisible in the heat haze. The sun, however, was going down, sinking behind the men, casting its light on the hill they had just climbed. In front of them, to the east, the fading light was gradually, magically, bringing the lost horizon back into view, at least before extinguishing it again in the darkness of night.

The Ain watering-hole and Wadi Dharbat, Ricketts surmised, were at the bottom of the eastern hill of the plateau, now safely out of sight. Perhaps for this reason, and knowing that they were to dig in here for the night, in order to call down support from the 25-pounders in the hedgehogs in Jibjat, the men were shaking off their bergens and lowering themselves to the ground, looking forward to slaking their thirst or having a smoke.

They were instantly disillusioned when Lampton and Parker came storming back from the eastern slopes, the latter saying in his soft-voiced, deadly way, 'What the hell do you troopers think you're doing?'

'Well, Sarge,' Jock began, 'we just thought . . .'

'That you'd won the fucking hill? You've won nothing, Trooper. You sit here on your arse, having a cigarette, and the *adoo* will come back over that ridge and blow the shit out of you. Now get back on your feet and start picking up rocks and build yourselves a sangar big enough to take all of you and that LAW. Is that understood?'

'Yes, boss!' Andrew said, loud and clear.

'Good,' Parker replied and started turning away.

'Just one thing, boss,' Gumboot said, looking surprisingly clear-eyed.

Parker turned back to face him. 'Yes, Trooper?'

'While we're building our sangar, boss, what will your *firqats* be doing?'

Parker stared steadily at Gumboot, burning up with an inner fire, then smiled, almost in admiration, and said, 'A fair enough question, Trooper. They'll be building another sangar, about a thousand metres from here, to the south, and I'll be with them, keeping in touch with the 319. While you, with Sergeant Lampton's help, call in grid references for the 25-pounders in Jibjat, we'll be foraging out over that eastern hill with the intention of bringing back a prisoner. Any problem, Trooper?'

'With you all the way, boss. No sweat.'

'Glad to hear that. Start building.'

As Parker walked away to rejoin his Arab fighters, Gumboot let his breath out in a lengthy sigh of relief.

'I've got to hand it to you,' Andrew said, 'you've got nerves of steel, Gumboot.'

'I thought I had,' Gumboot replied, 'until that cunt looked at me.'

Lampton laughed. He had been standing just

behind them. They all stared at him until he quietened down and said, 'Sorry, lads, but you're all being paranoid. Dead-eye's perfectly normal. Come on, let's build the sangar.'

As usual, they tore the rocks out of the earth with their bare hands and piled them one on top of the other to create a natural wall. It was a semi-circle, the open end to the rear, the curved wall overlooking the plateau and the vast, star-filled darkness beyond it. They placed their weapons around the wall, rolled out their sleeping bags – not for sleeping but to sit on – then checked their small-scale maps and button compasses by the light of pencil torches and, combining their readings with eyeball recces of the landscape, radioed back approximate calibrations to the big-gun teams in Jibjat.

All along the great length of the plateau overlooking the Wadi Dharbat and the Ain watering-hole, other OP teams were doing the same. Within minutes, they heard the dull, distant thumping of the big guns, followed seconds later by shells whistling overhead, then by the sound of explosions on the lower slopes of the eastern hill and the flatland beyond, with luck including the wadi and the watering-hole. Though only being targeted on a broad, general front, the big guns could not fail to do extensive damage before the assault force moved out, which would not be until first light the following day.

'Fucking hell,' Bill said, covering his ears, 'that's one hell of a noise.'

'No beauty sleep tonight,' Tom added. 'We'll move out deaf and dumb.'

'Better deaf and dumb than dead,' said Gumboot. 'Which is what a lot of those poor fuckers are going to be before first light dawns.'

'Dead right,' Andrew said.

When first light came, many hours later, the sky beyond the sunlit plateau was dark with drifting sand, dust and smoke. It was billowing up from the explosions far below, but the men could not see those. They broke the sangar up stone by stone, then began their long march down to the burning plain.

15

They had not gone very far across the plateau when they saw Parker coming up over the rim, holding his Lee Enfield sniper rifle across his chest. He was followed by his fierce-looking Arabs, who were dragging an *adoo* prisoner between them. The latter's ankles had been tethered with a short length of rope that made it difficult for him to walk. It ran up to his wrists, which were bound in front of him, thus making any other kind of movement just as difficult as walking.

Lampton stopped in front of them, letting Ricketts get a good look at the prisoner. The man had a gaunt, hungry face and darkly blazing, defiant eyes.

'Ah,' Lampton said, 'I see you had a good night.' Parker just nodded in agreement. 'Any other contact down there?' Lampton asked him.

'We terminated a few,' Parker said in his oddly disturbing manner, 'and saw that there's a lot of them. They were scattered all over the eastern hill, though I think they're making their way back down to regroup at the watering-hole. I heard a lot of trucks coming and going during the night, accompanied by the sounds of digging, so I think they were laying mines in the flatland leading up to the watering-hole.'

'Damn!' Lampton said softly. 'What about our 25-pounders? Did they do any good?'

'Yep. I think the shelling was what forced the *adoo* back down the hill. They were on the move while we were foraging about there. We terminated a few more before first light, taking them out with knives so as not to be noticed, then grabbed this prisoner for the green slime. I'm going to hand him over for questioning, then I'll come back and join you.'

'The green slime have set up in a tent in Jibjat, so you'll have to take him all the way back.'

'I'll send him with an escort of troopers and be with you in no time.'

'OK, Dead-eye. Excellent.' Lampton raised his right hand and waved it in a forward motion, indicating that the men should follow him.

They marched past Parker's group, heading across the plateau, towards where the ground sloped away to form the eastern hill. Once at the slope, they found themselves looking down on the broad stretch of desert leading to the watering-hole and the Wadi Dharbat. Both the lower slopes of the hill and the flatland at the bottom were covered in a pall of smoke and a lazily drifting cloud of sand and dust. The hill was strewn with rocks and littered with black shell holes. No dead bodies were visible.

'The *adoo* have removed their dead,' Lampton said. 'I respect them for that.'

Glancing in both directions, they saw other SF troops, including SAS, also crossing the plateau, weapons at the ready, and beginning their careful descent of the hill towards the flat plain. Ricketts saw the glint of water between curtains of smoke – the Ain watering-hole – surrounded by what looked like another horseshoe-shaped series of hills and ridges, forming a natural, presently ghostly amphitheatre.

'That's where the *adoo* will be waiting for us,' he said.

'Yes,' Lampton said. 'Let's go.'

Moving parallel with the others, they continued downhill, stepping carefully around the shell holes and scorched, blackened boulders while keeping their eyes peeled for signs of mines or *adoo* snipers.

The big guns were still firing at regular intervals as the men advanced. However, given new calibrations from the forward observers, they were firing on a much higher trajectory, dropping the shells on the flatland just short of the watering-hole, trying to force the *adoo* out of there and into the wadi.

Shells were exploding all over the flatland as the assault force made its way down the hillside. With no big guns of their own, the *adoo* were withholding fire until their targets were within range of their 81mm mortars, Shpagin heavy machine-guns, GPMGs and Katushka 122mm recoilless rocket launchers.

This was not something to contemplate with much enthusiasm, but Ricketts took some comfort from the softening-up barrage of the 25-pounders and assumed that his friends were doing the same.

There were no *adoo* snipers on the hill, nor were land-mines encountered. The men reached the bottom in thirty minutes and kept marching across the flat desert plain. In no time at all they left the bright sunlight of morning and found themselves advancing into the dense smoke and drifting dust created by the exploding shells. It was always nerve-racking in the smoke, with visibility reduced to zero, impossible to see land-mines or booby-traps and easy to become disorientated.

The range of the *adoo*'s Katushkas, Ricketts knew, was almost 11,000 metres, which meant that another five minutes' marching would put him and the other SAF troops within range. He was worrying about this and the possibility of mines when he saw a jagged flash well ahead, accompanied by an explosion, a dreadful scream of agony, the clashing of different voices bawling warnings or commands, some in Arabic, others in English, then the gradual grinding to a halt of the men around him.

'Land-mine!' someone bellowed up ahead. 'Don't move! Land-mine!' That fearful call was followed by, 'Medic!'

Pierced by a bolt of fear that had to be contained, Ricketts froze where he was, but glanced about him, seeing the others as barely recognizable, shadowy forms in the murk, all standing dead still just like him. Their presence was a comfort, though a residual fear nagged at him, and he knew that he would not have felt so bad had it happened in clear light. As it was, trapped in the fog of smoke, spiralling sand and drifting dust, his feeling of helplessness was greatly increased. But it was lucky at least, he told himself, that they were still out of range of the enemy's Katushka rocket launchers.

'What the fuck happens now?' Gumboot asked, standing beside Ricketts and talking just to hear the sound of a human voice.

'The SAF have a team of mine detectors spread out across the plain at the head of the column,'

Lampton said, positioned ahead of them and glancing back over his shoulder. 'They'll have to advance slowly, checking for more mines, and the assault force will break up into as many single files as are required to follow the men with the mine detectors. When I move, get into single file behind me and follow in my footsteps. Don't deviate one inch.'

They had to wait a long time, with the smoke still drifting around them, listening to the cont-inuing barrage of the big guns. Eventually, the shelling stopped, the gun crews having been alerted to the plight of the assault force, and the sand and dust gradually settled down. The smoke started thinning, too, letting Ricketts see farther ahead. Just as it cleared enough to let him glimpse the front of the column, which was on the move again, the men directly in front of him started moving too.

When Lampton raised and lowered his right hand, indicating 'Forward march', Ricketts and the others fell in behind him, but in single file, as ordered. Lampton moved very slowly, as if barefoot on broken glass, and Ricketts was careful to follow precisely in the footprints left in the sand.

Eventually, after ten minutes that seemed more like ten hours, the smoke cleared, and Ricketts saw the hundreds of men, advancing slowly, carefully in numerous long lines. Each man was following the footsteps of the man ahead, all tailing back from the men with the mine detectors, spread out across the front of the column over a distance of about a quarter mile.

It was a tortuous advance that would leave them sitting ducks for the *adoo* when they got within range. For that very reason the column was stopped again and instructions sent down the lines via the PRC 319s.

Lampton had been listening to his call from Major Greenaway and now he handed the phone back to Jock, in charge of the radio.

'The CO says we can't advance this way, at this speed, once we're within range of the *adoo* guns – we'd just become sitting ducks. So he's asked for the Skyvans to come over and clear the area with Burmail bombs. In the meantime, we wait.'

'Can we sit down?' Gumboot asked.

'I think that's safe enough,' Lampton said. 'Your arse is probably no wider than your big feet. Just don't move left or right.'

'Ha, ha,' Gumboot said.

Desperate for a rest, the men sat on the ground and saw many of the other soldiers doing the same, though some felt it more prudent to stay standing.

By now the sun was up, blazing out of a clear blue sky, and with the dispersal of the smoke, sand and dust, it felt hotter than ever. Even more irksome, the flies and mosquitoes returned, materializing out of the ether, buzzing, whining and dive-bombing in a feeding frenzy brought on by sweat and blood. A lot of the men put on dark glasses and covered their mouths with *shemaghs*, but the swarm just flew or crawled under them to get at their eyes and mouths.

The men baked in the sun, became nauseous in the heat, swatted and slapped to no avail, cursed and groaned while they waited. It was not a long wait, but it seemed like an eternity. Eventually, to their relief, the Skyvans were heard flying over the hill dividing the plain from Jibjat. When the three aircraft came into view, many of the men cheered.

In the brilliant sunlight, Ricketts could clearly see the rocky amphitheatre surrounding three sides of the watering-hole presently being held by the *adoo*. He judged it to be approximately 15,000 metres away, which was too far for him to pick out individual details, but left only 4000 metres between the column and the firing range of the *adoo*'s Katushka rocket launchers.

That danger was yet to come. For the moment, Ricketts took a great deal of pleasure from watching the Skyvans fly directly above him and on to the mined desert plain just ahead of the column. They were flying very low. Once they had passed overhead he saw that the rear cargo holds were open, with men standing in them, dangerously close to the edge, but behind the stacked Burmails. They simply pushed the oil drums out, probably sliding them off rollers. Ricketts saw the drums clearly, falling down through the sky, one after the other, with the Schermuly flares burning like firelighters on each side of them. They appeared to fall slowly, almost gliding, but that was an illusion.

When the first drum hit the ground, it bounced like a football, then exploded with a thunderous clap and became a boiling mass of brilliant flame spewing over the plain. The other Burmails did likewise, one after the other, some bouncing crazily before exploding, others seeming to burst open at once, and many catching fire from the great waves of flame that were boiling and leaping into one another to form an immense wall of fire capped by black, oily smoke.

As intended, the explosions set off the land-mines in another series of explosions covering most of the area between the stalled assault force and the entrance to the rocky amphitheatre surrounding the watering-hole. Mines not touched directly by the Burmails were set off by exploding mines in a domino effect that created a fantastic, awesome spectacle of boiling flame, billowing smoke and widly swirling columns of sand, dust and loose gravel. It went on and on, a constant roaring and burning so intense that the watching troopers felt relatively cool when the flames finally died away.

'Jesus Christ!' exclaimed Andrew, too stunned to get out his notebook.

'Fucking A!' Gumboot added.

A few minutes later the desert floor was smouldering, with isolated flames – the results of gaseous burning created by the oil – spiralling a few feet above the ground before sailing away like yellow threads and finally becoming mere wisps of smoke that also gradually disappeared. When nothing but the thinning smoke remained, the column moved on.

The *adoo* opened fire with their Katushka rocket launchers the instant the column had advanced another 5000 metres. As this placed most of the men within range of the rockets, the explosions erupted in their midst, causing devastation and death, with some soldiers being thrown up and smashed back to the ground in turbulent clouds of flame-filled smoke.

Instead of trying to take cover, since there was none available, the men started running, determined to get to the watering-hole before they were slaughtered. When the first of them reached the natural entrance, the *adoo* opened fire with a combination of Kalashnikovs, FN sniper rifles and GPMGs, cutting down even more troopers. This forced them to scatter north and south, to both sides of the amphitheatre, from where they could continue their advance by alternately hiding behind, and scrambling over, the rocks.

Three members of a four-man SAS GPMG team, trailing the SAF troops during the advance into the minefield, had been killed by the first mine explosion. The fourth man, now squatting on the ground beside his GPMG, was clearly in shock.

'Arrange to have that man sent back,' Lampton said to the medic on the scene. Then he turned to Ricketts and said, 'You lot are back on your original job. Pick up that GPMG and find a spot on those rocks.'

'Right, boss,' Ricketts said.

Andrew picked up the GPMG, using a sling to support it in a position conducive to firing from the hip. When Ricketts had slung the tripod onto his shoulders, helped by Gumboot, they all hiked it up to the rocky south wall of the opening, into the horseshoe-shaped area surrounding the watering-hole. They were soon joined by Major Greenaway, RSM Worthington and the redoubtable Sergeant Parker.

While Greenaway immersed himself in a briefing huddle with his RSM and two sergeants, the mortar and GPMG teams set up their weapons, aiming them across the watering-hole at the high ground opposite, which was hidden by thick thorn bushes and therefore ideal for a waiting enemy. The watering-hole itself was about 650 yards away, at the far end of the U-shape formed by the legs of the horseshoe, which opened up towards the SAF forces, including the SAS.

Lampton left the briefing huddle and returned to tell his men what was happening.

'The mortar teams and SAF will jointly hold this position,' he said, 'giving fire support to three SAF action groups and the Firqat Khalid bin Waalid. Those four groups, plus an SAS platoon coming up on the right flank, will advance tactically into the bowl and secure the watering-hole.'

Nodding his understanding, Ricketts opened the steel tripod and placed it firmly in the dusty ground. He then levelled the cradle and locked it. After centralizing the deflection and elevation drums, he fitted the GPMG, pushing the front mounting pin home until the locking stud clicked into position. Gumboot then flicked up the rear sight-leaf and set it on the 300-metre graduation, laying the sight on to a rocky outcrop on the tree line by use of the deflection and elevation drums. Finally, they sandbagged the legs and rechecked the sight. The gun was ready for firing.

The men then realized that they were in an excellently concealed firing position, with panoramic views of the whole area.

'Fucking perfect,' Gumboot said. 'We can see the whole show from here.'

'And it looks like it's just starting,' Andrew replied, pointing with his forefinger to where the *firqats*, about to move down the rocky gradient into the horseshoe, had stopped to have what appeared to be an excited argument with the SAF officers.

'Oh, oh!' Bill murmured, spitting on the rock between his knees.

'They've gone on strike,' Tom said drily.

Parker and Lampton hurried up to the group of *firqats* and SAF, listened to both sides of the argument, offered their suggestions, then nodded at each other, as if in agreement. Parker then went back to give his situation report, or sit rep, to Greenaway, while Lampton returned to his men to do the same.

'Having an argument, were they?' Gumboot asked sceptically.

'A Chinese parliament,' Lampton replied diplomatically. 'The *firqats* wanted us to mortar the high ground and fry the tree line with a mixed-fruit pudding before the action groups moved off.'

'A *what*?' Tom asked.

'A mixed-fruit pudding,' Lampton repeated impatiently, before remembering that his men were probationers. 'Two high-explosive shells to one white phosphorus, fired by mortar.'

'Ah!' Tom said. 'Right!'

'However,' Lampton continued, 'the actual action groups, the SAF, insisted that time is running out and that every *adoo* in the area will be homing in on the water-hole if they, the SAF action groups, don't make an immediate move to secure it.'

'Even before the mortars have time to get their bearings,' Gumboot said.

'Correct.'

'So what's the result?' Tom asked impatiently.

'We've vetoed the mixed-fruit pudding, but the *firqats* and action groups are moving off immediately on the basis that the mortar crew have already monitored the high ground and have possible *adoo* firing points on their plotter board.'

The men glanced over Lampton's shoulder to observe that the *firqats* were indeed already heading down into the horseshoe, followed by the SAF troops.

'Fucking terrific logic,' Gumboot said, as if he couldn't believe his own ears.

Lampton grinned. 'It's *their* logic, Gumboot. Now get ready to cover them.'

Ricketts closed the top cover of the GPMG on a belt of 200 rounds. Andrew then cocked the action and put the safety catch on 'Fire'. Gumboot scanned the area with binoculars while Jock, his jaws working on chewing gum, kept his ear to the radio.

The area around the watering-hole seemed unnaturally quiet. Dust was blowing across the wet sand surrounding the pool. The sun was blazing down on the white rocks and erasing the shadows. Flies clustered like bunches of black grapes over mounds of old excrement. The heat was fierce and oppressive.

The heavily armed *firqats* advanced in an extended line, holding their rifles out from their bodies, preparing to fire from the hip.

Suddenly, about halfway to the watering-hole, they fell one after the other belly-down on the ground, from where they frantically waved the action groups forward.

'What the hell . . .' Lampton looked confused. 'That's not what they're supposed to do. They're *supposed* to go all the way, because it's their watering-hole and tribal area. The SAF were letting them take that position to boost their morale. What the . . .?'

'They're on strike,' Gumboot said, sounding satisfied.

The SAF action groups were advancing through

the lines of prone *firqats* when the high-velocity rounds of the *adoo* suddenly shattered the silence.

The ground erupted around the SAS with fire from Kalashnikov AK-47s, RPD light machine-guns, and at least one Shpagin heavy machine-gun. A stream of green tracer floated towards the SAS mortar and GPMG positions, then whipped above their heads at incredible speed, only to expend itself harmlessly at the burn-out point of 1100 metres, well behind them.

'There!' Gumboot shouted, lowering his binoculars and pointing towards a cloud of blue smoke rising from the top of some thorn bushes on the high ground beyond the watering-hole. 'That's the heavy machine-gun! Range – 400 metres. A hundred metres right to take it out – behind those rocks, over there. Rapid fire! *Now*!'

Andrew obliged, firing off a lengthy burst, his ears ringing from the clamour, and saw his purplish tracer blending with the green tracer of the *adoo*.

'Too high,' Gumboot said. 'Reduce the elevation.'

Ricketts did this by unlocking the elevation drum and giving it a quick tweak downwards. This time, when Andrew fired, the tracer penetrated the thorn bushes where the smoke was rising, tearing them apart and making pieces of dust and stone fly off the rocks right beneath them. When the debris of the hit had settled down, the Shpagin machine-gun was silent.

The SAS mortars now began firing as well, with phosphorus rounds adding to the noisy spectacle and more silvery flashes exploding in the thorn bushes. Between the SAS mortars and GPMG, the thorn bushes along the high ground were blown apart and most of the *adoo*'s heavy guns were silenced.

Just then, however, as the SAS platoon was advancing on the exposed right flank, expecting cover from the advancing *firqats*, the latter stopped dead and started screaming in unison at the SAF troops just behind them. Incredibly, as *adoo* tracers whipped past them and bullets stitched the ground around them, the *firqats* engaged in a heated argument with the SAF troops, thus preventing the advance of the latter and allowing a group of *adoo* to come down off the high ground, take up positions behind rock outcrops and ambush the SAS troops advancing on the right flank.

'Christ!' Lampton exclaimed. 'I don't believe it!'

'That's the second group to go on strike,' Gumboot said as Lampton snatched the phone from Jock and got in touch with Sergeant Parker, who was crouched low beside a trooper with a PRC 319, near the arguing *firqats*. 'Lampton here! What the hell's going on?' Before Parker could answer, Lampton lowered the phone and bawled over his shoulder: 'Give them covering fire!'

Even as Lampton returned his attention to the radio, Andrew fired into the high ground on the right flank where the *adoo* were advancing on the SAS troops, some of whom were already wounded or dead.

'Randall's hit!' the radio crackled. 'McGuffin also hit! We're . . .'

The urgent voice was cut off when an exploding fragmentation grenade, thrown by one of the advancing *adoo*, blew the radio apart and flipped the operator onto his back. The assailant was then thrown onto his back when Parker took him out with a single shot from his 7.62mm Lee Enfield. Parker then jumped up and ran to help the platoon on the right flank, firing from the hip as he advanced, only stopping long enough to hurl a grenade into the midst of the *adoo* moving towards them. The explosion blew the group apart, flipping some of the men over, leaving others to stagger blindly to and fro, most soaked in blood, some blinded by shrapnel, all of them easy marks for the SAF riflemen, who soon picked them off.

The SAS platoon, almost lost in the ambush, then rushed forward, up to the high ground, joined by Parker. As they did so, Ricketts and the other probationers supported Andrew's noisy, murderous GPMG fire with their SLRs and M16s, followed by Tom and Bill's mortar. In doing so, they killed many *adoo* and forced the others back up the hill. The SAS action group then took control of the lower slopes and the SAF, having settled their argument with the *firqats*, continued their steady advance on the watering-hole.

'Day's work done,' Andrew said, releasing the trigger of the GPMG and waving the others into silence. 'I think we're home and dry, man.'

Even as he spoke, one of the SAS troopers threw a smoke grenade into the area chosen as a casevac point, marking it for the incoming chopper with a cloud of green smoke. Called in via a PRC 319, the casevac Huey soon arrived to land in a cloud of dust. Mere minutes later it was taking off with the casualties, some wounded, others dead. It headed back to the field surgical theatre of RAF Salalah without interference from the *adoo*, who had melted away.

'They've gone into the Wadi Dharbat,' Lampton said, 'adjacent to here. That's where we'll be going next.'

While the *adoo* were out of sight, the SAS

action groups, now followed by the *firqats* instead of being led by them, secured the watering-hole. Lampton then led Ricketts and the rest of the probationers in, saying, 'I'm really proud of you men. You've all done a great job.'

The whole area was littered with the evidence of battle – piles of 7.62mm shells and empty cases, bloodstained bandoliers and blood trails, pieces of flesh and torn clothing – but no bodies. The *adoo* had dragged them away. The air stank of burnt flesh, phosphorus and cordite. It also stank with human excrement over which bloated flies were relentlessly, frantically hovering, oblivious to the battle that had raged about them.

After a short break, Lampton made Ricketts and the other probationers take up new positions on the high ground above the watering-hole. Even up this high, they could smell the phosphorus and cordite from below, but after building another sangar, they broke out their hexamine blocks, lit the lightweight stove, boiled water from their water bottles and had a well earned brew-up.

'Why did the *firqats* stop advancing?' Bill asked when Sergeant Lampton dropped in for a chat.

'The *firqats* and the SAF soldiers despise each other,' Lampton explained, 'and when one of the latter accused the former of advancing too slowly, all hell broke loose. Thereafter, the *firqats* refused to lead the way into the watering-hole. It was as simple as that.'

'Well, fuck me with a bargepole,' Gumboot said, 'if that doesn't take the cake.'

'I wouldn't want to do that,' Andrew said, 'because you just might enjoy it. Pass the brew, Gumboot.'

Already the Skyvans were coming in with the resups, dropping such luxuries as mail from home, cigarettes, water, ammunition and fresh rations. The men drank their tea, swatting the flies away, ducking the mosquitoes and waiting patiently on the high ground, beneath the blazing sun, for the next phase of the bloody operation. When another Skyvan flew overhead, their friend, Corporal Whistler, stripped to the waist, waved at them from the rear cargo hold. He was pretty safe up there.

16

During a night and day spent in their sangars on the high ground, the men learnt that it was still not safe to wander about freely, as the *adoo*, though located mainly in the nearby Wadi Dharbat, were sending snipers back to do as much damage as possible. Therefore, though Lampton's blooded probationers spent most of that time in their sangar, other troopers were patrolling the high ground, flushing out the snipers, checking for land-mines, and generally securing the area. While this was largely successful, the snipers were persistent and no matter how many were caught or killed, others came in to replace them. Sporadic firing therefore continued unabated, with the odd soldier being wounded and no one able to properly rest up.

'Fucking bastards,' Bill said. 'They're just doing it to keep us awake and get us exhausted, the miserable shits.'

'Clever shits,' Andrew corrected him. 'They

don't have our fire-power – they're particularly lacking in heavy, long-range guns – so they fight us the only way they know how: with guerrilla tactics. You have to admire them.'

'Admire them! Are you fucking joking? They're just a bunch of miserable A-rabs, costing us sleep. They're murderous, mindless bastards, is all.'

'They're tenacious,' Ricketts said. 'Great marksmen. Courageous, as well. I agree with Andrew.'

'They're not courageous,' Gumboot said. 'They're just a bunch of fanatics. Brainwashed by the fucking commies in Aden and sent back here like zombies. They don't have the sense to think of dying; it means nothing to 'em. I don't call that courage.'

'You're just a racist,' Tom said.

'That's right, I'm a racist. I hate you bastards from the Midlands. I figure you're as mad as the *adoo* and should be put down at birth.'

Ricketts glanced down the hill at the sandy area around the watering-hole. It was now filled with back-up troops from Jibjat – SAF, Baluchi, *firqats* and SAS – with tents, sangars and hedgehogs springing up rapidly. Braying donkeys were being unloaded from a couple of Bedfords and passed on to the gathering *firqats*, who would use them for carrying heavy supplies up into the high hills. When Ricketts looked to the west, through the entrance to the amphitheatre, he saw Land Rovers and Saladin armoured cars creating billowing clouds of dust as they drove down the eastern hill, then across the sun-whitened plain pock-marked with black shell holes.

'The *adoo* aren't mad,' Andrew insisted, resting his notebook on his lap and tapping his teeth with his ball-pen, and pursing his lips, trying to think of something to write. 'They just think different from us. Born and bred in the desert, in a merciless environment, they view matters of life and death in a way we can't possibly imagine.'

'What he means,' Gumboot said, 'when you get past the fancy words, is that they'd slit your throat as soon as look at you. They don't think about death, you see.'

'We think about death in the West Midlands,' Tom said. 'The weather's so merciless, you don't want to get out of bed – you want to stay in the womb. You think of death a lot, then.'

Gumboot rolled his eyes. 'You hear that?' he said to Andrew. 'We have our home-brewed A-rabs in England and they're all from the Midlands. Mad as fucking hatters, and even think they're white men. What do you *do* up there,' he asked Tom, 'when you're not thinking about dying?'

'Lots of nice pubs where I live, ten-pin

bowling, darts. I've never missed a West Bromwich Albion game. Plus social evenings with old mates from the glassworks. Quite a nice life, really.'

'I'm breathless just thinking about it,' Gumboot said. 'What about you?'

Bill shrugged. 'Pretty varied life, really. The Four Furnaces, the Commercial, the Albion, the High Oak, the Elephant and Castle, the Fish, the Rose and Crown, and the Miners' Welfare Club on Commonside. Course on Wednesdays I'd play dominoes and on Tuesdays cribbage. Like Tom says, quite a nice life.'

'You hear that?' Gumboot said, addressing the distracted Andrew. 'The only time these bastards get out of the pubs is when they're called back to Hereford.'

'Wrong,' Andrew replied, jotting words down in his notebook. 'They play dominoes, cribbage and ten-pin bowling. They go to football matches. They check the weather and crawl into bed and think of death as they throw up. How *they* can look down on the Arabs, I just can't imagine!'

'Go fuck yourselves,' Bill said.

Flashing his teeth in a big smile, Andrew lowered his pen and glanced over the sangar wall at the watering-hole. The sun was blazing down, reflecting off the water, as the Land Rovers and

Saladin armoured cars drove into the clearing, the first of them braking to a halt near the braying donkeys, which were being herded away by the *firqats*.

'Donkeys and armoured cars,' Andrew said dreamily. 'The past and the future, the old and the new. We are straddling both worlds here.'

'The donkeys and the *firqats* are perfectly matched,' Gumboot said. 'I don't have to tell you why.'

Glancing down the hill, Ricketts saw Sergeant Lampton disengaging himself from a group of SAS men, including Major Greenaway, RSM Worthington and Sergeant Parker, who were grouped near the arriving Land Rovers and Saladin armoured cars.

'The Land Rovers and Saladins are coming in,' Ricketts said, 'to lend their support to the planned advance on the Wadi Dharbat.'

'I wish I was in a Saladin,' Andrew said, 'well protected by all that armour and those 76mm QF cannons, instead of having to do all this hiking, being shot at by snipers.'

'I'm not too sure I'd agree,' Ricketts answered thoughtfully. 'I like being in the open. I don't fancy the idea of being cooped up in an armoured car. They aren't all that easy to get out of. If they catch fire, you've had it. If a shell penetrates them, the shrapnel flies like crazy around the interior, slashing and burning everything inside. Even the turrets are a kind of trap. I keep remembering those poor bastards in the Saladin outside Um al Gwarif. They were probably killed because they couldn't get out in time. So, you know, there's certain advantages in being a foot soldier, out in the open. At least you can cut and run.'

'True enough,' Andrew said.

Glancing down again, Ricketts saw that Lampton was making his way laboriously up the hill, obviously heading for the sangar to impart the latest sit rep. Below him, on the level ground between the watering-hole and the parked Land Rovers and Saladins, Greenaway and Worthington were still in deep discussion with the granite-faced Parker.

'What do we know about Dead-eye Dick?' Ricketts asked, directing his question at the whole group.

'That he's fucking mad,' Gumboot said.

'A good soldier,' Bill added.

'A born killer if ever I saw one,' Jock said as he distractedly fiddled with the dials on his PRC 319. 'That bastard slits throats for breakfast.'

'He's pretty bloody frightening,' Tom said, glancing automatically down the hill to where Parker was. 'I mean, he doesn't seem normal.'

'He isn't normal,' Andrew said. 'He used to be,

but he isn't any more. He was in the Telok Anson swamp and that changed him for all time.'

Everyone stared intently at Andrew. 'The Telok Anson swamp?' Ricketts asked eventually.

Andrew nodded. 'Malaya, 1958,' he said. 'I got this from Sergeant Lampton. Parker was only twenty at the time, a probationer like us, and he was sent with D Squadron to Malaya. It was pretty hairy out there, always living in the jungle, but Parker proved to be a natural soldier and even better tracker. For that reason, in the spring of 1958, he was parachuted with two troops from D Squadron into the Telok Anson swamp, to go up against a bunch of CTs, or communist terrorists, led by the notorious Ah Hoi, nicknamed "Baby Killer". That swamp was a nightmare, the terrorists were even worse, and Parker was there for ten days, practically living in the water with the leeches and snakes. When he came out, he was changed for all time. Whatever happened in there, it obviously wasn't pleasant, and it certainly did something drastic to Parker. When he emerged, so Lampton said, he was no longer a baby-faced probationer – in fact, quite the opposite. He was . . .' Andrew shrugged, unable to find the correct words. 'The man we all know and revere. The one who makes us shit bricks.'

'And piss our pants,' Gumboot said.

'Right on, brother. Right on!'

Lampton, breathing heavily, had finally reached the sangar and gratefully sat on the wall, trying to get his breath back.

'Some climb,' he said.

'Piece of piss,' Gumboot replied. 'We run up and down it every five minutes without missing a breath. Of course, *we're* just probationers.'

Lampton grinned. 'I must be past it, Gumboot. I'm glad to know, however, that you're all fit enough to take what's coming.'

'What's that?' Jock asked, looking suspicious.

'The CO's decided that we've been here long enough, so he's going to deploy our forces on the plateau. We, the SAS, will be divided into two separate groups, each one being accompanied by *firqats* . . .'

'Oh, no!' Gumboot exclaimed.

'. . . with orders to advance down the western and eastern sides of the Wadi Dharbat, taking out the *adoo*. How does that grab you, gentlemen?'

'I'd rather let an *adoo* cut my throat,' Gumboot said, 'than depend on them fucking *firqats*. Come to think of it, if we're going to depend on them, we might as well cut our own throats and be done with it.'

Lampton grinned again. 'You exaggerate, Gumboot. I'm sure that now, with the differences between the *firqats* and the SAF troops resolved, you'll have no trouble at all with the former.'

'Very nicely put, boss. It shows you're educated. It also shows you're more optimistic than I am. Thanks, but no, thanks.'

'Orders are orders, Gumboot.'

'Please don't remind me, boss.'

'You have thirty minutes to break up the sangar and get down to the watering-hole.'

'Hear you loud and clear, boss.' When Lampton had slithered back down the hill, Gumboot raised his hands imploringly and looked to the heavens. 'What have we done to deserve this? What sin can be that bad?'

Andrew laughed, stood up, and placed his large hand on Gumboot's shoulder. 'It was the sin of being born, Gumboot. Now let's break up this sangar.'

They destroyed the sangar in no time, now expert at it, then moved carefully down the hill, spread well apart, keeping their eyes and ears alert for *adoo* snipers. Reaching the bottom without mishap, they joined the large group of other troops, including the *firqats*, gathered around Major Greenaway, who was standing up in the front of a Land Rover as if on a stage.

'As you doubtless know,' he said, 'the *adoo* are now entrenched in the Wadi Dharbat, eight kilometres' march from here. However, the high ground between here and that wadi is crawling with snipers. Your task will be to advance down the eastern and western sides of the wadi, taking out the *adoo* you encounter en route and, when you reach the wadi, clearing the remaining *adoo* off the plateau for good. For this purpose, you'll be divided into two groups – the Eastern Group and the Western Group – with each taking the side designated by its title. Both groups will be supported by members of the Firqat Khalid bin Waalid, who know the terrain and should be invaluable as scouts, trackers and support fighters. Your respective platoon leaders will now tell you what group you're in. We move out in thirty minutes, at noon precisely. Good luck, men.'

'Nice to know that the *firqats* are going to be our scouts,' Gumboot whispered sardonically to Ricketts. 'That means we'll be back in Um al Gwarif for supper – by accident, naturally.'

Nevertheless, despite Gumboot's doubts, they were assigned to the Eastern Group and moved out at noon on the dot, accompanied by a large contingent of *firqats*, who were at least, so Ricketts noted with relief, under the supervision of Dead-eye Dick Parker.

Spreading well apart, they clambered up the high ground, moving at the crouch, as Parker had taught them, and darting from one outcrop to another, leaving themselves exposed as little as possible. For this particular march, Andrew had discarded the GPMG tripod and was supporting it with the aid of a sling, intending to fire it from the hip. Tom and Bill were still struggling with the mortar components. Jock had the PRC 319 as well as his standard-issue weapons. Gumboot only had his standard-issue weapons, including an M16 semi-automatic rifle, and a pair of binoculars. Ricketts, relieved of the heavy, awkward GPMG tripod, was feeling as free as a bird with only his normal kit and weapons, including the SLR.

He was actually humming to himself when the first shot rang out and Tom jerked like a puppet on a string, dropping his M16, his left leg buckling, the weight of the mortar barrel pulling him back as the pain struck and he cried out. The men were falling low even as he hit the ground in a cloud of dust.

'Sniper 45 degrees east!' Lampton bawled from out front as Tom let out a piercing, long drawn-out scream and hammered the ground beside him with his clenched fist. Ricketts fired his SLR. Gumboot and Lampton let rip with their M16s, making the rocks above spit chipped stone and dust. 'I'm hit!' Tom yelled, getting his breath back after the scream. 'Oh, Jesus! The bastard!' Jock was speaking into the radio, calling for a medic, even as the sniper readjusted his aim and put a bullet through Tom's forehead, splitting his skull in two and turning it into a pomegranate with pieces of bone washed out on the blood that splashed over the sand.

'Purvis hit!' Jock screamed into his mike as the others kept firing and Parker appeared out of nowhere, higher up than the sniper. He rose up from behind a rock, taking aim with his Lee Enfield, fired a shot and then waved his right hand to send one of the *firqats* down. The latter ran down at the crouch, forcing the others to stop shooting, and stopped at the outcrop from which the *adoo* sniper had been firing. Having examined Parker's quarry, who must have been shot through the back, the *firqat* straightened up and waved his hand, indicating that the sniper was dead. Parker waved back, then turned away and hurried on up the hill, followed by the *firqat*.

'Tom is dead,' Andrew said.

'I can't bear to look,' Jock told him.

'Christ, what a mess,' Gumboot whispered. 'What the fuck do we do with him?'

Lampton slithered back down the hill, his feet kicking up clouds of dust. After glancing at Tom's bloody, shattered head, he asked, 'Did you call a medic, Jock?'

'Yes, boss. He's on his way up.'

'Then there's nothing more we can do here, so let's get moving, lads.' Lampton started turning away, then noticed Bill. He was staring at his friend, too shocked to speak, trying to reconcile that dreadful image of smashed bone and blood with the man he had shared a lot of good times with. Though trying, he failed.

'Get the fuck up,' Lampton snapped, grabbing Bill by the shoulder and tugging him to his feet. 'We haven't time to sit here brooding. Now get up that hill, Trooper.' Bill just stared at him. '*Go!*' Lampton screamed. Bill twitched as if slapped, blinked, glanced about him, said, 'Sorry, boss,' and turned away. He crouched low, his M16 at the ready, and hurried on up the slope.

'Gumboot!' Lampton snapped.

'Yes, boss.'

'Take that mortar tube off Purvis and then stick close to Raglan.'

'Shit, boss, he's all covered in . . .'

'Do it, Gumboot. Don't argue.'

'Right, boss. Will do.' Taking a deep breath and trying not to look, Gumboot rolled Tom over to get at his webbing and unstrap the mortar tube. When he had done so, which he only managed with great difficulty, avoiding the sight of the dead man's head, he strapped the tube to his own bergen, took another deep breath, then hurried to catch up with the others, falling in close to Bill. Though the latter's eyes were wet with tears, he was looking determined.

'He'll survive,' Gumboot whispered as he crouched behind a rock. Then he jumped up and zigzagged, crouching low, to another position.

The others were doing the same, zigzagging uphill, hiding behind rocks and leaping out and then dropping low again. They heard sporadic gunshots all around them – other snipers, more victims – but they managed to reach the crest of the hill without further incident.

It was only when they were starting down the other side that the *adoo* appeared. They might even have heard the gunshots first, but no one could be sure of that. It was a whole group of *adoo*, on a ridge just up ahead, about twenty yards away, some firing from behind the rocks, others advancing down the left flank. One of them jumped up in full view to swing his arm and hurl something.

'*Hand grenade*!' Lampton bellowed.

Ricketts turned away, pressing his back to a rock, lowering his head between his raised knees and covering his face with his hands. Nevertheless, he heard the explosion, felt the heat of the blast, choked as sand and dust rained on him, and felt gravel pepper him.

He turned around before it subsided, raising

his SLR, letting the barrel rest on the rock as he took aim and fired through the swirling, dust-filled smoke. Gumboot and Jock were doing the same, both covered in sand and dust, while Parker and Lampton covered the left flank with a hail of withering fire.

The *adoo* advance was stopped, some scattering, others falling, a few looking indecisive, the bullets turning the rocks and ground around them into a maelstrom of spitting dust and flying stones. The indecisive ones died in that turmoil, but one of them, having broken away from the others, suddenly bore down on Bill. His left hand had been shot off and was pumping blood like a fountain, but his right hand was holding a *kunjias*, which he was raising on high. Concentrating on the front, Bill failed to see his attacker. Ricketts saw him and fired a lengthy burst that made him dance like a demented doll, falling backwards and flipping over a rock and hitting the ground in a cloud of dust, his *kunjias* clanging noisily on the stones near his sandalled feet.

Ricketts looked to the front again, where the other *adoo* were still firing. He saw Parker jumping up to throw a grenade, ducking again as it sailed through the air and dropped behind the ridge. The explosion uprooted thorn bushes and sent up a column of soil and sand, and was followed immediately by the screaming of the wounded *adoo*.

Parker was up and running before the clamour died away, closely followed by his Arabs, some of whom were releasing macabre wailings and swinging their glittering *kunjias*. Ricketts gave them covering fire, aiming left of their advance, while the men beside him aimed to the right. Parker went up and over the rocks, jumping down on the *adoo*, firing his Lee Enfield from the hip as he disappeared over the other side, followed again by his *firqats*.

Ricketts saw a *firqat* swinging his gleaming *kunjias*, then jumped up and ran for the ridge without thinking about it. He reached the rim and stopped there for a short moment, aiming down with his SLR, but not firing immediately.

Parker was crouching low, holding his rifle in one hand, lunging upwards with his Fairburn-Sykes knife, to stab it into the stomach of an *adoo* who was trying to strangle him.

The *firqats*, still wailing in their strange, unearthly way, were slashing at the other *adoo*, whose jellabas were in tatters and soaked with blood.

Momentarily muddling the *adoo* with the *firqats*, Ricketts stood there, not firing, completely exposed, until he was pushed over the other side by someone behind him. Landing on his feet, he saw an Arab coming at him, swinging a *kunjias*, and he fired a burst that almost cut him in two. The *adoo*'s upper half leant forward – like an Oriental gentleman being very polite – as blood burst from his belly and mouth. His eyes, above the bloodsoaked *shemagh*, rolled up in their sockets.

Ricketts stepped back to let his victim fall forward, then Gumboot and Andrew jumped down beside him, followed almost instantly by Lampton and Jock, both of whom glanced left and right, at the dead, bloody *adoo*.

'Oh, man!' Andrew exclaimed softly.

'A real slaughterhouse,' Gumboot said.

'Damned lucky you're still in one piece,' Jock told them, 'let alone standing upright.'

'Serves the bastards right,' Bill said, 'for what they did to my mate.'

As they stood there, glancing about them, seeing clouds of flies feasting, more *firqats* were gathering along the ridge to wail in triumph and shout blessings for this victory. Then, realizing that no more could be done here, they jumped down and raced on towards the Wadi Dharbat, following the redoubtable Parker, whose OGs, Ricketts noticed, were soaked in the blood of his *adoo* victims.

'What the hell are you all standing here for?' Lampton bawled. 'Let's head for the wadi!'

Shocked back to reality and instantly oblivious to the dead men lying about their feet, they all followed the sergeant away from the ridge and on to the eastern side of the Wadi Dharbat, where all hell was breaking loose.

17

They advanced on the Wadi Dharbat in the late afternoon, when the sun was going down in the west, casting long shadows and turning the white hills a mellow golden colour. Lampton was leading his own group, but Parker and his *firqats* were well ahead of him, the latter now confident with victory and keen to fight again. More troops were advancing along the west side of the wadi, strung out in long lines that ran from the lowland to the crest of the high ground, appearing from behind rocks, disappearing, then reappearing, the sound of gunfire a clear indication that they were meeting resistance. Lampton's group had seen nothing since leaving the ridge an hour ago, but the sound of gunshots up ahead, where Parker's Arab fighters were merely part of a larger SAF force, including SAF and Baluchis, was an indication that they, too, were having to flush out *adoo* snipers as they advanced.

'Take five!' Lampton shouted, raising his right hand to signal that they could stop.

Sighing with relief, Ricketts used a smoothly rounded rock as a chair while he wiped sweat from his face and drank awkwardly from his water bottle, having to hold his hand over the spout to keep the frantic flies and mosquitoes out. After screwing the cap back on and clipping the bottle back on his webbing, he slid a stick of chewing gum into his mouth, hoping to get rid of the taste of sand and dust.

Gumboot lit a cigarette, inhaled luxuriously, then pursed his lips and blew a few smoke rings.

'Well, Gumboot,' Andrew said, wiping sweat from his glistening black forehead with a handkerchief and grinning mischievously, 'you've got to hand it to Parker's *firqats* – they fought like demons back on that ridge and proved they had courage.'

Gumboot looked carefully at Andrew, not too sure of his grounds here. 'I never said they didn't have courage,' he replied defensively. 'I just said the fuckers weren't dependable and I stand by that.'

'Admit it, Gumboot, they're OK.'

'They may have been OK back on the ridge, but that doesn't make them dependable. All whooping and hollering when we took out the *adoo*, but I'd still like to see them in a tight spot. I wouldn't exactly sit back with a smoke, letting them get on with it, I can tell you that, mate.'

Ricketts noticed that Bill was sitting slightly apart from the others, blowing thin clouds of cigarette smoke and looking decidedly unhappy, still shocked by the death of his friend. Lampton, who had been keeping his eye on him, said, 'Are you OK?'

Bill just stared at him, as if not understanding.

'I asked if you were OK,' Lampton repeated.

'Sure. Why shouldn't I be?'

'I know that Tom came as a shock. It always is the first time.'

'Are you telling me it gets better, boss?'

'You get used to it,' Lampton said.

Bill snorted derisively. 'Right,' he said. 'You get used to it.' He inhaled and blew another thin stream of smoke. 'His head,' he said, as if talking to himself. 'I keep seeing his head. I never thought . . .' He trailed off into silence, glanced left and right, blinked, then inhaled and exhaled, trying to keep himself steady.

'That's a form of self-indulgence,' Lampton said, 'and we haven't time for it. Put all thought of Tom out of your mind and concentrate on the task at hand. If you don't, you could make a mistake and endanger us all. Is that understood?'

'I'm OK,' Bill said.

'Good. Glad to hear it.' Lampton was just about to stand up and wave them all forward when he heard a distant, familiar, hollow thudding sound. '*Mortars*!' he bawled and dropped into a crouch as the shells came whistling in from a great height.

The others either looked up automatically or threw themselves to the ground as the first of the explosions erupted about twenty feet away, hurling soil and sand high in the air and deafening the men with its roar. As the afterblast struck and debris rained down on them, two more shells exploded, even closer than the first, and Lampton, already obscured by the smoke, bawled, '*Let's go*!' He advanced on the run, away from the swirling smoke, and the men did the same.

It was clear, as they ran, that a fire fight had broken out ahead, where the SAF, Baluchi and *firqat* troops were spreading across the irregular, rocky terrain at the crouch, with mortar explosions erupting between them. Before Lampton's group reached that area, however, a Shpagin fired on them from the high ground, making them take cover behind some rocks. They returned the fire with their SLRs and M16s, but as such weapons were largely ineffective at such a range, the *adoo* machine-gun kept firing, turning the terrain around them into an inferno of boiling dust and flying debris, including hot gravel and pieces of barbed thorn bushes.

'Set up the mortar!' Lampton shouted at Bill as sand, dust and gravel showered them. 'Take that bastard out!

The rest of the troop kept up a hail of return fire as Gumboot and Bill mounted the 7.62mm mortar on its steel baseplate. While they were doing so, Andrew ran up the lower slopes of the high ground, zigzagging from rock to rock, ignored by the machine-gun crew, still concentrating on the main group, though fired on by FN rifles from the same location. Eventually settling down behind some large boulders about halfway up the slope, south-west of the enemy position, he wrapped the GPMG sling around his body and waited for Bill and Gumboot to give him an opening.

From his position on high, Andrew was able to see both the enemy position on the high ground – revealed by the curling blue smoke from its roaring machine-gun – and the rest of his troop on the low ground, temporarily protected by a natural circle of rocks that was being devastated, and gradually torn apart, by the *adoo* machine-gunner.

Within the convulsion of sand and smoke created by the machine-gun fire, Bill and Gumboot had put the mortar together and were adjusting the alignment; Ricketts was giving covering fire with his SLR; and Sergeant Lampton was covering his left ear with one hand, blocking out the atrocious noise, while shouting into the radio mike.

Jock, though nominally in charge of the radio, was keeping watch with his M16 resting in the cradle of his left arm. Cocky as always, he waved at Andrew and then stuck his thumb up in the air.

An *adoo* sniper put a bullet through Jock's hand, making him scream and fall backwards, curling up and holding the wrist of his wounded hand with his free hand, amazed at the amount of blood pouring out.

Bill fired the mortar. The elevation was too low and the shell fell well behind the *adoo*'s machine-gun emplacement, though close enough to cover the gunners in a rain of soil and sand. As Bill and Gumboot increased the mortar's elevation, Ricketts kept up the covering fire with his SLR and Lampton took his first-aid kit out of his bergen and bandaged Jock's hand.

'It's bleeding a lot,' he said, wiping Jock's blood from his face, 'but the bullet went clean through and out the other side, so there's no lasting damage. You'll be in a lot of pain for a long time, but you won't be permanently damaged.'

'I'm fucking bleeding to death!' Jock responded, still holding his wrist and looking at the blood-stained bandage around his hand.

Lampton squeezed his shoulder. 'No, you're not. You're just bleeding a lot. It'll hurt and you'll have restricted mobility for a long time, but the hand will get better in due course. Now make sure that bandage stays tight – and keep in contact with the forward group through the radio. You can still work that, Jock.'

'OK, boss,' Jock said, then twitched when the mortar fired a second time. This time the shell fell even closer to the *adoo* sangar, but it still did not damage it. Jock rolled his eyes in mock despair. Lampton again squeezed his shoulder. 'You'll be OK,' he said, then turned away to do the leopard crawl up to Bill and Gumboot. 'You two couldn't hit a barn door,' he said, 'if the damned thing was stuck on your pricks. What the hell's going on?'

'We don't have a forward observer,' Bill said, 'so we can only guess the correct calibrations. But this time we'll get the cunts.'

'You will?'

'Yes, we will.'

'I depend on it,' Lampton said.

Ricketts was still blasting the hell out of the ground around the *adoo* sangar – not doing much damage, but keeping their heads down

– when Lampton crawled up to him and said, 'Good man. Keep it going.' Ricketts did not reply. He was too busy firing. Bill fired the mortar, making another awful racket, filling the vicinity with smoke, and the shell, which was clearly visible leaving the tube, arched over the hill at a very high elevation, then dropped down, like a bird shot in flight, on what seemed like the very heads of the *adoo*.

The explosion blew the stones of the sangar out a long way. When the smoke cleared, one dead body was clearly revealed, hanging over the remaining stones, his jellaba torn and bloody, with the bent and smouldering barrel of the machine-gun lying on top of him.

Some others, however, were clearly still alive and one of them stood up, screaming wildly, firing his Kalashnikov in a wide arc. Andrew stood up too, forgetting the rule book, supporting the GPMG with the sling around his body, holding the weapon in his right hand, the belt feed in his left, and spreading his legs to fire from the hip. The recoil pushed him back, but he leant forward, shaking visibly, and his sustained burst tore the remaining stones apart, exploding the sand and dust, then moved upwards to savage the *adoo* sniper and throw him back out of sight, his body riddled with bullets.

'Keep firing!' Lampton shouted and raced up

the hill, followed instantly by Ricketts, while Bill and Gumboot, forsaking the mortar, gave covering fire with their M16s.

Andrew kept firing, left and right, up and down, only stopping when Lampton and Ricketts almost reached the position. They raced into boiling dust, swirling smoke, the stench of cordite, and found Arabs slashed by shrapnel, scorched by the blast, peppered with bullets, pouring blood everywhere, with one of them still holding his *kunjias*, as if about to attack them. The bent barrel of the exploded machine-gun had crushed the skull of a gunner.

Lampton turned away and looked back down the hill, then he raised and lowered his right hand from shoulder level to hip, indicating, 'Follow me.'

'These diversions are holding us back,' he said to Ricketts. 'Let's catch up with the forward group.'

Without waiting for a reply, he waved to Andrew, still farther down the hill, then pointed forward with his forefinger. Understanding, Andrew waved back and started humping the GPMG onto his shoulders. Ricketts followed Lampton as he made his way obliquely down the hill, gradually falling back in front of the group on the rocky flatland that ran between the two sides of the wadi. Gumboot and Bill had broken the mortar down into its component parts and were now marching heavily burdened, holding their M16s at the ready. Bill looked less troubled now.

The fire fight was continuing where the forward group was located, with explosions from 81mm mortars and LAWS causing devastation. Though the sun was still sinking, painting the white rocks with gold, the troops were painfully advancing through an immense cloud of sand and dust. More accurately, they were moving left and right, between the eastern and western sides of the wadi, like men who did not quite know what to do. Though being devastated by *adoo* mortars and machine-guns, they still could not advance. Banked up behind them, spread across the flatland between the two sides of the wadi, were SAF and Baluchi soldiers, together with the SAS men who had advanced along the western side with their Land Rovers, Saladin armoured cars, and Omani suppliers with heavily laden donkeys. They had all stopped to find out what was happening.

'What the hell . . .?' As he often did, Lampton asked the question of no one in particular, then went off to look for an answer. In this case, he went no farther than another hundred yards, where, with Ricketts by his side and his other men behind him, he found Greenaway in heated consultation with Worthington and Parker.

'I'm sorry, boss,' Parker was saying, 'but they're adamant about this. They say it's the beginning of the religious festival of Ramadan, when they're forbidden to eat or drink between dawn and dusk. They're also forbidden to fight.'

'That's nonsense!' the CO replied, his face purple with rage. 'We know all about Ramadan, planned for it, discussed it, but because of the importance of this operation, the *firqats* were given a dispensation – not only by their religious leaders, but also by the Sultan himself. So they've no reason to lay down their arms.'

'Sorry, boss,' Parker replied, pointing to the mass of *firqats* who were leaving the assault force and heading back to the Ain watering-hole, 'but they aren't concerned with their religious leaders *or* the Sultan. Come what may, they're going to show proper respect for the religious festival of Ramadan. That means no eating, no drinking . . . and no fighting. They've already laid down their arms.'

'Damn it, Sergeant . . .!'

'Sorry, boss.'

'They can't desert us at this stage! We've already cleared most of the *adoo* off the plateau and driven them into the wadis around it. The

Sultan's forces can now control the area. If the *firqats* desert us at this point – just when we need to flush the remaining *adoo* out of the surrounding wadis – we'll have to abandon some of our positions and let the *adoo* come back in. If they do that, they'll mount a counter-attack.'

'They've just done it,' Worthington said, pointing towards the western hill.

Everyone looked automatically towards where he was pointing. They saw a vast, frightening number of *adoo* coming up over the rim of the western side of the wadi, all framed by a blood-red sun that appeared to be melting and dripping over them, painting the whole landscape in crimson. Even as the *adoo* marched down the hill, the dull thud of their firing mortars was heard.

'Damn!' Greenaway snapped.

The first shells exploded at the base of the western hill, throwing bodies into the air, shredding the flesh from some of the donkeys with flying red-hot shrapnel and obscuring those nearby in billowing sand and spiralling smoke. The bellowing of the donkeys did not drown the dreadful screams of the wounded men.

'We need the *firqats*,' Greenaway said.

'You won't get them,' Parker replied. 'Sorry, boss, they won't wear it.'

'I should have known,' Greenaway said.

'We live in hope,' Worthington told him. 'We either stand here and fight or make a tactical withdrawal and regroup where we have more support. What say you, boss?'

Greenaway looked at the western hill. The *adoo* were swarming down it. Their mortars were landing all along the base of the hill, killing animals and men, and clearing the way for an *adoo* advance back along the wadi, regaining what they had just lost. Greenaway scratched his nose, watched the mortar shells exploding, then turned to the radio operator beside Worthington. 'A tactical withdrawal,' he said, 'for the Western Group and its support teams, to regroup at the Ain watering-hole and wait for our instructions. The Eastern Group will . . .'

'Hold back those bastards,' Sergeant Parker interrupted, 'long enough for air support and for reinforcements to be transported in from Jibjat.'

'Yes, Sergeant,' Greenaway said. 'That sums it up nicely. RSM,' he said, turning to Worthington, 'get on that radio and do the necessary. Meanwhile, our Eastern Group will dig in here, out of range of the enemy mortars, and, if required, engage the enemy in hand-to-hand fighting. In short, we'll hold the hill as long as needs be. Any questions, gentlemen?'

'No, boss!' half a dozen voices sang out in unison.

'Good. Then let's do it.'

All along the line, while the *adoo* mortar explosions came closer and Major Greenaway was driven away to link up with the SAF, the radio operators communicated the CO's instructions to both action groups. Within minutes, the Western Group was making its withdrawal from the area being devastated by the *adoo* mortars – though some of the Saladin armoured cars, obviously given separate instructions, broke away from the retreating column and bounced across the rocky flatland to lend support to the Eastern Group.

'An encouraging sight,' Andrew murmured.

'We should turn those Saladins around,' Gumboot said, 'and send them after those fucking *firqats*. Blow the shit out of them'

'You can't dig in,' Lampton said, 'so I recommend sangars. The *adoo* will be here in half an hour, so don't hang around, lads.'

'With you all the way, boss,' Jock said. 'No need to say more.'

They all hurried to build their sangars, tearing the stones from the earth, but Gumboot, who was more scared than he looked, felt obliged to say something.

'Those dumb fucking *firqats*,' he said. 'I could shit on their couscous!'

Sergeant Parker walked up to him, grabbed

him by his webbing, tugged him forward until they were nose to nose, and said, 'Are you building a fucking sangar or aren't you?'

'Yes, boss, I am!'

'Then build it, Trooper. *Just build it*!'

Gumboot worked overtime – more scared of Parker than he was of the *adoo* – and the others, wanting no more aggravation, worked just as hard. They were encouraged in this not only by Parker's vehemence, but by the fact that the explosions from the *adoo* mortars were advancing from the base of the western hill to the SAS positions, even as the *adoo* troops – no longer impeded by the Western Group, which was now in tactical withdrawal – were advancing across the flatland and would soon be within the firing range of their AK-47 Kalashnikovs, FN rifles and RPD light machine-guns.

'Fuck!' groaned Gumboo. 'There's hundreds of them!'

'The man can count,' Andrew said.

They joked to quell the fear that even the hardiest felt when confronted with the possibility of death. Perhaps the jokes worked – at least they bought a breathing space – but when the *adoo* opened fire that primal fear was erased, leaving nothing but instinct and, as some thought, the lessons of Sickeners One and Two. By these they would now live or die.

'Fire at will!' Lampton bawled.

Gumboot and Bill had already set up their mortar and fired the first shell when Lampton shouted. Even before it had exploded in the midst of the advancing *adoo*, Andrew had opened up with his GPMG, and Ricketts and Lampton were firing their SLRs. Jock, who had the radio and could use it with one hand, was listening for incoming calls and wondering what he could do with his useless hand if the *adoo* overran them. He studied the bloody bandage around his hand and realized he was hurting.

'Shit!' Jock said as the first mortar shell fired by Bill exploded among the *adoo*. 'This is no fucking joke!'

Kneeling behind the wall, Ricketts fired his SLR, not knowing if he had hit anyone or not, only aware that he had to keep firing until he was stopped. He saw some of the enemy falling – shot by him or by someone else – and others blown apart in the explosions from the half-dozen SAS mortars in the sangars.

Almost deafened by a shocking roar, he glanced sideways and saw Andrew in the next sangar, standing upright, legs apart, firing the heavy GPMG from the hip and smiling in a distant, trancelike manner, unconcerned about dying.

'Get down, you stupid bastard!' Ricketts he screamed.

Andrew ignored him, being lost in his own world, seeing nothing but the hordes of *adoo* coming at him, skirting around mortar explosions, jerking epileptically in death, falling down and jumping up again to continue advancing.

Gumboot was with Bill, hurriedly reloading the mortar, fascinated by the sheer number of *adoo* coming at him and still unable to accept that the *firqats* had actually walked. He helped Bill adjust the elevation, then they fired another mortar round. Again, the shell exploded in the middle of the *adoo*, blowing some of them to hell, but those untouched emerged from the swirling smoke, still advancing determinedly. The pair were now loading and firing the mortar as quickly as possible. But the *adoo* kept advancing.

Like the others, Ricketts was convinced that his final hour had come, but he reloaded and fired with the expertise he had been given back in Hereford. Mortar shells were exploding around him, showering him with soil and sand, and gradually the thickening smoke obscured the advancing enemy. They were coming closer, however, firing on the march, making the sand spit viciously around the sangars, and sending bullets ricocheting noisily off the stones. An SAS trooper screamed, jerking backwards and collapsing. A whole sangar took a direct mortar hit and was blown to hell, with its troopers slashed by shrapnel and crushed by stones, their bodies covered in dust.

Ricketts fired his SLR. He saw the *adoo* drawing nearer. He thought of Maggie back home – it was just a flash of her lovely face – then he unholstered his Browning handgun and laid it down on the wall. He could hear the excited shouts of the *adoo*; which meant they were now very close. He saw the first of them emerging from the smoke, so he fired a sustained blast. They spasmed and collapsed. Others took their place. Some were firing Kalashnikovs or FN rifles, but others were waving their *kunjias*, prepared for hand-to-hand fighting.

Ricketts felt a bolt of fear. It shot through him, passing on. When it had gone, he experienced a great peace and heightened awareness. He fired his SLR until it was empty, then dropped it and picked up the Browning and climbed to his feet. The men around him were throwing grenades, which exploded and were followed by screaming. Jock was firing his Browning handgun with his good hand and Sergeant Lampton, standing beside him, was ducking to avoid the gleaming blade of a swinging *kunjias*.

Ricketts took aim with his Browning, holding it two-handed. He waited until he saw the whites of the *adoo*'s eyes above his *shemagh*, then he fired a double-tap and swung towards another man even before his first victim had fallen.

Before he reached his thirteenth shot, the ground around him roared and erupted, picking him up and slamming him back down into a whirlpool of light and pain. He passed out and regained consciousness, choking, spitting sand, then rolled painfully onto his back and looked directly above him.

An *adoo* with a *shemagh* across his mouth was standing above Ricketts, legs apart, holding a *kunjias* on high, about to split Ricketts in two with it.

Ricketts turned his head aside, not wanting to face the knife, and saw Gumboot rolling out of a subsiding cloud of dust as Bill ran forward, firing his Browning at the *adoo* standing over Ricketts. The Arab screamed and staggered back, dropping his *kunjias*. The long blade fell dangerously close to Ricketts's head as the Arab fell and the ground erupted under Bill.

Ricketts saw Bill picked up, flipped over and slammed down, screaming in an indescribable manner, with his lower half missing. Ricketts had to look away, but then he saw one of Bill's legs, severed at the hip and pumping blood from the mangled, scorched stump. Ricketts looked back and saw Bill's staring, dazed eyes. His arms and upper half were shaking in a spasm as the blood poured out of his legless torso to drain him completely.

As Bill died, his gaze freezing, Gumboot climbed to his feet. He withdrew his Fairburn-Sykes knife from his belt and launched himself at the *adoo* running at him with his raised *kunjias*. They collided and were lost in the general mêlée as the roaring of the Strikemasters and Skyvans came down from the sky.

Ricketts was in great pain, and passed out again. He recovered a few minutes later, brought back to painful consciousness by the fire in his left leg. Gritting his teeth to stop his groaning, he saw the men still fighting around him, most of them locked in mortal hand-to-hand combat, most screaming or shouting. Looking beyond them, through the dense, swirling smoke, he saw the Strikemasters diving on the high ground of the western hill with their guns roaring relentlessly. Even as they did so, one of the Skyvans came into view, flying low across the flat plain, its crew rolling out a series of Burmail bombs which exploded in the midst of the *adoo* still advancing, engulfing them in a vast wall of yellow flames.

Ricketts groaned again and tried to crawl out of his sangar, the walls of which had been badly damaged and scorched by a mortar blast. Even as he saw the reinforcements arriving in Bedfords, Land Rovers and Saladin armoured cars, all firing on the move, he was seized by another spasm of pain and passed out again. He drifted down a tunnel of darkness that took him to Maggie's face. There he found solace.

18

Ricketts recovered consciousness in Sergeant Whistler's Skyvan, which was flying the wounded and a lot of the dead back to RAF Salalah. The dead, mostly *adoo*, had been placed in body bags and just heaped on the aircraft floor, one on top of the other, then lashed down with web straps. Already, only halfway back to Salalah, the combined weight of the bodies was squeezing out body fluids and blood, creating what would soon become a foul smell.

When Ricketts had recovered enough to discuss the grisly scene around him, he was informed by Whistler that each time the Skyvans arrived at RAF Salalah, where the bodies were removed, the cargo compartment had to be hosed down by an RAF fire-engine. The SAF dead, he said, would be taken away for military burial. The *adoo* dead would be put on public display in the main square of Salalah as a demonstration to the locals that the Sultan's Armed Forces were winning the war.

Transferred from the Skyvan to the hospital in RAF Salalah, Ricketts learnt that his leg had been impregnated with many pieces of shrapnel, but that no lasting damage had been done. His mobility would be unimpaired once the wounds had healed. He also learnt that the *adoo* counter-attack in the Wadi Dharbat had been defeated with the arrival of the air support and reinforcements from Jibjat.

While resting up in hospital, waiting to be flown back to Hereford, he was visited by Sergeant Lampton and Gumboot, who informed him that Jock and Andrew had already been flown home, the former to have his wounded hand attended to, the latter to receive treatment for a minor wound in his left arm, received in hand-to-hand fighting with an *adoo* wielding a *kunjias*.

'Andrew won the fight,' Gumboot said, 'and he didn't stop crowing about it until he was flown back to Hereford.'

Ricketts was flown back on 3 October, just as the most dangerous phase of the operation in Oman was beginning. By that time B Squadron and G Squadron 22 SAS, the Firqat Khalid bin Waalid, and one company of the SAF had advanced some fifteen miles into communist-held territory and built three defensive positions on the sun-scorched Jebel Khaftawt. This became known as the Leopard Line. From there, the SAF moved out to dominate the surrounding area with an intensive 'aggressive-patrol' programme designed to clear the remaining *adoo* out of their lime caves and sangars in the wadis.

For ten days the SAS fought a running battle around the high plain, with SAF Skyvan tactical transporters, flown by British pilots, flying in supplies and ammunition, and SAS teams guiding Omani Strikemasters in strafing attacks on the *adoo* positions.

Again, the *firqats* threatened to stop fighting. This time they were insisting that their donkeys and camels be taken off the Jebel and transported to market. When this was done, with SAF jet fighters acting as escorts for the livestock, the *firqats* returned to the fray.

Eventually Operation Jaguar established the Sultan's Armed Forces on the Jebel Dhofar, which was seen as a significant defeat for the *adoo*. This success was crowned when the *adoo*, determined to rectify their great loss, launched and lost the legendary battle for Mirbat, which took place approximately nine months after Operation Jaguar, in July 1972.

Ricketts, Jock and Andrew had recovered from their wounds and were told about Mirbat when they were having drinks with Sergeant Lampton and Gumboot in the Paludrine Club at the SAS base in Hereford.

On 18 July a group of *adoo* deliberately allowed themselves to be seen by SAF forces in order to lure away the 60 *firqats* supporting the nine-man BATT team in Mirbat. This left only 30 *Askars* holding the Wali Fort and 25 gendarmes in the Dhofar Gendarmerie fort, located 900 yards north of the northern perimeter.

With the *firqats* gone, 250 of the *adoo*'s best warriors marched on Mirbat, armed with Kalashnikov AK-47s, light, heavy and medium machine-guns, two 75mm recoilless anti-tank rifles, an 84mm Carl Gustav rocket launcher, and mortars of various calibres, up to 82mm. Arriving at Mirbat, the *adoo* broke up into numerous combat groups and encircled the town. At 0530, the *adoo* attacked the DG fort, killing four of the gendarmes, but losing the element of surprise.

Once the fire fight had commenced, the guerrillas in the hills rained mortar bombs on the DG fort, the BATT house, and the town itself. On the roof of the BATT house, SAS corporals Peter Wignall and Roger Chapman were firing the settlement's only GPMG and an 0.5in Browning heavy machine-gun. With them on the roof was their 23-year-old commander, Captain Mike Kealy. Below them, in a pit at the base of the building, Lance-Corporal Harris was operating an 81mm mortar. In the gun-pit next to the DG fort, the enormous Fijian, Corporal Labalaba, was firing the 25-pounder with the aid of an Omani gunner, Walid Khamis. A second Fijian, Trooper Savesaki, was manning the gun-pit's short-range radio.

With the *adoo* swarming in on the town and settlement from all sides, Captain Kealy drafted an urgent request for reinforcements to provisional HQ at Salalah. As he was doing so, the *adoo* were firing on the DG fort and the settlement with Soviet RPG-7 rockets and their Carl Gustav 84mm rocket launcher. At approximately 0700 hours, Savesaki informed Captain Kealy by short-range radio that Labalaba had been badly wounded in the chin. Hearing this, Kealy called immediately for a helicopter to attempt a casevac.

While Lance-Corporal Chapman bravely ran from the BATT house, through the shell-torn town, to mark a helicopter landing zone near the beach for the casevac, Captain Kealy and a medical orderly, Trooper Tobin, crossed 400 yards of open ground, under enemy fire, to attend to the wounded Fijian. They found the Omani gunner, Walid Khamis, lying on his back, seriously wounded. Labalaba, though wearing a shell dressing on his face to staunch the flow of blood from his terrible chin wound, was still loading and firing the big gun, unaided. Savesaki, though bleeding from serious head and shoulder wounds, was propped up against the wall of the bunker and continuing to fire his rifle at the approaching *adoo*. One dead gendarme was lying in the gun-pit; another was on the parapet of the DG fort, sprawled across his machine-gun.

While the medical orderly attended to the wounded, Kealy sent a short-range radio message back to the BATT house, telling them to call for an air strike.

Shortly after, Labalaba was shot dead and Tobin had his jaw shot away. The latter was then also wounded badly in the back and hand by an *adoo* fragmentation grenade.

Meanwhile, on the beach, Chapman had thrown a green smoke grenade to mark the landing zone for the casevac helicopter. However, as the chopper approached the LZ, the *adoo*, now strongly reinforced and more heavily armed, fired on it from dead ground near the DG fort. Chapman therefore threw a red smoke grenade, warning off the helicopter. He dived for cover as the chopper flew away, its cabin peppered with machine-gun bullets, but luckily not damaged otherwise.

By now, the *adoo* were only thirty yards from

the gun-pit and adjoining ammunition bunker, hammering both positions, as well as the DG fort, with their rocket launcher, a hail of hand-grenades and a fusillade of small-arms fire.

The wounded Savesaki continued firing back, as did Captain Kealy, who was lightly grazed on the head by a bullet.

Just as the first of the *adoo* were about to overrun the gun-pit, two SAF Strikemasters, guided in by Kealy, now on the radio in the ammunition bunker, flew over the settlement, just above ground level, to attack the guerrillas with 7.62mm machine-guns and 500-lb bombs. Kealy was alternating his target guidance for the Strikemasters with instructions to his mortar team in the BATT house, 400 yards away.

In the BATT house's mortar pit, Lance-Corporal Harris found that the *adoo* were so close that he could not elevate the barrel high enough. He solved the problem by lifting the heavy steel tripod off the ground, pulling the burning-hot barrel against his chest, gripping the rest of the weapon between his legs and dropping the bombs down the barrel by hand. As Harris was doing this, Corporal Bob Bradshaw, in the BATT house, was directing the second wave of Strikemasters by radio.

The aircraft hammered the *adoo* machine-guns overlooking the town, then made several attacks on the guerrillas on the dead ground near the fort on the northern perimeter. One of the Strikemasters was damaged by machine-gun fire and had to return to Salalah.

At 0915, when Captain Kealy was giving water to the wounded and re-dressing their injuries, G Squadron 22 SAS flew by chopper, almost at sea level, from Salalah to the Mirbat beach, landing during the second Strikemaster attack on the hundreds of *adoo* massed around the northern perimeter.

Eighteen men from G Squadron marched inland in two groups to wipe out a position held by five guerrillas. A second group of SAS men, advancing south from the beach and operating in three-man teams, engaged in successful fire fights with three *adoo* positions.

Other guerrillas surrendered to SAS troopers guarding the helicopter LZ by the beach. By 1030, the wounded, including the Omani gunner, Walid Khamis, the Fijian trooper Savesaki, and the unfortunate medical orderly, Trooper Tobin, were casevacked by helicopter, though Tobin later died of his terrible wounds.

The retreating *adoo* lost at least forty men – perhaps thirty dead, and ten wounded and taken prisoner – as well as the last of their prestige. The battle begun with Operation Jaguar was completed with the Battle for

Mirbat, which became a turning-point in the war, ultimately leading to defeat for the *adoo*.

The 'secret' war in Oman remained secret for many years, but that night in July 1972, in the Paludrine Club, the survivors of the campaign, including Ricketts, Gumboot, Jock, Andrew and Sergeant Lampton, were able to toast their lost friends with a great deal of pride.

They did not discuss the dead, or those who had failed to 'beat the clock', but engaged in their traditional, good-natured bullshit before making their way back to their bashas.

'Where are we going next?' Gumboot asked as they entered the dark, silent spider.

'Belfast,' Lampton replied briskly. 'Have pleasant dreams, lads.'

The men groaned melodramatically, then crept off to the spider, and their beds.